About the Authors

Brenda Harlen is a multi-award winning author for Mills & Boon who has written over twenty-five books for the company.

Liz Fielding was born with itchy feet. She made it to Zambia before her twenty-first birthday and, gathering her own special hero and a couple of children on the way, lived in Botswana, Kenya and Bahrain. Seven of her titles have been nominated for RWA's Rita®; and she has won the Best Traditional Romance in 2000, the British Romance Prize in 2005 and the Best Short Contemporary Romance in 2006.

Born and raised just outside of Toronto, Ontario, **Amy Ruttan** fled the big city to settle down with the country boy of her dreams. After the birth of her second child, Amy was lucky enough to realize her life long dream of becoming a romance author. When she's not furiously typing away at her computer, she's a mum to three wonderful children who use her as a personal taxi and chef.

The Forever Family

COLLECTION

A Forever Family: Their Doorstep Delivery

BRENDA HARLEN

LIZ FIELDING

AMY RUTTAN

MILLS & BOON

First Published in Great Britain 2020
By Mills & Boon, an imprint of HarperCollins*Publishers*
1 London Bridge Street, London, SE1 9GF

A FOREVER FAMILY: THEIR DOORSTEP DELIVERY © 2020
Harlequin Books S.A.

Baby Talk & Wedding Bells © 2017 Brenda Harlen
Secret Baby, Surprise Parents © 2009 Liz Fielding
Alejandro's Sexy Secret © 2016 Amy Ruttan

ISBN: 978-0-263-28087-6

0220

MIX
Paper from
responsible sources
FSC™ C007454

This book is produced from independently certified FSC™ paper to ensure responsible forest management.

For more information visit: www.harpercollins.co.uk/green

Printed and bound in Spain
by CPI, Barcelona

BABY TALK &
WEDDING BELLS

BRENDA HARLEN

For Sheryl Davis – a fabulous friend, dedicated writer and librarian extraordinaire. Thanks for showing me 'a day in the life,' answering my endless questions and sharing my passion for hockey (which has absolutely nothing to do with this story but needed to be noted!)

Chapter One

By all accounts, Braden Garrett had lived a charmed life. The eldest son of the family had taken on the role of CEO of Garrett Furniture before he was thirty. A year later, he met and fell in love with Dana Collins. They were married ten months after that and, on the day of their wedding, Braden was certain he had everything he'd ever wanted.

Two years later, it seemed perfectly natural that they would talk about having a baby. Having grown up with two brothers and numerous cousins in close proximity, Braden had always envisioned having a family of his own someday. His wife seemed just as eager as he was, but after three more years and countless failures, her enthusiasm had understandably waned.

And then, finally, their lives were blessed by the addition of Saige Lindsay Garrett.

Braden's life changed the day his tiny dark-haired, dark-eyed daughter was put in his arms. Eight weeks later, it

changed again. Now, more than a year later, he was a single
father trying to do what was best for his baby girl—most
of the time not having a clue what that might be.

Except that right now—at eight ten on a Tuesday morning—he was pretty sure that what she needed was breakfast. Getting her to eat it was another matter entirely.

"Come on, sweetie. Daddy has to drop you off at Grandma's
before I go to work for a meeting at ten o'clock."

His daughter's dark almond-shaped eyes lit up with anticipation in response to his words. "Ga-ma?"

"That's right, you're going to see Grandma today. But
only if you eat your cereal and banana."

She carefully picked up one of the cereal O's, pinch-
ing it between her thumb and forefinger, then lifted her
hand to her mouth.

Braden made himself another cup of coffee while Saige
picked at her breakfast, one O at a time. Not that he was
surprised. Just like every other female he'd ever known,
she did everything on her own schedule.

"Try some of the banana," he suggested.

His little girl reached for a chunk of the fruit. "Na-na."

"That's right, sweetie. Ba-na-na. Yummy."

She shoved the fruit in her mouth.

"Good girl."

She smiled, showing off a row of tiny white teeth, and
love—sweet and pure—flooded through him. Life as a
single parent was so much more difficult than he'd anticipated, and yet, it only ever took one precious smile from
Saige to make him forget all of the hard stuff. He absolutely lived for his little girl's smiles—certain proof that
he wasn't a total screw-up in the dad department and tentative hope that maybe her childhood hadn't been completely ruined by the loss of her mother.

He sipped his coffee as Saige reached for another piece

of banana. This time, she held the fruit out to him, offering to share. He lowered his head to take the banana from her fingers. Fifteen months earlier, Braden would never have imagined allowing himself to be fed like a baby bird. But fifteen months earlier, he didn't have the miracle that was his daughter.

He hadn't known it was possible to love someone so instantly and completely, until that first moment when his baby girl was put into his arms.

I want a better life for her than I could give her on my own—a real home with two parents who will both love her as much as I do.

It didn't seem too much to ask, but they'd let Lindsay down. And he couldn't help but worry that Saige would one day realize they'd let her down, too.

For now, she was an incredibly happy child, seemingly unaffected by her motherless status. Still, it wasn't quite the family that Lindsay had envisioned for her baby girl when she'd signed the adoption papers—or that Braden wanted for Saige, either.

"I'm not going anywhere," he promised his daughter now. "Daddy will always be here for you, I promise."

"Da-da." Saige's smile didn't just curve her lips, it shone in her eyes and filled his whole heart.

"That's right—it's you and me kid."

"Ga-ma?"

"Yes, we've got Grandma and Grandpa in our corner, too. And lots of aunts, uncles and cousins."

"Na-na?"

He smiled. "Yeah, some of them are bananas, but we don't hold that against them."

She stretched out her arms, her hands splayed wide open. "Aw dun."

"Good girl." He moistened a washcloth under the tap to

wipe her hands and face, then removed the tray from her high chair and unbuckled the safety belt around her waist.

As soon as the clip was unfastened, she threw herself at him. He caught her against his chest as her little arms wrapped around his neck, but he felt the squeeze deep inside his heart.

"Ready to go to Grandma's now?"

When Saige nodded enthusiastically, he slung her diaper bag over his shoulder, then picked up his briefcase and headed toward the door. His hand was on the knob when the phone rang. He was already fifteen minutes late leaving for work, but he took three steps back to check the display, and immediately recognized his parents' home number. *Crap.*

He dropped his briefcase and picked up the receiver. "Hi, Mom. We're just on our way out the door."

"Then it's lucky I caught you," Ellen said. "I chipped a tooth on my granola and I'm on my way to the dentist."

"Ouch," he said sympathetically, even as he mentally began juggling his morning plans to accommodate taking Saige into the office with him.

"I'm so sorry to cancel at the last minute," she said.

"Don't be silly, Mom. Of course you have to have your tooth looked at, and Saige is always happy to hang out at my office."

"You can't take her to the office," his mother protested.

"Why not?"

"Because it's Tuesday," she pointed out.

"And every Tuesday, I meet with Nathan and Andrew," he reminded her.

"Tuesday at ten o'clock is Baby Talk at the library."

"Right—Baby Talk," he said, as if he'd remembered. As if he had any intention of blowing off a business meeting to take his fifteen-month-old daughter to the library instead.

"Saige loves Baby Talk," his mother told him.

"I'm sure she does," he acknowledged. "But songs and stories at the library aren't really my thing."

"Maybe not, but they're Saige's thing," Ellen retorted. "And you're her father, and it's not going to hurt you to take an hour out of your schedule so that she doesn't have to miss it this week."

"I have meetings all morning."

"Meetings with your cousins," she noted, "both fathers themselves who wouldn't hesitate to reschedule if their kids needed them."

Which he couldn't deny was true. "But…Baby Talk?"

"Yes," his mother said firmly, even as Saige began singing "wound an' wound"—her version of the chorus from the "Wheels on the Bus" song that she'd apparently learned in the library group. "Miss MacKinnon—the librarian—will steer you in the right direction."

He sighed. "Okay, I'll let Nate and Andrew know that I have to reschedule."

"Your daughter appreciates it," Ellen said.

He looked at the little girl still propped on his hip, and she looked back at him, her big brown eyes sparkling as she continued to sing softly.

She truly was the light of his life, and his mother knew there wasn't anything he wouldn't do for her.

"Well, Saige, I guess today is the day that Daddy discovers what Baby Talk is all about."

His daughter smiled and clapped her hands together.

The main branch of the Charisma Public Library was located downtown, across from the Bean There Café and only a short walk from the hospital and the courthouse. It was a three-story building of stone and glass with a large open foyer filled with natural light and tall, potted plants.

The information desk was a circular area in the center, designed to be accessible to patrons from all sides.

Cassandra MacKinnon sat at that desk, scanning the monthly calendar to confirm the schedule of upcoming events. The library wasn't just a warehouse of books waiting to be borrowed—it was a hub of social activity. She nodded to Luisa Todd and Ginny Stafford, who came in together with bulky knitting bags in hand. The two older women—friends since childhood—had started the Knit & Purl group and were always the first to arrive on Tuesday mornings.

Ginny stopped at the desk and took a gift bag out of her tote. "Will you be visiting with Irene this week?" she asked Cassie, referring to the former head librarian who now lived at Serenity Gardens, a seniors' residence in town.

"Tomorrow," Cassie confirmed.

"Would you mind taking this for me?" Ginny asked, passing the bag over the desk. "Irene always complains about having cold feet in that place, so I knitted her a couple pairs of socks. I had planned to see her on the weekend, but my son and daughter-in-law were in town with their three kids and I couldn't tear myself away from them."

"Of course, I wouldn't mind," Cassie told her. "And I know she'll love the socks."

Luisa snorted; Ginny smiled wryly. "Well, I'm sure she'll appreciate having warm feet, anyway."

Cassie tucked the bag under the counter and the two women continued on their way.

She spent a little bit of time checking in the materials that had been returned through the book drop overnight, then arranging them on the cart for Helen Darrow to put back on the shelves. Helen was a career part-time employee of the library who had been hired when Irene Houlahan was in charge. An older woman inherently distrustful of technology, Helen refused to touch the computers and spent most of her time finding books to fill online and call-in requests of patrons, putting them back when they were returned—and shushing anyone who dared to speak above a whisper in the book stacks.

"Hey, Miss Mac."

Cassie glanced up to see Tanya Fielding, a high school senior and regular at the Soc & Study group, at the desk. "Good morning, Tanya. Aren't you supposed to be in school this morning?"

The teen shook her head. "Our history teacher is giving us time to work on our independent research projects this week."

"What's your topic?"

"The role of German U-boats in the Second World War."

"Do you want to sign on to one of the computers?"

"No. Mr. Paretsky wants—" she made air quotes with her fingers "—real sources, actual paper books so that we can do proper page citations and aren't relying on made-up stuff that someone posted on the internet."

Cassie pushed her chair away from the desk. "Nonfiction is upstairs. Let's go see what we can find."

After the teen was settled at a table with a pile of books, Cassie checked that the Dickens Room was ready for the ESL group coming in at ten thirty and picked up a stack of abandoned magazines from a window ledge near the true crime section.

She put the magazines on Helen's cart and returned to her desk just as George Bowman came in. George and his wife, Margie, were familiar faces at the library. She knew all of the library's regular patrons—not just their names and faces, but also their reading habits and preferences. And, over the years, she'd gotten to know many of th on a personal level, too.

She was chatting with Mr. Bowman when the tall, dark
and extremely handsome stranger stepped into view. Her
heart gave a little bump against her ribs, as if to make
sure she was paying attention, and warm tingles spread
slowly through her veins. But he wasn't just a stranger, he
was an outsider. The expensive suit jacket that stretched
across his broad shoulders, the silk tie neatly knotted at
his throat and the square, cleanly shaven jaw all screamed
"corporate executive."

She would have been less surprised to see a rainbow-
colored unicorn prancing across the floor than this man
moving toward her. Moving rather slowly and with short
strides considering his long legs, she thought—and then
she saw the little girl toddling beside him.

The child she *did* recognize. Saige regularly attended
Baby Talk at the library with her grandmother, which
meant that the man holding the tiny hand had to be her
dad: Braden Garrett, Charisma's very own crown prince.

A lot of years had passed since Braden was last inside
the Charisma Public Library, and when he stepped through
the front doors, he had a moment of doubt that he was even
in the right place. In the past twenty years, the building
had undergone major renovations so that the address was
the only part of the library that remained unchanged.

He stepped farther into the room, noting that the card
catalogue system had been replaced by computer ter-
minals and the checkout desk wasn't just automated but
self-serve—which meant that the kids borrowing books
or other materials weren't subjected to the narrow-eyed
stare of Miss Houlahan, the old librarian who marked the
cards inside the back covers of the books, her gnarled fingers wielding the stamp like a weapon. He'd been terrified of the woman.

Of course, the librarian had been about a hundred years old when Braden was a kid—or so she'd seemed—so he didn't really expect to find her still working behind the desk. But the woman seated there now, her fingers moving over the keyboard as she conversed with an elderly gentleman, was at least twenty years younger than he'd expected, with chin-length auburn hair that shone with gold and copper highlights. Her face was heart-shaped with creamy skin and a delicately pointed chin. Her eyes were dark—green, he guessed, to go with the red hair—and her glossy lips curved in response to something the old man said to her.

Saige wiggled again, silently asking to be set down. Since she'd taken her first tentative steps four months earlier, she preferred to walk everywhere. Braden set her on her feet but held firmly to her hand and headed toward the information desk.

The woman he assumed was Miss MacKinnon stopped typing and picked up a pen to jot a note on a piece of paper that she then handed across the desk to the elderly patron.

The old man nodded his thanks. "By the way, Margie wanted me to tell you that our daughter, Karen, is expecting again."

"This will be her third, won't it?"

"Third *and* fourth," he replied.

Neatly arched brows lifted. "Twins?"

He nodded again. "Our seventh and eighth grandchildren."

"That's wonderful news—congratulations to all of you."

"You know, I keep waiting for the day when you have big news to share."

The librarian smiled indulgently. "Didn't I tell you just this morning that there's a new John Grisham on the shelves?"

Mr. Bowman shook his head. "Marriage plans, Cassie."

"You've been with Mrs. Bowman for almost fifty years—I don't see you giving her up to run away with me now."

The old man's ears flushed red. "Fifty-one," he said proudly. "And I didn't mean me. You need a handsome young man to put a ring on your finger and give you beautiful babies."

"Until that happens, you keep bringing me pictures of your gorgeous grandbabies," she suggested.

"I certainly will," he promised.

"In the meantime—" she picked up a flyer from the counter and offered it to Mr. Bowman "—I hope you're planning to come to our Annual Book & Bake Sale on the fifteenth."

"It's already marked on the calendar at home," he told her. "And Margie's promised to make a couple dozen muffins."

"I'll definitely look forward to those."

The old man finally moved toward the elevator and Braden stepped forward. "Miss MacKinnon?"

She turned toward him, and he saw that her eyes weren't green, after all, but a dark chocolate brown and fringed with even darker lashes.

"Good morning," she said. "How can I help you?"

"I'm here for…Baby Talk?"

Her mouth curved, drawing his attention to her full, glossy lips. "Are you sure?"

"Not entirely," he admitted, shifting his gaze to meet hers again. "Am I in the right place?"

"You are," she confirmed. "Baby Talk is in the Bronte Room on the upper level at ten."

He glanced at the clock on the wall, saw that it wasn't yet nine thirty. "I guess we're a little early."

"Downstairs in the children's section, there's a play area with puzzles and games, a puppet theater and a train table."

"Choo-choo," Saige urged.

Miss MacKinnon glanced down at his daughter and smiled. "Although if you go there now, you might have trouble tearing your daughter away. You like the trains, don't you, Saige?"

She nodded, her head bobbing up and down with enthusiasm.

Braden's brows lifted. He was surprised—and a little disconcerted—to discover that this woman knew something about his daughter that he didn't. "Obviously she spends more time here than I realized."

"Your mom brings her twice a week."

"Well, since you know my mother and Saige, I guess I should introduce myself—I'm Braden Garrett."

She accepted the hand he offered. He noted that hers was soft, but her grip firm. "Cassie MacKinnon."

"Are you really the librarian?" he heard himself ask.

"One of them," she said.

"When I think of librarians, I think of Miss Houlahan."

"So do I," she told him. "In fact, she's the reason I chose to become a librarian."

"We must be thinking of different Miss Houlahans," he decided.

"Perhaps," she allowed. "Now, if you'll excuse me, I need to check on something upstairs."

"Something upstairs" sounded rather vague to Braden, and he got the strange feeling that he was being brushed off. Or maybe he was reading too much into those two words. After all, this was a library and she was the librarian—no doubt there were any number of "somethings" she had to do, although he couldn't begin to imagine what they might be.

As she walked away, Braden found himself admiring

the curve of her butt and the sway of her hips and thinking that he might have spent a lot more time in the library
as a kid if there had been a librarian like Miss MacKinnon to help him navigate the book stacks.

Chapter Two

By the time he managed to drag Saige away from the trains and find the Bronte Room, there were several other parents and children already there—along with Cassie MacKinnon. Apparently one of the "somethings" that she did at the library was lead the stories, songs and games at Baby Talk.

She nodded to him as he entered the room and gestured to an empty place in the circle. "Have a seat," she invited.

Except there were no seats. All of the moms—and yes, they were *all* moms, there wasn't another XY chromosome anywhere to be found, unless it was tucked away in a diaper—were sitting on the beige Berber carpet. He lowered himself to the floor, certain he looked as awkward as he felt as he attempted to cross his legs.

"Did you bring your pillow, Mr. Garrett?"

"Pillow?" he echoed. His mother hadn't said anything about a pillow, but when he looked around, he saw that all of the moms had square pillows underneath their babies.

"I've got an extra that you can borrow," she said, opening a cabinet to retrieve a big pink square with an enormous daisy embroidered on it.

He managed not to grimace as he thanked her and set the pillow on the floor, then sat Saige down on top of it. She immediately began to clap her hands, excited to begin.

Ellen had told him that Baby Talk was for infants up to eighteen months of age, and looking around, he guessed that his daughter was one of the oldest in the room. A quick glance confirmed that the moms were of various ages, as well. The one thing they had in common: they were all checking out the lone male in the room.

He focused on Cassie, eager to get the class started and finished.

What he learned during the thirty-minute session was that the librarian had a lot more patience than he did. Even when there were babies crying, she continued to read or sing in the same soothing tone. About halfway through the session, she took a bin of plastic instruments out of the cupboard and passed it around so the babies could jingle bells or pound on drums or bang sticks together. Of course, the kids had a lot more enthusiasm than talent—his daughter included—and by the time they were finished, Braden could feel a headache brewing.

"That was a great effort today," Cassie told them, and he breathed a grateful sigh of relief that they were done. "I'll see you all next week, and please don't forget the Book & Bake Sale on the fifteenth—any and all donations of gently used books are appreciated."

Despite the class being dismissed, none of the moms seemed to be in a hurry to leave, instead continuing to chat with one another about feeding schedules and diaper rashes and teething woes. Braden just wanted to be gone but Saige had somehow managed to pull off her shoes, forcing him to stay put long enough to untie the laces, put the shoes back on her feet and tie them up again.

While he was preoccupied with this task, the woman who had been seated on his left shifted closer. "I'm Heather Turcotte. And this—" she jiggled the baby in her lap "—is Katie."

"Braden Garrett," he told her, confident that she already knew his daughter.

"You're a brave man to subject yourself to a baby class full of women," she said, then smiled at him.

"I'm only here today because my mom had an appointment."

"That's too bad. It would be nice to have another single parent in the group," she told him. "Most of these women don't have a clue how hard it is to raise a child on their own. Of course, I didn't know, either, until I had Katie. All through my pregnancy, I was so certain that I could handle this. But the idea of a baby is a lot different than the reality."

"That's true," he agreed, only half listening to her as he worked Saige's shoes back onto her feet. Out of the corner of his eye, he saw Cassie talking to one of the other moms and cleaning the instruments with antibacterial wipes, which made him feel a little bit better about the bells that his daughter had been chewing on.

"Of course, it helps that I have a flexible schedule at work," Heather was saying. "As I'm sure you do, considering that your name is on the company letterhead."

"There are benefits to working for a family business," he agreed.

Cassie waved goodbye to the other woman and her baby, then carried the bin of instruments to the cupboard.

"Such as being able to take a little extra time to grab a cup of coffee now?" Heather suggested hopefully.

He forced his attention back to her, inwardly wincing at the hopeful expression on her face. "Sorry, I really do need to get to the office."

She pouted, much like his daughter did when she didn't get what she wanted, but the look wasn't nearly as cute on a grown woman who had a daughter of her own.

"Well, maybe we could get the kids together sometime. A playdate for the little ones—" she winked "—*and* the grown-ups."

"I appreciate the invitation, but my time is really limited these days."

"Oh. Okay." She forced a smile, but he could tell that she was disappointed. "Well, if you change your mind, you know where to find me on Tuesday mornings."

"Yes, I do," he confirmed.

Somehow, while he'd been putting on her shoes, Saige had found his phone and was using it as a chew toy. With a sigh, he pried it from her fingers and wiped it on his trousers. "Are you cutting more teeth, sweetie?"

Her only answer was to shove her fist into her mouth.

He picked her up and she dropped her head onto his shoulder, apparently ready for her nap. He bent his knees carefully to reach the daisy pillow and carried it to the librarian. "Thanks for the loan."

"You're welcome," she said. Then, "I wanted to ask about your mother earlier, but I didn't want you to think I was being nosy."

"What did you want to ask?"

"In the past six months, Ellen hasn't missed a single class—I just wondered if she was okay."

"Oh. Yes, she's fine. At least, I think so," he told her. "She chipped a tooth at breakfast and had an emergency appointment at the dentist."

"Well, please tell her that I hope she's feeling better and I'm looking forward to seeing her on Thursday."

"Is that your way of saying that you don't want to see me on Thursday?" he teased.

"This is a public library, Mr. Garrett," she pointed out. "You're welcome any time the doors are open."

"And will I find you here if I come back?" he wondered.

"Most days," she confirmed.

"So this is your real job—you don't work anywhere else?"

Her brows lifted at that. "Yes, this is my real job," she said, her tone cooler now by several degrees.

And despite having turned down Heather's offer of coffee only a few minutes earlier, he found the prospect of enjoying a hot beverage with this woman an incredibly appealing one. "Can you sneak away for a cup of coffee?"

She seemed surprised by the invitation—and maybe a little tempted—but after a brief hesitation, she shook her head. "No, I can't. I'm working, Mr. Garrett."

"I know," he said, and offered her what he'd been told was a charming smile. "But the class is finished and I'm sure that whatever else you have to do can wait for half an hour or so while we go across the street to the café."

"Obviously you think that 'whatever else' I have to do is pretty insignificant," she noted, her tone downright frosty now.

"I didn't mean to offend you, Miss MacKinnon," he said, because it was obvious that he'd done so.

"I may not be the CEO of a national corporation, but the work I do matters to the people who come here." She moved toward the door where she hit a switch on the wall to turn off the overhead lights—a clear sign that it was time for him to leave.

He stepped out of the room, and she closed and locked the door. "Have a good day, Mr. Garrett."

"I will," he said. "But I need one more thing before I go."

"What's that?" she asked warily.

"A library card."

Cassie stared at him for a moment, trying to decide if he was joking. "*You* want a library card?"

"I assume I need one to borrow books," Braden said matter-of-factly.

"You do," she confirmed, still wondering about his angle—because she was certain that he had one.

"So where do I get a card?" he prompted, sounding sincere in his request.

But how could she know for sure? If her recent experience with the male species had taught her nothing else, she'd at least learned that she wasn't a good judge of their intentions or motivations.

"Follow me," she said.

He did, and with each step, she was conscious of him beside her—not just his presence but his masculinity. The library wasn't a female domain. A lot of males came through the doors every day—mostly boys, a few teens and some older men. Rarely did she cross paths with a male in the twenty-five to forty-four age bracket. Never had she crossed paths with anyone like Braden Garrett.

He was the type of man who made heads turn and hearts flutter and made women think all kinds of naughty thoughts. And his nearness now made her skin feel hot and tight, tingly in a way that made her uneasy. Cassie didn't want to feel tingly, she didn't want to think about how long it had been since she'd been attracted, on a purely physical level, to a man, and she definitely didn't want to be attracted to this man now.

Aside from the fact that he was a Garrett and, therefore, way out of her league, she had no intention of wasting a single minute of her time with a man who didn't value who she was. Not again. Thankfully, his disparaging remark about her job was an effective antidote to his good looks and easy charm.

Taking a seat at the computer, she logged in to create a new account. He took his driver's license out of his wallet so that she could input the necessary data. She noted that his middle name was Michael, his thirty-ninth birthday was coming up and he lived in one of the most exclusive parts of town.

"What kind of books do you like to read?" she inquired, as she would of any other newcomer to the library.

"Mostly historical fiction and nonfiction, some action-thriller type stories."

"Like Bernard Cornwell, Tom Clancy and Clive Cussler?"

He nodded. "And John Jakes and Diana Gabaldon."

She looked up from the computer screen. "You read Diana Gabaldon?"

"Sure," he said, not the least bit self-conscious about the admission. "My cousin, Tristyn, left a copy of *Outlander* at my place on Ocracoke and I got hooked."

For a moment while they'd been chatting about favorite authors, she'd almost let herself believe he was a normal person—just a handsome single dad hanging out at the library with his daughter. But the revelation that he not only lived in Forrest Hill but had another house on an island in the Outer Banks immediately dispelled that notion.

"My brothers tease me about reading romance," he continued, oblivious to her thought process, "but there's a lot more to her books than that."

"There's a lot more to most romance novels than many people believe," she told him.

"What do you like to read?" he asked her.

"Anything and everything," she said. "I have favorite authors, of course, but I try to read across the whole spectrum in order to be able to make recommendations to our patrons." She set his newly printed library card on the counter along with a pen for him to sign it.

He did, then tucked the new card and his identification back into his wallet. By this time, Saige had lost the battle to keep her eyes open, and the image of that sweet little girl sleeping in his arms tugged at something inside of her.

"Congratulations," she said, ignoring the unwelcome tug. "You are now an official card-carrying member of the Charisma Public Library."

"Thank you." He picked up one of the flyers advertising the Book & Bake Sale along with a monthly schedule of classes and activities, then slid both into the side pocket of Saige's diaper bag. "I guess that means I'll be seeing you around."

She nodded, but she didn't really believe him. And as she watched him walk out the door, she assured herself that was for the best. Because the last thing she needed was to be crossing paths with a man who made her feel tingles she didn't want to be feeling.

His daughter slept until Braden got her to the office. As soon as he tried to lay her down, Saige was wide-awake and wanting his attention. He dumped the toys from her diaper bag into the playpen—squishy blocks and finger puppets and board books—so that she could occupy herself while he worked. She decided to invent a new game: throw things at Daddy. Thankfully, she wasn't strong enough to fling the books very far, but after several blocks bounced across the surface of his desk, he decided there was no point in hanging around the office when he obviously wasn't going to get anything accomplished.

There were definite advantages to working in a family business, and since his baby wouldn't be a baby forever, he decided to take the rest of the day off to spend with her. He took her to the indoor play center, where she could jump and climb and swing and burn off all of the energy she seemed to have in abundance. Then, when she was finally tired of all of that, he took her to "Aunt" Rachel's shop— Buds & Blooms—to pick out some flowers, then to his parents' house to see how Ellen had fared at the dentist.

"Ga-ma!" Saige said, flinging herself at her grandmother's legs.

"I didn't think I was going to get to see you today," Ellen said, ruffling her granddaughter's silky black hair. "And I was missing you."

"I'm sure she missed you more," Braden said, handing the bouquet to his mother. "She was not a happy camper at the office today."

"Offices aren't fun places for little ones." Ellen brought the flowers closer to her nose and inhaled their fragrant scent. "These are beautiful—what's the occasion?"

"No occasion—I just realized that I take for granted how much you do for me and Saige every day and wanted to show our appreciation," he told her. "But now that I see the swelling of your jaw, I'm thinking they might be 'get well' flowers—what did the dentist do to you?"

"He extracted the tooth."

"I thought it was only a chip."

"So did I," she admitted, lowering herself into a chair, which Saige interpreted as an invitation to crawl into her lap. "Apparently the chip caused a crack that went all the way down to the root, so they had to take it out."

He winced instinctively.

"Now I have to decide whether I want a bridge or an implant."

"And I'll bet you're wishing you had oatmeal instead of granola for breakfast," he noted, filling a vase with water for her flowers.

"It will definitely be oatmeal tomorrow," she said. "How was Baby Talk?"

"Fine," he said, "aside from the fact that I was the only man in a room full of women, apparently all of whom know my life story."

"They don't know your whole life story," his mother denied.

"How much do they know?"

"I might have mentioned that you're a single father."

"Might have mentioned?" he echoed suspiciously.

"Well, in a group of much younger women, it was immediately apparent that Saige isn't my child. Someone—I think it was Annalise—asked if I looked after her while her mother was at work and I said no, that I looked after her while her dad's at work because Saige doesn't have a mother."

"Hmm," he said. He couldn't fault his mother for answering the question, but he didn't like the way she made him sound like some kind of "super dad" just because he was taking care of his daughter—especially when they both knew there was no way he'd be able to manage without Ellen's help.

"And you're not the only single parent with a child in the group," she pointed out. "There are a couple of single moms there, too."

"I met Heather," he admitted.

"She's a pretty girl. And a loving mother."

"I'm not interested in a woman who's obviously looking for a man to be a father to her child," he warned.

"She told you that?"

"She gave me the 'single parenthood is so much harder than most people realize' speech."

"Which you already know," she pointed out.

He nodded again.

"So maybe you should think about finding a new mother for Saige," she urged.

"Because the third time's the charm?" he asked skeptically.

"Because a little girl needs a mother," she said firmly. "And because you deserve to have someone in your life, too."

"I have Saige," he reminded her, as he always did when she started in on this particular topic. But this time the automatic response was followed by a picture of the pretty librarian forming in his mind.

"And no one doubts how much you love her," Ellen acknowledged. "But if you do your job as a parent right— and I expect you will—she's going to grow up and go off to live her own life one day, and then who will you have?"

"I think I've got a few years before I need to worry about that," he pointed out. "And maybe by then, I'll be ready to start dating again."

His mother's sigh was filled with resignation.

"By the way," he said, in a desperate effort to shift the topic of conversation away from his blank social calendar, "Cassie said that she hopes you feel better soon."

As soon as he mentioned the librarian's name, a speculative gleam sparked in his mother's eyes that warned his effort had been for naught.

"She's such a sweet girl," Ellen said. "Smart and beautiful, and so ideally suited for her job."

Braden had intended to keep his mouth firmly shut, not wanting to be drawn into a discussion about Miss MacKinnon's many attributes. But the last part of his mother's statement piqued his curiosity. "She's a librarian—what kind of qualifications does she need?"

His mother frowned her disapproval. "The janitor who scrubs the floors of a surgery is just as crucial as the doctor who performs the operation," she reminded him.

"But she's not a surgeon or a janitor," he pointed out. "She's a librarian." And he didn't think keeping a collection of books in order required any particular knowledge outside of the twenty-six letters of the alphabet.

"With a master's degree in library studies."

"I didn't know there was such a discipline," he acknowledged.

"Apparently there are a lot of things you don't know," she said pointedly.

He nodded an acknowledgment of the fact. "I guess, when I went into the library, I was expecting to find someone more like Miss Houlahan behind the desk."

His mother chuckled. "Irene Houlahan's been retired more than half a dozen years now."

"I'm relieved to know she's no longer terrifying young book borrowers."

"She wasn't terrifying," Ellen chided. "You were only afraid of her because you lost a library book."

"I didn't lose it," he denied. "I just couldn't find it when it was due. And you made me pay the late fines out of my allowance."

"Because you were the one who misplaced it," she pointed out logically.

"That's probably why I buy my books now—I'd rather pay for them up front and without guilt."

Which didn't begin to explain why he was now carrying a library card in his wallet—or his determination to put it to use in the near future.

Chapter Three

Cassie stood with her back against the counter as she lifted the last forkful of cheesy macaroni to her mouth.

"You might be surprised to hear that I like to cook," she said to Westley and Buttercup. "I just don't do it very often because it's not worth the effort to prepare a whole meal for one person."

Aside from the crunch of the two cats chowing down on their seafood medley, there was no response.

"Maybe I should get a dog," she mused. "Dogs at least wag their tails when you talk to them."

As usual, the two strays she'd rescued from a box in the library parking lot ignored her.

"Unfortunately, a dog would be a lot less tolerant of the occasional ten-hour shift at the library," she noted.

That was one good thing about Westley and Buttercup— they didn't really need her except when their food or water bowls were empty. And when she was away for several hours at a time, she didn't worry because they had one another for company.

But she did worry that she was turning into a cliché—the lonely librarian with only her cats and her books to keep her company. Since Westley and Buttercup were more interested in their dinner than the woman who fed it to them, she put her bowl and spoon in the dishwasher, then went into the living room and turned her attention to the tightly packed shelves.

The books were her reliable companions and steadfast friends. She had other friends, of course—real people that she went to the movies with or met for the occasional cup of coffee. But most of her friends were married now, with husbands and children to care for. It wasn't that Cassie didn't want to fall in love, get married and have a family, but she was beginning to wonder if it would ever happen. The few serious relationships she'd had in the past had all ended with her heart—if not broken—at least battered and bruised. When she'd met Joel Langdon three years earlier, she'd thought he was finally the one. Three months after he'd put a ring on her finger, she'd realized that her judgment was obviously faulty.

Thankfully, she was usually content with her own company. And when she wasn't, she could curl up with Captain Brandon Birmingham or Dean Robillard or Roarke. But tonight, she reached out a hand and plucked a random book from the shelf. A smile curved her lips when she recognized the cover of a beloved Jennifer Crusie novel.

She made herself a cup of tea and settled into her favorite chair by the fireplace, happy to lose herself in the story and fall in love with Cal as Min did. But who wouldn't love a man who appreciated her shoe collection, fed her doughnuts and didn't want to change a single thing about her? All of that, and he was great in bed, too.

She sighed and set the book aside to return her empty mug to the kitchen. Of course Cal was perfect—he was fictional. And she wasn't looking for perfect, anyway—she just wanted to meet a man who would appreciate her for who she was without trying to make her into someone different. He didn't have to be mouthwateringly gorgeous or Rhodes Scholar smart, but he had to be kind to children and animals and have a good relationship with his family. And it would be a definite plus if she felt flutters in her tummy when he smiled at her.

As she pieced together the ideal qualities in her mind, a picture began to form—a picture that looked very much like Braden Garrett.

Braden planned to wait a week or so before he tried out his library card to avoid appearing too eager. He figured seven to ten days was a reasonable time frame, and then, if he saw Cassie again and had the same immediate and visceral reaction, he would consider his next move.

He'd been widowed for just over a year and married for six years prior to that, so it had been a long time since he'd made any moves. How much had the dating scene changed in those years? Were any of the moves the same? Was he ready to start dating again and risk jeopardizing the precious relationship he had with his daughter by bringing someone new into their lives?

Except that Cassie was already in Saige's life—or at least on the periphery of it. And by all accounts, his little girl was enamored of the librarian. After only one brief meeting, he'd found himself aware of her appeal. Which was just one reason he'd decided to take a step back and give his suddenly reawakened hormones a chance to cool down.

But when he picked up his daughter's clothes to dump

them into the laundry basket, he found the red engine that she'd been reluctant to let go of at the train table earlier that day. He had a clear memory of prying the toy from her clenched fist and setting it back on the track, but apparently—maybe when he turned his back to retrieve her diaper bag—his daughter had picked it up again.

Wednesday morning he dropped Saige off at his parents' house, then headed toward his office as usual. But, conscious of the little red engine in his pocket, he detoured toward the library on his way. He'd considered leaving the train with his mother so that she could return it, but the "borrowed" toy was the perfect excuse for him to see the pretty librarian again and he was going to take advantage of it.

For the first six months after Dana's death, his mother hadn't pushed him outside of his comfort zone. Ellen understood that he was grieving for his wife and adjusting to his role as a new—and now single—dad. But since Christmas, she'd started to hint that it was time for him to move on with his life and urged him to get out and meet new people. More recently, she'd made it clear that when she said "people" she meant "women."

He knew she was motivated by concern—that she didn't want him to be alone. But whenever he dared to remind her that he wasn't alone because he had his daughter, she pointed out that Saige needed a mother. Saige deserved a mother. And that was a truth Braden could not dispute.

A real home with two parents.

He shook off the echo of those words and the guilt that weighed on his heart. He wasn't interested in getting involved with anyone right now. He had neither the time nor the energy to invest in a romantic relationship.

Getting some action between the sheets, on the other hand, held some definite appeal. But he knew that if he was just looking for sex, he should not be looking at the local librarian. Especially not when the woman was obviously adored by both his mother and his daughter.

But if he took the train back to the library, well, that was simply the right thing to do. And if he happened to see Cassie MacKinnon while he was there, that would just be a lucky coincidence.

Cassie didn't expect to ever see Braden again.

Despite his request for a library card, she didn't think he would actually use it. Men like Braden Garrett didn't borrow anything—if he wanted something he didn't have, he would buy it. And considering how busy the CEO and single father must be, she didn't imagine that he had much free time to read anything aside from business reports.

All of which made perfect, logical sense. What didn't make any sense at all was that she found herself thinking about him anyway, and wishing he would walk through the front doors in contradiction of her logic.

She tried to push these thoughts from her mind, annoyed by her inexplicable preoccupation with a man she was undeniably attracted to but wasn't sure she liked very much. A man who wasn't so very different from any other member of the male species who came through the library.

Okay, that was a lie. The truth was, she'd never met anyone else quite like Braden Garrett. But there were a lot of other guys in the world—good-looking, intelligent and charming guys. Some of them even came into the library and flirted with her and didn't regard her job as inconsequential. Rarely did she ever think about any of them after they were gone; never did she dream about any of them.

Until last night.

What was wrong with her? Why was she so captivated by a guy she'd met only once? A man who wasn't only gor-

geous and rich but a single father undoubtedly still grieving for the wife he'd lost only a year earlier.

Because even if he was interested in her, and even if it
turned out that he wasn't as shallow and judgmental as her
initial impressions indicated him to be, she had no intention
of getting involved with a man who was still in love with
another woman. No way. She'd been there, done that already, and she still had the bruises on her heart to prove it.

So it was a good thing she would probably never see
Braden Garrett again. A very good thing.

Or so she thought until she glanced up to offer assistance to the patron who had stopped at her desk—and
found herself looking at the subject of her preoccupation.

Her heart skipped a beat and then raced to catch up. She
managed a smile, determined not to let him know how he
affected her. "Good morning, Mr. Garrett. Are you looking for some reading material today?"

He shook his head. "Returning some smuggled mer-
chandise." He set a red engine on top of her desk. "Apparently Saige loves the trains more than I realized."

It wasn't the first toy to go missing from the playroom,
and she knew it wouldn't be the last. Thankfully, the "borrowed" items were usually returned by the embarrassed
parents of the pint-size pickpockets when they were found.

"Universal toddler rules," she acknowledged. "If it's in
my hand, it's mine."

"Sounds like the kind of wisdom that comes from experience," he noted, his gaze shifting to her left hand. "Do
you have kids?"

She shook her head and ignored the emptiness she felt
inside whenever she thought about the family she might
have had by now if she'd married Joel instead of giving
him back his ring. "No," she said lightly. "But I've spent
enough time in the children's section to have learned a lot."

"What about a husband?" he prompted. "Fiancé? Boy-friend?"

No, *no* and *no*. But she kept those responses to her-self, saying only, "Thank you for returning the train, Mr. Garrett."

"I'll interpret that as a no," he said, with just the hint of a smile curving his lips.

And even that hint was potent enough to make her knees weak, which irritated her beyond reason. "You should in-terpret it as none of your business," she told him.

Her blunt response had no effect on his smile. "Except that if you'd had a husband, fiancé or boyfriend, you would have said so," he pointed out reasonably. "And since there's no husband, fiancé or boyfriend, maybe you'll let me buy you a cup of coffee and apologize for whatever I did that put your back up."

Before she could think of a response to that, Megan hur-ried up to the desk. "I'm sorry I got caught up with Mrs. Lynch and made you late for your break, Cassie."

"That's okay," she said. "I wanted to finish logging these new books into the system before I left the desk."

"I can do that," her coworker offered helpfully.

Cassie thanked Megan, though she was feeling any-thing but grateful. Because as much as she was desperate for a hit of caffeine, she suspected that Braden would tag along on her break and his presence would make her jit-tery for a different reason.

"I guess you're free for that coffee, then?" he prompted.

"I'm going across the street for my break," she con-firmed, unlocking the bottom drawer of the desk to retrieve her purse. "And while I may not be a corporate executive, I can afford to buy my own coffee."

"I'm sure you can," he agreed. "But if I pay for it, you might feel obligated to sit down with me to drink it."

And apparently her determination to remain unaffected was no match for his effortless charm, because she felt a smile tug at her own lips as she replied, "Only if there's a brownie with the coffee."

Growing up a Garrett in Charisma, Braden wasn't accustomed to having to work so hard for a woman's attention. And while he was curious about the reasons for Cassie's reluctance to spend time with him, he decided to save the questions for later.

He pulled open the door of the Bean There Café and gestured for her to precede him. There were a few customers in line ahead of them at the counter, allowing him to peruse the pastry offerings in the display case while they waited. He ordered a lemon poppy-seed muffin and a large coffee, black; Cassie opted for a salted caramel brownie and a vanilla latte.

"How's this?" he asked, gesturing to a couple of leather armchairs close together on one side of the fireplace, further isolated by a display of gift sets on the opposite side of the seating.

"Looks…cozy," she said.

He grinned. "Too cozy?"

She narrowed her gaze, but he suspected that she wouldn't turn away from the challenge. A suspicion that was proven correct when she sat in the chair closest to the fire.

The flickering flames provided light and warmth and the soft, comfy seating around the perimeter of the room provided a much more intimate atmosphere than the straight-back wooden chairs and square tables in the center. Braden relaxed into the leather seat beside Cassie and set his muffin on the small table between them.

"Are you going to let me apologize now?" he asked her.

She eyed him over the rim of her cup as she sipped. "What are you apologizing for?"

"Whatever I said or did to offend you."

"You don't even know, do you?" she asked, her tone a combination of amusement and exasperation.

"I'm afraid to guess," he admitted. But he did know it had happened the previous morning, sometime after Baby Talk, because her demeanor toward him had shifted from warm to cool in about two seconds.

She shook her head and broke off a corner of her brownie. "It doesn't matter."

"If it didn't matter, you wouldn't still be mad," he pointed out.

"I'm not still mad."

He lifted his brows.

"Okay, I'm still a little bit mad," she acknowledged. "But it's not really your fault—you didn't do anything but speak out loud the same thoughts that too many people have about my work."

"I'm still confused," he admitted. "What did I say?"

"You asked if working at the library was my real job."

He winced. "I assure you the question was more a reflection of my interest in learning about you than an opinion of your work," he said. "And probably influenced by a lack of knowledge about what a librarian actually does."

"My responsibilities are various and endless."

"I'll admit, I was surprised to see so many people at the library yesterday. I figured most everyone did their research and reading on their own tablets or computers these days."

"To paraphrase Neil Gaiman, an internet search engine can find a hundred thousand answers—a librarian can help you find the right one."

"My mother's a big fan of his work," Braden noted.

"I know," she admitted. "Anytime we get a new book with his name on it, I put it aside for her."

"She's a fan of yours, too," he said.

Her lips curved, and he felt that tug low in his belly again. There was just something about her smile—an innocent sensuality that got to him every time and made him want to be the reason for her happiness.

"Because I put aside the books she wants," Cassie said again.

"I think there's more to it than that," he remarked. "How long have you known her?"

"As long as I've worked at CPL, which is twelve years."

"Really?" He didn't know if he was more surprised to learn that she'd worked at the library for so many years or that she'd known his mother for that amount of time.

"I started as a volunteer when I was still in high school," she explained. "And in addition to being an avid reader, Ellen is one of the volunteers who delivers books to patrons who are unable to get to the library."

"I didn't know that," he admitted. "Between the Acquisitions Committee of the Art Gallery, the Board of Directors at Mercy Hospital and, for the past year, taking care of Saige three to five days a week for me, I wouldn't have thought she'd have time for anything else."

"She obviously likes to keep busy," Cassie noted. "And I know how much she adores her grandchildren. Ever since Ryan and Harper got custody of little Oliver almost three years ago, I've seen new pictures almost every week.

"Of course, hundreds of pictures when Vanessa was born, and hundreds more when Saige was born," she continued. "And I know she's overjoyed that Ryan and Harper are moving back to Charisma—hopefully before their second child is born."

"You're probably more up-to-date on my family than I

am," he admitted. "I don't even know my sister-in-law's due date."

"August twenty-eighth."

"Which proves my point." He polished off the last bite of his muffin.

She broke off another piece of brownie and popped it into her mouth. Then she licked a smear of caramel off her thumb—a quick and spontaneous swipe of her tongue over her skin that probably wasn't intended to be provocative but certainly had that effect on his body and thoughts.

"I only remember the date because it happens to be my birthday, too," she admitted.

He sipped his coffee. "As a librarian, how much do you know about chemistry?"

"Enough to pass the course in high school." She smiled. "Barely."

"And what do you think we should do about this chemistry between us?" he asked.

She choked on her latte. "Excuse me?"

"I'm stumbling here," he acknowledged. "Because it's been a long time since I've been attracted to a woman—other than my wife, I mean."

She eyed him warily. "Are you saying that you're attracted to me?"

"Why else would I be here when there are at least a dozen coffee shops closer to my office?"

"I thought you came to the library to return the train Saige took home."

"That was my excuse to come by and see you," he said.

She dropped her gaze to her plate, using her fingertip to push the brownie crumbs into the center.

"You didn't expect me to admit that, did you?"

"I didn't expect it to be true," she told him.

"I was a little surprised myself," he confided. "When I

found the train, I planned to leave it with my mother, for her to return. And when I dropped Saige off this morning, I had it with me, but for some reason, I held on to it. As I headed toward my office, I figured I'd give it to her later. Except that I couldn't stop thinking about you."

She wiped her fingers on her napkin, then folded it on top of her plate.

"This would be a good time for you to admit that you've been thinking about me, too," he told her.

"Even if it's not true?"

He reached across the table and stroked a finger over the back of her hand. She went immediately and completely still, not even breathing as her gaze locked with his.

"You've thought about me," he said. "Whether you're willing to admit it or not."

"Maybe I have," she acknowledged, slowly pulling her hand away. "Once or twice."

"So what do you think we should do about this chemistry?" he asked again.

"I'm the wrong person to ask," she said lightly. "All of my experiments simply fizzled and died."

"Maybe you were working with the wrong partner," he suggested.

"Maybe." She finished her latte and set the mug on top of her empty plate. "I really need to get back to work, but thanks for the coffee and the brownie."

"Anytime."

He stayed where he was and watched her walk away, because he'd never in his life chased after a woman and he wasn't going to start now.

Instead, he took his time finishing his coffee before he headed back to his own office—where he thought of her throughout the rest of the day, because he knew he would be seeing the sexy librarian again. Very soon.

Chapter Four

When Cassie left work later that afternoon, she headed to Serenity Gardens to visit Irene Houlahan. Almost three years earlier, the former librarian had slipped and fallen down her basement stairs, a nasty tumble that resulted in a broken collarbone and femur and forced her to sell her two-story home and move into the assisted-living facility for seniors.

The septuagenarian had never married, had no children and no family in Charisma, but once upon a time, she'd changed Cassie's life. No, she'd done more than change her life—she'd saved it. And Cassie knew that she'd never be able to repay the woman who was so much more to her than a friend and mentor.

Since Irene had taken up residence at Serenity Gardens, Cassie had visited her two or three times a week. The move had been good for Irene, who was now surrounded by contemporaries who encouraged her to take part in various social activities on the property. And then, just after the New Year, Jerry Riordan had moved in across the hall.

His arrival had generated a fair amount of buzz among the residents and staff, and Cassie had overheard enough to know that he was seventy-two years old, a retired civil engineer and widower with three children and eight grandchildren, all of whom lived out of state. He was close to six feet tall, slender of build and apparently in possession of all of his own teeth, which made him the object of much female admiration within the residence.

But far more interesting to Cassie was her discovery that the newest resident of the fifth floor was spending a fair amount of time with the retired librarian. One day when Cassie was visiting, she'd asked Irene about her history with Jerry. Her friend had ignored the question, instead instructing Cassie to find *To Kill a Mockingbird* on her shelf. Of course, the woman's personal library was as ruthlessly organized as the public facility, so Cassie found it easily—an old and obviously much-read volume with a dust jacket curling at the edges.

"You've obviously had this a very long time."

"A lot more years than you've been alive," Irene acknowledged.

Cassie opened the cover to check the copyright page, but her attention was caught by writing inside the front cover. Knowing that her friend would never deface a work of art—and books undoubtedly fit that description—the bold strokes of ink snagged her attention.

Irene held out her hand. "The book."

The impatience in her tone didn't stop Cassie from taking a quick peek at the inscription:

To Irene—who embodies all the best characteristics of Scout, Jem and Dill. One day you will be the

heroine of your own adventures, but for now, I hope
you enjoy their story.
Happy Birthday,
Jerry

She closed the cover and looked at her friend. "Jerry—
as in Jerry Riordan?"

"Did someone mention my name?" the man asked from
the doorway.

"Were your ears burning?" Irene snapped at him.

Jerry shrugged. "Might have been—my hearing's not
quite what it used to be." Then he spotted the volume in
Cassie's hand and his pale blue eyes lit up. "Well, that
book is familiar."

"There are more than thirty million copies of it in
print," Irene pointed out.

"And that looks like the same copy I gave to you for
your fourteenth birthday," he said.

"Probably because it is," she acknowledged, finally
abandoning any pretense of faulty memory.

"I can't believe you still have it," Jerry said, speaking
so softly it was almost as if he was talking to himself.

"It's one of my favorite books," she said. "Why would
I get rid of it?"

"Over the years, things have a tendency to go missing
or be forgotten."

"Maybe by some people," the old woman said pointedly.

"I never forgot you, Irene," Jerry assured her.

Cassie continued to stand beside the bookcase, wondering if she was actually invisible or just felt that way. She
didn't mind being ignored and she had no intention of interrupting what was—judging by the unfamiliar flush in her
friend's usually pale cheeks—a deeply personal moment.

Years ago, when Cassie had asked Irene why she'd never

married, the older woman had snapped that it wasn't a conscious choice to be alone—that sometimes the right man found the right woman in someone else. Of course, Cassie hadn't known what she meant at the time, and Irene had refused to answer any more questions on the subject. Watching her friend with Jerry now, she thought she finally understood.

"Are you going to sit down and read the book or just stand there?" Irene finally asked her.

Cassie knew her too well to be offended by the brusque tone. "I was just waiting for the two of you to finish your stroll down memory lane," she responded lightly.

"I don't stroll anywhere with six pins in my leg and I wouldn't stroll with him even if I could," Irene said primly.

"Thankfully, it's just your leg and not your arms that are weak," Jerry teased. "Otherwise you'd have trouble holding on to that grudge."

Cassie fought against a smile as she settled back into a wing chair, turned to the first page and began reading while Jerry lowered himself onto the opposite end of the sofa from Irene.

She read three chapters before she was interrupted by voices in the hall as the residents started to make their way to the activity room for Beach Party Bingo. Irene professed to despise bingo but she was fond of the fruit skewers and virgin coladas they served to go with the beach party theme.

When Cassie glanced up, she noted that Jerry had shifted on the sofa so that he was sitting closer to Irene now. Not so close that she could find his ribs with a sharp elbow if the mood struck her to do so, but definitely much closer. Apparently the man still had some moves—and he was making them on her friend.

"I think that's a good place to stop for today," she decided, sliding a bookmark between the pages.

"Thank you for the visit," Irene said, as she always did.

Cassie, too, gave her usual response. "It was my pleasure."

She set the book down on the coffee table, then touched her lips to her friend's soft, wrinkled cheek.

Irene waved her away, uncomfortable with the display of affection.

"What about me?" Jerry said, tapping his cheek with an arthritic finger. "I'd never wave off a kiss from a pretty girl."

"Isn't that the truth?" Irene muttered under her breath.

Cassie kissed his cheek, too. "Good night, Mr. Riordan. I'll see you on Friday, Irene."

"There's a trip to Noah's Landing on Friday," her friend said. "We're not scheduled to be back until dinnertime."

"Then I'll come Friday night," Cassie offered.

"That's fine."

"No, it's not," Jerry protested. "You can't ask a beautiful young woman to spend her Friday night hanging out with a bunch of grumpy old folks."

"I didn't ask, Cassandra offered," Irene pointed out. "And she comes to visit *me*, not any other grumpy old folks who decide to wander into my room uninvited."

"Well, I'm sure Cassandra has better things to do on a Friday night," he said, glancing at Cassie expectantly.

"Actually, I don't have any plans," she admitted.

He scowled. "You don't have a date?"

She shook her head.

"What's wrong with the young men in this town?" Jerry wondered.

"They're as shortsighted and thickheaded now as they were fifty years ago," Irene told him.

"And on that note," Cassie said, inching toward the door.

"I'll see you in a few days," Irene said.

"Don't come on Friday," Jerry called out to her. "I'm going to keep Irene busy at the cribbage board."

"I have cataracts," she protested.

"And I have a deck of cards with large print numbers."

Cassie left them bickering, happy to know that her friend had a new beau to fill some of her quiet hours. And eager to believe that if romance was in the air for Irene, maybe it wasn't too late for her, either.

Of course, if she wanted to fall in love, she'd have to be willing to open up her heart again, and that was a step she wasn't sure she was ready to take. Because what she'd told Braden about her struggles with chemistry was only partly true. About half of her experiments had fizzled into nothingness—the other half had flared so bright and hot, she'd ended up getting burned. And she simply wasn't willing to play with fire again.

While Braden wouldn't trade his baby girl for anything in the world, there were times when he would willingly sacrifice a limb for eight consecutive hours of sleep.

"Come on, Saige," he said wearily. "It's two a.m. That's not play time—it's sleep time."

"Wound an' wound," she said, clapping her hands.

He reached into her crib for her favorite toy—a stuffed sock monkey that had been a gift from her birth mother—and gave it to Saige. "Sleep. Sleep. Sleep."

She immediately grabbed the monkey's arm and cuddled it close. Then she tipped her head back to look at him, and when she smiled, he gave in with a sigh. "You know just how to wrap me around your finger, don't you?"

"Da-da," she said.

He touched his lips to the top of her head, breathing in the familiar scent of her baby shampoo.

She was the baby he and Dana had been wanting for most of their six-year marriage, the child they'd almost given up hope of ever having. In the last few weeks leading up to her birth, they'd finally, cautiously, started to transform one of the spare bedrooms into a nursery. They'd hung a mobile over the crib, put tiny little onesies and sleepers in the dresser, and stocked up on diapers and formula.

At the same time, they'd both been a little hesitant to believe that this time, finally, their dream of having a child would come true. Because they were aware that the birth mother could decide, at the last minute, to keep her baby. And they knew that, if she did, they couldn't blame her.

But Lindsay Benson had been adamant. She wanted a better life for her baby than to be raised by a single mother who hadn't yet graduated from college. She wanted her daughter to have a real family with two parents who would care for her and love her and who could afford to give her not just the necessities of life but some extras, too.

Within a few weeks, Braden had begun to suspect that he and Dana wouldn't be that family. For some reason that he couldn't begin to fathom—or maybe didn't want to admit—his wife wasn't able to bond with the baby. Every time Saige cried, Dana pushed the baby at him, claiming that she had a headache. Every time Saige needed a bottle or diaper change, Dana was busy doing something else. Every time Saige woke up in the middle of the night, Dana pretended not to hear her.

Yes, he'd seen the signs, but he'd still been optimistic that she would come around. That she just needed some more time. She'd suffered so much disappointment over the years, he was certain it was her lingering fear of losing the child they'd wanted so much that was holding her back. He refused to consider that Dana might be unhappy because their adopted daughter was so obviously not their biological child.

Then, when Saige was six weeks old, Dana made her big announcement: she didn't really want to be a mother or a wife. She told him that she'd found an apartment and would be moving out at the end of March. Oh, and she needed a check to cover first and last month's rent.

And Braden, fool that he was, gave it to her. Because they'd been married for six years and he honestly hoped that the separation would only be a temporary measure, that after a few months—or hopefully even sooner—she would want to come home to her husband and daughter. Except that a few weeks later, she'd died when her car was T-boned by a semi that blew through a red light.

He hadn't told anyone that Dana was planning to leave him. He'd been blindsided by the announcement, embarrassed that he hadn't been able to hold his marriage together. As a result, while his family tried to be supportive, no one could possibly understand how complicated and convoluted his emotions were.

He did grieve—for the life he'd imagined they might have together, and for his daughter, who had lost another mother. But he was also grateful that he had Saige—her innocent smile and joyful laugh were the sunshine in his days.

If he had any regrets, it was that his little girl didn't have a mother. Her own had given her up so that she could have a real family with two parents. That dream hadn't even lasted three months. Now it was just the two of them.

"Well, the two of us and about a thousand other Garretts," he said to his little girl. "And everyone loves you, so maybe I should stop worrying that you don't have a Mommy."

"Ma-ma," Saige said.

And despite Braden's recent assertion, he sighed. "You've been listening to your grandma, haven't you?"

"Ga-ma."

"You'll see Grandma tomorrow—no," he amended, glancing at his watch. "In just a few hours now."

She smiled again.

"And I bet you'll have another three-hour nap for her, won't you?"

"Choo-choo."

"After she takes you to the library to play with the trains," he confirmed.

She clapped her hands together again, clearly thrilled with his responses to her questions.

Of course, thinking about the library made him think about Cassie. And thinking about Cassie made him want Cassie.

The physical attraction was unexpected but not unwelcome. If anything, his feelings for the librarian reassured him that, despite being a widower and single father, he was still a man with the usual wants and needs.

Unfortunately, Cassie didn't seem like the kind of woman to indulge in a no-strings affair, and he wasn't prepared to offer any more than that.

Cassie had updated the bulletin board in the children's section to suggest Spring into a Good Book and was pinning cardboard flowers to the board when Stacey found her.

"I've been looking all over for you," her friend and co-worker said.

"Is there a problem?"

"Nothing aside from the fact that I'm dying to hear all of the details about your hottie," Stacey admitted.

"Who?"

"Don't play that game with me," the other woman chided. "Megan told me you went for coffee with a new guy yesterday."

Cassie acknowledged that with a short nod. "Braden Garrett."

"As in the Garrett Furniture Garretts?"

She nodded.

"Not just hot but rich," Stacey noted. "Does this mean you've decided to end your dating hiatus?"

"Not with Braden Garrett," she said firmly.

"Because hot and rich men aren't your type?" her friend asked, disbelief evident in her tone.

"Because arrogant and insulting men aren't my type," Cassie clarified, as she added some fluffy white clouds to the blue sky.

"Which button of yours did he push?" Stacey asked, absently rubbing a hand over her pregnant belly.

"He asked if this was my real job."

"Ouch. Okay, so he's an idiot," her coworker agreed. "But still—" she held out her hands as if balancing scales "—a hot and rich idiot."

"And then he apologized," she admitted.

"So points for that," Stacey said.

"Maybe," Cassie allowed. "He also told me he's attracted to me."

"Gotta love a guy who tells it like it is."

"Maybe," she said again.

Stacey frowned at her noncommittal response. "Are you not attracted to him?"

"A woman would have to be dead not to be attracted to

him," she acknowledged. "But he's also a widower with a child."

"And you love kids," her friend noted.

"I do." And it was her deepest desire to be a mother someday. "But I don't want to get involved in another relationship with someone who might not actually be interested in me but is only looking for a substitute wife."

"You're not going to be any kind of wife if you don't start dating again," Stacey pointed out to her.

"I'm not opposed to dating," she denied. "I'm just not going to date Braden Garrett."

"How about my cute new neighbor?" her friend suggested. "He's a manager at The Sleep Inn, recently transferred back to Charisma after working the last three years in San Diego."

Cassie shook her head. "You know I don't do blind dates."

"In the past two years, you've hardly had *any* dates," Stacey pointed out. "You need to move on with your life."

She looked at her friend, at the enormous baby bump beneath her pale blue maternity top, and felt a familiar pang of longing. She was sincerely happy for Stacey and her husband who, after several years and numerous fertility treatments, were finally expecting a child, but she couldn't deny that her friend's pregnancy was a daily reminder that her own biological clock was ticking. "You're right," she finally agreed.

"So I can give your number to Darius?"

"Why not?" she decided, and left her friend grinning as she headed upstairs.

Toddler Time was scheduled to start at 10:00 a.m. on Thursdays. By nine fifty, almost all of the usual group were assembled, but Saige wasn't there yet. Cassie found herself watching the clock, wondering if she was going to show and, if she did, whether it would be her father or grandmother who showed up with her.

At nine fifty-seven, Ellen Garrett entered the room with the little girl. Cassie was happy to see the both of them—and maybe just a tiny bit disappointed, too.

The older woman's jaw still looked a little swollen and bruised, but she insisted that she was feeling fine. They didn't have time for more than that basic exchange of pleasantries before the class was scheduled to begin, and Cassie didn't dare delay because she could tell the children were already growing impatient. When the half hour was up, she noticed that Ellen didn't linger as she sometimes did. Instead, she hastily packed up her granddaughter's belongings, said something about errands they needed to run, then disappeared out the door.

It was only after everyone had gone and Cassie was tidying up the room that she discovered Saige Garrett's sock monkey under a table by the windows.

Chapter Five

Braden was just about to leave the office at the end of the day when his mother called.

"I need you to do me a favor," Ellen said.

"Of course," he agreed. Considering everything that his mother did for him, it never occurred to him to refuse her request.

"I can't find Saige's sock monkey. I think she might have left it at story time today."

His daughter never released her viselike grip on her favorite stuffed toy, which made him suspect that Saige hadn't *accidentally* left the monkey anywhere. "And you want me to go by the library to see if it's there," he guessed.

"Well, it is on your way from the office."

"Not really," he pointed out.

"If it's too inconvenient, I can get it tomorrow," Ellen said. "But you'll be the one trying to get Saige to sleep without it tonight."

Unfortunately, that was true. His daughter was rarely without the monkey—and she never went to sleep without it. Still, he could see what his mother was doing. She obviously liked Cassie MacKinnon and was trying to put the pretty librarian in his path as much as possible. And Braden didn't have any objection, really, but he suspected that Cassie might not appreciate his mother's maneuverings.

So he would stop by the library, per his mother's request, and apologize to Cassie for the situation. He would admit that Ellen was probably attempting to do a little matchmaking and suggest that maybe they should have dinner sometime, just to appease her.

Cassie might try to refuse, but he knew she liked his mother and he wasn't opposed to working that angle. In fact, he had the whole scenario worked out in his mind when he walked into the library just after five o'clock. He recognized the woman at the desk as the one who had nudged Cassie along to her coffee break. Megan, if he remembered correctly. He smiled at her. "Hi. I'm looking for Miss MacKinnon."

"I'm sorry, she isn't here right now," Megan told him.

"Oh." He felt a surprisingly sharp pang of disappointment, as if he hadn't realized how much he was looking forward to seeing her again until he was there and she wasn't.

"Is there something I can help you with?" she offered.

"I hope so," he said, because he did have a legitimate reason for this detour. "My daughter, Saige, was here for Toddler Time today and—"

"The sock monkey," Megan realized.

He nodded.

She pulled a clear zipper-seal bag out from under the

desk. Saige's name had been written on the bag with black marker, and her favorite soft toy was inside.

"That's it," he confirmed. "Now we'll both be able to get some sleep tonight."

She smiled. "Is there anything else I can help you with?"

"Can you tell me if Miss MacKinnon is working tomorrow?"

Megan shook her head. "I can't give out that kind of information." Then she sent him a conspiratorial wink. "But if you were to stop by around this time tomorrow, she might be able to tell you herself."

Braden smiled. "Thanks, I just might do that."

At first when Cassie put the phone to her ear and heard the deep masculine voice on the line, her pulse stuttered. When the caller identified himself as Darius Richmond, she experienced a twinge of regret followed by a brief moment of confusion as she tried to place the name.

"Stacey's neighbor," he clarified, and the conversation with her coworker immediately came back to her.

"Of course," she said, mentally chastising herself for thinking—and hoping—that it might have been Braden calling.

"I'm sorry it's taken me so long to call," he apologized. "Stacey gave me your number last week but I've been tied up in meetings with my staff."

"Understandable," she said. "Settling into a new job is always a challenge."

"But I'm free tonight and I'd really like to have dinner with you."

"Tonight," she echoed, her brain scrambling for a valid reason to decline. Then she remembered why she'd agreed to let Stacey give him her number: because she was trying to move on with her life. Because she'd only been out on a handful of dates since breaking up with Joel, and staying home and thinking about Braden Garrett—who, judging by his absence from the library for the past eight days, obviously wasn't thinking about her—wasn't going to help her move on.

"I know it's short notice," he said.

"Actually, tonight is fine," Cassie told him, determined not just to go out but to have a fabulous time.

"Seven o'clock at Valentino's?" he suggested.

"Perfect," she agreed, mentally giving him extra points for his restaurant selection. "I'll see you then."

Cassie disconnected the call and set her phone aside. As much as setups made her nervous, her friend and co-worker was right: she wasn't ever going to find her real-life happily-ever-after hanging out in the library.

She did have some lingering concerns about going out with one man when she couldn't get a different one out of her mind, but since the day Braden had bought her coffee, she hadn't heard a single word from him. She hadn't seen Ellen or Saige this past week, either, but at least Ellen had called to let her know that they would be absent from Baby Talk and Toddler Time because Saige had a nasty cold and Ellen didn't want her to share it with the other children.

And then, almost as if her thoughts had conjured the woman, Ellen was standing there.

"Who's the lucky guy?" she asked. Then she smiled. "Forgive me for being nosy, but that sounded like you were making plans for a date."

Cassie felt her cheeks flush. "I was. He's the neighbor of a friend."

"Oh," she replied, obviously disappointed. "A blind date?"

Cassie nodded, then asked, "How's Saige doing?"

"Much better," the little girl's grandmother said. "Though it's been a rough week for both of them."

"Both of them?"

"Braden was under the weather, too. Of course, that's what happens when you take care of a sick child. In fact, today will be his first day back at work—he's leaving Saige with me this afternoon and going into the office for a few hours."

"Well, I'm glad to hear they're both doing better—and that you managed to avoid whatever is going around. Because something is definitely going around," she noted. "Even Megan, who never calls in sick, did so today—and we have three school groups coming in for tours and story time this afternoon."

"In that case, I won't keep you from your work any longer," Ellen promised. "I really just wanted to check in to see if Braden stopped by last week to pick up Saige's sock monkey."

"He must have," Cassie told her. "I left it under the desk in a bag with Saige's name on it and it was gone when I got in the next morning."

"So you weren't here when he came in?" the other woman asked, sounding disappointed.

"No, I leave at two on Tuesdays and Thursdays, and then I'm back at seven for Soc & Study," she explained, referring to the teen study group that ran Monday through Friday nights.

Cassie was happy to supervise two nights a week and would have done more if required, because she understood how important it was for students to have a place to escape from the stress and drama of their homes. As a teen with three younger siblings and a short-tempered stepfather, she'd spent as much time as possible at the library. But of course she didn't mention that to Ellen, because she never told anyone about her past, and especially not about Ray.

In an effort to shift the direction of her own thoughts, she said, "Is there anything I can help you find today?"

"I'm just here to pick up a few travel books for Mabel Strauss," Ellen explained. "She hasn't left her own home in more than three years, but she still seems to find joy in planning trips that she's never going to take."

"What's her destination this time?" Cassie asked.

"Japan."

She smiled. "Well, if you're going to dream, dream big, right?"

"Absolutely," Ellen agreed. "Although, in Mabel's case, I think she's just going alphabetically now. It was Italy last week and India the week before that."

"Then you probably don't need me to steer you in the right direction," Cassie noted.

The older woman shook her head. "Thanks, but I know exactly where I'm going."

Several hours later, Cassie wished she wasn't going anywhere. After a busy day, she just wanted to go home, put her feet up and pet her cats. She considered canceling her plans with Darius, but she knew that she'd have to answer to Stacey if she did. She also knew that if she didn't want to spend the rest of her life alone with her cats, she had to get out and meet new people. Specifically, new men.

Unbidden, an image of Braden Garrett formed in her mind. Okay—he was new and she'd met him without leaving the safe haven of the library, but a man who'd lost his first wife in a tragic accident wasn't a good bet for a woman who'd vowed not to be anyone's second choice ever again.

She hadn't dated much since she'd given Joel back his ring. Her former fiancé hadn't just broken her heart, he'd made her question her own judgment. She'd been so wrong about him. Or maybe just so desperate to become a wife and a mother that she'd failed to see the warning signs. She'd fallen for a man who was all wrong for her because she didn't want to be alone.

That realization had taken her aback. For the first ten years of her life, her Army Ranger father had been away more than he'd been home, and her mother—unable to tolerate being alone—had frequently sought out other male companionship. Then her father had been killed overseas and her mother had dated several other men before she'd met and exchanged vows with Ray Houston.

Their marriage had been a volatile one. Naomi was a former beauty queen who basked in the adoration of others; Raymond was proud to show off his beautiful wife and prone to fits of jealousy if she went anywhere without him. Even as a kid, Cassie had decided she'd rather be alone than be anyone's emotional—and sometimes physical— punching bag, and she'd vowed to herself that she wouldn't ever be like her mother, so desperate for a man's attention that she'd put up with his mercurial moods and fiery temper.

For the most part, she was happy on her own and with her life. She had a great job, wonderful friends, and she was content with her own company and the occasional affectionate cuddle with her cats. And then Braden Garrett had walked into the library with his daughter.

So really, it was Braden's fault that she'd agreed to go out with Darius. Because he stirred up all kinds of feelings she'd thought were deeply buried, she'd decided those feelings were a sign that she was ready to start dating again. Because after more than two years on her own, she realized that she wasn't ready to give up. She wanted to fall all the way in love. She wanted to get married and have a family. And while she wasn't all starry-eyed and weak-kneed at the prospect of dinner with Stacey's new neighbor, she wasn't ready to write him off just yet, either.

So she brushed her hair, dabbed some gloss on her lips, spritzed on her perfume and headed out, determined to focus on Darius Richmond and forget about Braden Garrett.

Except that as soon as she walked through the front door of Valentino's, she found herself face-to-face with the man she was trying to forget.

"Hello, Cassie."

She actually halted in mid-stride as the low timbre of his voice made the nerves in her belly quiver. "Mr. Garrett—hi."

He smiled, and her heart started beating double-time. "Braden," he reminded her.

"I…um… What are you doing here?" Her cheeks burned as she stammered out the question. She never stammered, but finding him here—immediately after she'd vowed to put him out of her mind—had her completely flustered.

"Picking up dinner." He held up the take-out bag he carried. "And you?"

"I'm…um…meeting someone." And she was still stammering, she realized, with no small amount of chagrin.

"A date?" Braden guessed.

She nodded, unwilling to trust herself to respond in a complete and coherent sentence.

Of course, that was the precise moment that Darius spotted her. He stood up at the table and waved. She lifted a hand in acknowledgment.

"With Darius Richmond?" The question hinted at both disbelief and disapproval.

"You know him?" And look at that—she'd managed three whole words without a pause or a stutter.

"He went to school with my brother, Ryan," Braden

said, in a tone clearly indicating that he and Stacey's neighbor were *not* friends. "But last I heard, he was living in San Diego."

"He recently moved back to Charisma," she said, repeating what she'd been told.

"How long have you been dating him?"

"I'm not… I mean, this is our first date. And possibly our last, if I keep him waiting much longer." She glanced at the silver bangle watch on her wrist, resisting the urge to squirm beneath Braden's narrow-eyed scrutiny. She had no reason to feel guilty about having dinner with a man. "I was supposed to meet him at seven and it's already ten after."

"He knows you're here," Braden pointed out. "It's not as if he's sitting there, worrying that you've stood him up. Although, if that's what you want to do, I'd be happy to share my penne with sausage and peppers."

"Isn't your daughter waiting for her dinner?" she asked, relieved that she was now managing to uphold her end of the conversation.

But he shook his head. "I worked late trying to catch up after four days away from the office, so she ate with my parents."

"Your mom mentioned that you'd both been under the weather," she noted.

"Saige had the worst of it," he said. "But we're both fully recovered now."

"That's good," she said.

He looked as if he wanted to say something more, but in the end, he only said, "Enjoy your dinner."

"Thanks," Cassie said. "You, too."

Braden forced himself to walk out of the restaurant and drive home, when he really wanted to take his food into the dining room to chaperone Cassie on her date. Unfortunately, he suspected that kind of behavior might edge a little too close to stalking, even if he only wanted to protect her from the womanizing creep.

Because, yeah, he knew Darius Richmond, and he knew the guy had a reputation for using and discarding women. And, yeah, it bothered him that Cassie was on a date with the other man.

Or maybe he was jealous. As uncomfortable as it was to admit, he knew that his feelings were possibly a result of the green-eyed monster rearing its ugly head. Cassie's unwillingness to explore the attraction between them had dented his pride. Discovering that she was on a date with someone else was another unexpected blow, because it proved that she wasn't opposed to dating in general but to dating Braden in particular.

He couldn't figure it out. He knew there was something between them—a definite change in the atmosphere whenever they were in close proximity. What he didn't know was why she was determined to ignore it.

She was great with kids, so he didn't think she was put off by the fact that he had a child. Except that liking children in general was undoubtedly different than dating a guy with a child, and if she had any reservations about that, then she definitely wasn't the right woman for him.

Not that he was looking for "the right woman"—but he wouldn't object to spending time with a woman who was attractive and smart and interested in him. And the only way that was going to happen was if he managed to forget about his attraction to Cassie.

Which meant that he should take a page out of the librarian's book—figuratively speaking—and look for another woman to fulfill his requirement.

The problem was, he didn't want anyone but Cassie.

* * *

Cassie was tidying up the toys in the children's area late Saturday morning when Braden and Saige came into the library. The little girl made a beeline for the train table, where two little boys were already playing. Aside from issuing a firm caution to his daughter to share, Braden seemed content to let her do her own thing. Then he lowered himself onto a plastic stool where he could keep an eye on Saige and near where Cassie was sorting the pieces of several wooden puzzles that had been jumbled together.

"So…how was your date last night?" he asked her.

She continued to sort while she considered her response. "It was an experience," she finally decided.

"That doesn't sound like a rousing endorsement of Darius Richmond."

"Do you really want to hear all of the details?"

"Only if the details are that you had a lousy time and were home by nine o'clock," he told her.

She felt a smile tug at her lips. "Sorry—I wasn't home by nine o'clock." She put three puzzle pieces together. "It was after nine before I left the restaurant and probably closer to nine twenty before I got home."

He smiled. "Nine twenty, huh?"

She nodded.

"Alone?"

She lifted a brow. "I can't believe you just asked me that question."

"A question you haven't answered," he pointed out.

"Yes," she said. "Alone. As I told you last night—it was a first date."

"And you never invite a guy home after a first date?"

"No," she confirmed. "And why don't you like Darius?"

"Because he's a player," Braden said simply.

"So why didn't you tell me that last night?"

"I was tempted to. But if I'd said anything uncomplimentary about the man, you might have thought I was trying to sabotage your date, and I was confident that you'd figure it out quickly enough yourself."

"I knew within the first five minutes that it would be a first and last date," she admitted.

"What did he do?"

"When I got to the table, he told me that he'd ordered a glass of wine for me—a California chardonnay that he assured me I would enjoy. Which maybe I shouldn't fault him for, because he doesn't know me so how could he know that I generally prefer red wine over white? And maybe I wouldn't have minded so much if he was having a glass of the chardonnay, too, but he was drinking beer."

"You don't like guys who drink beer?" he guessed.

"I don't like guys who assume that women don't drink beer," she told him.

He nodded. "So noted."

"And when the waitress came to tell us about the daily specials, his gaze kept slipping from her face to her chest."

"You should have walked out then," he told her.

"Probably," she agreed. "Then he ordered calamari as an appetizer for us to share. And I hate squid."

"But again, he didn't ask you," Braden guessed, glancing over at the train table to check on his daughter.

"Not only did he not ask—he ignored my protests, as if he knew what I wanted more than I did.

"But still, I was hopeful that the evening could be salvaged," she admitted. "Because Valentino's does the most amazing three-cheese tortellini in a tomato cream sauce. And when I gave my order to the waitress—vetoing his suggestion of the veal Marsala—he suggested, with a blatantly lewd wink, that I would have to follow my meal with some intense physical activity to burn off all of the calories in the entrée."

Braden's gaze narrowed. "Is *that* when you walked out?"

"No," she denied. "I ordered the tortellini—with garlic bread—and I ate every single bite."

He chuckled. "Good for you."

"Then I had cheesecake for dessert, put money on the table for my meal and said good-night. And he seemed genuinely baffled to discover that I didn't intend to go home with him." She shook her head. "I mean, it was obvious early on that the date was a disaster, and yet he still thought I'd sleep with him?"

"When it comes to sex, men are eternally optimistic creatures."

"He was more delusional than optimistic if he believed for even two seconds that I would get naked with him after he counted the calories of every bite I put in my mouth."

"Note to self—never comment on a woman's food choices."

"I'm sure you didn't need to be told that."

"You're right," he admitted. "But obviously I'm doing something wrong, because you shot me down when I asked you to go out with me."

"You never actually asked me out," she said.

He frowned at that. "I'm sure I did."

She shook her head. "You only asked what we should do about the chemistry between us."

"And you said the chemistry would fizzle," he said, apparently remembering that part of the conversation.

She nodded.

"But it hasn't," he noted.

She kept her focus on the puzzles she was assembling. "So what do you propose we do now?"

"Right now, I'm trying to figure out how to tell Stacey that last night's date was a complete bust," she admitted.

"You could tell her you met someone that you like more," he suggested.

She finally looked up to find his gaze on her. "I do like you," she admitted. "But you're a widower with a child."

He frowned. "Which part of that equation is a problem for you?"

"It doesn't really matter which part, does it?" she said, sincerely regretful.

"You're right," he agreed. "But I'd still like to know."

Thankfully, before he could question her further, Saige came running over with a train clenched in each fist.

"Choo-choo," she said, in a demand for her daddy to play with her.

And Cassie took advantage of the opportunity to escape.

Chapter Six

She wasn't proud of the way she'd ended her conversation with Braden, but she'd done what she needed to do. If she tried to explain her reasons and her feelings, he might try to change her mind. And there was a part of her—the huge empty space in her heart—that wished he would.

She left the library early that afternoon and headed over to Serenity Gardens. When she arrived at the residence, she saw that a group of women of various shapes and sizes was participating in some kind of dance class in the front courtyard. Some were in sweats and others in spandex, and while they didn't seem to be particularly well choreographed, they all looked like they were having a good time.

"Geriatric Jazzercise," a familiar male voice said from behind her.

Cassie choked on a laugh as she turned to Jerry. "That's not really what they call it?"

He held up a hand as if taking an oath. "It really is."

"Well, exercise is important at any age," she acknowledged. "Unfortunately, I can't imagine Irene participating in something like this."

"Can't you?" he asked, his eyes twinkling. "Check out the woman in the striped purple top."

Cassie looked more closely at the group, her eyes widening when they zeroed in on and finally recognized the former librarian. "I don't know what to say," she admitted.

"You could say you'll have a cup of coffee with me," Jerry told her. "As I was told, in clear and unequivocal terms, that the jazzercise class is for women only."

"I'd be happy to have coffee with you," Cassie said, falling into step beside Jerry as he headed back toward the building.

"What's that you've got there?" he asked, indicating the hardback in her hand. "A new book for Irene?"

She nodded. "One of the advantages of being head librarian—I get dibs on the new releases when they come in."

"My name's on the waiting list for that one," he admitted.

"Irene's a fast reader—maybe she'll let you borrow it when she's done."

"I'm a fast reader, too," he told her. "Maybe *I* could give it to Irene when *I'm* done."

"That would work," she agreed.

Peggy's Bakery and Coffee Shop, on the ground floor of the residence, offered a variety of hot and cold beverages and baked goods, and the air was permeated with the mouthwatering scents of coffee and chocolate.

"What will you have?" Jerry asked her.

Cassie perused the menu, pleased to note that they had her favorite. "A vanilla latte, please."

"And I'll have a regular decaf," Jerry said.

"Can I interest you in a couple of triple chocolate brownies still warm from the oven?" Peggy asked.

"One for sure," Jerry immediately responded, before glancing at Cassie in a silent question.

"Brownies are my weakness," she admitted.

"Make it two," he said.

"You go ahead and grab a seat," Peggy said. "I'll bring everything out to you."

"Can we sit outside?" Cassie asked.

"Anywhere you like," the other woman assured them.

They sat on opposite sides of a small round table, beneath a green-and-white-striped awning. Peggy delivered their coffee and brownies only a few minutes later.

Jerry poured two packets of sugar into his coffee, stirred. "The first time I saw you here, visiting Irene, I thought you must be her granddaughter. Then I found out that she never married, never had any children."

"No, she didn't," Cassie confirmed.

"So what is your relationship?" he wondered. "If you don't mind me asking."

"I don't mind," she told him. "And although our relationship has changed a lot over the years, Irene has always played an important part in my life—from librarian to confidante, surrogate mother, mentor and friend."

"You've known her a long time then?"

"Since I was in fourth grade."

"I've known her a long time, too," Jerry said. "We grew up across the street from one another in the west end, went to school together, dated for a while when we were in high school. I'm sure both my parents and hers thought we would marry someday." He cut off a piece of brownie with his fork. "In fact, I was planning to propose to her at Christmas, the year after we graduated."

"What happened?"

He chewed on the brownie for a long minute, his eyes focused on something—or maybe some time—in the distance. "I met someone else that summer and fell head over heels in love." He shifted his attention back to Cassie, his gaze almost apologetic. "I'd fallen in love with Irene slowly, over a lot of years. And then Faith walked into my life and the emotions hit me like a ton of bricks. Everything with her was new and intense and exciting."

"And you married her instead," Cassie guessed.

He nodded. "She was the love of my life and I'm grateful for the almost fifty years we had together."

"And now you've come full circle," she noted.

"Do you disapprove of my friendship with Irene?"

"Of course not," she denied. "But I don't want to see her get hurt again."

"Neither do I," he told her.

She considered his response as she nibbled on her own brownie, savoring the rich chocolate flavor.

"Have you ever been in love, Cassie?"

"I was engaged once."

"Which isn't necessarily the same thing," he pointed out.

"I haven't had much luck in the love department," she acknowledged.

"It only takes once," he told her. "You only need one forever-after love to change your whole life."

She sipped her coffee. "I'll keep that in mind."

"It's not about the mind," Jerry admonished. "It's about the heart. You have to keep an open heart."

Cassie thought about Jerry's advice for a long time after she'd said goodbye to him and left Serenity Gardens. A week later, his words continued to echo in the back of her mind.

She headed to the library much earlier than usual, eager to get started on the setup for the Book & Bake Sale. The forecast was for partly sunny skies with a 25 percent chance of precipitation, but that was not until late afternoon. Cassie hoped they would be sold out and packed up before then.

The event was scheduled to start at 8:00 a.m. but she was on-site by six thirty to meet with a group of volunteers from the high school to set up the tents and the tables. There were boxes and boxes in the library basement—old books that had been taken out of circulation and donations from the community.

Over the past several weeks, Tanya and a couple of her friends from the high school had sorted through the donations, grouping the books into genres. Some of the books were horribly outdated—such as *Understanding Windows 2000*—but she decided to put them out on display anyway, because local crafters often picked up old books to create new things. In addition to the books, there were board games and toys and DVDs.

The student volunteers were almost finished setting up the tents when Braden showed up just after seven. It was the first time she'd seen him since she'd abruptly ended their conversation the previous Saturday morning—though she'd heard from Megan that he'd checked out some books when she was on her lunch break a few days earlier—and she wasn't sure what to make of his presence here now.

"The sale doesn't start until eight," she told him.

"I know, but I thought you might be able to use an extra hand with set up."

"We can always use extra hands," she admitted.

"So put me to work," he suggested.

"Where's Saige?" she asked.

"Having pancakes at my parents' house."

"Lucky girl."

He smiled. "My mom's going to bring her by later."

"Okay," she said. "Most of the tents have been set up, Tanya and Chloe know how to arrange the tables, which Cade and Jake are bringing out, so why don't you help Ethan and Tyler haul boxes up from the basement?"

"I can do that," he confirmed.

She led him down to the basement and introduced him to the other helpers, then went back outside to help Brooke arrange the goodies on the bake table. With so many volunteers from the high school—most of them students who were regulars at Soc & Study—there wasn't a lot for her to do, and she found herself spending an inordinate amount of time watching Braden and pretending that she wasn't.

"Is there somewhere else you're supposed to be?" he asked, when he caught her glancing at her watch for about the tenth time.

"Serenity Gardens in half an hour."

"Aren't you about fifty years too early for Serenity Gardens?"

"So maybe we were talking about the same Miss Houlahan," he mused.

"She's been retired for several years, but she never misses any of our fund-raising events."

"I didn't know she was still alive," he admitted. "She seemed about a hundred years old when I was a kid."

"I'm seventy-one," a sharp voice said from behind him. "And not ready for the grave yet."

Braden visibly winced before turning around. "Miss Houlahan—how lovely to see you again."

Behind square wire-rimmed glasses, the old woman's pale blue eyes narrowed. "You're just as cheeky now as you were when you were a boy, Braden Garrett."

Cassie seemed as surprised as he was that the former librarian had remembered him well enough to be able to distinguish him from his brothers and male cousins—all of whom bore a striking resemblance to one another.

"I was planning to pick you up," Cassie interjected.

"Jerry decided he wanted to come and get some books, and it didn't make sense to drag you away if he was heading in this direction," Miss Houlahan said.

"Where is Mr. Riordan?"

"He dropped me off in front, then went to park the car."

"Well, we're not quite finished setting up, but you're welcome to wander around and browse through the books we've got on display."

"I'm not here to shop, I'm here to work," Irene said abruptly.

Cassie nodded, unfazed by the woman's brusque demeanor. "Was there any particular section you wanted to work in?" she asked solicitously.

"Put me near history," the former librarian suggested. "Most people assume old people are experts on anything old."

"We've got history set up—" Cassie glanced at the tables queued along the sideway "—four tables over, just this side of the card shop. Give me a second to finish this display and I'll show you."

"I've got a box of history books right here," Braden said. "I can show her."

"It's 'Miss Houlahan' not 'her,'" Irene corrected him. "And I know where the card shop is."

"I'm heading in that direction anyway, *Miss Houlahan*," he told her.

But she'd already turned and started to walk away, her steps slow and methodical, her right hand gripping the handle of a nondescript black cane. Braden fell into step beside her, the box propped on his shoulder so that he had a hand free in case *Miss Houlahan* stumbled.

She didn't say two words to him as they made their way down the sidewalk. Not that they were going very far—the history/political science table wasn't more than thirty feet from the library's main doors—and not that he expected her to entertain him with chatter, but the silence was somehow not just uncomfortable but somehow disapproving. Or maybe he was projecting his childhood memories onto the moment.

When they reached the table, he eased the box from his shoulder and dropped it on the ground, perhaps a little more loudly than was necessary, and got a perverse sense of pleasure when she jolted at the noise, then glared at him. As he busied himself unpacking the books, he reminded himself that he was no longer a child easily intimidated but a CEO more accustomed to intimidating other people.

He'd just finished unpacking when he heard the sweetest sound in the world: "Da-da!"

Tucking the now-empty box under the table, he turned just in time to catch Saige as she launched herself into his arms. "There's my favorite girl," he said, giving her a light squeeze.

"Choo-choo, Da-da! Choo-choo!" she implored.

"Later," he promised.

Unhappy with his response, she turned her attention to her grandmother, who was following closely behind her. "Choo-choo, Ga-ma!"

"We can go find the trains in a minute," Ellen told her, before greeting Irene Houlahan.

While his mother was chatting with the old librarian, Braden slipped away to get a chair for Miss Houlahan. By the time he got back, his mother and Saige were gone again.

Miss Houlahan thanked him, somewhat stiffly, for the chair before she said, "Your daughter doesn't look much like you."

He smiled at her blunt statement of the obvious fact that so many other people tried to tiptoe around. "Her paternal grandmother was Japanese."

"You adopted her then?" she guessed.

He nodded.

"Adoption is a wonderful way to match up parents who want a child with a child who needs a family," she noted.

He appreciated not just the sentiment but her word choice. He didn't want to count the number of times that someone had referred to children placed for adoption as "unwanted," because that description couldn't be further from the truth. Perhaps untimely in the lives of the women who birthed them, those babies were desperately wanted by their adoptive parents. And in the case of his own daughter, he knew that Lindsay had wanted her child but, even more, she'd wanted a better life for Saige than she'd felt she would be able to give her.

"There was a time I considered adopting a child myself," Miss Houlahan surprised him by confiding. "But that was about forty years ago, when unmarried women weren't considered suitable to take on the responsibilities of raising a child, except maybe a child who was in the foster care system."

"I'm not sure much has changed," he admitted.

"Back then, not a lot of men would be willing to raise an infant on their own, either," she noted.

"I'm a Garrett," he reminded her. "There are currently thirty-one members of my immediate family in this town—believe me, I haven't done any of this on my own."

Miss Houlahan smiled at that, the upward curve of her lips immediately softening her usually stern and disapproving expression. "It takes a village," she acknowledged. "And a willingness to rely on that village."

"Believe me, I'm not just willing but grateful. I don't know how I would have managed otherwise."

"Where does Cassie fit into the picture?" Irene asked.

He didn't insult her by pretending to misunderstand the question. "I'd say that's up to her."

"Hmm," she said. Before she could expand on that response, a tall, silver-haired man ambled over. "I let you out of my sight for five minutes, and you're already chatting up other men," he teased Miss Houlahan.

She pursed her lips in obvious disapproval but introduced the newcomer as Jerry Riordan to Braden, and the two men shook hands.

"You're not trying to steal away my girl, are you?" Jerry asked.

Braden held up his hands in surrender. "No, sir. I can promise you that."

"I'm not anyone's *girl* and I'm not *your* anything," Miss Houlahan said firmly to her contemporary. "And Braden has his eye on Cassie."

"Then I'd say he's got a good eye," Jerry said, sending a conspiratorial wink in Braden's direction.

Miss Houlahan sniffed disapprovingly. "She's a lot more than a pretty face, and she deserves a man who appreciates her sharp mind and generous heart, too."

Braden silently acknowledged the validity of her concerns, because as much as he appreciated Cassie's pretty face and sharp mind, he had no interest in her heart—and even less in putting his own on the line again.

Chapter Seven

The library didn't spend much money to advertise the Book & Bake Sale, relying mostly on word of mouth to draw people to the event. As Cassie looked around the crowds gathered at the tables and milling on the sidewalk, she was satisfied the strategy had succeeded.

She wandered over to the children's tent—always one of the more popular sections—where, in addition to the books and games and toys for sale, balloon animals were being made and happy faces were being painted. Chloe, a straight-A student and an incredible artist, was turning boys and girls into various jungle animals and superheroes, and the lineup for this transformation seemed endless. While Cassie was there, a pint-size dark-haired toddler came racing toward her, baring tiny white teeth. "Raar!"

In response to the growl, Cassie hunkered down to the child's level. "Well, who is this?" she asked, peering closely at the little girl's face. "She looks a little bit like Saige and a lot like a scary lion."

"Raar!" Saige said again, then held out the train in her hand for Cassie's perusal.

"What have you got there?"

"Choo-choo."

She glanced at Braden. "Daddy finally caved and bought you a train, did he?"

Though the little girl probably didn't understand all of the words, she nodded enthusiastically.

"Not Daddy, Grandma," he corrected. "My mother spoils her rotten."

"If that was true, she'd be rotten and she's not," Ellen Garrett protested as she joined them. "In fact, she's so sweet I could gobble her right up." Then she scooped up her granddaughter and pretended to nibble on her shoulder, making Saige shriek with laughter.

"That doesn't change the fact that you indulge her every whim," Braden pointed out.

"Unfortunately, I can't give her what she really needs," his mother said.

He sighed. "Mom."

The single word was a combination of wariness and warning that gave Cassie the distinct impression she was in the middle of a familiar argument between the son and his mother.

"But I can give her a cookie," Ellen said, apparently heeding the warning.

"Kee?" Saige echoed hopefully.

Braden nodded. "*One* cookie," he agreed. "And then I need to get her home for her nap."

"I can take her back to my house," Ellen offered.

"You already had her for most of the morning," he pointed out.

"Is there a reason I shouldn't spend more time with my granddaughter?"

"You know there isn't," he said. "And you know how much I appreciate everything you do for us."

Cassie kept her attention on Saige, quietly entertaining the little girl with the "Handful of Fingers" song while her father and grandmother sorted out their plans.

"Then maybe you could do something for me," his mother suggested.

"Of course," he agreed readily.

"Stick around here to help Cassie with the cleanup—and make sure she gets something to eat."

"Oh, that isn't necessary," Cassie interjected. "We have plenty of volunteers."

"But you can always use extra hands," Braden reminded her of the statement she'd made only a few hours earlier.

"That's settled then," Ellen said happily. "Come on, Saige. Let's go get that cookie."

Braden stole a hug and a kiss from his daughter before he let her head off to the bake table with her grandmother.

"You really don't have to stay," Cassie told him. "You've already done so much to help."

"I do need to stay—my mother said so."

She smiled at that. "Do you always do what your mother tells you to?"

"Usually," he acknowledged. "Especially when it's what I want to do, anyway."

"There must be something else you'd rather do with your Saturday."

"You don't think supporting a community fund-raiser for the local library is good use of my time?" he countered.

"You're deliberately misunderstanding me."

"And you're tiptoeing around the question you really want to ask," he told her.

"You're right," she agreed, a teasing glint in her eye. "What I really want to know is why you got arrested."

He frowned. "Why would you think I was arrested?"

"Because your sudden determination to volunteer seems like a community service thing to me," she told him.

He chuckled at that. "You really do have a suspicious mind, don't you?"

"Not suspicious so much as skeptical," she told him.

"I wanted to help out," he said. "Although yes, I did have an ulterior motive."

"I knew it."

"To spend some time with you," he said, and slung a companionable arm across her shoulders. "Now let's go see if there's anything left at the bake table."

"There's probably not much more than crumbs," she warned. "I know for a fact that all of Mrs. Bowman's muffins were gone within the first half hour."

"How many of those did you take?"

"Four."

He lifted his brows. "Two were my breakfast," she explained. "I took the other two for Irene and Jerry."

"And none for me," he lamented.

"Sorry."

"You can make it up to me by going out with me for some real food when this is over and done," he suggested.

"Are you asking me on a date?"

"I am," he confirmed.

"Then I'm sorry to have to decline," she said. "Because the only reason half these kids are here to help with the takedown is that they know I always get pizza and soda for the volunteers when we're done."

"Does that mean I get to hang around for pizza and soda?"

"Only if you stop slacking and get back to work," she told him.

He grinned. "Yes, ma'am."

* * *

Cassie couldn't fault his work ethic. Braden did what he was told and with a lot less grumbling than she got from some of the teens who were helping out. He might spend his days sitting behind a desk, but he didn't look soft. In fact, the way his muscles bunched and flexed while he worked, he looked pretty darn mouthwatering and close to perfect.

And if she felt uncomfortable that he was hanging around, well, that was on her. He'd done absolutely nothing to suggest that his reasons for being there weren't as simple and straightforward as he claimed. But every once in a while, she'd catch a glimpse of him out of the corner of her eye, and she'd feel a little tingle course through her veins. Or she'd find him looking at her and he'd smile, unashamed to be caught staring, and her heart would flutter inside her chest as if she was a teenage girl. And maybe being surrounded by so many fifteen-to-seventeen year-olds was the reason for her immature and emotional response to the man.

"Is everything okay, Miss Mac?"

She dragged her attention away from Braden to focus on Ethan Anderson—a senior honor student and first-string football player. "Of course, Ethan."

"Who's the old guy hanging around?"

She couldn't help but smile at that. Not because Braden was old but because she understood that to most teens anyone over thirty was ancient—a status she was close to attaining herself. "Braden Garrett," she said. "His daughter is in a couple of the preschool programs."

"Is he your boyfriend?"

"No," she said quickly, unexpectedly flustered by the question.

"Then why is he here?" Ethan wanted to know.

"To help out," she said. "Just like everyone else."

"He's keeping a closer eye on you than anyone else," the teen noted.

"The tables," she reminded him, attempting to shift his attention back to the task at hand.

"You told me to keep this one set up for the pizza."

"Oh. Right."

Ethan eyed her speculatively, his lips curving. "Maybe he's not your boyfriend, but you like him, don't you?"

"What?" She pretended not to understand what he was asking, but she suspected the flush in her cheeks proved otherwise.

"I just noticed that you're keeping a pretty close eye on him, too," he remarked.

"It's my responsibility to keep an eye on *all* of the volunteers," she reminded him.

"So why haven't you told Cade and Jake to stop fooling around?"

She hadn't even noticed that the fifteen-year-old twins were roughhousing on the other side of the room until Ethan directed her gaze in that direction. "Cade, Jake," she called out. "If you don't stop fooling around, I won't sign off on your volunteer hours."

Cade reluctantly released his brother from his headlock and Jake took his elbow out of his twin's side.

Ethan's smile only widened.

Thankfully, before he could say anything else, Tanya announced that the pizza had arrived. While she and Chloe got out the drinks and plates and napkins, Cassie took out the money she'd tucked into her pocket. But when she looked up again, the delivery guy was already halfway back to his car.

"I didn't pay him," Cassie said, frowning.

"I did," Braden told her.

"You didn't have to do that—I've got the money right here."

But he shook his head when she tried to give it to him. "I'm beginning to suspect this might be the only way I ever get to buy you dinner."

Before she could respond, the volunteers descended on the boxes.

"You better grab a slice while you can," she told him.

He nodded and reached for a plate.

Although Braden knew this wasn't quite what his mother had in mind when she asked him to make sure that Cassie got something to eat, he was glad he'd stayed. Not only to lend a hand but to see her interact with the teen group. Although she was an authority figure, he could tell that they didn't just respect her, they genuinely liked her. And they were undoubtedly curious about who he was and why he was hanging around.

There was a lot of talk and laughter while everyone chowed down. The kids were an eclectic group: there was the good girl, the jock, the geek, the cheerleader, the artist. They probably didn't interact much at school, if their paths crossed at all, but here they were all—if not friends—at least friendly.

"Who's the kid in the red hoodie with the fat lip and angry glare?" he asked.

"That's Kevin," Cassie told him. "An eleventh grader at Southmount."

"What's his story?"

She looked at him curiously. "Why do you think he has any more of a story than any of the other kids here?"

"The way you look at him—like you understand what he's all about," he said.

"He hangs out at the library because he's got four

younger siblings at home, it's not all that difficult to understand," she told him.

Maybe not, but he suspected it wasn't quite that simple, either. "What happened to his lip?"

She shrugged. "How would I know?"

But her deliberately casual tone made him suspect that she did know—and wasn't nearly as unconcerned as she wanted him to believe.

"Does he get knocked around at home?" he asked quietly.

"Again—how would I know?"

But he saw it, just a flicker in her eyes, before she answered. And he realized that not only did she know, she'd been there. Who? When? These questions and more clamored for answers, but he knew this wasn't the time and place. Instead, he reached for another slice of pizza.

When everyone had eaten their fill, Cassie wrapped up the extra slices and discreetly slipped them into certain backpacks. After the food was cleared away, the teens started to head out.

Braden noticed that Ethan was the last to leave—after carrying the sole remaining table to the library basement, and even then he seemed reluctant to go.

"Are you sure you don't need anything else, Miss Mac?" the teen asked Cassie.

"I'm sure," she said. "Thanks for all of your help today."

"Anytime," Ethan said.

"So long as it's before June, right?" Cassie said. "After you graduate, you'll be throwing a football at college somewhere."

"Ohio State University," he told her proudly. "I'm going to be a Buckeye."

"Congratulations, Ethan. That's wonderful news."

"I'm glad you think so—Alyssa isn't so thrilled."

"Because she's got another year of high school before she goes off to college," Cassie acknowledged. "But I know she's proud of you."

Ethan checked his phone, grimaced. "And she's going to be annoyed with me if I'm late picking her up for our date tonight."

"Then you should get going," she advised.

He nodded, casting a sidelong glance toward Braden before he headed out. "Have a good night, Miss Mac."

"I don't think your football player likes me," Braden noted.

"He doesn't know you," Cassie clarified, heading into the building.

He followed. "And he's very protective of you."

"He does have a protective nature," she agreed. "But he's a good kid." She sighed when she saw the empty boxes all over the basement but didn't say anything else as she picked one up and broke it apart.

Braden picked up another and did the same. "I noticed most of the kids call you Miss Mac."

"They like nicknames."

But he knew it was more than that—it was a sign of acceptance and camaraderie. "I wonder if anyone ever considered giving Miss Houlahan a nickname," he mused. "How does 'Hoolie' sound?"

"Not very flattering," she said, but he could tell she was fighting a smile.

He grinned. "You don't think she'd like it?"

"I think you like to rile Miss Houlahan," she said, continuing to collapse the empty boxes.

"She was all about the rules and I was never a big fan of them," he explained.

"Your tune will change in a few years," Cassie warned

him. "When your daughter grows up and boys start coming around."

"Nah, I'll just put a padlock on her bedroom door," he decided.

"And then she'll sneak out her bedroom window," she warned.

"Is that what you did when you wanted to go out with a guy you knew your father wouldn't approve of?"

She shook her head. "My dad died when I was ten."

"I'm sorry."

"It was a long time ago," she said.

"Still, I imagine that losing a parent isn't an experience you forget about after a few years."

"No," she agreed. "But you shouldn't worry that Saige will be scarred by the loss of her mother—she's obviously happy and well loved."

"I wasn't thinking about Saige but about you," he told her.

"It was a long time ago," she said again.

She'd left only the biggest box intact and now stuffed the folded cardboard inside of it. "Thanks for your help today. We usually have a good number of volunteers, but the kids sometimes forget why they're here, so it was nice to have another adult around to keep them on task."

"You have an interesting group of kids," he said, turning his attention to stacking the stray chairs with the others that lined the wall. "I couldn't help but notice that they come from several different area high schools."

She nodded. "We advertise our programs widely—in all the schools and at local rec centers—to ensure all students are aware of our programs. For the most part, the ones who come here want the same thing, so they don't bring their issues or rivalries inside."

"That's impressive," he said. "Kids usually carry their grudges wherever they go."

"Only kids?" she challenged, doing a final visual scan of the basement.

"No." He breached the short distance that separated them. "But most adults have better impulse control."

She tipped her head back to meet his gaze. "You think so?"

"Usually," he clarified.

And then he gave in to his own impulses and kissed her.

Cassie was caught completely unaware.

One minute they were having a friendly conversation while they tidied up the basement storage area, and the next, his mouth had swooped down on hers.

In that first moment of contact, her heart stuttered and her mind went blank. And somehow, without even knowing what she was doing, she wound her arms around his neck and kissed him back.

It was all the encouragement Braden needed. He slid his hands around her back, drawing her closer. Close enough that her breasts grazed his chest, making her nipples tighten and the nerves in her belly quiver.

She was suddenly, achingly aware that it had been more than two years since she'd had sex. Twenty-eight months since she'd experienced the thrill of tangling the sheets with a man. For most of that time, she hadn't missed the sharing of physical intimacy. Truth be told, she'd barely thought about it.

But she was definitely thinking about it now.

Braden tipped her head back and adjusted the angle of his mouth on hers, taking his time to deepen the kiss and explore her flavor. Her fingers tangled in the silky ends of his hair, holding on to him as the world tilted on its axis. She sighed and his tongue delved between her parted lips to dance with hers in an erotically enticing rhythm.

He was turning her inside out with a single kiss, obliterating her ability to think. And she needed to think. She needed to be smart. And inviting this man to her home, to her bed, would not be smart.

But it would feel good.

If the man made love even half as masterfully as he kissed, she had no doubt that it would feel *really* good.

She forced herself to push that taunting, tempting thought aside, and to finally, reluctantly, push him away, too.

"What…" She took a moment to catch her breath. "What was that?"

"I think that's what happens when you try to douse a flame with gasoline," he said, sounding a little breathless himself.

"Explosive."

He nodded. "And proof that the chemistry between us hasn't fizzled. You're a dangerous woman, Cassie MacKinnon."

"Me? You're the one who started the fire."

"You're the first woman I've kissed in fifteen months," he admitted. "You're the only woman—aside from my wife—that I've kissed in eight years."

The ground was starting to feel a little more stable beneath her feet, but her heart was still struggling to find a normal rhythm. "That might explain why your technique is a little rusty."

But her unsteady tone belied her words, and his smile widened. "I'd be happy to show you a few other unpracticed talents."

She put her hand on his chest, holding him at a distance. "Maybe another time."

"Is that an invitation or a brush-off?" he asked.

She blew out a breath. "I'm not sure."

Chapter Eight

Several hours later, Braden couldn't stop thinking about the scorching hot kiss he'd shared with the sexy librarian.

Finally back home after picking Saige up from his parents' house and settling her into her crib, he sat down in front of the television as he did on so many other nights. Impulsively, he picked up the remote, clicked off the power and picked up the book he'd borrowed from the library.

But half an hour later, he hadn't turned a single page. He couldn't focus on the words because he couldn't stop thinking about Cassie. He closed the cover and set it aside.

Maybe he shouldn't have kissed her.

Maybe he shouldn't have *stopped* kissing her.

Maybe he should have his head examined.

Definitely he should have his head examined.

He wasn't accustomed to indecision. He was a Garrett— and Garretts didn't vacillate. Garretts set goals and devised clear strategies to get what they wanted.

Braden wanted Cassie, and he didn't doubt that she wanted him, too. But while he was confident that taking her to bed would satisfy their most immediate and basic needs, he knew that he had to think about what would happen after.

He wanted sex. After sleeping alone for more than fifteen months, he desperately wanted the blissful pleasure of joining together with a warm, willing woman. But he wanted more than that, too. One of the things he missed most about being married was the companionship—having someone to talk with about his day, someone to eat dinner with and watch TV with. Someone to snuggle with at night—not necessarily as a prelude to sex but as an affirmation that he wasn't alone in the world.

Oh, who was he kidding? A man snuggled when he wanted sex—other than that, he didn't want anyone encroaching on his territory. Except that after sleeping alone in his king-size bed for so many months, he realized he might not object to a little encroaching. Especially if Cassie was the one invading his space.

If he closed his eyes, he could picture her there—in his bedroom, sprawled on top of the covers in the middle of his mattress, wearing nothing but a smile. He didn't dare close his eyes.

The fact that she was acquainted with his mother and his daughter was both a comfort and a complication. If he decided to pursue a relationship with the librarian, he knew he wouldn't face any obstacles from his family. But if he subsequently screwed up that relationship, it could be incredibly awkward for all of them.

He wasn't looking for a one-night stand, but he wasn't looking to fall in love, either. He had no desire to go down that path again. And while he wasn't opposed to the idea of sharing his life with someone special, his main focus right now was Saige and what was best for his little girl.

But when he finally did sleep, it was Cassie who played the starring role in his dreams.

After she'd finished catching Irene up on all the latest happenings at the library and read a couple chapters of a new book to her, Cassie headed to the grocery store to do her weekly shopping. With her list in hand, she methodically walked up and down the aisles.

She paused at the meat cooler and surveyed the selection of pork roasts. Several weeks earlier, she'd found a recipe that she was eager to try, but the roasts seemed like too much for one person. Of course, she could freeze the leftovers for future meals—or maybe invite Irene and Jerry to come over.

After selecting what she needed from that department, she moved to the fresh food section and from there on to the nonperishable aisles. Cat food was on sale, so she stocked up on Westley's and Buttercup's favorite flavors. Then she remembered that she needed kitty litter, too, and added a bag of that to her cart.

And then she rounded the corner and nearly collided with Braden Garrett.

"I guess it's a popular day for grocery shopping," she said lightly.

Saige was seated in the cart facing her father, but twisted around when she recognized Cassie's voice, a wide smile spreading across her face.

"I'm here at least three times a week," Braden admitted. "Because I never seem to remember everything I need to get it all done in one trip."

"You don't make a list?"

"I usually do, and then I usually forget the list on the table at home."

Cassie smiled as Saige offered her a package of string cheese. "Those look yummy," she commented.

The little girl nodded her enthusiastic agreement.

"What other treats does Daddy have for you in there?"

Saige dropped the package of cheese and picked up a box of yogurt tubes. "Chay-wee."

The flavor noted on the box helped Cassie interpret. "You like the cherry ones best," she guessed.

Saige nodded again.

"Me, too," Cassie confided, as she glanced from Braden's shopping cart to her own. His was almost filled with family-size boxes of cereal, multipacks of juice, and bags of fresh fruits and vegetables; Cassie's basket wasn't even half full and her biggest purchases were the cat food and kitty litter.

"We're on our way to the prepared foods section, because I forgot to take dinner out of the freezer this morning," Braden told her. "Why don't you come over to eat with us?"

"Thanks, but I have to get my groceries home and put away."

"You could come over after," he suggested.

She considered the offer for about two seconds before declining. Because as much as she didn't want to be the lonely old cat lady, she also didn't want to be the broken-hearted librarian. Again. And since the kiss they'd shared in the basement of the library four days earlier, it would be foolish to continue to deny the chemistry between them. The only thing she could do now was avoid situations in which that chemistry might heat up again.

"I could get a tray of three-cheese tortellini," he said enticingly. "It's not Valentino's, but it's not bad."

She ignored the temptation—of the food and the man. "Maybe another time."

His direct and steady gaze warned that he could read more of what she was thinking and feeling than she wanted him to.

"We're at twenty-eight Spruceside in Forrest Hill, if you change your mind," he finally said.

But she knew that she wouldn't—she couldn't. "Enjoy your tortellini."

When Cassie was finished making and eating her own dinner, she turned on her tablet to check her email. Then she snapped a picture of the cats wrestling on the carpet in front of her and posted it to her Facebook page. Scrolling through her newsfeed, she saw that a friend from high school—who had married in the Bahamas just before Christmas—was expecting a baby. She noted her congratulations, adding hearts and celebratory confetti emojis to the message.

Buttercup jumped up onto the couch and crawled into her lap. She stroked her back, her feline companion purring contentedly as Cassie's fingers slid through her soft, warm fur.

She had so many reasons to be grateful: terrific friends and a great job that allowed her to spend much of her time working with children. But recently, after spending even just a little bit of time with Braden and Saige, she was suddenly aware of the emptiness inside herself, a yearning for something more.

She was twenty-nine years old with a history of broken or dead-end relationships—it would be crazy to even think about getting involved with a widowed single father to an adorable baby girl who made all of her maternal instincts sit up and beg "pick me." And while Braden had flirted with her a little, and kissed her exactly once, she didn't know what he wanted from her. But she knew what she wanted: a husband, children, a house with a second chair on the front porch and a tire swing in the backyard.

Unfortunately, she had a habit of jumping into relationships, falling in love before she had a chance to catch her breath. Most of the time, it was infatuation rather than love, but she usually only realized the truth after the relationship was over.

She wondered whether it was some kind of legacy from her childhood, if losing her family had created a desperate yearning in her for a meaningful connection. She didn't have a list of qualities that she was looking for in a partner, although she wouldn't object to meeting a man who would make her heart beat from across a room and her insides quiver with a simple touch—and Braden Garrett checked both of those boxes.

She also liked the way he interacted with his little girl, leaving absolutely no doubt about how much he loved his daughter. And she liked the way he talked about his family—not just his parents and siblings but his aunts, uncles and cousins and all of their kids.

And she really liked the way she felt when he looked at her.

She hadn't felt that stir of attraction in a long time—and she didn't want to be feeling it for this man now. Because as gorgeous and charming as he was, she'd vowed to stay away from men who had already given their hearts away.

But she couldn't deny that she was intrigued to see his house in Forrest Hill—or maybe she was just looking for an excuse to see him again. Whatever the reason, she set her tablet aside and picked up her keys.

Braden settled Saige into her high chair with a bowl of tortellini while he put the groceries away. She used both of her hands to shove the stuffed pasta into her mouth, ignoring the spoon he'd given to her. When her bowl was empty, she had sauce—and a happy grin—spread across her face.

"Did you like that?" he asked her.

She nodded and pushed her empty bowl to the edge of her tray. "Mo'."

"Do you want more pasta or do you want dessert?"

She didn't hesitate. "Zert!"

"Yeah, that was a tough question, wasn't it?" He chuckled as he wiped her face, hands and tray.

He was looking in the fridge, considering dessert options, when the doorbell rang.

He unbuckled Saige and lifted her out of her high chair, then went to respond to the summons. He wasn't expecting company, but it wasn't unusual for his parents or his brother Justin, or any of his cousins to stop by if they were in the neighborhood. The absolute last person he expected to see when he opened the door was Charisma's sexy librarian.

"I changed my mind," Cassie said.

Despite the assertion, she looked a little uncertain, as if she might again change her mind and turn right back around.

"I'm glad," he said, and moved away from the door so that she could enter. "Saige and I have already eaten, but there is some pasta left."

"Zert!" Saige said.

Cassie smiled at his daughter. "I had dinner," she said. "And then I decided I was in the mood for ice cream, so I went back to the grocery store and came out with all of this."

He glanced at the bags as she stepped into the foyer. "That looks like a lot of ice cream."

"It's not just ice cream. There's also chocolate sauce,

marshmallow topping, chopped peanuts, toffee bits, sprinkles and maraschino cherries."

"I cweam?" Saige said hopefully.

Braden chuckled. "Yes, Cassie brought ice cream. And it sounds like a whole sundae bar, too," he noted, taking the bags and leading her through the living room.

Cassie shrugged. "I didn't know what you and Saige liked."

"What do you like?"

"Everything," she admitted.

He grinned. "A woman after my own heart."

But Cassie shook her head. "I'm only here for the ice cream." Then her gaze shifted, to take in the surroundings as she followed him toward the kitchen. "How long have you lived here?"

"Almost six years."

"So you've had time to paint—if you wanted to," she noted.

"Dana picked the colors," he admitted.

She squinted at the walls, as if looking for the color, and he chuckled.

"I know it's hard to see the difference, but the foyer is magnolia blossom—no, the original color was magnolia blossom," he remembered. "Now it's spring drizzle or summer mist or something like that, the living and dining rooms are vintage linen…I think, and the kitchen is French vanilla."

"In other words, every room is a different shade of white," she commented.

"Pretty much," he admitted, depositing the grocery bags on the counter so he could put Saige back in her high chair.

"I cweam!" Saige demanded.

"Yes, we're going to have ice cream," he promised.

His little girl clapped her hands together.

"Do you like chocolate sauce?" Cassie asked his daughter.

"Chay-wee."

"I brought some cherries, too," she said. Then, to Braden, "What I didn't bring was an ice-cream scoop."

He opened a drawer to retrieve the necessary implement, then reached into an overhead cupboard for bowls while she unpacked the bags.

"You should make Saige's sundae," she said, nudging the tub of vanilla ice cream toward him. "Because you know what she likes and what she can have."

"She likes everything, too," he told her. "Although she probably shouldn't have the toffee bits or peanuts. Or a lot of chocolate."

"Which is why you should do it," she said again.

So he scooped up a little bit of ice cream, added a drop of chocolate sauce, a dollop of marshmallow topping, a few sprinkles and three cherries on top.

"You need to use a spoon for this," he told Saige, setting the bowl in front of her.

"'Kay," she agreed, wrapping her fingers around the plastic handle of the utensil.

"How many scoops do you want?" Cassie asked him.

"How many can I have?"

She put three generous scoops of ice cream into the bowl, covered them with chocolate sauce, nuts, toffee bits, marshmallow topping, sprinkles and cherries. Then she prepared a second, much smaller bowl of the same for herself.

"I'm not sure why you came all this way to bring us dessert, but I'm glad you did," he told her, digging into his sundae.

"Bingeing on ice cream seems like one of those things that shouldn't be done alone."

"I seem to be the only one bingeing," he pointed out.

"And as good as this ice cream is, I can think of other and more satisfying things that shouldn't be done alone, either."

Her cheeks turned a pretty shade of pink as she dipped her spoon into her bowl.

"And maybe I wanted to have a real conversation with another human being as much as I was craving ice cream," she admitted.

"Conversation, huh?" He scooped up more ice cream. "That wasn't exactly what I had in mind, but okay. Anything in particular you want to talk about?"

"No." She slid her spoon between her lips, humming with pleasure as she closed her eyes. "Oh, this is good."

He knew she wasn't being deliberately provocative, but he recognized her expression as that of a woman lost in pure, sensual pleasure, and he found himself wishing that he'd been the one to put that look on her face. Because her blissful smile, combined with the sensual sound emanating from deep in her throat, had all of the blood draining from his head into his lap. To cool the heat pulsing in his veins, he shoved another spoonful of ice cream into his mouth.

"What did you have for dinner?" Braden asked, hoping that conversation would force her to open her eyes and stop making those noises that were making him aroused.

"A microwaveable chicken and rice bowl," she admitted.

"That sounds…incredibly unappealing," he decided.

She licked her spoon. "It wasn't that bad." And then she shrugged. "I do occasionally cook, but it's not a lot of fun to prepare meals for only one person."

"You can make dinner for me anytime," he told her.

"That's a generous offer," she said dryly.

He grinned. "I'm a generous guy."

"Hmm," was all Cassie said to that, as she spooned up more ice cream.

"Aw dun!" Saige announced.

He shifted his attention away from Cassie. "And it looks like you put more in your belly than on your face this time," he noted. "Good girl."

She smiled and rubbed her belly. "Mo?"

He shook his head. "No more ice cream for you or I'll never get you to sleep tonight."

"Chay-wee?" she said hopefully.

Before he could respond, Cassie had scooped one of the cherries out of her bowl and held her spoon out to Saige, who snagged the piece of fruit and popped it into her mouth. Then she smiled again, showing off the cherry caught between her front teeth, making Cassie laugh.

His attention shifted back to her, noted her curved lips and sparkling eyes. He'd always thought she was beautiful, but looking at her here now—in his kitchen, with his daughter—she almost took his breath away.

"Chay-wee?" Saige said again.

"I've got one more," Cassie said, this time looking to Braden for permission before she offered it.

He shrugged. At this point, he didn't think one more cherry was going to make any difference.

So Cassie gave Saige her last cherry, then pushed away from the table to clear away their empty bowls. While she was doing that, he got a washcloth to wipe off Saige's face and hands. He was returning the cloth to the sink just as Cassie closed the dishwasher and turned around, the action causing her breasts to brush against his chest.

She sucked in a breath and took half a step back—until she bumped against the counter. "Oh. Um. Sorry."

He held her gaze, watched her pupils dilate until there was only a narrow ring of dark chocolate around them. "Close quarters," he noted.

She looked around, managed a laugh. "This is not close quarters. You should see my kitchen."

"Is that an invitation?" he asked.

She tilted her head, as if considering. "Maybe."

He smiled and took a half step forward, so there was barely a breath between them. "I think we're making progress."

The tip of her tongue swept over her bottom lip, leaving it glistening with moisture. "Are we?"

He dipped his head, so that his mouth hovered above hers. "I haven't stopped thinking about our first kiss," he admitted.

"First implies the beginning of a series," she pointed out.

He'd noticed that she had a habit of reciting definitions and facts when she was nervous. Apparently he was making her nervous; she was definitely making him aroused.

"Uh-huh," he agreed.

"And I haven't decided if there's going to be a second," she said, the breathless tone undercutting her denial.

"That's okay—because I have," he said, and brushed his lips against hers.

Her eyelids fluttered and had just started to drift shut when the phone rang.

She immediately drew back; he cursed under his breath but didn't move away.

"Aren't you going to answer that?" she asked him.

"If my choices are answering the phone or kissing you, I opt for door number two," he told her.

But when the phone rang again, she lifted her hands to his chest and pushed him away. "I need to get home," she said.

With a resigned sigh, he stepped back.

A cursory glance at the number on the display panel had a whole different kind of tension taking hold of him.

"I'm sorry," he said, "but I do have to answer this."

"Of course," she said easily.

Nothing was easy about the emotions that coursed through his system as he lifted the receiver to his ear. "Hello?"

"Hi, Mr. Garrett."

"Lindsay?"

"Yeah, it's me," she confirmed.

He hadn't heard from Saige's biological mother in months, and the last he'd heard, she was in London. The 330 exchange, though, was Ohio, which meant that she was back at her parents' house.

As endless thoughts and questions tumbled through his mind, he vaguely registered Cassie lifting a hand in a silent goodbye before she stepped out of the room and then, out the front door.

Chapter Nine

Cassie didn't hear from Braden again until Friday afternoon when he came into the library. She was guiding an elderly patron through the self-checkout process and showing her how to unlock the DVDs she wanted to borrow. He waited patiently until she was finished, pretending to peruse the books on the Rapid Reads shelf, but she felt him watching her, his gaze almost as tangible as a caress.

"Can I help you with something, Mr. Garrett?" she asked when Elsa Ackerley had gone.

"You could accept my apology," he said.

"What are you apologizing for?"

"Not having a chance to say good-night before you left the other night."

"You were obviously focused on your conversation with…what was her name?"

"Lindsay," he told her.

"Right—Lindsay." She kept her tone light, feigning an

indifference she didn't feel. Pretending it didn't bother her that less than a minute after his mouth had been hovering over hers and anticipation had been dancing in her veins, he'd forgotten she was even there as he gave his full and complete attention to *Lindsay*. Proving to Cassie, once again, how unreliable her instincts were when it came to the opposite sex.

"And it's not what you think," Braden said to her now.

"I'm not thinking anything," she lied.

He opened his mouth as if to say something else, then closed it again when Helen approached the desk. After retrieving the basket of recently returned DVDs, she steered her cart away again.

"Have dinner with me tonight and give me a chance to explain," he said when Helen had gone.

"You don't owe me any explanations," she assured him. "And I'm working until seven, anyway."

"Then you'll probably be hungry when you're done," he pointed out.

"Which is why I have a pork roast in my slow cooker at home." Although she hadn't been able to firm up plans with Irene and Jerry, she'd impulsively decided to cook the roast anyway, figuring she'd take the leftovers to her friend on the weekend.

"I was offering to take you out for dinner, but that sounds even better," he decided.

She blinked. "What?"

"Dinner at your place is an even better idea than going out."

"I didn't—"

But he'd already turned and walked away.

Cassie huffed out a breath as she watched him disappear through the door. She didn't know if she was more amused or exasperated that he'd so easily manipulated the situation to his advantage, but there was no doubt the man knew how to get what he wanted—though she was still uncertain about what he wanted from her.

And while the prospect of sharing a meal with Braden filled her with anticipation, she couldn't help but wonder if he only wrangled dinner with her because Lindsay had other plans.

He wasn't waiting outside the door when she left the library and he wasn't in the parking lot, either. Cassie exhaled a sigh as she headed toward home and told herself that she was relieved he'd changed his mind. But she was a little confused, too. Braden had deliberately twisted her words to suggest an invitation she'd never intended, and then he didn't even bother to follow up on it. Maybe she hadn't planned to invite him, but she still felt stood up.

She shook off the feeling that she refused to recognize as disappointment and focused on admiring the many colorful flowers that brightened her path as she walked to her modest one-and-a-half story home that was only a few blocks from the library. The spring season was evident in the sunny yellow jessamine, vibrant pink tulips, snowy bloodroot and bright purple irises, and she felt her mood lifting a little with every step.

Her steps slowed when she spotted an unfamiliar vehicle parked on the street in front of her house. A late model silver Mercedes sedan. And leaning against the hood of the car, looking ridiculously handsome, was Braden Garrett with a bottle of wine in one hand and a bouquet of flowers in the other.

He smiled when he saw her, and her resolve melted away like ice cubes in a glass of sweet tea on a hot summer day.

"You said you were cooking a pork roast," he said by

way of greeting. "And while some people claim that pork is the other white meat, you once mentioned that you preferred red wine so I picked up a bottle of my favorite Pinot Noir." He offered her the bouquet. "I also brought you flowers."

"Why?" she asked, unexpectedly moved by the commonplace gesture. Because commonplace or not, it had been a long time since any man had brought her flowers.

"It's been a long time since I've had a first date, but I always thought flowers were a nice gesture."

"This isn't a date," she told him.

"Then what is it?"

"It's you mooching my dinner."

"I offered to take you out," he reminded her.

She nodded in acknowledgment of the point. "And then you deliberately misinterpreted my refusal as an invitation."

"You weren't asking me to come here for a meal?" he asked, feigning surprise—albeit not very convincingly.

"The pork roast isn't anything fancy," she told him, as she unlocked the front door. "And there's nothing for dessert."

"No cheesecake?" he asked, disappointed.

She was helpless to prevent the smile that curved her lips. "Sorry—no."

"Well, I'm glad to be here, anyway," Braden said, following her into the house.

Waning rays of sunlight spilled through the tall windows that flanked the door, illuminating the natural stone floor. The walls in the entranceway were painted a warm shade of grayish blue and the wide trim was glossy and white.

He was barely inside the door when he felt an unexpected bump against his shin. "What the—" He glanced down to see a cat with pale gold fur rubbing against his pant leg. "You have a cat."

"Two actually." She glanced over her shoulder. "That's Buttercup. She's much more sociable than Westley."

It took him a minute to figure out why the names sounded familiar. "*The Princess Bride*?" he guessed, carefully stepping around the cat to follow her into the bright and airy kitchen.

She seemed surprised that he'd connected the names to the story. "You've read the book?"

He frowned. "It's a book?"

Cassie shook her head despairingly, but another smile tugged at the corners of her mouth. "It was a book long before it was a movie."

"I haven't read the book," he admitted, as he looked around to admire the maple cupboards, granite countertops and mosaic tile backsplash. "But it was a great movie."

"One of my favorites." She took a meat thermometer out of a drawer and lifted the lid of the slow cooker to check the temperature of the roast. "And the book was even better."

"You're a librarian—you probably have to say that."

"Why don't I lend it to you, then you can judge for yourself?" she suggested.

"Sure," he agreed. "Mmm…that smells really good."

"Hopefully it tastes as good," she said. "It's a new recipe I'm trying out."

"So I'm a guinea pig?" he teased.

"As a result of your own machinations," she reminded him.

"I'm here for the company more than the food, anyway." He looked over her shoulder and into the pot. "Are those parsnips?"

"You don't like parsnips?" she guessed.

"Actually, I do. And sweet potatoes, too," he said, chunks of which were also in the pot. "I just didn't think anyone other than my mother cooked them."

"How lucky that you decided to invite yourself to dinner tonight," she said dryly, replacing the lid.

He grinned. "I was just thinking the same thing."

"Why don't you open the wine while I take care of these flowers?"

"Corkscrew?"

She pointed. "Top drawer on the other side of the sink. Glasses are above the refrigerator."

While he was opening the bottle, she slipped out of the room. The cat stayed with him, winding between his legs and rubbing against him.

He glanced down at the ball of fur and remarked, "Well, at least one of the females here is friendly."

"She's an attention whore," Cassie told him, returning with a clear glass vase.

"Where's Westley?"

"Probably sleeping by the fireplace—he spends most of his day lazing in his bed until he hears his food being poured into his bowl." Setting the vase aside, she opened the door of the pantry and pulled out a bag. She carried it to an alcove beside the fridge, where he saw now there were two sets of bowls neatly aligned on mats, and crouched down to pour the food.

As the first pieces of kibble hit the bottom of the bowl, he heard a distant thump of paws hitting the floor then saw a streak of black and white shoot across the kitchen floor. The plaintive meow made Braden realize it wasn't his bowl that Cassie had filled first. Her attention diverted by her sibling's call, Buttercup padded over to her bowl and hunkered down to feast on her dinner while Westley waited for his own.

"I've never seen a cat reluctant to eat out of another animal's bowl," he noted.

"Neither of them does," she told him. "Which makes it easier for me when I need to put drops or supplements in their food, because I know they've each gotten the right amount."

"Did you train them to do that?"

She smiled at that. "You've obviously never tried to train a cat to do anything."

"I'm guessing the answer to my question is no."

"No," she confirmed. "It's just a lucky quirk of their personalities. Or maybe it has something to do with the fact that, as kittens, they were crammed into a boot box with four other siblings. Now they appreciate having their own space—not just their own bowls but their own litter boxes and beds." Although they usually curled up together in one or the other when it was time to go to sleep, because apparently even feline creatures preferred not to sleep alone.

"Six kittens and you only ended up with two?" he teased.

"I wanted to take them all," she admitted. "But I'm not yet ready to be known as the crazy old cat lady."

"You're too young to be old," he assured her.

She lifted a brow. "I notice you didn't dispute the 'crazy' part."

"I don't really know you well enough to make any assertions about your state of mind," he pointed out. Then, "So what happened to the other kittens?"

"Tanya—you met her at the Book & Bake Sale—took Fezzik, Mr. and Mrs. Bowman—regular patrons of the library—chose Vizzini, Mr. Osler—the old bachelor who lives across the street—wanted Inigo, and Megan—one of the librarian assistants—took Prince Humperdinck, but she just calls him Prince."

"You named them all," he guessed.

"I found them," she said logically.

"That seems fair," he agreed, watching as she snipped the stems of the flowers and set them in the vase she'd filled with water. She fussed a little with the colorful blooms, so he knew she liked them. A fact she further confirmed when she set the vase on the windowsill above the sink and said, "Thank you—they're beautiful."

"They are beautiful," he agreed. "That's why they made me think of you."

"You always have the right line, don't you?"

"Do I?" he asked, surprised. "Because I often feel a little tongue-tied around you."

"I find that hard to believe."

"It's true," he told her.

While Cassie sliced the meat, Braden set the table, following her directions to locate the plates and cutlery. Then they sat down together to eat the pork roast and vegetables and drink the delicious Pinot Noir he'd brought to go with the meal.

"You're not going to ask, are you?" Braden said, as he stabbed his fork into a chunk of sweet potato.

She shook her head. "It's none of my business."

"Well, I'm going to tell you anyway—Lindsay is Saige's birth mother."

"Oh." Of all the possible explanations he might have given, that one had never occurred to her.

"When Dana and I adopted Saige, we promised Lindsay that we would keep in touch. But not long after the papers were signed, she went to London to do a year of school there, and although I routinely sent photos and emails, I hadn't actually spoken to her in more than a year."

"Why was she calling?" Cassie asked curiously.

"Because she's back in the US and wants to see Saige."

"Oh," she said again. "How do you feel about that?"

"Obligated," he admitted. "We agreed to an open adoption—of course, we would have agreed to almost anything to convince Lindsay to sign the papers—so I can't really refuse. And I do think it is important for Saige to know the woman who gave birth to her, but I'm a little concerned, too."

"About?" she prompted gently.

He picked up his glass of wine but didn't drink; he only stared into it. "Lindsay gave up her baby because she wanted her to be raised in a traditional family with two parents who would love her and care for her. And now that I'm a single parent, I can't help worrying that Lindsay will decide she wants Saige back."

She considered that as she sipped her wine. "I don't know much about adoption laws, but I would think it's a little late for her to change her mind, isn't it?"

"Most likely," he acknowledged. "The first thing I did when I hung up the phone after talking to Lindsay was call my cousin, who's a lawyer. Jackson assured me that judges generally don't like to reverse adoptions. But he also warned me that if Lindsay decided to take it to court and got a sympathetic judge, she *might* be able to claim a material change in circumstances and argue that Saige's best interests would be served by vacating our contract."

Cassie immediately shook her head, horrified by the possibility. "There's no way anybody who has ever seen you with your daughter would believe it's in her best interests to be anywhere but with you."

He managed a smile at that. "I appreciate the vote of confidence."

His smile did funny things to her insides—or maybe she was hungry. She decided to stop talking and start eating.

Braden's plate was almost empty before he spoke again. "Tell me something about you," he said.

"What do you want to know?"

"Have you been dating anyone—other than Darius Richmond—recently?"

She shook her head. "No. In fact, until a few months ago, I hadn't dated at all in a couple of years."

"Bad break-up before that?" he asked sympathetically.

But she shook her head. "The break-up was good—the relationship was bad."

His dark green eyes took on a dangerous gleam. "Was he abusive?"

"No, nothing that dramatic," she assured him. "I was twenty-six when I met him and eager to move on to the next stage in my life."

"Marriage," he guessed.

She nodded. "And kids. I wanted so desperately to get married and start a family that I saw what I wanted to see…right up until the minute the truth slapped me in the face—figuratively speaking."

"Were you married?"

"No," she said again. "Just engaged for a few months."

She thought back to that blissful moment when Joel Langdon proposed. They'd quickly set the date for their wedding and booked the church and the reception venue, and she'd been so excited for their future together, believing they were on their way to happily-ever-after.

"Until I discovered that he was still in love with his ex-wife," she continued.

Braden winced. "How did that happen?"

"As we talked about the wedding, I realized that Joel had some specific ideas about how he wanted his bride to look. A strapless dress wasn't appropriate for a church wedding, white satin would make my skin look pasty, and the princess-style ball gown would overwhelm my frame.

Instead, he'd suggested a more streamlined style, perhaps ivory in color with long sleeves covered in ecru lace."

"That's pretty specific," he noted.

She nodded. And although she'd been disappointed by her fiancé's assessment, she'd been pleased he was taking such an interest in the details of their special day.

"He also suggested that I should let my hair grow out, so that I could wear it up under my veil—but I hadn't planned to wear a veil. And maybe I could consider adding a few blond highlights, to tone down the auburn. The more suggestions he made, the more I realized that he was trying to change who I was—or at least how I looked."

She shook her head, lamenting her own foolishness for not seeing then what was so obvious to her now. She knew he'd been married before, but Joel hadn't talked about his ex-wife. He certainly never said or did anything to suggest to Cassie that he was still in love with her.

"It was only after I moved in with him that I found his wedding album with the date engraved on the front—the same month and day he'd chosen to marry me."

And the date had been *his* choice. She'd thought that a fall wedding might be nice, but he'd urged her to consider spring, so that she could carry a bouquet of white tulips—her favorite flowers. She hadn't much thought about what flowers she wanted for the wedding, and while she wouldn't have said tulips were her favorite, she liked them well enough.

"Then I opened the cover and saw a picture of his ex-wife, in her long-sleeved lace gown with a bouquet of white tulips in her hand." She'd slowly turned the pages, trying to make sense of what she was seeing. "And on the last page, the close-up photo of the bride's and groom's hands revealed that my fiancé had proposed to me with his ex-wife's engagement ring.

"The rest of it I might have been able to ignore," she admitted. "But when I saw the diamond cluster on her finger—the same diamond cluster that was on my finger— I felt sick to my stomach.

"And when I confronted him about it, he didn't even try to deny it—he just said he'd paid a lot of money for the ring. So I took it off my finger and told him that I hoped the next woman he gave it to wouldn't mind being his second choice."

All of which was why she'd barely dated in the more than two years that had passed since her broken engagement. Because in the space of the few hours that had passed between finding the wedding album hidden in the back of her fiancé's closet and his return to the apartment, she'd been shocked—and a little scared—by some of the thoughts that had gone through her own mind.

During that time, she'd actually tried to convince herself that she was making the discovery of those photos into more than it needed to be. She'd even considered putting the album back and pretending that she'd never seen it, to let it go so they could move forward with their plans.

Because she'd been desperate to feel connected to someone, desperate to be part of a family again. Even aware that marriage to a man who was still in love with another woman didn't bode well for their long-term future together, her eagerness to be a wife and then a mother almost made her willing to overlook that fact. *Almost.*

In the end, it was this desperation to not be alone that made her rethink her plans. Her mother hadn't ever been able to find happiness or even contentment on her own. Not even her daughters had been enough for her. She'd needed to be with a man; she'd needed his adoration and approval to justify her existence. The possibility that she might be like her mother—that she could make the same destructive choices and ruin not only her own life but that of any children she might have in the future—compelled her to take that step back.

Actually, she'd taken a lot of steps back. For a long time after she'd given Joel back the ring, she'd been afraid to even go out on a date. Her desperation to be a wife and a mother had made her question her own judgment and fear her own motivations. Thankfully, she had her job at the library to give her another focus, and she found both pleasure and fulfillment in working with children and teens.

She'd vowed then not to waste any more time with the wrong men. Unfortunately, the wrong men didn't always come with a warning label, as her recent experience with Darius Richmond had demonstrated. And if she wanted to find the right man, she had to be open to meeting new people.

Over the past few months, she'd started to do that, but none of the guys she'd gone out with had made her think "maybe this one." None of their good-night kisses had made her pulse race and her heart pound. In fact, none of their kisses made her want a second date.

No one had made her want anything more—until Braden kissed her.

Chapter Ten

"Cassie?"

She glanced up to find Braden watching her, his expression one of concern. She forced a smile. "Sorry—my mind just wandered off for a moment."

"How long ago was it that you gave him back the ring?" he wondered.

"Two years."

He set his cutlery on his empty plate and swallowed the last of the wine in his glass. "Did you live with him here?"

"No," she said again, smiling a little at this happier memory as she pushed away from the table to begin the cleanup. "I found this place when Stacey and I spent most of a rainy Sunday afternoon going through open houses. I think this was the third—or maybe the fourth—house we saw, and as soon as I saw the den with the fireplace and the built-in bookcases, I wanted it."

"I think I need to see the den," he remarked.

So she led the way through the dining room to her favorite room in the house. As he stepped inside, she tried to see it through his eyes. She knew it was modestly sized, as was the rest of the house, but there wasn't anything else about the room that she would change. Not the hardwood floors or the natural stone fireplace or the trio of tall narrow windows—each with a cushy seat from which she could enjoy the view of her postage-stamp-sized backyard—and especially not the floor-to-ceiling bookcases that covered most of three walls and were filled with her books.

"Well, it doesn't look as if you'd ever run out of reading material." He ventured farther into the room to examine the array of titles that filled her shelves and reflected her eclectic taste. From Jane Austen's *Pride and Prejudice* to J.R. Ward's *Dark Lover*; from Anthony Burgess's *A Clockwork Orange* to Shel Silverstein's *The Giving Tree*; from John Douglas's *Mindhunter* to Eckhart Tolle's *The Power of Now*. There were also biographies of historical figures, entrepreneurs and movie stars; books about auto mechanics and dogs and feng shui. "You have almost as many books here as there are at the library."

"Hardly."

"How many have you actually read?" he wondered.

"All of them—except for that bottom shelf," she said, pointing. "Those are new."

"You've read every other book on these shelves?" he asked, incredulous.

"Some of them more than once." She moved to the other side of the room and reached up to the third shelf. "Do you want to borrow this one?"

He took the book from her hand and glanced at the cover. "*The Princess Bride: S. Morgenstern's Classic Tale of True Love and High Adventure* by William Goldman."

He frowned. "Who's the author—Morgenstern or Goldman?"

She just smiled. "Read the book."

They returned to the kitchen and the task of cleaning up. "I'm sorry I don't have anything for dessert," she said.

"But you weren't expecting company," he said, speaking the words before she could.

"I guess I've made the point a few times."

"A few," he acknowledged, starting to load the dishwasher while she packed the rest of the meat and vegetables into a plastic container. "I'm still not sorry that I crashed your dinner party for one."

"I'm not sorry you did, either," she said, lifting her glass to her lips. "This is good wine."

He smiled. "I didn't think you'd admit that."

"That I like the wine?"

"That you like my company."

She opened the refrigerator to put the leftovers inside. "I never said that."

He chuckled as he closed the dishwasher. "I was reading between the lines."

She put the stoneware from the slow cooker in the sink and filled it with soapy water, then dried her hands on a towel.

When she turned away from the sink, he was right in front of her, trapping her between the counter and his body. *Déjà vu*, she thought. And in her kitchen, they really were in close quarters.

Braden lowered his head toward her. She went still, completely and perfectly still, as his lips moved closer to her own. Then he shifted direction, his mouth skimming over her jaw instead. The unexpected—and unexpectedly sensual caress—made her breath catch in her throat, then shudder out between her lips.

"Wh-what are you doing?"

"Well—" his mouth moved toward her ear, nibbled on the lobe "—you said there wasn't anything for dessert, and I was in the mood for something sweet."

Lust pulsed through her body, a relentless and throbbing ache. "And you think I'm...sweet?"

"I think you are incredibly sweet," he told her, his mouth skimming leisurely down her throat.

"Um—" she had no idea what to say to that "—thank you?"

She felt him smile, his lips curving against the ultra-sensitive spot between her neck and collarbone. "You really have no idea how you affect me, do you?"

"I know how you affect me," she admitted.

"Tell me," he suggested, his mouth returning to brush lightly over hers.

"You make me feel things I haven't felt in a very long time."

His lips feathered across her cheekbone. "What kind of things?"

Her fingers dug into his shoulders. "Hot. Needy. Weak."

"You make me feel all of those things, too," he assured her.

"When you kiss me...when you touch me...you make me forget all the reasons this is a bad idea."

He put his hands on her hips and lifted her onto the counter so that they were at eye level. He spread her thighs and stepped between them. "So maybe this isn't such a bad idea," he suggested, then covered her mouth again.

As if of their own volition, her legs wrapped around him, drawing him closer. So close that she could feel the ridge of his arousal beneath his zipper. She pressed shamelessly against him, wanting to feel his hardness against her. Inside her.

His hands slipped under her top, skimming up her belly to her breasts. She couldn't remember what kind of underwear she'd put on that morning—whether it was cotton or satin or lace. Lace, she decided, as his thumbs brushed over the nipples through the whisper-thin fabric, sending sharp arrows of sensation from the beaded tips to her core.

He made her want with an intensity and desperation that she'd never experienced before. Even in high school, when many of the other girls were slaves to their hormones, she'd spent most nights at home, alone. She'd been the quiet girl, the geeky girl. Most of the boys hadn't looked at her twice. She was too smart and flat-chested to warrant their notice. And that was okay—because she didn't want to be distracted from her plans and she especially didn't want to be like her mother.

She imagined that Braden had been one of the popular boys. Smart and rich and devastatingly good-looking. He certainly kissed like a man who had a lot of experience. And he knew just where and how to touch her so that her only thoughts were *yes* and *more*.

He was the type of guy who'd dated the most popular girls—the cheerleaders or varsity athletes. The type who never would have noticed her. And although they weren't in high school now, he was the CEO of a national corporation and she was a small-town librarian. In other words, he was still way out of her league.

But somehow, by some twist of fate, he was here with her now. Kissing her and touching her, and she was incredibly, almost unbearably, aroused. "Braden—"

He clamped his hands on the edge of the countertop and drew in a deep breath. "You want me to stop?"

She should say yes. She should shout it at the top of her lungs. What was happening between them was too much, too fast. She hadn't known him long and she certainly didn't know him well, but she knew that she wanted him and she hadn't felt such an immediate and intense attraction to a man in a very long time.

"Cassie?" he prompted.

"No." She shook her head. "I don't want you to stop."

"Tell me what you do want."

She lifted her eyes to his. "I want you to take me to bed."

The library had been Cassie's absolute favorite room in the house when she bought it, but since she'd converted the attic to a master bedroom suite, that had become a close second. The deeply sloped ceilings and dormer-style windows created a bright and cozy space that was, in her mind, the perfect place to snuggle under the covers.

To Braden, who stood about six inches taller than her, the space probably felt a little cramped. But he didn't complain when she led him up the narrow stairs and over to the queen-size four-poster bed set up in the middle of the room. Of course, that might have been because his mouth was preoccupied with other matters—namely kissing her senseless.

And his hands, those wide and strong hands, were touching her in all the right places, further heating the blood that coursed through her veins. He found the tiny zipper at the back of her skirt with no trouble at all, and then the skirt itself was on the floor at her feet. Less than a minute later, her blouse had joined it, leaving her clad in only a pale pink bra and matching bikini panties.

She wanted to touch him, too, but her fingers fumbled as they attempted to unfasten the buttons of his shirt. She'd only worked her way through half of them when he eased his lips from hers long enough to yank the garment over his head and toss it aside. Then her hands were sliding over warm, taut skin and deliciously sculpted muscles. He was so strong, so male, so perfect.

He hooked his fingers in the straps of her bra and tugged them down her arms as he skimmed kisses down her throat, across her collarbone. Then the front clasp of her bra was undone and he slowly peeled back the cups. She bit down on her tongue to prevent herself from apologizing for the small size of her breasts, because Braden didn't seem to have any complaints. And when his thumbs scraped over the nipples...*ohmy*, the frissons that sparked through her body.

Then he lowered his head to continue his exploration, and her own fell back as pleasure coursed through her body. He teased her with his tongue and his teeth, and when he took her breast in his mouth and suckled, her knees almost gave way.

He must have felt her tremble, because he eased her back onto the bed, and she drew him down with her. Though he was still half-dressed, she automatically parted her legs to fit him between them. His arousal was unmistakable and as her hips tilted instinctively to meet his, the glorious friction of the thick denim against the wisp of lace caused a soft, needy moan to escape from between her lips.

He pulled away from her just long enough to shed the rest of his clothes, then yanked her panties over her hips and tossed them aside, too. She wiggled higher up on the mattress, so that her head was cushioned on the mountain of pillows and so that his legs wouldn't be hanging off the end. He rejoined her on the bed and his mouth came down on hers again. Stealing a kiss. Stealing her breath.

If she'd thought about it, she would have come up with all kinds of reasons that this shouldn't happen. But with his mouth on hers and his hands stroking over her body, rational thought was impossible. Even coherent speech seemed beyond her grasp as she responded with only throaty sighs and needy whimpers.

And then, one desperate word, as common sense nudged its way into the middle of her true-life erotic fantasy.

"Condom," she gasped.

He groaned. "I don't have one."

Which probably wasn't surprising considering that he'd been married for so many years and, by his own admission, celibate in the year since his wife had died. Thankfully, she'd prepared for this possibility, remote though it had seemed at the time when she'd hidden the box of condoms among a variety of other items she'd purchased from the pharmacy.

"Top drawer of the night table."

He yanked open the drawer and found the box, tearing it open in his haste and scattering the strips of condoms all over the floor.

He swore; she giggled.

Finally, he had one of the little square packets in hand. Cassie tried to take it from him, but he held it out of reach.

"Not this time," he said. "I'm afraid if you touch me now, it will be over before we even get started."

"I think we've started," she said. "I'm so ready for you, I feel as if I'm going to explode."

"Sounds promising." He covered himself with the latex sheath, then parted her thighs and drove into her in one smooth thrust that made her cry out with pleasure.

Braden groaned his assent. "This...being inside of you... is even more incredible than I imagined."

Her cheeks flushed with pleasure. "You've imagined this?"

"Every night since I met you," he admitted.

She tilted her pelvis, pulling him even deeper. "So what happens next?"

He proceeded to tell her, in raw and graphic detail, how he wanted to pleasure her body. His words both shocked and aroused her, further heightening her anticipation. When he stopped talking, he focused his attention on doing everything that he'd promised. And it was exactly what she'd needed—and so much more.

When he was able to summon enough energy to move, Braden rolled off Cassie and onto his back. Now that blood flow had been restored to his brain, his mind was going in a dozen different directions. "I think we just shattered the world record for fastest simultaneous orgasms."

A surprised laugh bubbled out of her. "I feel so proud."

"You feel so good," he said, tightening his arms around her.

"If I'd had even an inkling that this might happen tonight, I would never have let you into my house," she told him.

"I didn't plan this. If I had, I would have been prepared," he said. "But I'm not the least bit sorry."

"Right now, I'm not sorry, either," she admitted.

It had been nearly a decade since he'd made love with a woman who wasn't his wife, and he'd expected to feel a little bit guilty after doing so. Regardless of the fact that his relationship with Dana had been deteriorating over the past several years, she'd still been his wife. But the minute he'd taken Cassie in his arms, all thoughts of Dana had been swept from his mind.

From the first moment that his lips touched hers, he hadn't thought of anyone but Cassie. He hadn't wanted anyone but Cassie.

"So where do we go from here?"

She nudged him toward the edge of the mattress. "You need to go home."

He didn't know whether to be insulted or amused by her ineffectual efforts to push him out of her bed. "You're kicking me out?"

"Don't you have to pick up Saige from your parents' house?"

He shook his head. "She's sleeping over tonight."

"Oh."

He slid his arm up her back and drew her closer. "Why are you so determined to draw lines and boundaries around what's happening between us?"

"Because if I don't, I'll try to turn this into something that it isn't," she admitted.

"Something like what?" he asked curiously.

"Like a happily-ever-after fantasy."

The admission gave him pause. Because he liked Cassie—and he *really* liked making love with Cassie—but he had no intention of falling in love with her. "You don't believe we can have a mutually satisfying physical relationship without making a big deal out of it?"

"I know that a couple of orgasms are not the foundation of a lasting relationship—"

"Three," he interjected. Then, in response to her blank look, he clarified. "You had three orgasms."

She blushed but didn't dispute his count. "The number is irrelevant. You have to—"

He silenced her words with a quick kiss. "Hold that thought."

She frowned at the command but didn't say anything else when he slipped from her bed. He'd noticed the small three-piece bathroom tucked near the stairs when she led him up to her bedroom. Thinking only of the necessity of dispensing with the condom, he wasn't paying attention to the shape of the space and, when he turned, rapped his head smartly on the sloped ceiling.

When he returned to the bedroom, rubbing his head, he saw that Cassie had wrapped herself in a short, silky robe and had scooped up the condoms that were scattered on the floor and stuffed them back into the broken box. He caught the edge of the drawer as it was closing and withdrew a strip from the box to set it on top of the table.

She looked at him, the arch of her brow as much a challenge as a question.

"I want to see if we can set another record," he told her. "For the world's slowest simultaneous orgasms this time."

"I'm not sure there really is such a record," she said dubiously.

"I don't care," he admitted. "I want to make love with you again."

Make love.

Those two little words stirred something inside of Cassie's heart. She was probably reading too much into the expression, especially considering that she would have been offended if he'd used the common crude vernacular. Still, there were other ways to describe the act, various euphemisms that he might have relied upon—such as the "mutually satisfying physical relationship" he'd already referenced. But she wanted to believe that what they'd shared was lovemaking, because she wanted to believe that hers wasn't the only heart involved in what was happening between them.

Except that she was trying to keep her heart *un*involved.

Yes, the experience of being naked with Braden had been beyond incredible, but she needed to maintain perspective here. He was a single father with a young daughter—a widower who had lost his wife barely a year earlier. It would be a mistake to believe that what they'd just shared was anything more than the result of an intense and mutual attraction or that it could lead to anything more than that.

"I have a habit of falling hard and fast," she admitted, as he eased her back down onto the mattress.

"Don't fall for me," he said. But with his lips skimming down her throat, and lower, it was really hard to concentrate on his words.

"I know I shouldn't," she acknowledged. "Because falling in love with a man who's still in love with the woman he married is a heartbreak waiting to happen."

He lifted his head to look at her. "You think I'm still in love with my dead wife?"

"It's okay, I know—"

"No," he said. "You don't."

She frowned at the certainty in his tone as much as the interruption.

He took a moment to gather his thoughts before he finally said, "The truth is, I'm only a widower because my wife was involved in a fatal car accident before she could divorce me."

"What?" she said, unable to make sense of what he was telling her.

"A few weeks before the crash…Dana told me that she wanted to move out," he admitted.

She couldn't imagine why a woman—especially a new mother—would choose to break up her family. Unless her husband was abusive or unfaithful. And though she couldn't imagine Braden being guilty of either of those offences, she was obviously missing something. "But… why?"

"Things hadn't been good between us for a long time," he confided. "I thought it was the stress of not being able to have a baby, and maybe that was a contributing factor, but obviously there was more going on than I realized. Only six weeks after we brought Saige home, Dana decided she couldn't do it—that she didn't really want to be a mother after all."

Cassie was stunned. She didn't understand why anyone would pursue adoption unless they were desperate to have a baby—or how anyone, when finally given the incredible gift of a child to raise, would suddenly decide that they didn't want to be a parent. "Oh, Braden," she said, her tone filled with anguish for him and what he'd been through.

"I'm only telling you this so you know that I'm not still missing my dead wife. I did grieve that her life was cut so tragically short—and I grieved for the loss of the life that I thought we were building together. But the truth is, the love we'd shared died long before she did."

"I'm so sorry," she said.

"The point of sharing that sordid tale wasn't to elicit sympathy," he told her. "It was to let you know that I'm with you because I want to be with *you*, because I don't want anyone but you."

Her heart began to fill with cautious joy and tentative hope. "Then this isn't…a one-night stand?"

"I sincerely hope not," he said.

The simple and earnest words tugged at her, but she struggled to maintain her balance. Because there was still a lot of distance between "not a one-night stand" and "forever after" and it would be a mistake to believe otherwise.

He tipped her chin up and brushed his lips over hers. "Now can we stop talking and start taking advantage of the hours we have left in this night?"

She lifted her arms to link them behind his head. "You don't want to hear all of my deep dark secrets?" she teased, in an effort to lighten the mood.

"Everyone has secrets," he said. "But unless you have six previous lovers buried in your backyard, I don't need to know all of them right now."

"Not six previous lovers, only one."

He paused, just a beat. "You only had one previous lover?"

She smiled sweetly. "No, I only buried one in the back-yard."

His lips curved just before they settled on hers. "I'm willing to take my chances."

Chapter Eleven

Saturday dawned bright and sunny—a perfect day for a trip to Frazer's Butterfly Farm made even more perfect by the fact that Braden had persuaded Cassie to join him and Saige on their outing. As they toured the facility, his daughter was mesmerized by the graceful fluttering wings of the colorful insects and happy to watch them swoop and glide. When one landed on Braden's shoulder, he slowly bent down so that she could get a closer look. Saige's eyes grew wide and she clapped her hands excitedly.

Of course, the sudden movement and sharp noise startled the butterfly and it flew away again. But there were so many of them that it wasn't long before another one—and then two and three—ventured over to feed from the sugar paper Cassie carried in her hand. And while Saige obviously enjoyed watching them from a distance, she screamed like a banshee when one of them dared to land on the guardrail of her stroller.

But the winged creature didn't go far—flying away from Saige's stroller only to settle again on top of Cassie's head.

"I'm holding sugar paper in my hand—why do they keep landing on my head?" Cassie wondered.

"Because your hair smells like peaches," Braden noted.

"You think that's what's attracting the butterflies?" she asked skeptically.

"It's attracting me," he told her, dipping his head to nuzzle her ear.

Despite the warmth of the day, Cassie felt shivers trickle down her spine and goose bumps dance over her skin. She put a hand on his chest and pushed him away. Braden grinned but backed off—for now.

They walked through the education center, where they could view butterflies at various stages of development—from egg to larva to chrysalis to butterfly. They even got to see a butterfly emerging from its chrysalis. One of the expert guides advised them that it was about to happen, pointing out the wings clearly visible through the now-translucent casing and contrasting it to other encasements that were opaque and green in color. The emergence didn't take very long, and though Saige didn't really seem to understand what was happening, she was content to sit in her stroller and munch on some cereal O's while Braden and Cassie watched.

"I've never seen anything like this before," Braden admitted, as the butterfly unfurled its vibrant orange-and-black wings.

"It is incredible, isn't it?" she said.

"One of Saige's favorite stories is that one about the caterpillar that eats and eats and eats until it becomes a beautiful butterfly."

Of course, as a librarian, Cassie was familiar with the story. "She's probably disappointed to see these caterpillars aren't eating through cherry pie and lollipops."

"I think she's just enjoying being here," Braden countered. "But speaking of eating—are you hungry?"

"A little," Cassie admitted.

"Why don't we go find someplace to have our lunch?" he suggested.

"That sounds like a good idea to me."

So they made their way outside, where there were walking paths and gardens and picnic areas and play structures. As they followed along the path, Cassie noticed a trio of butterflies circling around the stroller. She leaned down beside the little girl to draw her attention to the pretty insects, only to discover that Saige was fast asleep.

"If she's tired, she can sleep anywhere, anytime," Braden told her.

Which she remembered from the first day he was with Saige at the library, when the little girl had fallen asleep in his arms. "It must be nice, to be that young and carefree, with no worries to keep you awake or interfere with happy dreams," she mused.

"What kind of worries keep you awake?" he asked, steering the stroller off the path and toward the dappled shade of a towering maple tree.

"Oh, just the usual," she said dismissively.

He took a blanket from beneath the stroller and spread it out on the grass. "Job? Bills? Family?"

Cassie helped him arrange the cover, then sat down on top of it, leaning back on her elbows and stretching out her legs. "Actually, I love my job, I live within my means and I don't have a family."

After checking on Saige to ensure that she was comfortable, he stretched out beside Cassie. "No one?"

She shook her head.

"I can't imagine what my life would be like without

my parents, brothers, aunts, uncles and cousins and their spouses and children," he said.

"You're lucky to have them," she noted. Then, "This is an unexpected side of you—I never would have guessed that you were the type to watch butterflies in the sky or eat lunch on the grass."

"It's a new side," he admitted. "I used to be focused on the business of Garrett Furniture almost to the exclusion of all else. And then, when Dana and I decided it was time to start a family, I shifted my focus to the business of having a baby."

"Sounds romantic," she said dryly.

He managed a wry smile. "It was at first. Candlelight dinners and midday trysts. But when nearly a year passed with no results, it became an endless succession of tests and doctor appointments and schedules."

"Did they ever figure out why she couldn't conceive?"

"She had a condition called anovulation. It's a pretty generic term with numerous possible causes and, depending on the origin, there are various treatment options, some of them highly successful. But not for Dana."

"I'm sorry," she said sincerely.

"It was a difficult time for both of us," he said. "And then, six months after we finally decided to pursue adoption, we got a call to meet Saige's mom."

"That must have been exciting."

"Exciting and daunting, because we knew that she was meeting with four other couples, too, in an effort to find the best home for her baby. Our odds were, at best, twenty percent, because there was always the possibility that she would decide none of the couples was suitable and expand her search.

"And then, even when she did choose us, we knew there was still a possibility that she might, at the last minute, change her mind about the adoption entirely and decide to keep her baby."

"I can only imagine what an emotional roller coaster that must have been."

He nodded. "We were so excited—and so afraid to admit that we were excited in case the baby that was finally so close at hand would be snatched out of our grasp." He looked at that baby stretched out and sleeping in her stroller now, and a smile touched the corners of his mouth. "Since she was born, not a single day has passed that I haven't thought about how incredibly lucky I am to have her in my life.

"But still, aside from the fact that I was getting a lot less sleep, my day-to-day life didn't change a lot. And I was pretty proud of myself that I managed to squeeze fatherhood into my busy schedule.

"Then, one morning when I was getting Saige dressed, she was looking at me and babbling nonsense and I saw something in her mouth. Actually two somethings. She'd cut her first teeth. Not that they looked much like teeth at that point—more like tiny little buds poking through her gums. But it suddenly struck me that those two teeth hadn't been there the day before. Except, when I thought about it, I couldn't say for certain that was true. It was a normal milestone in a baby's life—but it was huge to me because I'd almost missed it.

"That was when I forced myself to slow down a bit and vowed to not just appreciate but savor at least five minutes with my daughter every day."

"She's a lucky girl," Cassie said softly.

"I'm the lucky one," he insisted. "I just wish..."

"What do you wish?" she prompted.

"Lindsay said that she chose us because we could give her daughter what she couldn't—two parents."

"There was no way you could have known that your wife would die only a few months after Saige was born."

"But even if the accident had never happened, we wouldn't be together now," he reminded her. And he'd been devastated not just that Dana's senseless death obliterated any hope of a reconciliation, but because it meant he'd failed his daughter, that the family he'd promised to give to her wasn't ever going to exist.

Cassie touched a hand to his arm, a silent show of support.

"When I got to the hospital and talked to the officer who had responded to the accident scene and he told me what had happened, do you know what my first thought was?"

She shook her head.

"I thought, 'Thank God, the baby wasn't in the car with her.' Even through the shock of losing my wife, there was relief that Dana didn't have Saige with her when she was hit—that our baby was safe."

"And you feel guilty about that," she realized.

"Hell, yes," he admitted. "I'd just found out that my wife was dead and, instead of being grief-stricken, I was relieved."

"You weren't relieved that she'd died—you were relieved that you hadn't lost your child, too," Cassie pointed out gently.

Braden nodded, accepting that she was right. And he was grateful that he'd found the courage to tell her about the feelings he'd never been able to speak about before, because her understanding helped him to finally attain a small measure of peace.

Cassie gave his hand a reassuring squeeze.

"Now—you said something about food," she reminded him.

He unpacked the contents of the cooler: buns piled high

with meats and cheeses, carrot and celery sticks, seedless grapes and miniature chocolate chip cookies. There was even a bottle of sweet tea for them to share and a couple of juice boxes for Saige, paper plates and napkins—and antibacterial hand wipes.

"You sure know how to pack a picnic," Cassie remarked.

"There's nothing very complicated in here."

"Those cookies look homemade," she noted.

"Not by me."

"Your mom?" she guessed.

He nodded.

"Did you tell her that you'd invited me to spend the day with you and Saige?"

"No," he assured her. "The last thing I want to do is encourage my mother's matchmaking efforts."

Cassie smiled at that as she unwrapped a sandwich. "Are you sure that's what she's trying to do?"

"There's no way she would ever 'forget' Saige's sock monkey anywhere unless it was on purpose."

"And what do you think was her purpose?"

"To put you in my path—or attempt to."

"She did seem disappointed to learn I wasn't there when you showed up to get the monkey," she acknowledged, nibbling on her sandwich.

"And since that failed, I'm guessing her next move will be to invite you to dinner at her house—and then she'll invite me and Saige, too," he warned.

"Do you really think she'd be that obvious?"

"She thinks she's subtle," Braden told her. "She invited the neighbor's single granddaughter to my brother Justin's thirty-fifth birthday party because she felt it was time he met a nice girl and settled down."

"And how did that work out?"

"Not the way she'd planned. Of course, she didn't

know—no one knew—that he'd already hooked up with Avery by then. And since they're happily married now, my mother considers it a win, especially since they've given her another grandchild. But she wants lots of little ones running around, which is why she's turned her attention to me again."

Cassie popped a grape into her mouth. "And how do you feel about that?"

"Well, I certainly can't fault her taste," he said.

"I have a horrible track record with men," she confided. "I tend to fall hard and fast and always for the wrong guys. Megan thinks that's because I grew up without a dependable father figure."

"Because your dad died when you were young," he remembered.

"And because he was an Army Ranger who, even before he died, was gone a lot more than he was home."

"Do you remember much about him?"

"Not really," she admitted. "Mostly I remember my mom always being so excited when he was coming home. She'd make sure the house was clean from top to bottom, she'd buy a new outfit, spritz on her favorite perfume, cook his favorite foods. She'd even dress me up in my prettiest clothes and braid ribbons into my hair.

"I loved my dad, but I didn't know him. Even when he was home, he seemed so distant and unapproachable. Now I would probably say haunted, although back then I just thought he was grumpy. I didn't look forward to him coming home, because I always knew he would go away again. And when he did, my mom would cry for days.

"She was a true Southern belle," Cassie explained. "Born in Savannah and accustomed to the attention and adoration that were her reward in the beauty pageant circuit. From what I've been told, my father fell for her, hard and fast. They had a whirlwind courtship and married after knowing each other only three weeks.

"After he died, she dated a few other guys, but none of them stuck around for long. I think I was twelve when she met Ray—an Episcopalian minister, widowed, with two sons. Eric and Ray Jr.—we called him RJ. My mom was a widowed military spouse with two daughters. I think she had some kind of image of us being a modern day Brady Bunch."

"So you have a sister?" he prompted.

She shook her head and wrapped her sandwich up again, her gaze focused on the task. "Had. Amanda was four years younger than me, and only ten when she died."

"What happened?"

Cassie took a minute, carefully wiping her fingers on a napkin, sipping the sweet tea he'd poured for her. "She'd gone fishing with Eric and RJ—just out to the pond at the back of Ray's property. They didn't usually catch anything, but they would spend hours out there trying, anyway. Amanda loved to follow the boys around—" she shook her head, her eyes shining with unshed tears "—no, she loved to follow *me* around, to pepper me with questions about everything until I told her to get lost.

"She wanted me to play some kind of game with her... I don't even remember what it was...but I told her I was busy and suggested that she go bug the boys. So she did, and they gave her a fishing pole and let her tag along. And I stayed in the house, studying for a science test because I was barely holding on to an A-minus and I knew I wouldn't be able to get a scholarship if my grade dropped."

"You were thinking about scholarships in tenth grade?" he asked, not just because he was surprised by the fact but because the anguish in her voice warned him where the story was going and he wanted to give her the option of a detour.

"When you grow up with limited financial resources, you need to think about all other options," she told him matter-of-factly. Then she fell silent for a moment before she steered the conversation back onto its original path. "So Amanda went off with the boys and I went back to my books, grateful for the peace and quiet.

"It was a long time later before RJ came racing back to the house. Apparently Amanda caught a small sunfish and was leaning forward to pull it out of the water when she lost her balance and fell in. But she was a good swimmer, so the boys weren't worried at first. They just watched the surface of the water, waiting for her to come up." Her gaze dropped away, but not before he saw that tears were now trembling on the edge of her lashes.

"Mom and Ray weren't home, so I was the only one there when RJ came running back to the house. I jumped into the pond where they said she'd gone in, and I pulled her out of the water."

There was nothing he could say to ease the pain he heard in her voice, a pain he knew she still felt deep in her heart, so he only put his arms around her and held her tight.

"Eric called 9-1-1 while I tried to remember the basic CPR I'd been taught in my babysitting course, but I knew she was already gone."

"I'm so sorry, Cassie."

"I was devastated." The admission was barely a whisper. "But my mother…my mother never recovered from losing Amanda. I don't know if she blamed herself for not being there or if losing both a husband and a child proved to be too much for her.

"She started to drink, as if the alcohol might fill up the emptiness inside of her, and she didn't stop. Six months later, she was dead, too—hit by a car when she was walking home from the bar one night."

And as horrific as it must have been for her mother to have lost that husband and child, he could not begin to imagine how much worse it had been for Cassie to have lost her father, her sister and then her mother. He wondered how she'd survived the devastation—and marveled over the fact that she had.

"The police ruled it an accident, but I'm not so sure," she admitted. "Maybe she was so drunk that she unknowingly stumbled into the middle of the road—or maybe she saw the headlights and wanted to make the pain go away forever."

He didn't know what to say to that. He wanted to reassure her that no mother grieving the loss of one child would willingly abandon another, but he didn't really know what her mother's state of mind had been. Maybe she had been so focused on everything she'd lost, she couldn't see what she had left.

"Ray, regularly prone to fits of temper, was always angry after that. He was furious with my mother for leaving him—and for leaving him with another kid. He'd frequently used scripture not as a comfort but as a weapon, and after my mother died, it got even worse. I went to church every Sunday, and sat beside the boys as he pontificated about sin. But even at home, the preaching never stopped, and when the words stopped being enough to satisfy his rage…he started to use his hands."

"He hit you?"

"Not just me," she said quietly, then shrugged. "Although I was the usual target."

"Did you tell anyone?"

"Who was I going to tell? I had no one. My father, my sister, my mother…they were all gone."

Listening to her talk about the experience, he couldn't even imagine what she'd gone through, how she must have felt. He only knew how he felt right now—furious and impotent—and he knew that if he could, he would go back in time and use his own hands on her stepfather.

"Please tell me that somebody did something," he implored.

"I spent a lot of time at the library when I was in high school," she reminded him. "And there's not much that gets past Irene. She took me to the hospital so there would be a documented record of my bruises, which prompted interviews by the police and family services. Of course, Ray had alternate explanations for my injuries—not the least of which was that I was absentminded and clumsy, never paying attention to where I was going and walking into things.

"The police officer who came to talk to Ray was sympathetic to the twice-widowed father trying to raise a teenage stepdaughter who wouldn't listen to anything he said—as Ray described the situation. Family services took a slightly harder line, offering counseling and insisting that he take an anger management course."

Braden was incredulous. "They didn't remove you from the home?"

"He was a minister—a pillar of the community."

He shook his head. "Sometimes the system really sucks."

"Sometimes it does," she agreed. "But the next time he knocked me around, Irene insisted on taking me to church for the Sunday service, and she wouldn't let me cover up any of the bruises. After the service, she met with the church elders, who later suggested that Ray might benefit from a change of scenery and offered him a position in Oregon."

"They should have offered him a position in the chaplain's office at Central Prison."

She managed a small smile. "He might have preferred that. In his eyes, losing the church in Charisma—where both his father and grandfather had preached before him— was a harsher punishment than being behind bars."

"Not harsh enough," Braden insisted.

"So Ray went to Oregon, RJ and Eric went to live with their maternal grandparents and I was supposed to be placed in a group home."

"Why a group home?"

"Because not many foster parents want an angry and grieving teenager living under their roof," she explained. "But I got lucky. By some miracle, a woman came forward for consideration as a foster parent and she was willing to take in an older child. A few days later, I was placed in her care."

And though Cassie didn't mention the woman's name, Braden knew—and he realized that he had severely misjudged Irene Houlahan.

Chapter Twelve

Cassie enjoyed the time she spent with Braden and Saige at the Butterfly Farm, but she was glad to go home alone at the end of the day. She'd poured her heart out to him—told him things that she'd never told to anyone else. And she suspected he'd done the same when he'd revealed the personal details of his marriage.

Somehow, the sharing of confidences seemed more intimate even than the physical joining of their bodies. As a result, she needed some space and time to think about everything that had happened on the weekend—and how to categorize their relationship. Were they friends? Friends with benefits? More?

Did he want more?

Did she?

She had yet to answer that question in her own mind when he called Wednesday afternoon while she was still at the library.

"How about dinner at my place tonight?" he suggested.

"What are you making?"

"Shrimp and grits," he told her.

"Mmm… I haven't had shrimp and grits in…years," she admitted.

"Is that a yes to dinner?"

"That's a definite yes."

"What time do you want to eat?" he asked.

"I finish at four today, so anytime after is good," she told him.

"Our usual dinner time is six, so we'll stick with that," he decided. "Do you want us to pick you up?"

"No, I'll drive myself so that you don't have to drag Saige out again to take me home."

"Okay," he relented. "I'll see you tonight."

"I'll see you tonight," she confirmed, and disconnected the call.

"Who are you seeing tonight?" Megan asked curiously from behind her.

Cassie sighed. "There is absolutely no privacy around here."

"What do you expect in a *public* library?" her friend teased.

"Good point," she acknowledged.

"So?" Megan prompted. "Was that the very handsome and rich Braden Garrett on the phone?"

"Yes," she admitted.

"And what is the plan for tonight?"

"Dinner."

"At his place," her friend mused.

Cassie frowned. "How long were you listening?"

"Long enough to know that shrimp and grits are on the menu," her coworker admitted unapologetically. "But the real question is…what's for dessert?"

Of course, that inquiry made Cassie remember the night she hadn't offered Braden any dessert, when his craving for something sweet had led to him kissing her—and the kissing had led to her bedroom.

"Well, well, well." Megan folded her arms on the counter and grinned. "The man is certainly doing something right if that dreamy look in your eyes and the flush in your cheeks is any indication."

"It's not the big deal you're making it out to be," Cassie protested.

"But the two of you are...dating?"

"No." She wondered how her friend would respond if she said, "just sleeping together," but decided the shock value of the revelation wasn't worth the plethora of questions that would inevitably follow.

Her friend arched a brow. "Having dinner together sounds like a date to me."

"I'm having dinner with Braden *and his daughter.*"

Megan ignored the clarification. "And you and Braden have really hot chemistry together."

Cassie shook her head. "I never should have told you about that kiss."

"The way the temperature soars whenever he's around you, I'm thinking there's been more than that one kiss." Which proved that she'd been keeping a close eye when Braden visited the library to return books he'd borrowed and check out new ones.

"It doesn't matter how many kisses—" or how much more than kisses "—there have been," she told her.

"I'm just happy to see that you're putting out—I mean, putting yourself out there," Megan teased.

Cassie felt her cheeks burn. "I think I'm going to call him back and cancel."

"Don't you dare," her friend admonished.

"Why not?"

"Because in the end, we always regret the chances we didn't take."

She lifted her brows. "Why does that sound like 'quote of the day' relationship advice?"

"Maybe because I read it on Pinterest."

Cassie couldn't help smiling as she shook her head. "Isn't that Introduction to Social Media group waiting for you in the Chaucer Room?"

"I'm on my way. But remember," Megan said, as she headed away from the desk, "those who risk nothing often end up with nothing."

"Apparently you spend too much time on Pinterest."

"It's an addiction," her friend admitted. "But since I don't have a handsome man offering to make me dinner, I've only got a computer to go home to at night."

Of course, Megan disappeared before Cassie could respond, leaving her alone with her thoughts and concerns— and a niggling suspicion that her friend was right, and if she didn't take a chance with Braden, she might regret it.

But taking a chance required opening up her heart, and that was easier said than done. It wasn't just her failed engagement that made her reluctant to want to risk loving— and losing—again. In fact, her relationship with Joel was the least cause of concern to Cassie. Far more troubling was the fact that everyone she'd ever loved had left her in the end: her father, her sister, her mother and, yes, most recently her fiancé. Was it any wonder that she'd put up barriers around her heart when she found herself alone— again—after giving back Joel's ring?

Maybe she was a coward. Certainly she knew plenty of other people who had just as much reason to be wary but still found the courage to open up their hearts again. Like her coworker Stacey, who was thirty-nine years old,

twice divorced and finally about to become a mother for
the first time. Her first marriage had ended after only ten
months when her husband decided that he just didn't want
to be married anymore; her second marriage lasted for
almost ten years before she finally left her abusive partner. It had taken years of counseling for Stacey to move
on after that, but she'd finally done so, and she was bliss-
fully happy with her new spouse and excited about having a family with him.

Obviously Stacey was braver than Cassie. Because as
much as she wanted the happily-ever-after that her coworker had finally found, she was starting to suspect that
some people were just meant to be alone. And maybe that
was okay. Irene Houlahan was a perfect example of someone who'd never married or had any children of her own,
and she seemed perfectly content with her life.

But even Cassie had to admit that, after seeing Irene
in the company of Jerry Riordan these past few weeks,
her friend had seemed more than content—she'd seemed
happy. So maybe there was no harm in spending some
time with Braden and enjoying his company.

Besides he'd promised her shrimp and grits, and she
was hungry.

Cassie made a quick stop at home to feed the cats and
change her clothes, opting for a pair of jeans and a short-
sleeved knit sweater layered over a tank top because the
wrap-style dress she'd worn to work only required a tug
of the bow at her waist to come undone. And then, not
wanting to show up at his house empty-handed after he'd
brought wine and flowers for her, she made another quick
stop on the way to his Forrest Hill address.

The contemporary two-story brick home on Spruceside Crescent was set back from the road and surrounded

by large trees that gave the illusion of privacy despite the neighbors on each side. She pressed a finger to the bell, and heard the echo of a melodic chime that somehow suited the house and upscale neighborhood. He greeted her with a warm smile and a quick kiss, and it was only when he stepped carefully away from the door that she realized Saige was holding on to her father's pant leg.

The little girl tipped her head to peek around him and grinned at Cassie. "Hi."

"Hello, Saige."

"What's in the bag?" Braden asked curiously.

"It's for your daughter," she said, offering it to the little girl.

Saige reached her hand inside and pulled out the package of box cars. Not knowing what trains she had, Cassie had opted for the accessory cars that would attach to any of the engines. When the little girl realized what they were, her eyes grew wide.

"Ope!" she said, shoving the package at her daddy. "Ope!"

"Please," he reminded her.

"Ope, p'ease," she said obediently.

He tore open the package, freeing the box cars for his daughter.

"Now you say thank you to Cassie," he said, when he gave Saige the cars.

"Dan-koo," she piped up.

"You're very welcome," Cassie told her.

"P'ay?" Saige implored.

"You want me to play?"

The little girl nodded so vigorously her ponytails bounced up and down.

"I'd love to play, if your daddy doesn't need any help in the kitchen."

"I certainly wouldn't object to your company," he told Cassie, 'but if you'd rather play with Saige, that's okay with me."

So Cassie let Saige lead her to the living room where, in place of the coffee table she'd seen on her last visit, there was an enormous train table covered with curving tracks that went over bridges and through tunnels, winding this way and that with switches and turnouts and railway crossings, ascending pieces and risers, towers and moving cranes and even a roundhouse.

"Wow," Cassie said. "This is quite the setup."

"P'ay," Saige said again, setting her box cars on the track and linking them to the red engine—obviously her favorite.

She looked at the various engines and specialty cargo cars on the track. "What train do I get to play with?"

The little girl crinkled her forehead as she considered. She decided on a green engine and turned to hand it to Cassie, then abruptly changed her mind and set it back down again. Next she selected a blue engine, then put that one down again, too. At last she decided on an orange one.

"I'm guessing orange is not your favorite color," Cassie said.

Of course, Saige didn't respond. She was already engrossed in driving her engine and box cars around the track, halting obediently at a railway crossing as she steered a purple engine pulling a passenger coach through on another part of the track.

After about ten minutes, Cassie realized why it had been so difficult for the little girl to decide which engine to let her play with, because she took turns with all of them, hitching and unhitching box cars and cargo cars to each of them in turn as she did laps around the table. Cassie stayed near the quarry, using her engine to haul imaginary cargo from the work site to the storage shed—and moving out of Saige's way whenever she raced past with one of her engines, obviously driving an express and in a hurry to get wherever she was going.

"Who's hungry?" Braden asked, poking his head into the living room.

Saige responded by immediately abandoning her trains and racing to the kitchen.

"Your daughter's definitely worked up an appetite," Cassie told him.

"She loves that train table," he noted.

"Who wouldn't?" she agreed.

"Now to see if you love my shrimp and grits," he told her.

"Well, they smell delicious."

He had a bottle of his favorite Pinot Noir in his wine rack and though she protested that she had to drive home, he opened it, anyway. She decided she would have one glass and no more—because she didn't want to give herself any excuses for staying, no matter how much she wanted to.

Of course, the man himself was much more potent than any amount of alcohol, and the more time she spent with him the more time she wanted to spend with him. And after her first taste of the meal he'd prepared, she realized that he'd seriously understated his culinary capabilities. The flavors enticed her tongue—his shrimp and grits every bit as good as what her mother used to make.

"Is something wrong?" Braden asked.

"No," she immediately responded. "Why would you think that?"

"Because you stopped eating and started pushing your food around on your plate."

"This is really delicious," she assured him, stabbing her fork into a shrimp, and then popping it into her mouth.

"So where did your mind wander off to?"

She finished chewing, swallowed. "I was remembering the last time my mom made shrimp and grits."

"Good memories?" he prompted hopefully.

She nodded. "Very good."

He topped up her glass of wine.

"I'm driving," she reminded him.

"Eventually," he agreed.

She picked up her glass and took a tiny sip. "Your daughter is obviously a fan of your cooking," she remarked.

"Saige is a fan of food," he told her.

"You're lucky—some kids can be finicky eaters."

He nodded. "My cousin's daughter, Maura, was an incredibly finicky eater when she was little. For almost two years, she hardly ate anything more than chicken fingers, sweet potatoes—but only if they were in chunks, not mashed—and grapes."

"Well, at least she was getting some protein, vegetable and fruit," Cassie noted.

"True," he acknowledged. "And while Saige doesn't turn her nose up at too many things, I'm not sure how much food actually ends up *in* her rather than *on* her."

Cassie had noticed that the little girl's determination to feed herself resulted in a fair amount of food on her face, dribbled down her shirt and in her hair. "I'm guessing that bath time follows dinnertime."

"And you'd be right."

"Mo," Saige said, shoving her empty plate toward him.

"How about dessert?" Braden suggested, catching the plate as she pushed it over the edge of the high chair tray.

"Zert!" she agreed happily, clapping her sticky hands together.

"Cassie?" he prompted.

"I very rarely say no to dessert," she admitted. "But I don't think I could eat another bite."

"Not even a bite of lemon meringue pie?"

She groaned. "You do know how to tempt a girl."

He grinned. "Is that a yes?"

"It's an I wish but still no."

"Zert!" Saige demanded.

"Coming right up," Braden promised his daughter.

He carried the stack of dinner plates into the kitchen. Cassie wanted to help him clear up, but she didn't want to leave Saige unattended, so she stayed where she was and did her best to clean up the little girl with her napkin.

When Braden returned, she saw that he carried a wet cloth in addition to the bowl containing his daughter's dessert. He set the bowl on the table and pretended to look around for her. "Saige? Where are you?"

The little girl giggled.

He turned his head from left to right and back again. "I can hear her but I can't see her."

Saige giggled again.

"Wait a minute—" He held out the cloth, then swiped it over his daughter's face, scrubbing away the remnants of her dinner. "There you are. You were hiding behind all those cheesy grits."

Saige grinned as she held out her hands for him to clean, too, in what was obviously a post-dinner ritual. Braden complied, then set the bowl on her tray table.

The little girl's dessert was flavored gelatin cut into squares that she could easily pick up, and she immediately dipped her hand into the bowl.

"Apparently you are a man of many talents," Cassie noted.

Braden shook his head. "I can't take credit for dessert.

My mother made the Jell-O squares, and the pie that you said you don't want came from The Sweet Spot."

The downtown bakery he credited was legendary for its temperamental pastry chef—and its decadent desserts. "Now I'm really sorry I don't have room for pie."

"We can always have our dessert after."

"After what?" she asked warily, watching as Saige curled her fingers around a square and lifted it from the bowl to her mouth.

He smiled. "Whatever."

"Braden," Cassie began, but the rest of what she intended to say was forgotten as Saige held a second square of gelatin out to her in silent offering. "Oh…um…is that for me?"

"Zert," Saige told her.

"Well, there's always room for Jell-O, isn't there?" she said, and opened her mouth.

It was his own fault that he'd been caught unaware.

Braden had been so focused on enjoying the time that he was spending with Cassie—and watching Saige and Cassie together—that he'd forgotten about Lindsay's telephone call only a week and a half earlier. He'd forgotten that his happiness was like a precarious house of cards, and that an unexpected puff of air—or an unannounced visitor—could cause it to tumble down around him.

Saige was finishing up her Jell-O when the doorbell rang, and he left Cassie in the kitchen with his daughter while he responded to the summons.

He opened the door, and his heart stalled. "Lindsay."

"Hello, Mr. Garrett." A smile—quick and a little uncertain—immediately followed her greeting. "I'm sorry to drop by uninvited, but I've been driving around for hours, not sure if I was actually headed in this direction."

"Did you want to come in?"

She nodded. "I want to see Saige."

Braden stepped away from the door. "You know you're always welcome."

"I know that visitation was part of our original agreement—but a lot of things have changed since Saige was born. In fact…I'm getting married at the end of the summer."

"Congratulations."

"Thanks." She tucked her hands in her pockets and rocked back on her heels. "The thing is…"

Whatever else she intended to say was temporarily forgotten as her gaze moved past him, and he knew, even before he turned, that Cassie was there with Saige in her arms.

"There's your daddy," Cassie said, halting abruptly when she saw that he wasn't alone. "Oh, I'm sorry. I didn't realize you had company."

"This is Lindsay," he told her. "Saige's birth mother."

"Oh," she said again, her gaze shifting from Braden to Lindsay and back again. "Hi."

Lindsay returned the greeting stiffly.

"Da-da!" Saige, oblivious to the tension, lifted her arms to reach out to him, and Cassie transferred the baby to him.

Lindsay's tear-filled gaze followed the little girl. "She's grown so much," she said softly. "She's even bigger than she was in the photos you sent of her first birthday."

He nodded.

"I'm, um, going to finish up in the kitchen," Cassie said, backing away.

"Nanny?" Lindsay asked, when Cassie had gone.

"No." He set Saige on her feet by the train table and settled into a chair, then gestured for Lindsay to sit.

She perched on the edge of the sofa, her hands twisting the strap of her oversize purse as if she needed to keep them busy to prevent herself from reaching out to the little girl.

"Saige doesn't have a nanny. She's with me most of the time and, when I'm at work, my mom takes care of her."

"It's nice that your family helps out," Lindsay acknowledged, opening her purse now and withdrawing an envelope. "But a little girl needs a mother." Then she lifted her chin and handed the envelope to him. "And I *am* her mother."

Chapter Thirteen

Even before Braden opened the flap and pulled out the papers, he knew what he would find inside: an application to reverse Saige's adoption. And though he understood and even—to an extent—empathized with her position, he had to believe that the law was on his side. That belief was all that allowed him to maintain a semblance of calm when he was feeling anything but.

"Not according to the State of North Carolina," he finally responded to her claim, his tone gentle but firm.

"An adoption can be reversed," she insisted.

He slid the papers back into the envelope and set it on the table beside him. "Usually only with the consent of the adoptive parents."

She frowned at that.

"I don't know who's giving you legal advice, Lindsay, but I can assure you that no judge is going to overturn an adoption sixteen months after the fact."

"But what if it's in the best interests of the child?" she persisted.

"She hasn't seen you in more than a year," he pointed out. "Do you really think it would be in her best interests to be taken away from everything she knows, and everyone who loves her, and placed in your care just because there's a biological bond between you?"

Lindsay's lower lip quivered as her eyes filled with tears. "I love her, too."

"I know you do," he acknowledged. "That's why you wanted a better life for her than you could give her on your own."

"But I'm not on my own now. And when I told Charles that I had a child, why I gave her up, and about you now being a single parent to Saige, he said she would be better off with us."

"I appreciate that you're thinking about what's best for Saige," he said, "but I promise you, staying here—where she's lived her entire life and where she has the love and support of my extended family and with whom she's bonded emotionally—is the best thing for her."

Lindsay swiped at the tears that spilled onto her cheeks.

"Look at her, Lindsay," he instructed, though the young woman hadn't stopped doing that since Saige had entered the room. "Do you really want to tear her away from the only home she's ever known? The only parent she's ever known?"

She choked on a sob, the ragged sound drawing Saige's attention from her trains to her visitor.

"Choo-choo," she said, holding up her favorite red engine.

Lindsay sniffled. "That's a pretty awesome choo-choo," she said, and was rewarded with a beaming smile.

"P'ay?" Saige invited.

She dropped to her knees on the floor beside the table and reached for a green engine. Saige immediately snatched it away.

"Saige," he admonished softly. "What have I told you about sharing?"

She set the green engine on Braden's knee, indicating her willingness to share with her daddy, then selected a yellow engine from the track for the visitor.

Lindsay, apparently happy just to be interacting with the little girl, began to move it around the winding track.

"So…the woman in the kitchen," she said, glancing up at him through red-rimmed eyes. "Is it serious?"

He knew that the question didn't indicate a shift in the topic of their conversation but was actually an extension of it. And of course, the honest answer was that his relationship with Cassie was still too new to be categorized. However, he knew that response wouldn't assuage her concerns, so he gave her one that would. "Yes, it is."

Lindsay was quiet for a moment before she said, "Saige seems to like her."

"Saige adores Cassie—and the feeling is mutual."

She watched the little girl play for several more minutes. "She seems happy," she finally acknowledged. "Here. With you."

"She is happy," he confirmed.

Her eyes again filled with tears as she watched Saige abandon her trains and raise her arms toward Braden, a silent request to be picked up. He lifted her onto his lap, and she immediately rubbed her cheek against his shoulder and stuffed a thumb in her mouth.

"I guess I just needed to see her again, to know it was true," she admitted softly. "I thought maybe she needed me…but it's obvious that she doesn't."

"Not being needed isn't the same as not being wanted," he told her.

She seemed surprised by that. "You'd still be willing to let me visit?"

"That was always our agreement," he reminded her.

She managed a smile. "Maybe I knew what I was doing when I chose you for Saige."

"I like to think so."

"I'll talk to my lawyer about withdrawing the court application," she said.

"I'd appreciate that."

His daughter yawned and tipped her head back to look at him. "Kee?"

"You can have your monkey after your bath," he promised.

Lindsay blinked. "Monkey?"

He nodded. "The sock monkey you gave to her when she was born—she won't go to sleep without it."

This time, Lindsay's smile came more easily. "And she's obviously ready for sleep now," she decided. "So I should be going."

Braden rose from the chair with Saige in his arms. "Can you say bye-bye to Lindsay?"

"Bye-bye," she said, and yawned again.

After a brief hesitation, Linday stepped forward and touched her lips to Saige's cheek. "Night-night, sweetie."

"Bye-bye," the little girl repeated.

"I'll come back to visit again," Lindsay told him. "But next time, I'll call first."

Cassie was just putting the last pot away when Braden and Saige returned to the kitchen. "Where's Lindsay?"

"She's gone," Braden told her.

"That was a short visit," she said cautiously. "Is everything okay?"

"I hope so," he said. "We cleared the air about a few things while you were clearing up in here—so thank you."

Though she had a ton more questions about the young woman's obviously impromptu visit, she held them back, saying only, "Thank *you* for the delicious meal."

"Why don't you relax with a glass of wine now while I get this one—" he glanced at Saige "—bathed and ready for bed?"

"Can I help?"

"If you want, but I should warn you—the whole bathroom can become a splash zone."

"I won't melt," she assured him.

As Cassie followed Braden up the stairs, she saw that the monochromatic color scheme continued on the upper level. His house was beautiful but incredibly bland and she wondered why he hadn't made any changes to the decor since his wife's death. Of course, the little girl in his arms was probably the answer to that question—no doubt Saige kept him so busy that painting was the last thing on his mind. But she couldn't help but think his daughter would benefit from a little color being added to her surroundings.

So she was pleasantly surprised to see that Saige's bedroom was beautiful and colorful. The room was divided horizontally by white chair rail, with the lower part of the walls painted a rich amethyst color and the upper part done in pale turquoise. On the wall behind Saige's crib, her name had been painted in dark purple script with the dot above the *i* replaced by a butterfly. A kaleidoscope of butterflies in various shapes and sizes flew across the other three walls so that the overall effect was colorful and fun and perfect for a little girl.

"This is amazing," Cassie said, as she traced the outline of a butterfly and realized it wasn't a decal but hand-painted.

"My cousin, Jordyn, helped decorate in here."

"She's incredibly talented," she noted. "Of course, she is Jay Addison, the illustrator of graphic novels."

"How did—" He shook his head, realizing the answer even before he'd finished asking the question. "My mother."

Cassie nodded. "She was at the library when I was unpacking the latest installment of A. K. Channing's series."

"Apparently she spends a lot more time at the library than I ever realized."

"Some people golf, others knit, your mother likes to read." She noted the bookshelf above the little girl's dresser. "And she's obviously passed her love of books on to her granddaughter."

"Saige never goes to sleep without a story," he admitted.

"Wee?" his daughter echoed hopefully.

"*After* your bath."

Which turned out to involve a lot of plastic toys and plenty of splashing, resulting in a more exhausting and time-consuming process than Cassie had anticipated. When Saige was finally clean and dry and dressed for bed, Braden asked Cassie if she could keep an eye on the baby while he cleaned up the bathroom. She happily agreed.

"P'ay?" Saige said hopefully.

"No play," her father said firmly. "It's bedtime."

"Wee?"

"Yes, Daddy will read you a story in a little bit," he promised. "Why don't you let Cassie help you pick out a book?"

His daughter took Cassie's hand and led her across the room to the bookshelf. Apparently she knew what story she wanted, because as soon as Cassie lifted her up, she grabbed *Goodnight Moon* and hugged the book to her chest.

"Kee," Saige said.

"Hmm…you're going to have to help me with that one," Cassie said. At the Book & Bake Sale, the little girl had said "kee" when she wanted a cookie, but Cassie didn't think that was what she wanted now.

"Kee," she said again, stretching out her free hand toward her bed.

"Ahh, *mon*key," Cassie realized, plucking the toy out of the crib.

Saige took the monkey from her and hugged it to her chest, too.

"All set now?"

The little girl nodded, even as her mouth opened wide in a yawn.

Cassie carried her to the rocking chair by the window and sat down with the baby in her lap.

Saige looked toward the door. "Da-da?"

"He'll be finished up in a minute—after he wipes up all the water you splashed on the bathroom floor," Cassie guessed.

Saige responded by snuggling in to her embrace, the back of her head dropping against Cassie's shoulder. She lifted a fist—the one still clutching the sock monkey—to rub her eye.

"You're a sleepy girl, aren't you?"

Saige's only response was another yawn.

"Do you want me to read your story or are you waiting for Daddy?"

"Wee," Saige replied, offering her the book.

So Cassie took it from her hand and opened the cover. She began to read, not needing to look at the page to recite the words of the classic story she'd read aloud at the library more times than she could count.

And although it wasn't a long story, Saige's eyelids had

drifted shut before the little bunny had wished good night to half of the objects in the great green room. But Cassie read all the way to the last page before setting the book aside. Still, the baby didn't stir.

Cassie continued to sit with her, the weight of the little girl in her arms filling her heart and reminding her of the dreams she'd tried to put aside. Dreams that had teased and tempted for many years but so far remained unfulfilled.

Tonight, Braden had given her a glimpse of the life she'd always imagined in her future. A home, a husband, a family. It wasn't so much—and yet it was everything she'd always wanted. And being with Braden and Saige, she was tempted to let herself dream again. To believe that she might one day be part of a family again, maybe even *this* family.

Of course, she was getting way ahead of herself. She hadn't known Braden very long and didn't know him very well, and it would be foolish to hope that one night could lead to a lifetime together.

You can't start the next chapter of your life if you keep rereading the last one.

Great—not only was Megan quoting words of wisdom from Pinterest, now those words were echoing in the back of Cassie's head.

Maybe it was clichéd advice—and maybe it was true. Maybe it was her own past experiences that were preventing her from moving forward with her life. And maybe, if she let herself open her heart, she might discover that Braden and Saige weren't just characters in her next chapter but in every chapter of the rest of her life.

It didn't take Braden long to wipe out the tub and dry off Saige's toys, but when he made his way across the hall after completing those tasks, his daughter was already asleep. And in that moment, looking at Saige snuggled contentedly in Cassie's arms, he knew: she was the one.

Cassie was the perfect mother for his little girl—the mother that Saige deserved.

Now he only had to convince her of that fact.

He didn't think it would be too difficult. Cassie had admitted that she wanted to be a wife and a mother and, coincidentally, he needed a wife and a mother for his daughter. It was, from his perspective, a win-win.

The fact that he didn't—wouldn't—love her, didn't have to be a barrier to a future for them together. He could be a good husband—affectionate and faithful—without opening up his heart. And he would do everything in his power to make Cassie happy, to show her how much he appreciated her presence in their lives.

"I think you have the touch," he said, speaking quietly from the doorway.

"It doesn't require any special magic to get an exhausted child to sleep," Cassie pointed out.

"If you were ever here at two a.m., you'd know that's not true," he commented dryly.

"She doesn't sleep through the night yet?"

"Most nights she does," he acknowledged. "But lately she's decided that two a.m. is playtime. She doesn't wake up because she's wet or hungry, she just wants to play. And then, after being up for half the night, she has a three-hour nap at my mother's house."

"Fiona, one of the moms in Toddler Time, went through something like that with her little guy," Cassie told him. "He would sleep at day care but not at home. According to her pediatrician, it's not uncommon with babies who want to spend time with their working parents."

"Well, giving up my job isn't really an option," he noted.

"And my mom's trying to break her of the habit by limiting her naptime during the day."

"That might be why she fell asleep so easily tonight," Cassie noted.

"Or maybe you tired her out, making her chase all of those trains around the track."

"You're giving me too much credit," she told him.

He shook his head. "I don't think so. I've seen you with the kids at the library—from babies to teens," he reminded her. "You have an instinctive ability to empathize and relate to all of them."

"I love working with kids."

"Did that broken engagement destroy all hope of having your own?"

"No," she denied. "But I would like to have a husband before the kids and, so far, that hasn't worked out."

"Well, maybe you'll luck out someday and meet a fabulous guy who already has a child," he suggested. "Perhaps an adorable little girl."

"That would be lucky," Cassie said lightly.

"Or maybe you've already met him."

"Maybe I have," she acknowledged. "And maybe I specifically recall the fabulous guy with the adorable little girl warning me not to fall for him."

He leaned down to lift his sleeping daughter from her arms and touch his lips to Cassie's. "But that was before he started falling for you."

He tucked Saige into her crib, ensuring that her sock monkey was beside her, then he took Cassie's hand and led her back downstairs.

"Why don't you sit down by the fire?" he suggested. "I'll be there in just a sec."

She went into the living room, but when he returned with their glasses and the rest of the bottle of wine, he saw that she was standing by the fireplace, looking at the photographs lined up on the mantel. Several were of Saige, the rest were various other members of his family.

She set down the picture in her hand—a candid shot taken at Lauryn and Ryder's wedding—and accepted the wine he offered.

"It was big news when they got married," she commented. "A daughter of Charisma's most famous family stealing the heart of America's hottest handyman."

He nodded. "But not quite as big as when my brother Ryan married Harper, daughter of soap actor Peter Ross. We had actual paparazzi in town to cover that event."

"It really is a small world, isn't it?" she mused. "The first time I ever saw Ryder Wallace was on *Coffee Time with Caroline*, which was produced by your sister-in-law, and now he's married to your cousin."

"And his sister is married to my brother Justin."

"Apparently it's even smaller than I realized."

"Especially if you're a Garrett," Braden remarked. "I swear, I can't move in this town without bumping into someone I'm related to. And it will only get worse when Ryan and Harper move back from Florida and Lauryn and Ryder return from Georgia."

"But you don't really mind," Cassie guessed. "I can tell by all these photos—and your mother's stories—that your family is close."

"We are," he agreed. "As much as they drive me crazy at times, I don't know what I would do without them."

"I miss that," she admitted.

"Being driven crazy?"

She smiled as she shook her head. "Being part of a family."

"A Day with the Garrett Clan might cure you of that,"

he suggested. And if she didn't run screaming, that would be his cue to take the next step.

"A Day with the Garrett Clan sounds like an event you'd sell tickets to," she teased.

"Maybe I'll suggest that in advance of the next family gathering, but this one is an informal welcome home barbecue at my parents' place on Sunday for Ryan, Harper and Oliver. You should come."

"If the whole family is going to be there, I'm sure your parents won't want extra people underfoot."

"Are you kidding? My mother is happiest in complete chaos—and I know she'd be thrilled to see you there."

"Aren't you worried that she might make a big deal out of me being there with you?" she asked cautiously.

He grinned. "*Everyone* will make a big deal out of you being there with me."

"Are you trying to talk me *into* or *out of* going to this barbecue?"

"Into," he assured her. "I very much want you there with me. I want you to meet my family and I want them to meet you."

Still, she hesitated. "I just think it might be too soon."

"Why?"

"Because I have a really lousy track record with relationships," she admitted.

"Most people go through a few failed relationships before they figure out how to make it work—or even realize that they want to." He slid his arms around her, drawing her closer. "We can make this work, Cassie."

"Do you really think so—or are you just saying that to get me into bed again?"

"If I wanted to get you into bed again, I wouldn't waste my breath on words," he said.

"What would—" She shook her head. "Forget it. I don't want to know."

He dipped his head, but paused with his lips hovering just a fraction of an inch above hers. "I think you do want to know. And I think you really want me to kiss you."

She responded by lifting her chin to breach the scant distance and press her mouth to his.

He believed what he'd said to her—that they could make a relationship work—and the powerful chemistry between them was only one of the many reasons. And when she was in his arms, it was an unassailable reason.

He knew a relationship required more than physical attraction. Passion was the icing on the cake rather than the base layer, more decorative than essential. But it was also able to transform something good into something spectacular. And making love with Cassie was spectacular.

He liked who she was and everything about her. She was warm and kind and compassionate, beautiful and smart and funny. He enjoyed spending time with her, talking to her and making love with her—but he wasn't going to fall in love with her.

It wasn't just that he was unwilling to risk heartbreak again—it was that he didn't have anything left in his heart to give to anyone else. The failure of his marriage—and the sense that he had failed the woman he'd vowed to love, honor and cherish—had undoubtedly broken a piece of his heart. But only a piece, because the rest was filled with the pure love he felt for Saige, and he didn't want or need anything more than that.

But his daughter did, and he owed it to Saige to give her the life that her birth mother wanted for her. A real family. A whole family. He didn't believe Lindsay would ever be able to take Saige away—and hopefully, after their conversation today, she wouldn't even try—but he did agree that his little girl needed a mother. And he couldn't imagine a woman who would be more perfect for the role than the one he was kissing right now.

They were both breathless when she finally eased away from him. He lifted a finger to her chin, tilting her head back so that he could look into her beautiful dark eyes. "Will you stay with me tonight?" he asked.

"For a while," she agreed.

"That's a start," he said, and led her down the hall.

Chapter Fourteen

Cassie was in way over her head.

She knew it, and she didn't care. When she was with Braden, when his hands were on her body, it was difficult to care about anything but how good he made her feel. And he instinctively knew how to make her feel really good.

She'd never had a lover who was so closely attuned to the wants and needs of her body, but Braden was nothing if not attentive. He used her sighs and gasps and moans to guide his exploration of her body, and his own lips and his hands to lead her slowly and inexorably toward the ultimate pinnacle of pleasure.

She followed not just willingly but eagerly, their discarded clothing marking the path to his bedroom. Somewhere in the back of her mind, she knew that they were venturing into dangerous territory—but she didn't care. Her body already knew him and wanted him and her heart refused to heed the warnings of her mind.

His hands stroked down her back, over the curve of her bottom, drawing her closer. She touched her mouth to his chest, and let her tongue dart out to taste his skin. He tasted good. Hot. Salty. Sexy. She skimmed her lips down his breastbone, then flicked her tongue over his nipple, eliciting a low growl of approval. She reached down between their bodies as her mouth moved to his other nipple, and wrapped her hand around the rigid length of him. She felt him jerk against her palm, and was pleased to know that he wanted her as much as she wanted him.

She started to move lower, her mouth trailing kisses down his belly, but he caught her arms and hauled her up again, his tongue sliding deep into her mouth in a kiss that was so hot and hungry it made her head spin and her knees tremble.

She tumbled onto the mattress, dragging Braden down with her. He pulled away only long enough to sheathe himself with a condom, then he parted her thighs and thrust into her. She gasped with pleasure, instinctively tilting her hips so that they were joined as deeply and completely as possibly.

He filled all her senses. She could see nothing but the intensity of his deep green eyes locked with her own; hear nothing but the roar of blood through her veins; taste nothing but the sweetest passion when his mouth covered hers again; feel nothing but the most exquisite bliss as their bodies merged and mated and…finally…leaped over the precipice together.

She was still waiting for her heart to stop racing when she heard a soft sound somewhere in the distance. While she was attempting to decipher what it was and from where it had come, Braden was already sliding out from beneath the covers that he'd yanked up over their naked bodies sometime after they'd collapsed together.

"I'll be right back," he said, brushing a quick kiss over her lips, having shifted gears from lover to father in the blink of an eye.

A moment later, she heard the soft murmur of his voice through the baby monitor that she now realized was on the bedside table. She couldn't hear what he was saying, but his tone was soothing, reassuring.

A few minutes later, she heard his footsteps enter the room again. She lifted her arm away from her forehead and peeled open one eyelid—then the second, when she saw that he was carrying an enormous wedge of lemon meringue pie on a plate.

"I thought you went to check on Saige."

"I did. She's fine," he assured her. "But I thought you might be ready for dessert now."

"That's for me?"

"It's for both of us," he said.

She wiggled up to a sitting position, tucking the sheet under her armpits to ensure she was covered.

He grinned. "It's a little late for modesty, don't you think?"

"I'm not going to sit here naked and eat pie," she protested.

He shrugged, broke off the tip of the pie with the fork and held it toward her—then pulled it away and ate the bite himself.

She frowned.

"Mmm…this is really good. The lemon is the perfect balance of sweet and tart and the meringue—" he cut off another piece, popped it into his mouth "—is so incredibly light and fluffy."

"You said that was to share," she reminded him.

"You give up the sheet and I'll give you some pie."

"Seriously?"

"Those are my terms," he told her.

She hesitated; he took another bite of the pie.

Her mouth watered as she watched the fork slide between his lips, swallowing up the flaky crust, tart filling and fluffy meringue, and she decided he was right—it was a little late for modesty.

She dropped the sheet; he grinned. This time, when he scooped up a forkful of pie, he held it close for her to sample. She could smell it—the tangy sweet scent—just before she parted her lips to allow him to slide the fork into her mouth.

She closed her eyes and sighed with blissful pleasure. "Oh, yeah. This is really good."

He lifted the fork again, but the pie slid off the tines and onto her thigh, near her hip. She yelped. "That's cold."

"Sorry," he said, even as he lowered his head to clean up the dessert with his mouth. He licked her skin thoroughly, making her suspect that the mishap might not have been an accident after all.

"Two can play that game," she warned him, and scooped some of the meringue off the pie with her finger, then smeared it on his belly before cleaning it up with her mouth.

He retaliated by dabbing lemon filling on each of her nipples and suckling the rigid peaks until she was gasping and squirming.

And so they went back and forth, taking turns savoring the dessert from one another's bodies. Then they made love again, the remnants of the pie creating a sticky friction between them and necessitating a quick shower afterward.

A shower that ended up not being so quick, as the slow, sensual soaping of one another's bodies had their mutual passion escalating again. When Braden finally twisted the knob to shut off the spray, it had started to go cold, and they were still dripping with water when they tumbled onto his bed again.

As Cassie drifted to sleep in his arms, she realized that she'd gone and done what she'd promised herself she wouldn't: she'd fallen head over heels in love with Braden Garrett.

Braden's maternal grandmother had been a resident of Serenity Gardens for the last ten years of her life. Of course, she'd passed away more than a dozen years earlier and the residence had undergone significant renovations and benefitted from a major addition since then. Thankfully, the main reception desk was in the same place and, after buzzing up to Irene Houlahan's room, he and Saige were cleared to find their way to Room 508 in the North Wing.

When they arrived at her door, it was ajar. He remembered that his grandmother had often left her door open, too, to welcome any neighbors who wanted to drop in for a visit. Still, he knocked on the portal and waited for Miss Houlahan's invitation before pushing the door wider.

The old woman was seated at one end of an overstuffed sofa in the living room, a thick hardcover book open in her lap. The permanent furrow between her brows relaxed marginally when her gaze lit on his daughter by his side, and she closed her book and set it aside. "Hello, Saige."

His little girl didn't have a shy bone in her body, and while he hovered on the threshold, she happily toddled across the room to the sofa. Once there, she climbed up onto the cushions, surprising Braden as much as Irene when she pursed her lips and kissed the old woman's wrinkled cheek.

"Well," Irene said, as if she wasn't quite sure how to

respond to the gesture. "It's not often that I have the plea-sure of such a young visitor." Then she lifted her gaze to Braden's. "And since you're not the Grim Reaper, you can come in, too."

He fought against a smile as he stepped farther into the room.

"I don't imagine you were just 'in the neighborhood,'" Irene said.

"Not really," he admitted, setting the vase on the table beside the sofa. "We came to deliver these."

Saige, having noticed the stack of photo books on the coffee table, slid off the sofa again and reached for the one on top. Braden caught her hands and gently pried them from the cover. "Those are Miss Houlahan's books—they're not for little girls."

"I always believed books were intended to be read by anyone who was interested," Irene contradicted him. "But I don't imagine pictures of coffee tables would be of much interest to a toddler."

Braden had been so focused on ensuring his daughter didn't damage the item he hadn't taken note of the cover, but he did now. "A coffee table book about coffee tables?"

"Cassie's idea of a joke." She shifted forward and re-moved a different book from the bottom of the pile: *A Vibrant History of Pop Art.*

"This has some strange stuff in it but at least the pic-tures are colorful," she told him. Then she turned to his daughter and asked, "Do you want to look at this one?"

Saige nodded and Irene set the book on the table in front of her, then opened it up to the middle. Saige lifted all of the pages from the front cover and pushed them over so that she could start at the front.

"She knows how to read a book," Irene noted.

"We read every night before bed, and my mother takes her to the library a couple of times a week."

"A child who reads will be an adult who thinks," the former librarian said approvingly. "Now tell me what the flowers are for, because I'm not so old that I've forgotten when my birthday is and I know it's not today."

"Why does there need to be an occasion?" he countered.

"Because I've never known a man to bring flowers to a woman without one."

"Then maybe you've known the wrong men," he told her.

"You're trying to sweeten me up so I'll say good things about you to Cassie, aren't you?" she guessed.

He suspected it would take a lot more than a bouquet of flowers to do that, but he bit down on his tongue to prevent the thought from becoming words. "No," he denied. "I'm trying to say thank you."

"For what?" she asked, obviously still suspicious.

"For being there for Cassie when no one else was."

She scowled. "I don't know what you think I did—"

"I think you saved her life."

Irene snorted. "I did nothing of the sort."

"I don't mean literally," he explained. "But she told me about everything that happened the year her sister—and then her mother—died."

Irene peered at him over the rim of her glasses, her gaze speculative. "Cassie doesn't often talk about her family," she noted.

"She also told me that you appealed to the church to have her stepfather sent away—and gave family services the evidence they needed to ensure that he couldn't take Cassie with him."

"I didn't realize that she knew anything about that," Irene admitted.

"And then, because you recognized that she was just as terrified of the system as she was of her abusive step-father, you took her into your home."

"It wasn't a sacrifice to give her an extra bedroom."

He glanced at Saige, who was braced on her arms on the table, leaning close to scrutinize the details in the pictures.

"You gave her more than that," he said to Irene. "You gave her security, guidance and direction. You helped her focus on and achieve her goals."

"I didn't do any of it for thanks," she told him.

"I know, but I'm thanking you, anyway."

"Well, it was a nice gesture," she admitted, just a little begrudgingly.

He held back his smile. "If you give me a chance, you might find that I'm a nice guy."

"Maybe I will," she conceded, with just the hint of a smile tugging at her mouth.

The next day, when Cassie was visiting Irene, she saw the vase of colorful blooms prominently displayed on the coffee table.

"I see Jerry brought you flowers again," she noted.

"Those aren't from Jerry," Irene told her.

"Really?" She grinned. "You have another suitor in competition for your affections?"

Her friend sniffed. "Not likely. Those are from *your* suitor."

Cassie lifted a brow.

"Braden Garrett came to see me yesterday."

"He did?"

Irene nodded. "Brought his little girl with him—goodness, she's just a bundle of sweetness and joy, isn't she?"

"Saige is a very happy child," Cassie agreed.

"You've been spending a lot of time with them lately?"

"I guess I have," she agreed cautiously.

"A man like that, with a young child to raise, is a package deal," Irene warned her.

"I know."

"And you love them both already, don't you?"

There was no point in telling the old woman it wasn't any of her business. When Irene had taken an angry and grieving fifteen-year-old girl into her home, Cassie's business had become her business. Since that time, she'd been Cassie's legal guardian and surrogate mother, and she'd never hesitated to ask Irene for guidance and advice when she needed it. In the current situation, she decided that she needed it because her feelings for Braden and Saige had become so muddled with her own hopes and dreams that she feared she'd lost perspective.

"I do," she admitted.

"Why don't you sound happy about it?"

"Because I didn't want to fall in love with Braden," she admitted. "I didn't want to give him the power to break my heart."

"Loving someone is always a risk," Irene acknowledged.

"Please don't start quoting Pinterest advice to me."

"You don't need any advice—you just need to follow your heart."

"Because that's never steered me wrong in the past," Cassie noted dryly.

"Stop dwelling on the past and focus on the future," her friend suggested.

"That definitely sounds like Pinterest advice."

Irene handed Cassie the book she'd been reading during her previous visit.

"There's a lot of good stuff on Pinterest," she said. "But not a lot of men like Braden Garrett in the world."

* * *

Maybe Cassie should have made an excuse to get out of attending the welcome home party for Braden's brother and sister-in-law, but she was curious to see him interact with the whole family, and she wanted to be able to tell Megan—who was a huge fan of *Ryder to the Rescue*—that she'd met Ryder Wallace. Although his crew was still in Georgia finishing up the restoration of an antebellum mansion, he and his wife and their kids had returned to Charisma for the family event.

"It's a good thing your parents have a huge backyard," Cassie said, when they arrived at Ellen and John's residence.

"And that the weatherman was wrong in forecasting rain for today," Braden noted.

She looked up at the clear blue sky. "I guess even Mother Nature knows not to mess with Ellen Garrett's plans."

He chuckled. "You might be right about that."

As they made their way around the gathering, he introduced her to his aunts, uncles and cousins. When they crossed paths with Ellen, who was in her glory with so many little ones underfoot, she immediately whisked Saige away to play with her cousins. It seemed that everywhere Cassie looked, there were children and babies. And more than one expectant mother in the crowd, too.

Not long after they'd arrived, John dragged Braden away to man one of the extra grills that had been set up in the backyard. He was reluctant to leave Cassie's side, but she assured him that she would be fine. Although the words were spoken with more conviction than she felt, he took them at face value and accepted the chef's apron and long-handled spatula his father gave him.

"There's a gate by the garage," a pretty dark-haired woman said to her.

"Sorry?"

"You had that slightly panicked look in your eyes, as if you were searching for the nearest exit."

"Oh." Cassie blew out a breath and managed a smile. "I guess I am feeling a little overwhelmed. And I'm sorry— I know Braden introduced us, but I don't remember your name."

"Tristyn," the other woman said. "And there's no need to apologize. I sometimes feel overwhelmed at these gatherings, too, and I'm related to all of these people."

"When Braden said the whole family would be here, I didn't realize what that meant."

"There are a lot of us," his cousin agreed. "More and more every year, with all the babies being born."

"Do any of the little ones belong to you?"

"No," Tristyn said quickly, firmly. "I'm just a doting aunt—actual and honorary—to all of the rug rats running around."

The words were barely out of her mouth when a preschooler raced over to them, giggling as he was chased by a chocolate Lab that was as big as the child. Tristyn swept the little boy up into her arms and planted noisy kisses on each of his cheeks.

The dog plopped on its butt at their feet, tail swiping through the grass and tongue hanging out of its mouth.

Since Tristyn was fussing over the child, Cassie dropped to her knees beside the dog. Pleased with the attention, she immediately rolled onto her back. "Aren't you just the cutest thing?" she said, dutifully rubbing the animal's exposed belly.

The dog showed her agreement by swiping Cassie's chin with her tongue.

She chuckled softly. "Who does she belong to? And will they notice if I take her home with me?"

"What do you think, Oliver?" Tristyn asked the boy. "Would you notice if Cassie took Coco home with her?"

Oliver nodded solemnly.

"Well, as adorable as she is, I would never want to come between a boy and his dog," Cassie said.

"But there is supposed to be a leash between the boy and his dog," a different female voice piped up.

Cassie turned to see Braden's sister-in-law Harper with the leash in hand.

"But Coco wanted to meet Cassie," Oliver told her.

"Is that so?" his mother said, a smile tugging at her lips as she glanced at Cassie. "And have they been properly introduced now?"

Oliver nodded. "Coco gave her kisses and she didn't say 'yuck.'"

"That doesn't mean her kisses aren't yucky," Harper noted, bending down—not an easy task with her pregnant belly impeding her—to clip the leash onto the dog's collar. "Just that Cassie has better manners than your dog."

Coco looked at Harper with big soulful eyes, silently reproaching her for putting restrictions on her freedom.

She handed the leash to her son. "Please take her into the house so that she's not underfoot while Grandpa's grilling. And don't bug Grandma for a snack before dinner."

The little boy sighed but obediently trotted away with the dog in tow.

Harper watched him go, then her gaze shifted to encompass all of the people gathered in the backyard. "Now that we're back in Charisma, I find myself wondering how we ever stayed away so long."

"It might have had something to do with your contract with WMBT and *Mid-Day Miami*," Tristyn noted.

Harper nodded. "And maybe it was the right move for us at the time, but now...I'm so glad we're home."

"We all are," Tristyn told her. "If you'd stayed in Florida to have that baby, there would have been a convoy of Garretts down the I-95."

The expectant mother laughed. "Somehow, I don't doubt it," she said, then she turned her attention to Cassie. "Is this your first family event?"

Cassie nodded. "I've known Ellen for years and, through her, Saige since she was about six months old, but I only met Braden in March."

"The man moves fast," his sister-in-law noted, a suggestive sparkle in her eye.

Cassie felt her cheeks heat and hoped the reaction might be attributed to the afternoon sun. "We're friends," she said.

"Uh-huh," Harper agreed, smiling.

"It's true," Tristyn piped up in Cassie's defense. Or so she thought until the other woman spoke again. "In fact, they were very friendly in the shed just a little while ago."

"We were looking for a soccer ball for the kids," Cassie explained.

"And Braden thought a soccer ball might be hiding in your clothes?"

Now her cheeks weren't just hot, they were burning.

Harper chuckled but showed mercy by shifting her cousin's attention away from Cassie. "I'm going to make sure Coco isn't tripping up everyone in the kitchen."

"I should probably go in, too," Cassie said. "To give Ellen a hand."

"She has all the help she needs in the kitchen," Tristyn assured her. "The aunts have been managing family get-togethers for more years than I've been alive, and the meal preparation is more expertly choreographed than the dancers in a Beyoncé video."

Cassie couldn't help but smile at the mental image the other woman's words evoked. "I don't doubt that's true."

"The bar, on the other hand, looks abandoned," Tristyn said, linking her arm through Cassie's and guiding her in that direction.

"We're going to work the bar?"

Braden's cousin grinned. "No, we're going to get you a drink to accompany the dish I'm going to give you on my cousin."

Chapter Fifteen

Cassie would gladly have paid admission to spend a Day with the Garrett Clan—as Braden referred to it. It was a little chaotic and a lot of fun and she loved watching the interactions of his family. There was also much talking and teasing and more food than she'd ever seen in one place in her life. So she ate and she mingled and she found herself falling even more in love—not just with the man but with his whole family.

It was hard to keep track of who were siblings and who were cousins, because they were all "aunt" and "uncle" to little ones. Cassie had no experience with close-knit families like the Garretts. Growing up, she vaguely remembered a set of grandparents in Utah—her father's parents—who had sent cards at Christmas and on birthdays, but they'd both died a couple of years before Amanda did. Her mother had refused to talk about her family, so if she had any relatives on that side, Cassie had never known them.

For almost two years, the first two years after her mom had married Ray, Cassie had felt as if she was part of a real family. For the first time that she could remember, she'd lived with both a mother and a father, her sister and two stepbrothers, and it had been nice. Normal.

Even when she'd cringed at demonstrations of Ray's temper, she'd thought that was normal because she'd never really known anything different. But this was even better than that—this was the family she'd always dreamed of having someday, and being here with Braden gave her hope that the dream might be within her grasp.

"You sure do know how to throw a party," Cassie said to the hostess, when Ellen brought out a fresh pitcher of sweet tea and set it on the table with a stack of plastic glasses.

Braden's mom beamed proudly. "It's always fun getting the family together."

"It's nice that they could all be here," she commented.

And she meant it. She envied Braden having grown up with Ellen and John as parents, and she was glad that Saige, despite not having a mother, would grow up secure in the knowledge that she was loved.

"Family means a lot to all of us," Ellen said. "And although I understood why Ryan and Harper wanted to move to Florida, I can't deny that—for the past three years—I've felt as if a part of my heart was missing."

"I guess a mother never stops worrying about her children—even when they have children of their own."

"That's the truth," Ellen confirmed. "But now that all of my boys are home and happy, I'm looking forward to focusing on and enjoying my grandchildren—and maybe planning another wedding in the not-too-distant future."

Cassie suspected that Ellen was hoping for some insights about her relationship with Braden, but she had none to give her. "Speaking of your grandchildren," she said, because she didn't dare comment on the latter part of Ellen's remark, "it looks like Saige wore more ice cream than she ate. I'm going to wash her up before she puts her sticky fingers on everything."

"There's a change table in the first bedroom at the top of the stairs," Ellen told her.

"Great," Cassie said, then scooped up the little girl and made her escape.

Braden was catching up with his middle brother when he caught a glimpse of Saige out of the corner of his eye. She'd been sitting on a blanket spread out on the grass with several other kids, all of them enjoying ice-cream sandwiches under the watchful eye of Maura, one of the oldest cousins. Having finished her frozen treat, Saige stood up and turned toward the house. He saw then that she hadn't actually eaten her dessert but painted her face and shirt with it.

He started to excuse himself to take her inside to wash up, but before he could interrupt Justin's ER story, he saw Cassie pick up his daughter and carry her toward the house. He couldn't hear what she said, but whatever it was, it made Saige giggle.

He never got tired of watching Cassie with Saige. She was so good with his daughter, so easy and natural. The first day he'd attended Baby Talk at the library, he'd been impressed by her humor and patience. If there was ever a woman who was meant to be a mother—and hopefully Saige's mother—it was Cassie.

"You haven't heard a word I've said," Justin accused.

"What?"

His brother shook his head. "Never mind."

"Why are you grinning?" Braden asked suspiciously.

"Because I never thought I'd see you like this," Justin admitted.

"Like what?" Braden asked.

"Head over heels. And—more important—happy."

He scowled. "What are you talking about?"

"I don't know if you really thought you were fooling anyone, but we could all tell that you were miserable in the last few years of your marriage, at least until Saige came along."

Braden couldn't deny it.

"It's nice to see you happy again," Justin said. "And if Cassie's the reason for that, you'd be smart to hold on to her."

"I intend to," he said, and headed into the house.

He found Cassie in the nursery—formerly Ryan's childhood bedroom that his parents had redone in anticipation of their first grandchild. It had been several more years before they'd actually needed it, but the room was in frequent use now whenever Ellen and John looked after Vanessa for Justin and Avery, or—even more frequently—Saige for Braden. In fact, his parents were talking about adding a second crib and a couple of toddler beds to ensure they'd be able to accommodate all of the grandchildren now that Ryan and Harper were back in Charisma with Oliver and another baby on the way.

"I wondered where you disappeared to," Braden said to Cassie.

She glanced over and smiled at him. "Saige had ice cream all over her, so I brought her in to wash up and change her clothes, then she started yawning and I realized it was getting close to her bedtime, so I decided to put her pajamas on her instead."

"You could have asked me to do it," he protested.

"You were busy with your brother, and I didn't mind," she said, as she fastened the snaps of Saige's one-piece sleeper.

The little girl lifted her arms, indicating her desire to be picked up. As soon as Cassie had done so, Saige laid her head on her shoulder and closed her eyes.

"I think all the excitement today has worn her out," Cassie said.

"No doubt," he agreed. "How about you?"

"I had a great day," she said. "I really enjoyed being here, watching you with your family. It's rare to see so many members of three different generations and all of them so close."

He lifted Saige from her arms and carried his daughter over to the crib, setting her gently down on the mattress, before turning back to Cassie again. "I'm glad that Saige has cousins of a similar age, although I haven't given up hope that she might have a brother or a sister—or both—someday, too."

"You should have more kids," Cassie said. "You're a wonderful father."

"Thanks, but first I'd have to find a woman who's willing to take on the challenges of a widower and his adopted daughter."

"I don't think you'll have too much trouble with that," she said, her tone light and teasing. "Your little girl is pretty darn cute."

"What about her dad?" he prompted.

Cassie smiled. "He's not hard to look at, either."

"Of course, she'd also have to be willing to put up with my family."

"Your family is wonderful," she assured him.

"Most of the time," he agreed. "I'm glad to see that you survived your first Garrett family gathering without any visible signs of trauma."

"First?"

He took her hands and linked their fingers together. "I

hope it's only the first of many, because being here with you today, I realized that this is where you belong—with me and Saige."

And then he released one of her hands to reach into the side pocket of his cargo shorts and pull out a small velvet box.

Cassie's eyes went wide when he offered it to her, but she made no move to take it.

So he flipped open the hinged lid with his thumb, revealing a princess-cut diamond solitaire set on a simple platinum band. "I'm asking you to marry me, Cassie. To be my wife and a mother to my daughter—and any other children we may have."

She stared at the ring in his hand, stunned.

Because while she had undeniably thought about the possibility of a future with Braden and Saige, she'd counseled her eager heart to be patient. Even if she believed Braden's claim that he wasn't still mourning the death of his wife, he'd experienced a lot of changes in his life over the past seventeen months and she didn't imagine that he was eager to make any more right now. And although he'd recently hinted that he was falling for her, she hadn't expected this.

"I know it's fast," he acknowledged, when she failed to respond. "And if it's too soon, I can wait. But I don't want to wait. I want to start the rest of my life with you as soon as possible."

And with those words, her heart filled with so much joy, her chest actually ached. "I want that, too," she finally said.

His lips curved then, and the warmth and happiness in his smile arrowed straight to her heart. Maybe this was fast—certainly a lot faster than she'd expected—but it felt so right. And when he took her hand and slid the ring onto her finger, it fit right, too.

* * *

"I didn't think we were ever going to get away," Braden said, when they finally left his parents' house a few hours later.

"It's your own fault," Cassie told him. "After you announced our engagement, your mother insisted on opening half a dozen bottles of champagne, and then everyone wanted to toast to something."

"Maybe I should have waited for a more private venue," he acknowledged. "But seeing you with my family today, how perfectly you fit, I knew there wouldn't be a more perfect moment.

"And Tristyn, in particular, was thrilled about the engagement, because our impending wedding plans ensure that the focus of attention will be shifted away from her, at least until after the ceremony."

"Is she usually the focus of attention?"

"Only since Lauryn and Ryder got married," he told her.

"And her other sister, Jordyn, is the artist married to Marco Palermo and who has the twin boys?"

"You must have been taking notes," he mused.

"A notebook would have come in handy," she told him. "Because not fifteen minutes after meeting Tristyn, I couldn't remember her name."

"Well, I'm impressed," he said. "And the combination of Lauryn's recent wedding with Jordyn's pregnancy has everyone wanting to know when Tristyn's going to settle down."

"But she's with Josh, right?"

Braden scowled. "Where did you ever get that idea?"

"From the fact that he didn't take his eyes off her the whole day."

The furrow in his brow deepened. "Really?"

"Or maybe I just assumed they were together, because

everyone else was paired up," she offered as an alternate explanation, attempting to appease him.

"Well, they're not together," he assured her. "Josh is a friend of Daniel's and his partner in Garrett/Slater Racing."

"So is Tristyn the only one who isn't married?"

"No, Nora is single, too, but her half-sister status provides a little bit of insulation from most of the familial nosiness," he told her.

"They're not nosy," she protested. "They're interested."

"Wait until they all want to help plan the wedding—then you can let me know if they're interested or interfering."

Cassie didn't get a chance to announce her engagement to her coworkers on Monday, because as soon as Stacey saw the ring on her finger, she squealed with excitement—an instinctive reaction that prompted a fierce shushing from Helen. She immediately grabbed Cassie's arm and dragged her into the staff room where they could talk without fear of reprisal.

"Ohmygod," Stacey said, her gaze riveted on the rock. "Is that thing real?"

"I haven't actually tried to cut glass with it, but I assume so," Cassie told her friend.

"Braden?"

"No, Mr. Pasternak," she said dryly, giving the name of one of their oldest patrons, who had a habit of falling asleep in the magazine section.

Stacey rolled her eyes. "Okay—stupid question. But when? Where? How?"

She smiled at the barrage of questions, happy to share the details and some of her own euphoria. "Last night. During a barbecue at his parents' house."

"He proposed to you in front of everyone?"

She shook her head. "No, it was just me and Braden. And Saige—but she was sleeping."

Her friend sighed dreamily. "So…when's the wedding?"

"We haven't set a date yet."

"What are you thinking—summer? Fall?"

"I really haven't had a chance to think about it," Cassie admitted. "Everything has happened so fast. In fact, when I woke up this morning, I had to look at my finger to be sure it wasn't a dream."

"It's a dream come true," Stacey said. "You're going to be Braden Garrett's wife and a mother to his baby girl." She sighed again. "Who would have guessed, the first day he came in here, that you'd be engaged to him less than three months later?"

"Everything did happen fast, didn't it?"

"Love doesn't have any particular timetable," Stacey said. "It's more about the person than the days."

Cassie rolled her eyes. "Are you giving me Pinterest advice now, too?"

"No, that's something I learned from my own experience," her friend said. "I knew that when you met the right man, he would love you as much as you love him."

Cassie smiled at that, but as she glanced at her engagement ring, the usual joy was tempered by doubts and questions.

And when she sat back down at her desk to prepare the schedule for the kids' summer reading club, Stacey's words echoed in the back of Cassie's mind, making her wonder: Did Braden love her as much as she loved him?

Did he love her at all?

Because now that she was thinking about it, she couldn't recall that he'd ever actually spoken those words to her. Not even after they'd made love, when she'd been snuggled in his embrace and whispered the words to him. Instead, he'd kissed her again, and she'd assumed that was proof he felt the same way. Now she wasn't so sure—and she hated the uncertainty.

But she pushed aside her worries and concerns. After all, a lot of men weren't comfortable putting their feelings into words. The fact that he'd asked her to marry him told her everything that she needed to know about his feelings.

Still, she was immensely grateful when a trio of seventh graders came in and asked her to help them find some books for a research project and she was able to focus on something other than the words Braden had never spoken.

It was nearly three weeks after the barbecue at his parents' house before Braden saw Ryan again. Of course, he knew his youngest brother was busy getting his family settled into a new house and transferring his job back to his old office, so he was pleased when Ryan showed up at his door after dinner on Wednesday night.

"There's a Prius in your driveway," Ryan noted.

Braden smiled. "Yeah, it's Cassie's car."

"Has she moved in with you then?"

"No," he admitted. "So far I've only managed to persuade her to bring a few things over, but she's sleeping here most nights."

"Does that mean I've come at a bad time?" his brother wondered.

"It depends on what you want."

"A beer?"

"I've got a few of those," he agreed. "Come on in."

Ryan followed him to the kitchen, where Braden took two bottles from the fridge and twisted off the caps, then handed one to his brother.

"Are you settled into the new house?"

"Mostly," Ryan said, following him out onto the back deck. "Of course, it's a lot bigger than the condo we had in Florida, so some of the rooms are still empty."

"Too bad there isn't a furniture store anywhere in this town," Braden said dryly.

Ryan grinned as he settled back in an Adirondack chair, his legs stretched out in front of him. "Yeah, Harper's already been to the showroom three times."

"She doesn't like anything?"

"She likes *everything*."

"Well, maybe we'll set you up with a friends and family discount."

"Speaking of friends and family—"

"Why do I sense that you're now getting to the true purpose of your visit?"

Ryan tipped his bottle to his lips, drank. "Maybe it's none of my business—Harper told me it's none of my business," he admitted.

"It's generally good advice to listen to your wife," Braden told him.

"It probably is, but I can't deny that I'm a little worried you're rushing into marriage with Cassie."

He frowned at that. "Do you have a problem with my fiancée?"

"No," his brother quickly assured him. "She's great. In fact, she just might be perfect for you."

"Then why the concern?" he asked warily.

"Because I know you haven't known her very long. And because I know you were unhappy in the last few years of your marriage to Dana. And because you told me, after her funeral, that you felt guilty about failing in your promise to Saige's birth mom to give her daughter a real family."

"I'm still not seeing your point," he said, although he was beginning to suspect that he did.

"I can't help wondering—are you marrying Cassie because you want her for your wife? Or because you want her to be Saige's mother?"

"Considering that our marriage will put her in both of those roles, why do the reasons matter?" Braden countered. "And why are you in my face about this when you got married to give Oliver a family?"

"Because Oliver's aunt was suing for custody and we needed to ensure that he stayed with us, because that's what his parents wanted."

"And Saige's birth mother wanted her to have two parents—to grow up in a real family. And just as you would do anything for your son, I will do anything for my daughter."

"The difference being that when Harper and I decided to get married, we both knew why we were doing it."

"I want to marry Cassie," Braden assured his brother. "She's an incredible woman—warm and kind and generous. And Saige absolutely adores her."

"But do you love her?" Ryan pressed.

He tipped his bottle to his lips. "I will honor the vows I make to her on our wedding day," he finally said.

His brother shook his head, clearly unsatisfied with that answer. "She's in love with you, Braden. How long do you think it's going to take her to figure out that her feelings aren't reciprocated? And," he continued without giving Braden an opportunity to respond, "what do you think she'll do when she figures it out?"

"Getting married will give us both what we want," Braden insisted.

"I hope you're right," Ryan said. "Because losing another mother will be a lot harder on your daughter than growing up without one."

* * *

Cassie stood by the open window in Saige's bedroom, frozen by the conversation that drifted up from the deck as she lifted Braden's sleepy daughter into her arms. She'd just finished reading a story to the little girl and intended to take her downstairs to say good-night to her daddy when she heard voices from below and realized that he had company.

She hadn't intended to eavesdrop, but she couldn't avoid overhearing their conversation—and couldn't stop listening when she realized that they were talking about her.

I want to marry Cassie. She's an incredible woman—warm and kind and generous. And Saige absolutely adores her.

But do you love her?

Her breath caught as she waited for Braden to reply.

I will honor the vows I make to her on our wedding day.

The response answered not just his brother's question but her own, and with those few words, the joy leaked from her wounded heart like air from a punctured tire.

How long do you think it's going to take her to figure out that her feelings aren't reciprocated?

Well, Ryan's conversation with his brother had taken care of that for her. While she'd managed to disregard her own niggling doubts for the past few weeks, she could do so no longer.

And what do you think she'll do when she figures it out?

Cassie forced herself to move away from the window, but she couldn't force herself to answer that question. She didn't want to answer that question. She didn't want to do anything except go back ten minutes in time and never overhear Braden and Ryan's conversation.

Because she could live with her own doubts and uncertainties. As long as she had Braden and Saige, she could live with almost anything. But the one thing she could not live with was the absolute knowledge that the man she planned to marry—the man she loved with her whole heart—didn't love her back.

Unshed tears burned the back of her eyes as she rocked Saige to sleep for what she knew might be the very last time. She couldn't blame Braden. There had been so many clues as to his motivation—most notably Lindsay's visit and her threat to have the adoption revoked—but Cassie had refused to see them.

I will do anything for my daughter.

She'd always known he wanted a mother for Saige—he'd made no secret of that fact. But she'd let herself hope and believe that he wanted her, too. That when he took her in his arms and made love to her, it was because he did love her.

I will honor the vows I make to her...

An admirable sentiment but not the words she'd wanted to hear. Not what she needed from him.

Saige exhaled a shuddery sigh as her thumb slipped out of her mouth, a signal that the little girl was truly and deeply asleep. Cassie reluctantly pushed herself out of the chair and touched her lips to the top of the baby's head before she gently laid her in the crib and tucked her sock monkey under her arm.

Then she walked across the hall to Braden's room and the bed that she'd shared with him almost every night for the past several weeks. Peering through the window, she saw that his brother's car was still in the driveway. Though it was much earlier than she usually went to bed, she put on her pajamas, picked up a book and crawled between the covers. And when Braden finally came upstairs, she pretended to be asleep.

She heard his footsteps cross the floor, then he gently removed the book from her hand and set it on "her" bedside table before turning off the lamp. He moved away again, and she heard the quiet click of the bathroom door closing. A few minutes later, he crawled into bed with her, his arm automatically snaking around her waist and drawing her close, nestling their bodies together like spoons.

She'd been surprised to discover that he liked to sleep snuggled up to her. He protested, vehemently, when she accused him of being a cuddler, so she stopped teasing him because it didn't matter what he called it—the simple truth was that she slept so much better when she was in his arms. It was something that had become a habit far too easily and one that she would have to break. But not tonight.

It didn't take long for his breathing to settle into the slow, regular rhythm that told her he'd succumbed to slumber. And only then, when she was certain he was sleeping, did she let her tears fall, confident that they would dry by morning, leaving no evidence of her heartbreak on the pillowcase.

Chapter Sixteen

It was harder than she'd thought it would be to go through the motions the next day. She was distracted and unfocused at work, unable to concentrate on the most menial tasks. Though she hated to do it, she called Stacey to cover the Soc & Study group that night so that she could take some time at home and figure out her life and her future.

Truthfully, she knew what she had to do, but that didn't make the doing any easier. She loved Braden and Saige and she wanted nothing more than to be part of their family. She wanted to marry the man she loved, but she couldn't marry a man who didn't love her.

She needed to talk to Braden about the conversation she'd overheard, and she didn't want to fall apart when she did. So she spent the afternoon at home with her cats, trying to prepare herself for the inevitable confrontation. But whenever she thought about saying goodbye, the tears would spill over again. When she reached for a tissue to wipe her nose, Buttercup jumped up onto the sofa and crawled into Cassie's lap—which only made her cry harder. And Westley, who rarely paid attention to anything that wasn't dinner, eventually took pity on her and crawled into her lap beside his sister, too.

She gave them tinned food for dinner, because she figured they deserved a reward for their unsolicited support and comfort. And as she watched them chow down, she decided that maybe being a crazy cat lady wasn't so bad.

When they were finished eating, she knew that she'd stalled as long as she could. She dried her eyes again, got into her car and drove to Forrest Hill.

"I thought you had the Soc & Study group tonight," Braden said when he responded to the doorbell and found her standing on the porch. "And why didn't you use your key?"

"Stacey agreed to fill in for me," she said, ignoring the second part of his comment.

He stepped away from the door. "Are you hungry? Saige and I ate a while ago, but I can heat up some leftover lasagna for you."

She shook her head. "No, thanks."

"Well, I'm glad you're here," he said, his tone as sincere as the smile that tugged at her heart. "I got official notice from the court today that Lindsay withdrew her application to reverse the adoption."

"Oh, Braden, that is wonderful news," she said, genuinely thrilled that he wouldn't have to battle for custody of his daughter.

"And to celebrate, Saige has been working on something for you."

At that revelation, her carefully rehearsed words stuck in her throat. "For me?"

"Uh-huh." He took her hand and led her into the living

room where the little girl was playing at the train table. "Look who's here, Saige."

The toddler looked up, her lips immediately stretching into a wide smile when she saw Cassie. "Ma-ma."

Cassie instinctively squeezed Braden's hand as her throat constricted and her eyes filled with tears. Then she remembered why she was here, and she extricated her fingers from his.

"P'ay?" Saige asked hopefully.

"Not right now, sweetie."

Braden lifted a hand and gently brushed away the single tear that she hadn't realized had escaped to slide down her cheek. "What's wrong, Cassie?"

She could only shake her head, because her throat was too tight for words.

He took her hand again and led her to the sofa. "Tell me what's going on. Please."

She drew in a slow, deep breath and lifted her gaze to his. "I need to ask you something."

"Anything," he said.

"Do you love me?"

He drew back, instinctively and physically, which she recognized as his answer even before he said anything.

"Where is this coming from?" he asked.

"It's a simple question," she told him.

"It's a ridiculous question," he said, obviously still attempting to dance around it. "I asked you to marry me—doesn't that tell you how I feel about you?"

"Maybe it should," she acknowledged. "But I'd still like to hear it."

"I want to spend my life with you," he told her, and he sounded sincere. But even if it was true, it wasn't a declaration of love.

"Because Saige needs a mother? Because I complete your family?"

"Where is this coming from?" Braden asked again, his uneasiness growing as she tossed out questions he wasn't sure he knew how to answer.

"I heard you talking to your brother last night," she admitted. "When you told him that you were marrying me to give Saige the family you'd promised she would have when you adopted her."

And to think that he'd actually been happy when his brother had moved back to town.

"Why is it wrong to want a family for my daughter?" he said, still hoping to sidestep her concerns and smooth everything over.

"It's not," she said. "In fact, many people would say it's admirable. Especially the lengths to which you're willing to go to give it to her."

"You're losing me," he told her. But even more frustrating was the realization that *he* was in danger of losing *her*.

"Maybe I'm almost thirty years old, maybe I won't ever have a better offer, but I want not just to fall in love, but to be loved in return. I want the fairy tale." She slid her engagement ring off and set it on the table. "And I'm not willing to settle for anything less."

The sadness and resignation in her tone slayed him as much as her removal of the ring he'd put on her finger. "Cassie—"

She shook her head. "Don't."

"Don't what?" he asked, torn between bafflement and panic.

"Don't tell me again that you care or that we're really good together. Don't tell me again that Saige adores me. Don't paint rosy pictures of the future we can have together." She looked at him, the tears in her eyes slicing like knives through his heart. "Please don't tempt me to settle for less than I deserve, because I love you so much I might be willing to do it."

She was right. As much as Braden didn't want to admit it, she was right. When he'd asked her to marry him, he'd been selfish. He'd been thinking only of what he wanted—for himself and his daughter. He'd wanted to give Saige the security of the family that he knew they could be if Cassie agreed to be his wife.

And all the while that he'd been courting her, he'd known that he wasn't going to fall in love with her. It was no defense that he'd warned her against falling in love with him—because he'd then done everything in his power to make her forget that warning.

She did deserve more—so much more than he could give her. Because it was the only thing left to say, he finally said, "I'm sorry."

"So am I," she told him. Then, with tears still shining in her eyes, she turned and walked away.

And he let her go.

"Ma-ma?" Saige said as the door closed behind Cassie.

With a sigh, Braden lifted her into his lap and hugged her tight.

Losing another mother will be a lot harder on your daughter than growing up without one.

"I guess your uncle Ryan is smarter than he looks," he said regretfully.

But he knew the emptiness he felt inside wasn't just for Saige. An hour earlier, he'd been looking toward his future with Cassie and his heart had been filled with hope and joy. Now he was looking at the ring she'd taken off her finger and he felt as cold and empty as the platinum circle on the glass table.

* * *

Megan dropped a pile of bridal magazines on Cassie's desk when she came into the library Friday morning. "I've been planning my wedding for years and since I'm not any closer to finding a groom now than when I started, I thought you might want to look through these to get some ideas for your big day."

"Thanks," Cassie said. "But I'm not going to need them."

"Don't you dare tell me you're planning to elope," Megan warned.

"No, we're not planning to elope."

"You're hiring a wedding planner," was her coworker's second guess.

Cassie shook her head. "We're not getting married."

Her friend stared at her, stunned. "What are you talking about?"

"I gave Braden back his ring last night."

"What?" Megan's gaze dropped to her now-bare left hand. *"Why?"*

"Because I want to be someone's first choice."

Her friend frowned. "Is this because he was married before?"

"No. It's because he doesn't love me," she admitted softly, her heart breaking all over again to admit the truth aloud.

"Why would you say that?" Megan demanded.

"Because it's true."

"The man asked you to marry him," her coworker reminded her.

She nodded. "And fool that I was, it took me almost three weeks to realize that every time he talked about our future, he never once said that he loved me. Even when I said it first, he never said it back."

"A lot of men aren't comfortable with the words," Megan noted.

"A man who claims he's ready to commit himself in marriage should be."

Unable to dispute the truth of that, her friend picked up the pile of magazines again. "I'll put these in the staff room…just in case."

Cassie didn't argue, but she knew there wasn't going to be any "just in case." She also knew that the awkward and difficult conversation with Megan was only the first of many she would have over the next few weeks.

The problem with sharing the happy news of her engagement with so many people was that she had to either pretend she was still happily engaged—albeit not wearing a ring—or admit that the shortest engagement in the history of the world was over.

Okay, she knew that was probably an exaggeration. After all there were plenty of celebrity marriages that hadn't even lasted as long as her engagement. Or at least one, she mentally amended, thinking of Britney Spears's famous fifty-five hour nuptials.

Of course, everyone had words of advice ranging from "give him another chance" to "you'll find someone else." Cassie knew they meant well, but no advice could heal a heart that was cracked wide-open.

Almost as bad as the aching emptiness in her chest was the realization that she dreaded going into work Tuesday morning. When she woke up, she wanted to pull the covers over her head and pretend that she was sick so she could stay home with her cats and avoid seeing Braden's mother and daughter. The apprehension was an uncomfortable weight in her belly, but it also helped her stiffen her spine. Because she loved her job and she wasn't going to let a failed relationship take that joy from her.

Still, she had to force a smile for her Baby Talk class. It was all she could do to hold back the tears when Saige released her grandmother's hand and ran to Cassie, wrapping herself around her legs, but she went through the motions. And because all of the caregivers were focused on their children, no one seemed to realize anything was wrong.

But after class had ended and everyone else was gone, Ellen approached her. Cassie braced herself, not sure what to expect from the woman she'd always liked and respected but who didn't understand the concept of boundaries. So she was surprised when Ellen didn't say anything about the failed engagement. In fact, she didn't say anything at all; she just reached for Cassie's hand as she walked past her on the way out, giving it a gentle but somehow reassuring squeeze.

If she was surprised by Braden's mother's discretion and unexpected show of support, she was even more surprised when Irene defended Braden, insisting that his feelings for Cassie were probably deeper than he was willing to acknowledge.

Cassie appreciated the sentiment but she refused to believe it, refused to let herself hope and have her hopes trampled again.

Braden didn't want to talk about the break-up with Cassie, so he didn't. Whenever anyone asked about her, he said she was doing great. If someone wanted to chat about the wedding, he just said they hadn't figured out any details yet. And while he knew the truth would eventually come out, he was feeling too raw to deal with it right now.

Of course, his mother didn't care about that.

"I'm a little confused," she said, when he picked Saige up after work on Tuesday. "On the weekend, we were talking about potential wedding venues, and then, when I took Saige to the library for Baby Talk today, I discovered that Cassie wasn't wearing her engagement ring."

"Maybe it needs to be sized," he suggested.

"Even if that was true, it doesn't explain why your supposed fiancée looked as if her heart was broken."

"I don't know why her heart would be broken," he grumbled, finally giving up the pretense that everything was status quo. "She was the one who decided to give me back the ring."

"And I've known Cassie long enough to know that she wouldn't have done so without a good reason, so what was it?"

He busied himself sorting through a pile of miscellaneous stuff—junk mail, flyers and the book Cassie had lent to him from her personal library—on the kitchen island. "Because I didn't echo the words back when she told me that she loved me," he finally admitted.

Ellen frowned. "And why didn't you?"

"Because I was trying to be honest about my feelings and I didn't want our marriage to be based on a deception."

His mother stared at him for several long seconds before she let out a weary sigh. "Now I see the problem."

"I'm not going to fall in love again."

She shook her head. "The problem is that you actually believe that's true."

"Because it *is* true," he insisted.

"Honey, you wouldn't be this miserable if you didn't love her."

He set the book on top of the pile so that he could return it to her. Except she might think he was using the book as an excuse to see her again—and maybe he would be. "I'm miserable because I let my daughter down. Again."

"If that's your biggest concern, maybe you should give Heather Turcotte a call," Ellen suggested. "She was asking about you at the library again today."

"Geez, Mom, can you give me five minutes to catch

my breath before you start tossing more potential Mrs. Garretts at me?"

"Why do you need time?" his mother challenged. "If you aren't in love with Cassie—if all you want is a mother for Saige—why aren't you eager to move ahead toward that goal?"

He opened his mouth, closed it again. "I really am an idiot, aren't I?"

"As much as it pains me to admit it—in this situation— I have to answer that question with a resounding yes."

He sighed. "What am I supposed to do now?"

"You figured out how to screw it up all by yourself, I have faith that you can figure out how to fix it."

He sincerely hoped she was right.

Braden knew that after refusing to say the words Cassie had wanted to hear, she would doubt their veracity when he said them to her now. But how was a man supposed to prove his feelings? What kind of grand gesture would convince her how much she meant to him?

It took him a while to come up with a plan—and a lot longer to be able to implement it. So it was almost three weeks after she'd given him back his ring before he was ready to face her again—to put his heart and their future on the line.

The moment Cassie saw him waiting on her porch, her steps faltered. He forced himself to stay where he was, to wait for her to draw nearer, but it wasn't easy. The last few weeks without her had been the emptiest weeks of his life, and he wanted nothing more than to take her in his arms and just hold her for a minute. An hour. Forever.

She came up the stairs slowly, pausing beside the front door. "What are you doing here, Braden?"

"I needed to talk to you and you haven't returned any of my calls."

"Maybe I didn't return your calls because I didn't want to talk to you," she suggested.

"I considered that possibility," he acknowledged. "But it's not in my nature to give up that easily."

"Where's Saige?"

"With my parents. I didn't want this to be about anything but you and me."

"I have things to do," she said. "So please say whatever you need to say and then go."

"I love you, Cassie."

She looked away, but not before he saw the shimmer of tears in her eyes. She didn't say anything for a long moment, and then she shook her head. "It's not enough to say it—you have to mean it."

"But I *do* mean it," he told her. "I meant it even when I couldn't bring myself to say it, but I didn't want to admit the truth of my feelings because I'd promised myself that I wouldn't fall in love again.

"I want you in my life, Cassie. I *need* you in my life. I don't even care if you don't want to put the ring back on your finger—not yet. I want to marry you, I want to spend my life with you, and yes—I do want you to be Saige's mother because you're so great with her and I know how much she loves you. But most importantly, I just want to be with you, because my life is empty without you.

"When I finally realized I loved you, I tried to figure out why—what it was about you that made me fall in love with you. And I discovered that it wasn't any *one* thing—it was *every*thing. And every day I'm with you, I discover something new that makes me love you even more than the day before."

"You're doing it again," she whispered softly. "Saying all of the right things."

"But?" he reluctantly prompted, because he could hear the unspoken word in the tone of her voice.

"But you're a businessman. You know how to close a deal. I don't know if you really mean what you're saying or if you're saying it because you know it's what I want to hear."

"You have every reason to be wary," he acknowledged. "I'm asking you to trust in feelings that I wouldn't even acknowledge a few weeks ago."

She nodded.

"So give me a chance to prove my feelings are real," he suggested.

"How?" she asked, obviously still skeptical.

"Come home with me so that I can show you something."

Home.

The word wrapped around her like a favorite sweater—warm and comforting and oh-so-tempting.

Except that the home he was referring to wasn't her home, only where he lived with his daughter.

"The last time I fell for that line was my first year at college," she said, feigning a casualness she didn't feel.

"It's not a line," he assured her.

Cassie sighed, but her resistance had already crumbled. It wasn't just that she couldn't say no to him but that she didn't want to. She didn't want to shut him out—she wanted him to force open the doors of her heart and prove that he loved her.

She didn't know what, if anything, could make her trust that the feelings he claimed to have for her now were real, but she was willing to give him a chance. The past three weeks without him had been so achingly empty, because she loved him so much she wanted to believe a future for them was possible.

"I need to feed the cats," she said.

"I'll wait."

Cassie noticed the changes as soon as she stepped through the front door and into the wide foyer of Braden's house. The previously bland off-white walls had been painted a warm pale gold. The color was still subtle but it drew out the gold vein in the floor tile and provided a sharper contrast for the white trim.

The living room was a pale moss green and the furniture was all new—the off-white leather sofa and armchairs having been replaced by a dark green sectional with a chaise lounge, and the contemporary glass-and-metal occasional tables replaced by mission-style tables in dark walnut. The only piece of furniture that remained from her last visit was Saige's train table.

"End of season sale at Garrett Furniture?" she asked, her tone deliberately light.

"Something like that," he agreed.

"And the paint?"

"My cousin Jordyn. You seemed to like what she did in Saige's room, so I asked her to pick out the colors."

"She has a good eye," she noted.

As they continued the tour, she discovered that every single room—aside from Saige's—had been redone. Not all of them had new furnishings, but each had at least been repainted with decorative accents added.

"Why did you do all of this?"

"It's partly symbolic," he confessed. "To illustrate the warmth and color you brought back into my life. But it's mostly practical, because I hoped that if you actually liked my house you might want to spend more time here, and maybe reconsider moving in. Of course, if there's anything you don't like, we can change it. We can change everything, if you want."

"I do like your house," she told him. "And everything looks fabulous, but—"

"Hold that thought," he said. "There's still one more room to see."

She'd been so amazed by the changes he'd made throughout the house, she hadn't realized that he'd ushered her past the main floor den until he paused there now. He seemed more nervous about this room than any other, which made her even more curious about what was behind the closed doors.

"The painting was simple and, with a full crew of men working round the clock, pretty quick," he told her. "But I wanted some more significant changes made in this room—which is what took so long. Thankfully, Ryder put me in touch with the right people or I'd still be waiting."

Then he opened the doors.

The room, originally a simple main floor office with a desk and a few bookcases, had been transformed to include floor-to-ceiling bookcases, lots of comfortable seating and a fireplace that was almost an exact replica of the one in Cassie's living room.

She had to clear the lump out of her throat before she could speak. "The bookcases are empty," she finally said.

"Not completely," he said, taking her hand and drawing her over to a shelf between two windows where she could see a single book lying on its side: *The Princess Bride: S. Morgenstern's Classic Tale of True Love and High Adventure* by William Goldman.

"Did you read it?" she asked him.

He nodded. "I'm not sure I agree it was better than the movie, but it was a good book," he acknowledged.

"You did this for me—so that I would have a place in your house for my books?"

"*Our* house," he said. "You only have to say the word and it's our house."

"What word is that?"

He pulled his hand out of his pocket and showed her the ring she'd given back to him three weeks earlier. "Yes," he told her. "When I ask again, 'Will you marry me, Cassie?' you just have to say yes."

Then he dropped to one knee and took her hand in his. "Cassie MacKinnon, I love you with my whole heart, and there's nothing I want more in this world than to spend every day of the rest of my life with you by my side. Will you marry me?"

She held his gaze, her own steady and sure, and finally answered his question, not with a yes but with the words that came straight from her heart. "As you wish."

Epilogue

February 14th

Every morning when she woke up in her husband's arms, Cassie took a moment to bask in the sheer joy of her new life.

In the five months that they'd been married, Braden had given her everything she'd ever wanted: a home, a family, love. He never missed a chance to tell her that he loved her, and though her heart still swelled each time she heard the words, he showed her the truth of those words in even more ways. Every day with Saige brought new joys and experiences, too. After waiting for so long to be a mother, Cassie was loving every minute of it.

On Valentine's Day, Cassie made a pork roast with sweet potatoes and parsnips, which Saige hated, followed by ice-cream sundaes, which Saige loved. After dinner, Braden presented Cassie with two gifts. A diamond-encrusted heart-shaped pendant and a homemade Valentine. The former was stunning, but the latter took her breath away: Braden's handprints—in red paint—were upside down and overlapped at the thumbs to form a big heart inside which Saige's handprints—in pink paint—formed a smaller heart. On the outside, making a border around the edge, he had written:

> *For Cassie—on our first Valentine's Day together with tons of love and thanks for being such a fabulous wife and mother and making our family complete. We love you more than you will ever know. Braden & Saige xoxoxoxoxo*

Cassie's eyes filled as she read the printed words, but she didn't know the tears had spilled over until Saige asked, "Why you cwyin', Mama?"

She wiped at the wet streaks on her cheeks. "Because I love both of you more than you will ever know, too," she said.

Of course, Saige continued to look perplexed. Braden dropped a kiss on the little girl's forehead and told her to go play with her trains. She skipped out of the room, happy to comply with the request.

"Cassie?" he prompted when their daughter had gone.

"Sometimes I can't believe how much my life has changed since I met you."

"But in a good way, right?"

She managed to smile. "In the very best way," she assured him.

He plucked a tissue from the box and gently dabbed at the streaks of moisture on her cheeks. "So these are... happy tears?"

She nodded.

"Okay," he said, obviously relieved.

"But I should warn you," Cassie said, lifting her eyes to his, "I think I'm going to be one of those women who is really emotional in the first trimester."

Braden stared at her for a minute, his hand dropping away from her face as the confusion in his gaze slowly gave way to comprehension and joy. "Are you saying…?"

They'd decided to stop using birth control as soon as they were married, because they didn't know how long it might take for Cassie to get pregnant and they were hoping that Saige would have a little brother or sister sooner rather than later—which was apparently going to happen even sooner than either of them had anticipated.

But she could understand why he'd be hesitant to ask the question. Although she didn't know all the details of everything he and Dana had gone through in their efforts to conceive a child, she knew how disappointed he'd been by their lack of success—and that he would, naturally, be reluctant to hope that it would happen now.

"Yes." She took his hand and laid it on her abdomen. "I'm pregnant."

He whooped and lifted her off the chair and into his arms, spinning her around in circles. Then he stopped abruptly and set her carefully back on her feet and framed her face with his hands. "Are you all right? Have you been to see a doctor? How are you feeling?"

She laughed, a little breathlessly, before she answered each of his questions in turn. "Yes. Not yet. Happy and excited and so incredibly lucky."

The grin that spread across his face assured her that he was feeling happy, too. Even if he still looked a little dazed.

"Wow. That was…fast," he decided.

"Too fast?" she wondered.

He immediately shook his head. "No, it's not too fast," he promised. "And this news is the second best Valentine's Day present ever."

She lifted her brows. "*Second* best?"

"Second best," he confirmed. Then he lowered his head to kiss her. Softly. Deeply. "Second only to you."

* * * * *

SECRET BABY, SURPRISE PARENTS

LIZ FIELDING

With many thanks to Carol O'Reilly for her insight into the legal aspects of surrogacy in the UK.

CHAPTER ONE

GRACE MCALLISTER restlessly paced the entrance to Accident and Emergency, punching yet another number into her cellphone in a desperate attempt to contact Josh Kingsley.

It would be Sunday evening in Australia and she'd tried his home number first. A woman had picked up.

'Anna Carling.'

'Oh…' The sound of her voice, the knowledge that she was in Josh's apartment answering his phone, for a moment drove everything else from her mind. Then, gathering herself, she said, 'Can I speak to Josh, please?'

'Who's calling?'

'Grace… Grace McAllister. I'm his…his…'

'It's okay, Grace, I know who you are. His brother's wife's sister, right?'

The woman was in his apartment and knew all the details of his personal life….

Grace gripped the phone tighter until it was hurting her fingers. 'Could I speak to him, please?'

'I'm sorry, Josh is away at the moment. I'm his personal assistant. Is there anything I can do to help?'

'Do you know where he is?'

'He's moving about a lot. Hong Kong. Beijing. Can I pass on a message?' she prompted when Grace didn't reply.

'No. Thank you.' This wasn't news she could ask a member of his staff—no matter how personal—to deliver second-hand. 'I need to speak to him myself. It's urgent.'

Anna didn't waste time asking questions, playing the dragon at the door, but gave her a string of contact numbers. His cellphone. The number of his hotel in Hong Kong in case there was no signal. The private number of the manager of the Hong Kong office, since it was evening there. Even the number of Josh's favourite restaurant.

There was no signal. She left a message asking him to call her, urgently, then called the hotel. He wasn't there and the manager of the Hong Kong office informed her that Josh had flown to mainland China. Apparently Anna had already called the office and primed the manager to expect her call and again, when she wouldn't leave a message, he helpfully gave her the number of Josh's hotel there, and his partner in Beijing.

Beijing? He had a partner in Beijing? That was new since the last time he'd been home. Or maybe not. He hadn't stayed for more than a few hours and no one had been talking about business…

Calling the number she'd been given, she was told that Josh was out of the city for a few days and that the only way to contact him was through his cellphone.

She felt as if she were going around in circles, but at least it helped take her mind off what was happening at the hospital, even if she was dreading the moment she found him.

This time it rang. Once, twice, three times and then she heard him. His voice, so familiar, so strange as he briefly instructed the caller to leave a message.

'Miss McAllister…'

She spun round as a nurse called her name. Then wished she'd taken her time.

She'd been trying so hard not to think about what was happening to Michael. She'd only caught a glimpse of him lying unconscious on the stretcher while the emergency team worked on him before they'd rushed him away to the operating theatre and she'd been told to wait.

One look told her everything she needed to know. Her warm, loving brother-in-law had not survived the accident that had already killed her sister.

'Josh…' She forced his name out through a throat aching with unshed tears. There would be time for tears, but not yet. Not now. 'Josh… You have to come home.'

A day, even an hour ago, the very thought of seeing him would have been enough to send her into the same dizzy spin that had afflicted her as a teenager.

Numbed with the horror of what had happened, she was beyond feeling anything but rage at the unfairness of it.

Rage at the cruelty of fate. With Josh for being so blind. For refusing to understand. For being so angry with them all.

She didn't know what he'd said to Michael.

Remembered little of what he'd said to her, beyond begging her to think again.

All she could remember was his bloodless face when she'd told him that it was too late for second thoughts. That she was already pregnant with her sister's child. She would never forget the way he'd lifted a hand in a helpless gesture, let it fall, before taking a step back and opening the front door, climbing into the car waiting to take him back to the airport.

The nurse, no doubt used to dealing with shocked relatives, put her arm around her. Said something about a cup of tea. Asked if there was someone she could telephone so that she would not be alone.

'I've called Josh,' Grace said, stupidly, as if the woman would understand what that meant. 'He'll come now.' He had to come.

Then, realising she still had the phone clutched tightly to her ear as if she might somehow catch his voice in the ghostly static, she snapped it shut, pushed it into her pocket and allowed herself to be led back inside the hospital.

Josh Kingsley looked up at the majestic sight of Everest, pink in a freezing sunset.

He'd come here looking for something, hoping to recapture a time when he and his brother had planned this trip to Base Camp together. Older, a little wiser, he could see that it had been his big brother's attempt to distract him from his misery at their parents' divorce.

It had never happened. Now he was here alone but for the Sherpa porters, drawn to make this pilgrimage, take a few precious days out of a life so crowded by the demands of business that he was never entirely on his own. To find a way to come to terms with what had happened.

Now, overcome with the sudden need to talk to him, share this perfect moment, make his peace with the only member of his immediate family he cared about, he peeled off his gloves and took out the BlackBerry that he'd switched off three days ago.

Ignoring the continuous beep that signalled he had messages—work could wait, this wouldn't—he scrolled hurriedly through his numbers. Too hurriedly. The slender black miracle of computer technology slipped through fingers rapidly numbing in the thin atmosphere. And, as if he, too, were frozen, he watched it bounce once, then fly out across a vast chasm, not moving until he heard the faint sound of it shattering a thousand feet below.

When he finally looked up, the snow had turned from pink to grey and, as the cold bit deeper, he shivered.

Josh would come, but not yet, not for twenty-four hours at the earliest. Now, numb with shock, incapable of driving, she let the nurse call Toby Makepeace. He was there within minutes, helped her deal with the paperwork before driving her home to Michael and Phoebe's home and their three-month-old baby.

'I hate to leave you,' he said. 'You shouldn't be alone.'

'Elspeth's here,' she said, struggling with the simplest words. 'She stayed with Posie.' Then, knowing more was required, she forced herself to concentrate. 'Thank you, Toby. You've been a real friend.'

'I'm here. If you need anything. Help with arrangements…'

She swallowed, not wanting to think about what lay ahead. 'Josh will be here.' Tomorrow or the next day. 'He'll see to everything.'

'Of course.' He left his hand briefly on her arm, then turned and began to walk away.

Elspeth, a close friend of Michael and Phoebe, had answered Grace's desperate call and stayed with Posie. Now she said nothing, just hugged her and made her a cup of tea and then shut herself in Michael's study, taking on the task of calling everyone to let them know what had happened. She even rang Michael's parents—his mother in Japan, his father in France.

Grace had never met either of them—Michael and Josh had only minimum contact with either parent since their divorce—but Elspeth had at least known them, could break the news without having first to explain who she was. Then she stayed to answer the phone, field the calls that came flooding in.

Calls from everyone but the one person she was waiting to hear from.

Friends arrived with food, stayed to give practical help, making up beds in the spare rooms in the main part of the house while Grace did the same in Josh's basement flat. Even when her world was spinning out of control, she couldn't bear to let anyone else do that.

Then she set about putting her own life on hold, leaving a

message on the answering machine in the self-contained flat she occupied on the top floor, before taking her laptop downstairs.

Sitting in the armchair that had been a permanent fixture beside the Aga for as long as she could remember, Posie within reach in her crib, she scrolled through her schedule of classes, calling everyone who had booked a place, writing the cheques and envelopes to return their fees as she went. Anything to stop herself from thinking.

After that she was free to concentrate on Posie. Bathing her, feeding her, changing her, shutting out everything else but the sound of the telephone.

She'd insisted that she tell Josh herself.

'It's night in China,' Elspeth said, after the umpteenth time the phone rang and it wasn't him. 'He's probably asleep with the phone switched off.'

'No. My call didn't go straight to the message service. It rang…'

'Asleep and didn't hear it, then.'

'Maybe I should have told someone in his office—'

'No. They've given you all the numbers they have and if you can't get hold of him, neither can they.'

'But—'

'You're the only person he'll want to hear this from, Grace.'

'Maybe.' Was she making too much of that? What did it matter who gave him the news?

'No question. You're the closest thing he has to family.'

'He has parents.'

Elspeth didn't bother to answer, just said, 'Come and have something to eat. Jane brought a quiche…'

She shook her head. 'I can't face anything.'

'You don't have the luxury of missing meals,' Elspeth said firmly. 'You have to keep strong for Posie.'

'What about you?' Grace asked. Elspeth had lost her best

friend. She was suffering, too. 'You've been on the go all day and I haven't seen you eat a thing.'

'I'm fine.'

'No, you're not.' She lay Posie in the crib. 'Sit down. Put your feet up while I boil us both an egg.'

'Do I get toast soldiers?' Elspeth asked, managing a smile.

'Of course. It's my turn to look after you, Elspeth.'

'Only if you promise to take one of those pills the doctor left for you. You haven't slept…'

'I can't,' she said. 'Not until I've spoken to Josh.'

'But then?'

'I promise,' she said. And, because it was the only way to get Elspeth to eat, she forced down an egg, too, even managed a yoghurt.

She had a bath and might have dropped off in the warm water, but Posie was fretful. It was almost as if she sensed that something was out of kilter in her world and Grace put on Phoebe's dressing gown so that she would have the comfort of her mother's scent as she held her against her shoulder, crooning softly to her, walking the long night away—waiting, waiting, waiting for the phone to ring.

Finally, when she knew it was day on the other side of the world, she called again. Again, it was the answering service that picked up. 'Where are you?' she cried out in desperation. 'Call me!' All she got back was a hollow emptiness. 'Michael's dead, Josh,' she said hopelessly. 'Phoebe's dead. Posie needs you.'

She covered her mouth, holding back her own appeal. Refusing to say that she needed him, too.

She'd always needed him, but Josh did not need her and, even *in extremis*, a woman had her pride.

'Did Grace McAllister manage to get hold of you, Josh?'

He'd flown direct to Sydney from Nepal, stopping at his

office to pick up urgent messages before going home to catch up on sleep.

'Grace?' He frowned, looking up from the list of messages his PA handed him. 'Grace rang me?'

'Last week. Sunday. I gave her the Hong Kong numbers but I knew you'd be on the move so I gave her your cellphone number, too,' she said. 'She said it was urgent. I hope I did the right thing.'

'Yes, yes,' he said, reassuring her.

Last week? On Sunday he'd been in the mountains, thinking about his brother. Thinking about Grace. There had been a message alert on his phone, but he'd ignored it....

'I dropped the damn thing off a mountain. Can you get me a replacement?' Then, 'Did Grace say why she was calling?'

'Only that it was urgent. It's the middle of the night there now,' she reminded him as he picked up the phone, hit the fast dial for her number.

'It doesn't matter. She wouldn't have called unless it was…' He stopped as the call went immediately to the answering machine.

"This is Grace McAllister. I'm sorry that I can't take your call at the moment. Due to a family bereavement, all classes have been cancelled until further notice. Please check the Web site for further details."

Bereavement?

He felt the blood drain from his face, put out a hand to grasp the desk. Posie…

It had to be Posie. Small babies were so vulnerable. Meningitis, cot death… After so many years of waiting, so much heartache.

'Cancel everything, Anna. Get me on the next available flight to London,' he said, dialling his brother's number.

Someone whose voice sounded familiar, but wasn't Michael, wasn't Phoebe, wasn't Grace, answered the phone.

'It's Josh Kingsley,' he said.

There was a momentary hiatus and then she was there—Grace, her familiar voice saying his name.

'Josh...'

It was all it took to stir up feelings that he'd done his level best to suppress. But this last year he hadn't been able to get her out of his head....

'Josh, I've been trying to get hold of you....'

'I know. I rang your number. Heard your message,' he said, ignoring her question. 'What's happened? Who died?'

He heard her take a long shuddering breath.

'Grace!'

'There was an accident. Michael, Phoebe... They were both killed.'

For a moment he was too stunned to speak. His brother was dead. 'When? How?'

'Last Sunday morning. I've been calling, leaving messages. When you didn't get back to me I thought... I thought...'

'No!' The word was wrenched from him. He knew what she'd thought and why, but it didn't hurt any less to know that she could believe him so heartless.

But then she already believed that.

She had been so happy that she was having a baby for her sister, couldn't understand why he'd been so desperate to stop her. And he hadn't been able to tell her.

'What happened?' he asked.

'The police said that the car skidded on a slick of mud. It went through a fence and then it rolled. It happened early in the morning and no one found them...'

'The baby, Grace,' he pressed urgently. 'Posie...'

'What? No! She wasn't with them. She was here with me. Michael and Phoebe were away for the weekend. It was their wedding anniversary but they left the hotel early. They couldn't wait to get back....'

Long before she'd stumbled to a halt, he'd clamped his hand over his mouth to hold in the cry of pain.

'Josh?'

'It's okay. I'm okay,' he managed. 'How are you coping?'

'One breath at a time,' she said. 'One minute. One hour…'

He wanted to tell her how sorry he was, but in a situation like this words were meaningless. And in any case she would know exactly how he was feeling. They were faced with the same loss. Or very nearly the same.

Grace wouldn't have to live with his guilt….

Instead, he kept to the practical. He should have been there to deal with this, make the necessary arrangements, but it had been over a week already.

'Who's with you? What arrangements have been made? When is the…' He couldn't bring himself to say the word.

'We buried them on Friday, Josh. Your father insisted on going ahead and, when you didn't call back, no one could reach you…' He heard her swallow, fight down tears, then she furiously said, 'Where were you?'

'Grace…'

He looked up as his PA returned. 'There's a car waiting to take you to the airport. You have to leave now,' she said, handing him a replacement BlackBerry.

'Grace, I'm leaving now for the airport.' Then, 'Keep breathing until I get there.'

Grace let Elspeth take the phone from her as she leaned weakly against the wall.

'Maybe you could get some sleep now,' she said gently, handing her the pills the doctor had left when he'd called after hearing the news. 'You've left plenty of milk in the fridge for Posie. I'll manage if you want to take a rest.'

'I know.' She put the pills in her pocket, knowing she wouldn't take them. She didn't want to go to sleep because when she woke she knew there would be a moment when she'd think it was just another day.

Then she'd remember and have to live through the loss all over again.

But she didn't say any of that. Instead, she hugged her and said, 'Thank you.'

'We're here, Mr Kingsley.'

Josh glanced up at the façade of the tall Georgian town house that Michael had bought when he had married Phoebe McAllister. It was a proper family home with a basement and an attic and three floors in between. Endless rooms that they'd planned to fill with children.

Instead, they'd got him and Grace. A seventeen-year-old youth whose parents had split up and who, wrapped up in their own concerns with new partners, didn't want a moody cuckoo in the nest. And a fourteen-year-old girl for whom the only alternative was to be taken into the care of the local authority.

Exactly what every newly-wed couple needed.

They'd taken on each other's damaged siblings without a murmur. Had given him his own space in the basement, had decorated a room especially for Grace. Her first ever room of her own.

She'd been such a pathetic little scrap. A skinny rake of a kid, all straight lines when other girls her age had been testing out the power of their emerging attraction on impressionable youths. Only her eyes, a sparkling green and gold mix that could flash or melt with her mood, warned that she had hidden depths.

Like her nose and mouth, they'd been too big for her face. And, until she'd learned to control them, they'd betrayed her every thought.

Eyes like that should carry a health warning.

'Is there anything I can do, Mr Kingsley?'

Josh realised that the chauffeur—a regular who his PA had arranged to pick him up from the airport—was regarding him with concern.

He managed a smile. 'You can tell me what day it is, Jack. And whether it's seven o'clock in the morning or seven o'clock at night.'

'It was Tuesday when I got up this morning. And it's the evening. But I'm sure you knew that.'

'Just testing,' he said, managing a smile.

He'd counted every one of the last twenty-four hours as he'd travelled halfway round the world, coming to terms with the loss of his brother. And of Phoebe, who'd been the nearest thing to a big sister he'd ever had. By turns motherly, bossy, supportive. Everything that he'd needed.

Knowing that he would have to live with a world of regrets for the hard words he'd said. Words that could never be taken back. For holding on to his righteous anger, a cover for something darker that he could never admit to…,

But the hair shirt would have to wait. Grace needed him. The baby would need them both.

He climbed from the car. Grace's brightly painted 'Baubles and Beads' van was parked in its usual place but the space where he expected to see his brother's car was occupied by a small red hatchback that underlined, in the most shocking way, the reality of the situation.

Realising that Jack was waiting until he was inside, he pulled himself together, walked up the steps to the front door as he had done times without number to a house that had always felt as if it were opening its arms to him. Today, though, even in the spring sunshine, with tubs of bright yellow tulips on either side of the front door, it seemed subdued, in mourning.

The last time he'd been here he'd tossed the keys to both the house and his basement flat on his brother's desk—his declaration that he would never return. For the first time since he'd moved in here as a seventeen-year-old, he would have to knock at the door but, as he lifted his hand to the antique knocker, it was flung open.

For a moment he thought it was Grace, watching out for him, racing to fling her arms around him, but it wasn't her. Why would it be? She had Toby Makepeace to fling her arms around, to offer her comfort. At least she had the last time he'd come home on a visit. He hadn't been in evidence on the day he'd turned up without warning, but then discovering his girl-friend was pregnant with someone else's baby must have put a crimp in his ardour.

The woman who opened the door was older, familiar—a friend of Phoebe's. Elizabeth? Eleanor? She put her finger to her lips. 'Grace is in the kitchen but she's just dropped off. Try not to wake her. She hasn't been sleeping and she's exhausted.'

He nodded.

'You must be, too,' she said, putting her hand on his arm. 'It's a terrible homecoming for you. I'm so sorry about Michael. He was a lovely man.' She didn't wait for him to answer, just said, 'I'll go now you're here, but tell Grace to ring me if she needs anything. I'll call in tomorrow.'

'Yes. Thank you…' Elspeth. 'Thank you, Elspeth.'

He watched her until she was in her car, then picked up the bags that Jack had left on the top step, placed them inside and shut the door as quietly as he could. Each movement slow, deliberate, as if he could somehow steady the sudden wild beating of a heart that was loud enough to wake Grace all by itself.

He told himself that he should wait.

Go down to the basement flat, take a shower. But to do that, he'd need the key and the key cupboard was in the kitchen.

For the first time for as long as he could remember, he was frozen in indecision, unable to move. Staring down at the hall table where a pile of post—cards, some addressed to Grace, some to him—waited to be opened. Read.

He frowned. Cards?

He opened one, saw the lilies. *In sympathy...*

He dropped it as if burned, stepped back, dragged his hands over his face, through his hair as he looked down the hall. Then, because there was nothing else to do, he turned and walked slowly towards the kitchen.

He pushed the door very gently. It still squeaked. How many times had he heard Michael promise Phoebe that he'd do something about it?

He'd offered to do it himself, but Phoebe had just smiled. She liked the warning squeak, she'd told him. Liked to have something to complain about once in a while. It wasn't good for a man to believe he was perfect.

He could have told her that Michael didn't believe that. On the contrary. But that had been a secret between the two of them and, somehow, he'd managed to smile back.

He paused, holding his breath, but there was no sound and he stepped into the room that had always been the hub of the house. Warm, roomy, with a big table for everyone to gather around. An old armchair by the Aga that the fourteen-year-old Grace had taken to like a security blanket, homing in on it when she'd arrived clutching a plastic bag that contained everything she possessed under one arm, a small scruffy terrier under the other.

The pair of them had practically lived in it. And it was the first place she'd taken the puppy he'd given her when old Harry had died a few months later and he'd been afraid her heart was going to break.

The puppy, too, had finally died of old age, but now she had a new love. Posie. The baby she had borne with the purest heart as surrogate for the sister who had given her a home and who was now lying, boneless in sleep, against her shoulder.

Michael, hoping that if Josh saw the baby he would finally understand, forgive him even, had e-mailed him endless photographs of Posie, giving him a running commentary on her progress since the day she'd been born, refusing to be deterred by Josh's lack of response.

There had been no photographs of Grace until the christening and then only in a group consisting of Grace, as godmother, holding Posie, flanked by Michael and Phoebe. A happy picture in which everyone had been smiling and sent, he suspected, with just a touch of defiance. A 'see what you're missing' message.

He hadn't cared about that. He'd only cared about Grace and he'd cropped the picture so that it was only of Grace and Posie. He'd had it enlarged and printed so that he could carry it with him.

Her face had been outwardly serene, but a photograph was just a two-dimensional image. It was without warmth, scent. You could touch it, but it gave nothing back. But then it had been a very long time since Grace had given anything back to him. Keeping her distance, her eyes always guarded on his visits home.

At least he'd had time to get over his shock that, some time in the last year, she'd cut her beautiful long hair into a short elfin style. He'd come to terms with the fact that her boyish figure had finally filled out in lush womanly curves.

But this scene was not a photograph.

This was an intimate view of motherhood as only a husband, a father would see it and he stood perfectly still, scarcely daring to breathe, wanting to hold the moment, freeze this timeless image in his memory. Then, almost in slow motion, he saw the empty feeding bottle that had dropped into her lap begin a slow slide to the floor.

He moved swiftly to catch it before it hit the tiles and woke her, but when he looked up he realised that his attempt to keep her from being disturbed had failed.

Or maybe not. Her eyes were open and she was looking at him, but she wasn't truly awake. She wasn't seeing him. He froze, holding his breath, willing her to close them again and drift back off to sleep.

She stirred. 'Michael?' she said.

Not quite seeing him, not yet remembering. Still he hoped…

She blinked, focused, frowned.

He saw the exact moment when it all came flooding back, and instinctively reached out to her as he had a year ago. As if he could somehow stop time, go back, save her from a world of pain. 'Grace…'

'Oh, Josh…'

In that unguarded moment, in those two little words, it was all there. All the loss, all the heartache and, sinking to his knees, this time he did not step back, but followed through, gathering her into his arms, holding her close.

For ten years he'd lived with a memory of her in his arms, the heavy silk of her hair trailing across his skin, her sweet mouth a torment of innocence and knowing eagerness as she'd taken him to a place that until then he hadn't known he had wanted to go.

He'd lived with the memory of tearing himself away from her, fully aware that he'd done the unforgivable, then compounded his sin by leaving her asleep in his bed to wake alone.

He'd told himself that he'd had no choice.

Grace had needed security, a settled home, a man who would put her first while, for as long as he could remember, he'd had his eyes set on far horizons, on travelling light and fast. He'd needed total freedom to take risks as he built an empire of his own.

But nothing he had done, nothing he had achieved, not even a hastily conceived and swiftly regretted marriage, had ever dulled the memory of that one night they'd spent together and still, in his dreams, his younger self reached out for her.

It had been unbearably worse during the last twelve months. Sleep had been elusive and when he did manage an hour he woke with an almost desperate yearning for something precious, something that was lost for ever.

This. This woman clinging to him, this child…

He brushed his lips against her temple and then, his head full of the warm, milky scent of baby, he kissed Posie and for one perfect moment all the pain, all the agony of the last twenty-four hours fell away.

Grace floated towards consciousness in slow, confused stages. She had no idea where she was, or why there was a weight against her shoulder, pinning her down. Why Michael was there, watching her. Knowing on some untapped level of consciousness that it couldn't be him.

Then, as she slowly, unwillingly surfaced, he said her name. Just that.

'Grace…'

Exactly as he had once, years and years ago, before gathering her up in his arms. And she knew that it wasn't Michael, it was Josh. Josh who had his arms around her, was holding her as if he'd never let her go. A rerun of every dream she'd had since he'd walked out of her life, gone away ten years ago without a word, leaving a vast, gaping hole in her world. And she clung to him, needing the comfort of his physical closeness. Just needing him.

She felt the touch of his lips against her hair as he kissed her. The warmth of his mouth, his breath against her temple. And then she was looking up at him and he was kissing her as he had done every night of her life in dreams that gave her no peace.

There was the same shocked surprise that had them drawing back to stare at one another ten years ago, as if suddenly everything made sense, before they had come together with a sudden desperate urgency, his mouth branding her as his own, the heat of their passion fusing them forever as one. A heat that had been followed by ten years of ice….

Now, as then, it was the only thing in the world that she wanted.

It was so long since he'd held her.

Not since he'd left her sleeping. Gone away without a word. No, 'wait for me'. Nothing to give her hope that he'd return for her. Not even a simple goodbye.

He had come back, of course, full of what he'd seen, done, his plans. Always cutting his visits short, impatient to be somewhere else, with someone else.

But she'd never let her guard down again, had never let him see how much he'd hurt her, never let him get that close again. She'd avoided the hugs and kisses so freely bestowed on the prodigal on his increasingly rare visits home, keeping away until all the excitement was over. Making sure she had a date for the celebratory family dinner that had always been a feature of his homecoming—because there had always been some new achievement to celebrate. His own company. His first international contract. His marriage…

Yet now, weakly, she clung to him, drinking in the tender touch of his lips, the never-to-be-forgotten scent of his skin.

Needing him as he'd never needed her. Knowing that even now, in his grief, he would be self-contained, in control, his head somewhere else.

He was holding her now, not because he needed comfort, but because he knew that she did. Just as she had all those years ago.

He'd hold her, kiss her, lie with her even if that was what she wanted. It was how men gave closeness, comfort to women.

That was all it had ever been, even then. When, after years

of keeping her feelings to herself, doing a pretty good job of being the teasing friend who criticised his choice in clothes, girls, music, she'd finally broken down the night before he'd gone away—not to university this time, or on some backpacking gap year adventure with his friends—but to the other side of the world to start a new life.

Distraught, unable to express her loss in mere words, she'd thrown herself at him and maybe, facing the risk of the unknown, he'd been feeling a little uncertain, too.

She didn't blame him for taking what she'd so freely offered, so freely given. It was what she had wanted, after all. Had always wanted. Her mistake had been in believing that once he understood that, he'd stay.

He couldn't do it then and he wouldn't now.

He'd comfort her. He'd deal with the legal stuff and then, once everything had been settled, made tidy, the tears dried away, he'd fly off to Sydney or Hong Kong, China or South America. Wherever the life he'd made for himself out there in the big wide world took him. He'd go without a backward glance.

Leave her without a backward glance.

At eighteen she'd been so sure she could change him, that once she'd shown him how much she loved him he would never leave her.

At twenty-eight she knew better and, gathering herself, she pulled back, straightened legs that, curled up beneath her, had gone to sleep so that Josh was forced to move, sit back on his heels.

But, try as she might, she couldn't look away.

It was as if she were seeing him for the first time in years. Maybe she was. Or maybe she was looking at him for the first time in years instead of just glancing at him as if he was someone to be remembered only when he passed through on his way to somewhere else, forgotten again the minute he was out of sight.

She'd perfected that glance over the years.

Now she was really looking at him.

He seemed to have grown, she thought. Not physically. He'd always been a larger-than-life figure. Clever, with a touch of recklessness that lent an edge to everything he did, he'd not only dominated the school sports field but stood head and shoulders above the crowd academically, too.

He'd had those broad shoulders even then, but he'd grown harder over the years and these days he carried himself with the confidence of a man who'd taken on the world and won. And the close-clipped beard that darkened his cheeks—new since his last brief, terrible visit—added an edge of strangeness to a face that had once been as familiar to her as her own.

But this Josh Kingsley *was* a stranger.

She'd known him—or thought she had—and for one shining moment he had been entirely hers. But dawn had come and she'd woken alone, her illusions shattered beyond repair.

Older, wiser, she understood why he'd gone. That it had been the only thing he could do because if he'd stayed ten years ago, he would, sooner or later, have blamed her for his lost dreams. It was so easy for love to turn to hate. And nothing had changed.

He was home now, but once everything was settled, tidied away, he'd go away again because Maybridge was—always had been—too small for Josh Kingsley.

CHAPTER TWO

'GRACE,' he said, repeating her name. Calling her back from her thoughts, her memories. That was all. Just her name. Well, what else could he say? That he was sorry about his last visit? Sorry he'd got it all so wrong?

It was far too late for that and, without warning, she found herself wanting to slap him, yell at him for being such a fool. For staying away when coming home would have made his brother so happy. When it would have meant something.

'Where were you?' she demanded.

Josh shook his head. 'In the mountains. Everest. I was so close that I took a few days to go to a place with no work, no phone…'

He looked so desolate that she wanted to reach out and gather him close. Comfort him. Instead, she turned to the baby at her shoulder, kissed her precious head.

How two brothers could be so different—one gentle, caring, the other so completely cut off from emotional involvement—was a total mystery to her and falling in love with him had been the biggest mistake of her life. But, too young to know better, how could she have done anything else?

He had been her white knight.

Fourteen years old, in a strange town, faced with yet another school—when school had only ever been a place of torment—it could have been, would have been a nightmare if Josh hadn't ridden to her rescue that first terrifying day.

He'd seen her fear and, by the simple action of tossing her a spare crash helmet and taking her into school on the back of his motorbike, he'd turned her life around. He'd made everything all right by giving her instant street cred, an immediate 'in' with the cool girls in her class, who'd all wanted to know Josh Kingsley. And with the cool guys, who'd wanted to be him. At this school there had been no shortage of girls who'd wanted to be her friend.

Not that she'd been stupid enough to believe that she was the attraction.

She'd known it was Josh they all wanted to be near, but that had never bothered her. Why would it when she'd understood exactly how they felt? Not that she had worn her heart on her sleeve. A ride was one thing, but a sixth-form god like Josh Kingsley was never going to stoop to taking a fourth-year girl to a school dance.

She's almost felt sorry for the girls he did date. Each one had thought that her dreams had come true, but she'd known better. He'd shared his dreams with her and she'd always known that he couldn't wait to escape the small-town confines of Maybridge. Discover the life waiting for him beyond the horizon.

Not that it had stopped her from having the same foolish fantasies. Or, ultimately, making the same mistake.

Maybe he read all that in her face—she was too tired to keep her feelings under wraps—because he stood up, took a step back, placed the baby feeder he was holding on the table beside her.

'It was about to fall,' he said. 'I didn't want it to wake you. Elspeth warned me not to disturb you when she let me in.'

Too late for that. Years too late.

'Has she gone?'

He nodded. 'She said to tell you that she'll call in the morning.'

'She's been wonderful. She's stayed here, manned the phones, organised food for after the funeral. But she's grieving, too. She needs to rest.' Not that Josh looked particularly great. He might have had the luxury of a first-class sleeping berth to take the edge off the long flight to London, but there was a greyness about his skin and his eyes were like stones. 'How are you?'

'I'll think about that later.'

'When you're back in Sydney?' she asked, reminding herself that this, like all his visits, was only a break from his real life.

'I'm not going anywhere,' he said. 'Not until everything is settled.'

'Everything?'

'I'm Michael's executor. I have to arrange for probate, settle his estate.'

'A week should do it,' she retaliated, and immediately regretted it. He had to be hurting, whether he was showing it or not. 'I'm sorry.'

'Don't! Don't apologise to me.' He looked up, took another deep breath. 'You and Phoebe were so close. She was like a mother to you.'

'A lot better than the real thing.'

'Yes.' He looked at her, and for a moment she thought he was going to say something she'd find hard to forgive. In the end he just said, 'Have you managed to contact your mother? Let her know what happened?'

She shook her head.

Her mother turned up occasionally, stayed for a week or two before drifting off again, a constant wanderer. Phoebe had bought her a mobile phone, but she had refused to take it and there was never anything as substantial as an address.

'There was a card from somewhere in India a couple of months ago. Whether she's still there…' She shook her head. 'Elspeth rang the consulate and she left messages with everyone who might be in contact with her, but she's even harder to get hold of than you.'

'I'm sorry, Grace. I flew back to Sydney from Nepal so I missed any messages you left at the office.'

'Nepal?' Then she remembered. 'Everest. What on earth were you doing there?'

'Making a pilgrimage.'

And if she felt lost, he looked it.

'I was going to call Michael, tell him I was looking at the sun setting on the mountain, but my hands were so cold that I dropped the phone.' He pushed his hands deep into his pockets as if, even now, he needed to warm them. 'We once planned to take that trip together.'

'Did you? I never knew that.'

He shrugged. 'It was when our parents first split. Before he met Phoebe.'

She frowned. 'She wouldn't have stopped him going.'

'Maybe he couldn't bring himself to leave her, even for a month. She was everything he ever wanted.'

While he'd had nothing, Grace thought. At least her mother did, occasionally, put in an appearance. It was disruptive, unsettling, but it was better than the nothingness that Josh had been left with when his parents had chosen to follow their own desires.

'Michael would have been happy to know that you finally made your dream trip,' she told him.

'Yes, he would. He wanted everyone to be happy. While I suspect all I wanted to do was make him feel bad…'

'No…' Her hand was on his arm before she could even think about it, but he stared at the floor as if unable to meet her gaze. 'Why would he feel bad? You were there. You were thinking of him.' Then, 'Did it match the vision?'

'The mountains were beyond anything I could describe, Grace. They made everything else seem so small, so unimportant. I wanted to tell him that. Tell him…'

'He knows, Josh,' she said, swallowing down the ache in her throat. 'He knows.'

'You think?' Josh forced himself to look up, face her. 'I should have been here. I can't bear the thought of you having to go through all this on your own….'

'I wasn't on my own. Everyone helped. Toby was wonderful.'

Toby.

Josh felt his guts twist at the name.

Toby Makepeace. Her ideal man. Reliable. Solid. Always here.

'Michael's partners took care of all the arrangements for the funeral. And once your father arrived and took charge—'

'He's here?'

'He flew back straight after the funeral. There was some big debate at the European Parliament that he couldn't miss.'

About to make some comment about his father's priorities, he thought better of it. Who was he to criticise?

'And my mother? Has she raced back to the toy boy in Japan?'

'She's staying with friends in London.'

'Waiting for the will to be read,' he said heavily.

'Josh!' Then, 'She said she'd come back when you got here. I sent her a text.'

'I refer to the answer I gave earlier.' Then he shook his head. His issues with his family were solely his concern. 'I'm sorry. That was uncalled for.' He pushed his parents from his mind and said, 'Thank you for sticking with it, Grace. Not just leaving a message with the Sydney office.'

'I wanted to tell you myself, although if I'd realised how long it would take…'

'It must have felt like a year.'

'A lifetime.' Then, quickly, 'Your staff were terrific, by the way. Will you thank them for me? If I'd thought about it, I'd have anticipated resistance to handing out contact numbers to someone they don't know.'

'Of course they know you,' he said. 'Do you think I don't talk about you all? Then, almost as if he were embarrassed by this brief outburst, 'Besides, they have an any time, any-where list.'

'And I'm on that?'

'We both know that the only time you'd ever call me would be with news I had to hear.'

Once Grace would have laughed at that.

If only he knew how many times she'd picked up the phone, her hand on the fast dial number, not to speak to him, but simply to hear his voice. How she'd longed to go back to the way it had once been, when they had been friends…teased one another…told one another everything.

Almost everything.

'Grace—'

'I'm going to miss Michael so much,' she said quickly. Taking a step back from the memory of a night that had changed everything. When she'd thrown all that away. 'There wasn't a kinder, sweeter—'

'Don't.' He closed his eyes for a moment, then, gathering himself, he opened them and looked straight at her. 'Don't put him on a pedestal, Grace. Michael wasn't perfect. He had his faults like the rest of us.'

Grace was too angry to answer him. Even now he wouldn't let go of whatever had been driving him…

Instead, she held Posie close as she got to her feet, sup-porting her head with her hand. Then, when she didn't stir, she laid her in the crib beside her chair.

For a moment her tiny arms and legs waved as if searching for her warmth and her face creased up, as if she was about to cry. Grace laid her hand on her tummy until, reassured by the contact, the baby finally relaxed.

Once she was settled, Grace crossed to the kettle, turned it on, not because she wanted something to drink, but because anything was better than doing nothing.

'Your flat is ready for you,' she said, glancing at him. 'The bed's made up and you'll find the basics in your fridge. It's too late to do anything today and I'm sure you need to catch up on your sleep.'

'I'll hang on for a while. The sooner I slot back into this time zone, the sooner I'll beat the jet lag.'

'Is that right? As someone whose only trip overseas was the Isle of Man, I'll have to take your word for it.'

'The Isle of Man isn't overseas, Grace.'

'Isn't it?' she asked. 'I wouldn't advise walking there.'

That earned her one of those smiles that never failed to light up her insides and, feeling instantly guilty, she looked away.

'There's a casserole in the oven and I'm just about to eat. I'm not sure what meal time you're on but, if you're serious about keeping local hours, you'd be wise to join me.'

He shook his head. 'I'm not hungry.'

'Oddly enough,' she said, 'neither am I, but unlike you I can't indulge in the luxury of missing meals.'

She stopped herself. His body clock must be all over the place and while snapping at him might make her feel better, would certainly help distract her from an almost irresistible urge to throw caution to the winds, fling herself at him and beg him to make it better, it wasn't fair on him.

'Look, why don't you go and take a shower? Maybe have a shave?' she suggested. 'See how you feel then?'

He ran a hand over his chin. 'You don't like the beard?'

'Beard?' Under the pretext of assessing the short dark beard that covered his firm chin, cheeks hollowed with exhaustion, she indulged herself in a long look. Finally shaking her head as if in disbelief, she said, 'Are you telling me that the stubble is deliberate?'

And for a moment, just for a moment, his mouth twitched into a whisper of the smile that had once reduced the hearts of teenage girls to mush. If her heart-racing response was anything to go by, it had much the same effect on mature and otherwise sensible women.

But then she was a long-lost cause.

'I'm sorry, Josh,' she added. 'I just assumed that you'd forgotten to pack your razor.'

'If that were true, you'd have had no doubt about the beard, but I'm still carrying the bag I had with me in China and Nepal so I hope the washing machine is up to the—'

He broke off as a tiny mewl emerged from the crib. A tiny mewl that quickly grew into an insistent wail.

Grace sighed. 'I thought it was too good to be true. She's been so fretful for the last couple of days. Clingy. It's almost as if she knows there's something wrong.'

Josh took a step towards the crib and, very gently, he laid his hand, as she had done, on the baby's tummy.

Posie immediately stopped crying and, eyes wide, stared up at the tall figure standing over her. Then, as if demanding more from her uncle, she reached out a tiny fist and Grace caught her breath as Josh crouched beside the crib and touched her hand with the tip of one finger.

He'd been beyond angry when she'd told him that he was too late to stop the surrogacy, that she was already pregnant with her sister's baby. News that she hadn't even shared with Phoebe, determined not to raise false hopes until the doctor had confirmed it.

She hadn't known how he would react to Posie. As a youth, a young man, he'd been adamant that he would never have children of his own. His marriage to a girl he'd never even mentioned had been so swift, so unexpected that it seemed at the time as if everyone was holding their breath, sure that only the imminent arrival of a baby could have prompted it. But there had been no baby and within a year the marriage had been over.

Now, as he gazed down at this small miracle, she waited, heart in her mouth, for his reaction. For the inevitable question.

How could she do it?

How could she have felt the first tiny movements, watched that first scan, listened to the squishy beat of her heartbeat, cherished the baby growing inside her for nine long months, only to surrender her to her sister and his brother?

Other people had asked.

Not friends, true friends. They had understood. But a reporter from the local paper who'd somehow picked up the story had called her, wanting to know the whys, the hows, the financial deal she'd signed up to. If the woman had done her research, she'd have known that anything but expenses was against the law and Grace hadn't needed or wanted even that. It was the people who didn't know them who'd seemed most indignant that she could do such a thing. People who clearly had no concept of unselfish love.

None of those people had mattered, but she so wanted Josh to understand. Even though he disapproved of what she'd done, she needed him to understand, without asking, why she'd done it.

Don't, she silently begged him. Please don't ask....

'Michael rang me minutes after Posie was born,' he said, after what felt like an eternity. 'He was almost incoherent with joy.' For a moment he too seemed to find difficulty in speaking. 'I was in the back of beyond somewhere, the line was terrible but even through the static it came through loud and clear. His world was complete.' He looked up, looked at her. 'You gave him that, Grace.'

She let out a breath she hadn't been aware she was holding. He understood.

Then, catching up, 'Michael phoned you?'

'He didn't mention it?'

She shook her head. Why wouldn't he have told her? Had Phoebe known?

'What did you say to him, Josh?' she demanded.

'I asked him if you were all right and, when he assured me that you had sailed through the whole thing, I asked him if he was sure you had no doubts about giving up the baby. Urged him not to rush you…'

She waited, sure there was something else, but he shook his head.

'I didn't,' she said. 'He didn't.'

Why had it mattered so much to him? And why wouldn't they have told her that he'd cared enough to ask about her? Had been concerned that she was all right. Hadn't Phoebe known how much it would have meant to her?

Or was that it?

Had her sister suspected what had happened between them all those years ago? Had they been afraid that, in the hormonal rush after Posie's birth, a word from Josh might have been enough to change her mind?

Not wanting to think about that, she crossed to the crib, picked Posie up, cradled her briefly, cherishing the weight of her in her arms, the baby scent of clean hair, warm skin. Then she turned and offered her to Josh.

'Here,' she said. 'Take her. Hold her.' When he didn't move, she looked up to find him staring, not at the baby but at her. 'What?'

He shook his head. 'I thought you'd be married to your Toby by now, Grace. With a home, children of your own. Wasn't that what you always wanted?'

'You know it was.'

She'd wanted what her sister had wanted. A settled home, a good man, children. She also wanted Josh Kingsley and the two were incompatible. No one could have everything they wanted.

Her sister had never borne the children she had yearned for.

And she had never found anyone who could erase her yearning for a man for whom risk was the breath of life, the horizon the only place he wanted to be.

'Unfortunately,' she said, 'life isn't that simple.'

'Maybe men just have it too easy these days. All of the comforts with none of the responsibility.'

'Excuse me?'

'Well, it wasn't for lack of choice, was it? You appeared to be dating someone different every time I came home.'

'Not *every* time, surely?' Her well-schooled, careless tone was, she knew, ruined by a blush.

'You don't remember?'

She remembered.

Given a few days warning of his arrival, it hadn't been difficult to drum up some hungry man from the crafts centre who was glad of a home-cooked meal. Camouflage so that it wouldn't look as if she was living in limbo, just waiting for Josh to come home and sweep her up into his arms, tell her that he'd been a fool. Pick up where they'd left off.

These days, only Toby was left. He'd been brighter than most, quickly cottoning on to what she was doing and apparently happy to play the possessive suitor whenever Josh came home.

Why she'd still been going through the motions after so long she couldn't say. Unless it was because she still wanted it so badly. That it was herself she was fooling rather than him....

Whatever, she could hardly get indignant if he'd been fooled by her deception. Assumed that she'd fallen into bed with every one of them as easily as she'd fallen into his.

'Maybe they could sense the desperation,' she said, burying

her hot cheeks in Posie's downy head, before holding her out
to Josh. 'Here,' she said, placing the baby in his arms. 'Say
hello to Phoebe Grace Kingsley. Better known as Posie.'

Josh held her awkwardly and Posie waved her arms nervously.

'Hold her closer to you,' she said, settling her against
Josh's broad chest, taking his arm, moving it, so that it was
firmly beneath the baby. 'Like this. So that she feels safe.'

She was desperately anxious for him to bond with this little girl who would never know her real father. For whom
Josh, no matter how reluctantly, would have to be the male
role model.

'She has a look of Michael, don't you think?' she suggested. 'Around her eyes?'

'Her eyes are blue. Michael has…had brown eyes.'

'All babies have blue eyes, Josh, but it's not the colour.'
The tip of her finger brushed the little tuck in Posie's eyelid.
'It's something about the shape. See?'

She looked up to see if Josh was following her and found
herself looking at the same familiar feature, deeper, stronger
in the man. Remembered the still, perfect moment ten years
ago when, after a long, lingering kiss, a promise that all her
dreams were about to come true, she'd opened her eyes and
that tuck had been the first thing she'd seen.

Josh felt as if he were carrying a parcel of eggs. Just one
wrong move and they'd be crushed. Maybe Grace was just as
anxious because she'd kept her arm beneath his, laid her long,
slender fingers over his hand, as if to steady him.

This was so far from anything he'd imagined himself
doing. He'd never wanted children. Had never wanted to
be responsible for putting children through the kind of
misery he'd endured. The rows. The affairs. The day his
father had walked out and his mother had become someone
he didn't know.

After a while, as he became more confident, Grace stepped back, leaving him holding this totally unexpected baby, who bore not the slightest resemblance to his brother.

If she looked like anyone, it was Grace, which was strange since she didn't much resemble her sister. He'd always assumed that they were half-sisters, although Michael had said not. The little tuck in the eyelid was familiar though, and he said, 'So long as she hasn't got Michael's nose.'

Grace laughed at that and the sound wrapped itself around his heart, warming him, and he looked up.

'I wish...' he began, then stopped, not entirely sure what he was wishing for.

'Michael never gave up hoping you'd turn up for the christening,' she said. 'He so wanted you to stand as her godfather.'

'He knew why I couldn't be there.'

'Too busy conquering the world?' Then, when he didn't answer, didn't say anything, 'Here, let me take her,' she said, rescuing him. 'I'll change her and put her to bed while you have a shower. Then we'll eat.'

He lifted his head and, glad of a change of subject, said, 'Actually, something does smell good. How long have I got?'

'Oh, half an hour should do it,' she said, not waiting to see whether he took her advice, but heading for the stairs and the nursery.

Josh let the shower pummel him, lowering the temperature gradually until it was cold enough to put the life back into his body, wake up his brain.

Doing his best to forget the moment when he'd come so close to breaking the promise he'd made to his brother. A promise he'd refused to free him from. Would never be able to free him from.

To forget the look on Grace's face as she'd looked up, and

for just an instant he could have sworn that she'd seen the truth for herself.

He stared in the mirror. He favoured Michael—no one would have doubted they were brothers—but there were not by any means identical. Still he could have sworn she'd seen something.

He tugged on an old grey bathrobe that had been hanging behind the bathroom door for as long as he could remember, waiting for him whenever he was passing through London and could spare a little time to visit Maybridge, see his family.

He tied the belt and crossed to the alcove that still contained the desk he'd used when he was at school. Where he'd plotted out the future. Where he'd go. What he'd do.

His old computer was long gone, but the corkboard was still there. He reached over and pulled free a picture, curling with age, that Phoebe had taken of Michael and him building a barbecue in the garden years ago, when his brother had been about the same age he was now.

The likeness was striking, but Michael had more of their mother, her brown eyes.

He tossed the photograph on the desk and, turning to the wardrobe, hunted out a pair of jeans that weren't too tight, a sweatshirt that didn't betray his adolescent taste in music.

Then he checked his new BlackBerry for messages, replied to a couple that wouldn't wait. By then it was time to go back upstairs—to Grace, and to the miracle and disaster that was Posie.

Grace took her time putting Posie to bed.

She hadn't been so close, so intimate with Josh in years and she needed to put a little time and space between them. Get her breathing, her heart rate back under control.

She didn't hurry over changing her, washing her hands and face, feeding her little arms and legs into a clean sleep suit, all the time talking to her, tickling her tummy, kissing her toes. Telling her that she was the most beautiful baby in the world, just as Phoebe would have done.

Using the sweet little smiles to distract herself from vivid memories of Josh, naked in the shadowy light from a single lamp. His grey eyes turning molten as that first kiss had turned into hot, feverish, desperate need.

He'd been so beautiful. So perfect…

Posie waved a foot at her and she caught it, kissed it, peered into her eyes. Did all babies really have blue eyes? People said that, but was it true? Weren't Posie's a little bit grey? Then she saw the tiny flecks of brown and smiled.

'You're a beautiful, clever girl,' she said, doing up the poppers, then picking her up and nuzzling her tummy before putting her in the cot, 'and you're going to be just like your daddy.'

She carried on talking to her as she wound up the musical mobile, teasing, laughing and, once she'd set it gently turning, singing to her, very softly.

Upstairs, Josh stopped at the open door to his brother's small study. As always, it was immaculately tidy, with only his address book and an antique silver photograph frame on the desk.

He picked it up, stared at the picture of Phoebe cradling her new baby daughter. It looked perfect, but it was all wrong. A lie.

Even his perfect brother, who everyone had loved and thought could do no wrong, had one, unexpectedly human, frailty.

He carefully replaced the picture and left the room, closing the door behind him.

Later. He'd go through his papers later. Not that it would take long. He knew that all bills would be paid, life insurance up to date, will filed with the family lawyer.

Then he frowned. Had he changed it since Posie had been born? There hadn't been much time but Michael had never, in the normal way of things, believed in leaving a mess for other people to clear up. But playing fast and loose with life, keeping secrets, even with the best of intentions, had a way of coming back to bite you. And that tended to make things very messy indeed.

Whatever he'd done, it seemed likely that Grace would be the person most affected.

He wondered if she had the least idea how her life was about to change. How, on top of the loss of her closest family, she might also lose the home she loved. The baby who she'd so selflessly surrendered and yet hadn't totally surrendered, knowing that she would always be close to her. That she would still be hers to comfort. To hold.

He wiped those thoughts from his mind, took a breath, pushed open the kitchen door.

'Sorry,' he began. 'I had to make…'

He stopped. Looked around. He could have sworn he'd heard her talking to Posie but the kitchen was empty.

He shrugged, crossed to the cutlery drawer, planning to lay the table. He'd barely opened it when he heard her again. 'Night-night, Rosie Posie…' she said, laughing softly. 'Daddy's gorgeous little girl.'

He spun around, then saw the baby monitor on the dresser. Was it two-way? Could she hear him? No, of course not. But even so he stepped away from the drawer, planning to escape before she came down and found him eavesdropping on her private conversation with her baby.

There was the sound of something being wound up, the gentle tinkling of a lullaby.

'Night-night, sweetheart. Sleep tight…'

His imagination supplied the vivid image of her bending over to kiss this very precious baby.

And then she began to sing and nothing could have torn him away.

CHAPTER THREE

GRACE came to an abrupt halt at the kitchen door. The table was laid. A bottle of red wine had been uncorked. A jug of water beside it on the table. Everything ready for them to eat.

'Oh, Lord,' she said. 'Have you been waiting long?'

'I guessed you were still busy and made a start, that's all' he said, pulling out a chair. 'Sit down. I'll get the casserole.'

'No, I'll do that…'

'I'm here to help, not add to your burdens, Grace.' He picked up a cloth, took the casserole out of the slow oven and placed it on the heatproof mat. 'Did Posie go off to sleep?' he asked, looking up.

'Like a lamb. Until her next feed.'

'And when is that?'

'Whoa… Enough,' she said as he heaped the meat and vegetables on her plate. Then, answering his question, 'Around ten. There are jacket potatoes in the top oven.' She leapt up to get them, but he reached out and, with a hand on her shoulder, said, 'Stay. I'll get them.'

She froze and he quickly removed his hand. It made no difference. She was certain that when she took off her shirt, she would see the imprint of his fingers burned into her skin.

He turned away, took the potatoes from the oven, placed one on each of their plates.

'No—'

'You have to eat,' he reminded her.

'Yes, but…'

But not this much.

She let it go as, ignoring her, he fetched butter from the fridge, then picked up the bottle of wine, offering it to her. She shook her head and he beat her to the water, filling her glass.

'Michael told me that Posie was sleeping through the night,' he said when, all done, he sat down, picked up a fork.

'She was, but she's started waking up again. Missing her mother.' Then, not wanting to think about that, she said, 'Michael told you?'

'He e-mailed me daily bulletins. Sent photographs.'

Why was she surprised? That was Michael. Josh might have walked away, but they were brothers and he would never let go.

'He wanted you to share his happiness, Josh.'

'It was a little more complicated than that.'

'Your understanding, then,' she said, when he didn't elaborate.

'I understood.'

'You just didn't approve.'

'No.'

'Why? What was your problem?' She hadn't understood it then and didn't now. 'He didn't pressure me. Neither of them did. It was my idea. I wanted to do it.'

For a moment she thought he was going to explain but, after a moment, he shook his head, said, 'When did you have your hair cut?'

Her hair? Well, maybe that was better than a rerun of a pointless argument. Although, if the general male reaction to her cutting her waist-length hair was anything to go by, maybe this was less a change of subject than a change of argument.

'About six months ago,' she said, trying not to sound defensive. Every man she knew seemed to have taken it as a personal affront. She, on the other hand, had found it liberating. 'When did you grow the beard?' she retaliated.

'About six months ago.'

'Oh, right. It's one of those clever/dumb things, then.'

He thought about it, then shook his head. 'No. Sorry. You're going to have to explain that one.'

'Whenever someone does something clever, in another part of the world another person does something stupid to balance it out,' she said, as if everyone knew that. She shook her head and then, unable to help herself, grinned. 'Sorry. It's just a ridiculous advert on the television that drove Phoebe...' She stopped.

'Say it, Grace. Talking about her, about Michael keeps them with us.'

'That drove Phoebe nuts,' she said slowly, testing her sister's name on her tongue. How it felt. It brought tears to her eyes, she discovered, but not bad tears. Thinking about her sister being driven mad by Michael, them both laughing, was a good memory. She blinked back the tears, smiled. 'Michael used to tease her with versions he made up.'

'Like you're teasing me?'

'Oh, I'm not teasing, Josh. I'm telling it the way I see it.'

'Is that right? Well, you're going to have to live with it. But while I'm not prepared to admit that the beard is dumb, I have to agree that your new style is clever. It suits you, Grace.'

'Oh...'

She picked up her fork, took a mouthful of casserole. Touching her hair would have been such a giveaway gesture—

'I really, really hate it,' he added, 'but there's no doubt that it suits you.'

—and much too soon.

'Pretty much like the beard, then,' she said. And, since the food hadn't actually choked her, she took another mouthful.

'Grow your hair again and I'll shave it off.'

It was an update of the arguments they'd used to have about the clothes she'd worn. The girls he'd dated. The music she'd listened to.

'If you hold shares in a razor-blade company, sell them now,' she advised.

Perhaps recognising that step back to a happier time in their relationship, he looked up, smiled.

And it was as if he'd never been gone.

For a moment they allowed the comfortable silence to continue, but finally Josh shifted, said, 'Do you want to tell me about the funeral?'

She sketched a shrug. 'Michael and Phoebe had left instructions…' She swallowed. 'How could they do that? They were much too young to be thinking about things like that.'

'I imagine they did it for one another. So that whoever went first wouldn't be faced with making decisions. What did they want?'

'A simple funeral service in the local church, then a woodland burial with just a tree as a marker for their grave. I imagine that was Phoebe's choice. Your father wasn't impressed, but there was nothing he or your mother could do.'

'One more reason for Michael to lay it all out in words of one syllable.'

'Josh… He was their son,' she said helplessly.

'Not in any way that matters. His mother is living in Japan with someone she isn't married to. His father is in Strasbourg, raising his second family. He hadn't spoken to either of them in years.'

'You're their son, too. Have you spoken to them?'

'We have nothing to talk about.'

She said nothing. What could she say? That they had both been dealt rubbish hands when it came to parents?

In a clear attempt to change the subject, Josh said, 'How

are you coping with your business? I heard your answer-phone message cancelling your classes for the time being and obviously Posie needs full-time care at the moment, but what are you doing about the craft centre workshop? Private commissions?'

'Beyond asking someone to hang a "closed until further notice" sign on the workshop door?' she asked. 'Not much.'

'Have you actually been out of the house in the last few days? Apart from the funeral?'

She shook her head.

'Go into Maybridge tomorrow. Pick up your post, at least. You need to keep some semblance of normality in your life.'

'Normality?'

How on earth did he expect her to think about something as frivolous as jewellery at a time like this?

'It's all you can do, Grace. It's what Michael and Phoebe would want.'

Of course it was. She didn't need Josh to tell her that. But knowing it and doing it were two entirely different things.

'I'll drop you off there when I go into town tomorrow,' he said. 'I have to talk to Michael's lawyers. I spoke to them from the car on the way from the airport. They're expecting me first thing.'

'Right. Well, I suppose I should go to the workshop. Process what orders I can fill from stock, send notes to people about anything that's going to be delayed, give them the chance to cancel.'

'Maybe you should think about taking someone on to help out for the time being,' he suggested. 'Who takes care of things when you're gallivanting off to the Isle of Man?'

'I wasn't gallivanting. The craft centre received an invitation from a fair being held over a holiday weekend and a group of us went.'

'You're getting very adventurous.' Then, 'A group?'

'I wouldn't have gone on my own, but Mike Armstrong sent some of his smaller pieces of furniture, there was a candlemaker, Toby took some of his toys and one of his rocking horses and there was—'

'So who took care of the shop while you were away?' he asked, cutting her off.

'Abby. She started as one of my students. She's very gifted.'

'Then call her. You can't afford to turn down business.'

'That's the tycoon speaking. I'm sorry, Josh, but the world won't end if Baubles and Beads is closed for a few weeks. I promise you it's never going to trouble the FTSE 100.'

'No? You don't see yourself as a franchise operation with a shop in every shopping mall five years from now?' he asked, with a smile that she remembered from the days when he'd been planning to be the world's youngest billionaire.

Did he make it?

'Er… No.' She liked the way things were. Controllable. Totally hers.

'No surprise there,' he said.

Did he look a touch disappointed in her lack of ambition? He was the one who, when she had made jewellery for college fund-raisers, her friends, had pushed her into taking a Saturday stall at Melchester market. It was Josh who'd printed flyers on his computer, handed them out, called the local press who'd sent out a photographer to take pictures. He'd gone out of his way to prove to her that it wasn't only friends and family who would pay good money for something original, different.

'I'm not into mass production, Josh. People come to me because they know they'll never see anyone else wearing the same pair of earrings. The same necklace.'

'Then you need to find some other way to grow. A static business is a dying business.'

'Possibly, but not now.' Then she groaned.

'What?'

'I promised Geena Wagner that I'd make a wedding tiara for one of her brides. It's almost done. I can bring it home, finish it here.'

'No,' he said, and she looked up, startled by the insistence in his voice. 'I really don't think that's wise.'

'But Posie…'

'You need to keep your work and your home life separate.' Again he had the look of a man with something on his mind.

'Easy to say. Elspeth would take care of her, but Posie needs continuity, Josh. She's already confused. Leaving her with anyone who has an hour to spare just so that I can keep working won't do.'

'I know,' he said. Then, more gently, 'I know.'

'I suppose I could take her with me.' Was that his point? That she was about to become a single mother with a business to run and she needed to think about how she was going to manage that. Answering herself, she said, 'I'd have to install some basic essentials if it's going to be a permanent thing.'

'Like what?'

'You want a list?' she asked, smiling despite everything. 'How long have you got?'

'I'm in no hurry.'

'Do you have the slightest idea how much stuff a baby on the move needs?' It was a rhetorical question and she wasn't expecting an answer. 'Actually, I suppose I could ask Toby to partition off the far end of the workshop so that I could turn it into a little nursery.' Then, irritated at how easily he'd manipulated her into thinking about the future when she didn't want to think about anything, she said, 'Okay, that's my life sorted. Now tell me about yours. About Nepal. China. What are you doing there?'

He began to talk about a major engineering project which

should have bored her witless, but just being the centre of his attention, being able to listen to him without pretence was such a rare treat that she didn't actually care what he was saying.

And when he turned the conversation to the jewellery-making workshops she ran, showing a keen interest in what she did, her stories about some of the odder characters who came to them made him laugh.

He told her about places he'd visited, both fabulous and foul. The wonders of the world, natural and man-made. The remote, the exotic, the emptiness of a tropical beach lit only by the stars.

She told him about her recent trip to Brighton for a jewellery convention.

Finally, long after they'd finished eating, Josh stood up. 'It's late, you're tired,' he said, clearing the dishes.

She didn't bother to fight with him over it—he was right, she was finding it hard to stay awake—but instead rinsed plates and cutlery, stacking them in the dishwasher as he cleared the table. She wiped mats as he put away the butter, the wine. Their hands momentarily entangled as they both reached for the cruet and she found herself looking up at him.

'I'll take the pepper. You take the salt,' he said after a moment.

'No,' she said, pulling back. 'It's all yours, Josh. You're right. I'm done and by the time I've had a bath, Posie will be awake again, demanding food.'

'Are you okay up there by yourself now that Elspeth's gone home?' he asked. 'I could just as easily sleep in one of the spare rooms.'

'I'll be fine.'

He lifted a hand, laid his palm against her cheek. 'Sure?' he asked.

She swallowed. 'Really. Besides, if Posie is restless she'll keep you awake.'

'I have to fall asleep first. I'm going to look through some of Michael's things before I go down to the flat.'

'Right, but don't forget you're supposed to be working on UK time.'

He smiled. 'I won't.' Then, before she could move, he leaned close and kissed her cheek. 'Good night, Grace.'

'Um…good night,' she said, backing away until she reached the door, then turning and running up the stairs before she said or did something stupid.

She took a steadying breath before she glanced in at Posie and then, in the safety of the bathroom, she leaned back against the door, her hand to her cheek, still feeling the soft prickle of his close-cropped beard as it brushed against her skin.

Remembering the shock of his kiss as he'd woken her—when she was anything but Sleeping Beauty—knowing how easy it would have been for her to have asked him to stay with her. How easy it would have been to turn into his arms for the comfort they both craved.

Wondering what would it be like to lie beside Josh Kingsley on a white beach in the starlight with only the sound of the ocean shirring through the sand, the chirruping of tree frogs, the scent of frangipani on the wind.

He'd made it sound so magical. Doubtless it had been. And she wondered who had shared that tropical night with him?

He hadn't said and, unable to bear the thought of him with another woman, she hadn't asked.

He'd only once brought someone home. They'd been expecting him, but not the tall, tanned Australian girl he'd married without telling a soul. A girl who was, in every way, her opposite. Outgoing, lively, ready to follow him to the ends of the earth. Or so she'd said. It had lasted a little over a year. Since then he'd never brought anyone home, never even talked about anyone in his life, at least while she was around and although he was, by any standards, a rich and eligible bachelor, he didn't seem to live the kind of lifestyle that brought him into contact with gossip magazines. But just because he didn't date the kind of glamorous women who were pursued by the paparazzi meant absolutely nothing.

Only that he preferred to keep his private life just that.

Private.

She ran a bath, added a few drops of lavender oil. But even up to her neck in soothing warm water she discovered that once having thought about it, it was impossible to get the image of Josh, of her, their naked bodies entwined, limbs glistening in the surf, out of her head.

Horrified that she could be thinking about such things at a time like this, she sank beneath the water in an attempt to cleanse the thoughts from her mind. Or maybe just to blot out everything. Only to erupt in a panic when she thought she heard Posie crying.

Her ears full of water, she couldn't hear anything, but when she threw a bathrobe around her and checked, she found the baby lying peacefully asleep.

She rubbed her hair dry, then eased herself into bed in the room next to the nursery. Closed her eyes and slept.

Josh replaced the telephone receiver in Michael's study, then opened the door, pausing at the foot of the stairs, listening. Everything was quiet. Grace couldn't have heard the phone—his Chinese partner hunting him down with impatient need to set up a meeting—or she'd surely have come down. Unless she'd fallen asleep in the bath?

The dark hollows beneath her eyes told their own story and, knowing he wouldn't rest until he'd reassured himself, he kicked off his shoes and, as quietly as he could, went upstairs. The bathroom door was unlocked. He opened it a few inches and said, 'Grace?' When there was no response, he glanced inside and saw, with relief, that it was empty. Then, as he turned away, he saw the nursery door was slightly ajar and, unable to help himself, he pushed it open, took a step inside.

He stood for a moment by the cot, looking down at the sleeping infant. Listening to her soft breathing, assailed by a torment of confused emotions as he considered every possible future. For Posie. For Grace.

Grace laughed as, her bottle empty, Posie turned to nuzzle at her breast, searching for more.

'Greedy baby,' she chided softly.

It was just getting light and, miraculously, they had both slept through.

She looked up as the squeak of the door warned her that she was no longer alone.

As Josh padded silently across the kitchen floor on bare feet, unaware that he had company, her first thought was that he didn't look so hot.

Then, as he reached the kettle, switched it on and stood by the window, staring out of the window at a pink and grey dawn while he waited for it to boil, she thought again.

He might have the hollow-eyed look of a man who'd spent the night staring at the ceiling but, in washed thin jogging pants and nothing else, he looked very hot indeed.

'Tea for me,' she said, before that train of thought joined last night's beach fantasy and got completely out of hand. Then, as he spun around, 'If you're offering.'

'Grace... I didn't see you there. Why are you sitting in the dark?'

'I've been feeding Posie,' she said. 'There's more chance that she'll go back to sleep if I leave the light off.' Then, 'Is the kettle playing up again?'

He looked at the kettle, which was clearly working, then at her.

'The one in your flat,' she said. 'Phoebe was going to buy

a new one before…' Before the christening. But Josh had been 'too busy' to fly home, so she hadn't bothered.

'What? No,' he said. Then, 'I don't know. It was claustrophobic in the basement. Since I moved last year I've got used to seeing the sky when I wake up.'

'You have to go to sleep before you wake up,' she pointed out.

He shrugged. 'I managed an hour or two. I don't need a lot of sleep.'

'I remember,' she said.

'Do you?'

It was just as well the half-light was pink because she blushed crimson. That wasn't what she'd meant….

'I remember Michael saying that you'd moved to some fabulous new penthouse with views to the end of the world.' They'd gone out there to visit, just after he'd moved in and BP. Before pregnancy. 'He said you wanted a closer look at all those horizons still waiting to be conquered.'

'Is that what you think?'

'I haven't the first idea what you want, Josh.' She shifted the baby to a more comfortable position, then said, 'So? What's it like?'

He regarded her for a full ten seconds before he turned away, dropped a couple of tea bags into two mugs and poured on boiling water. Then, his back to her, he said, 'It's like standing on the high board at the swimming pool without a handrail. You'd hate it.'

That hurt, cut deep, mostly because he was right, but, refusing to let it show, she said, 'I don't have a problem with views. I just don't have your unstoppable urge to find out what lies beyond them.'

'Still clinging to the safety net of home, Grace?' he said, lifting his head to challenge her.

'Still searching for something to cling to, Josh?' she came back at him.

He was the one who looked away and she realised that she'd touched an unexpected nerve.

'Will you stay and keep an eye on Posie while I go and take a shower?' she asked, easing herself to her feet, laying the sleepy babe in her crib, then fetching the milk jug from the fridge. 'Milk?' she asked, after fishing out the tea bags.

He didn't answer and, when she looked up, she realised that he was staring down at the overlarge dressing gown she was wearing, or rather at the way it was gaping open where she'd held Posie against her breast as she'd fed her from the bottle, as Phoebe had, giving the same skin to skin closeness as breastfeeding.

'This is Phoebe's,' she said, self-consciously pulling it around her, tightening the belt. 'It's a bit big, but I've been wearing it so that Posie has the comfort of her scent.'

'Until yours and hers become indistinguishable?'

'No! It was just while she was away.' Except, of course, her sister wasn't ever coming back. 'I hadn't thought that far ahead.'

'No,' he said, with a heavy finality that suggested she hadn't thought very much about anything. 'Although I suspect that, unless her table manners improve, all she's going to get is the smell of stale milk or dribble.'

She frowned.

'There's a damp patch,' he said, then, when she looked down. 'No, on the other side...'

'Oh, nappy rash! I'm leaking.'

'Leaking?'

She opened a cupboard, grabbed a sealed pack of sterilised bottles. 'Make yourself comfortable. I may be a while,' she said, heading for the door.

'Wait!' He caught her arm. 'You're feeding Posie with your own milk?'

He sounded shocked. Instantly on the defensive, she said, 'Of course. Why wouldn't I?'

'You have to ask?'

Confused by his reaction, she said, 'Apparently.'

He shook his head. 'You're expressing your own milk, putting it in a bottle and then sitting down and feeding Posie with it. Do I really have to explain what is wrong with that picture?'

'There's not a thing wrong with it. Breast milk is the very best start for a baby. Everyone knows that.'

'In an ideal world,' he replied, 'but I suspect that precious few surrogate mothers stick around to play wet nurse.'

'I'm not!'

'As near as damn it, you are.'

She stared at him, shaken by the fierceness of his reaction. 'You know this isn't a normal surrogacy, Josh.'

'Really?'

How could anyone invest such an ordinary word with such a mixture of irony, disdain, plain old disbelief? Grace didn't bother to respond, defend herself, since clearly he was a long way from finished.

'In what way isn't it normal?' he asked. 'You're not married, so there was nothing to stop Michael's name being put on the birth certificate. I assume that happened?'

'Of course.'

'And presumably you went through all the legal hoops with the court-appointed social worker? Signed all the paperwork so that the Parental Order could be issued, along with a new birth certificate in which Phoebe and Michael were named as Posie's parents?'

'Of course. We were really lucky. It can take up to a year to get everything settled, but there was space in the court calendar and, since the social worker was happy, the paperwork was completed in double quick time.'

'So you are aware that you've surrendered any legal rights you had as Posie's birth mother?'

Grace clutched the plastic container of feeding bottles

against her breast, a shield against words that meant nothing and yet still had the power to hurt her.

'You've done your homework,' she said, more than a little unnerved at his thoroughness in checking out the legal formalities. Trying to figure out what, exactly, he was getting at.

'I did, as a matter of fact,' he replied, 'although, since Michael explained everything in his regular progress bulletins, it was more for my own peace of mind than necessity.'

That was Michael, she thought. He would never have given up trying to make Josh see how perfect it all was. Trying to break down whatever his problem had been with this arrangement.

Poor Michael....

'So why are you asking me all this?' she demanded, making an effort to concentrate, trying not to think about what had happened, but how totally happy Michael had been. 'Since you already seem to have chapter and verse.'

'I just wanted to be sure that you fully understand the situation.'

'Of course I understand. And I didn't "surrender" Posie. She was always Phoebe's baby.'

'Truly?'

He slipped his hand inside the gown and laid his hand over the thin silk of her nightgown, fingers spread wide across her waist to encompass her abdomen in a shockingly intimate gesture. Her womb quickened to his touch, her breast responding as if to a lover's touch.

'Even while she was lying here? When you could feel her moving? When it was just the two of you in the night? You didn't have a single doubt?'

It was as if he were reading her mind. Had been there with her in the darkness, the restless baby in her womb keeping her awake, thinking about how different it could have been. How, all those years before, she'd longed for the protection he'd used to have failed, knowing that a baby was the one thing that would have brought him back to her.

She'd hated herself for wishing it, knowing how wrong it was to want a baby only to bind him to her. If he'd loved her, he would not have left. Or, if he had, would not have been able to stay away.

Knowing that carrying his brother's child for her sister was the nearest she was ever going to get to having Josh's child growing within her womb. But that was for her to know. No one else.

She knew she should move, step back, stop this, but the warmth, strength of his hand against her body held her to him like a magnet.

'Well?' he demanded, pressing her for an answer.

'No,' she mouthed, no sound escaping. Then again, 'No!' No doubts. Not one. 'It isn't unknown for a woman to carry a baby for her sister,' she told him. 'It was once quite normal for a woman to give a childless sister one or even two of her own babies to raise.'

'This isn't the nineteenth century.'

'No. And I've no doubt some of the neighbours believe I actually had sex with Michael in order to conceive but, since you've done your homework, you couldn't possibly think that. Could you?'

'Of course not—'

'Only, for your information, he was at a conference in Copenhagen when all the planets were in alignment but since the clinic already had his contribution in their freezer that wasn't a problem.'

'I know how it's done, Grace.'

'You have been thorough.'

'I didn't need to look that up on the Internet,' he said, his face grim now.

'No? Well, know this. Since I was here, living under the

same roof, it made perfect sense to give Posie the very best start possible.'

'Did it? And whose idea was that? The whole breast is best thing.'

'Does it matter?' He didn't answer, just waited for her to tell him what he already believed he knew. And, infuriatingly, she couldn't deny it. 'Phoebe would never have asked.'

'No, I didn't think it was her idea. So how long had you planned to stretch it out, Grace? Six, nine months? Or were you planning to be one of those earth-mother types—?'

'That's enough!' she said, finally managing to step away from his hand. 'This wasn't about me. You told me that Michael was incoherent with joy. Well, I want you to imagine how Phoebe felt. After years of tests, hoping, waiting, longing for a baby of her own. The fertility treatment. All those failed IVF cycles. How do you think she felt when the midwife put Posie in her arms?'

'No one would deny that you did a generous, beautiful thing, Grace.'

'You thought I was wrong then and you still do.'

'No… Not you.'

'Michael, then?' Now she was confused. Who exactly did he blame for what had happened? 'Phoebe?'

'They were desperate. Beyond reason…' He shook his head. 'It no longer matters. All I'm saying is that it might have been better if you'd gone away for a while. Afterwards. Cut the cord, not just physically, but emotionally.'

He was so obviously concerned for her that she couldn't be angry with him.

'Or were you already planning to do this all over again a year from now so that Posie could have a brother or sister?'

She took a step back. He followed her.

'Are you really so terrified of getting out there and making a life for yourself that you were ready to settle for having a second-hand family? One without the risk of making a commitment to a relationship? Leaving the comfort of the nest?'

On the other hand...

'So what if I did,' she retaliated defiantly. 'What possible business is it of yours?'

'It's my business because, unless either of them left specific guardianship instructions,' he said, 'as Michael and Phoebe's executor, I'll be the one playing Solomon with Posie's future.'

She felt the blood drain from her face. 'What are you saying?' And then she knew. 'No. You can't take her from me. You wouldn't. She's mine....'

The words were out before she could stop them.

'I thought we'd just established that she's anything but yours. That you have no rights.'

'No...' It wasn't like that. Okay, so maybe he was right. Maybe she'd never given Posie up in the way that a true surrogate would have done. But she was her aunt. Her godmother. Obviously she was going to be close. Be there for her if ever she needed her. And she needed her now. Then, more fiercely, 'No!' she said again, this time with a touch of desperation. 'You don't want her! You couldn't even be bothered to come home for the christening!'

He bit down hard, clearly fighting an angry retort. Then, very calmly, very quietly, he said, 'Forget me, Grace. Where Posie is concerned, I'm the last person you need worry about.'

Confused, she frowned. 'So what are you saying?'

Before he could answer, the phone began to ring.

Josh, closer, reached out and unhooked the phone from its cradle on the kitchen wall, responding with a curt, 'Kingsley.' He listened impassively for what seemed like forever, then said, 'We'll expect you when we see you.'

'Who was it?' she asked as he hung up, turned back to face her.

'My mother. Michael's mother—'

'Is she coming to see you?'

'—Posie's grandmother,' he said, his face set, his expression grim, 'who will be here some time this morning.'

On the point of objecting to his rudeness, she thought better of it. He clearly had something on his mind.

'Thank you. Now I'll finish what I was saying when the phone rang.' He looked so angry, so fierce. 'When I was telling you that I was the last of your worries.'

'Last? When did you ever come last in anything?' she demanded.

Least of all where she was concerned.

'Last,' he repeated. 'I come a long way down the list of next of kin. The only person who's lower than me on this particular list is you. After my father, my mother, *your* mother even…'

He let the words hang, giving her time to work it out for herself. And, when she did, her heart stopped beating, her legs buckled and there was a crash as the pack she was carrying fell to the floor.

If Josh hadn't reached out and caught her, she'd have followed it but, his arms around her, he supported her, held her close.

'I won't let it happen,' he said fiercely, as she subsided weakly against his naked chest, a rock in a world that was disintegrating around her. Stroked his hand over her hair in a gesture meant to calm her. 'Trust me, Grace. Whatever it takes. You have my promise.'

The temptation to stay in the safety of his arms almost overwhelmed her. To call him on that promise. Leave him to fight her corner. But he wasn't always going to be around to make things right for her. If there was to be a battle, she would fight for her daughter. But she didn't think it would be necessary.

'It's all right, Josh,' she said, lifting her cheek from the steady beating of his heart, the warm silk of his skin. 'They wouldn't want her,' she said, looking up at him. 'They didn't want us.'

'No,' he said, his face grim. 'But then, neither of us had the legacy of a fine house, a couple of generous life insurance policies and whatever Michael's partnership in his architect's practice is worth. Even after the Chancellor has taken his cut in inheritance tax, it's still going to provide a very nice expense account for anyone who can prove their case for bringing up Posie.'

'What?' Then, 'Are you suggesting any of them would take her just for the money?'

'There are other factors. My father has a second family. A young wife. Three little girls who would no doubt welcome a baby sister.'

'But she's *my* baby!' The betraying words flew from her lips and in that instant she knew he'd spoken no more than the truth. She'd given her sister her baby, but she hadn't been able to totally let go.

'My mother would, I'm sure, give up her present precarious existence for this house, a steady income. She would, of course, employ a first-class nanny to take care of Posie. Might even offer you the job.'

Grace shook her head. 'She's mine,' she repeated. 'If it comes to a fight, any court would have to recognise that.'

He shook his head. 'I spent a long time last night researching this on the Internet. You carried a fertilised egg for your sister but, once you've completed the formalities, that's it. In law you're no more to Posie than her aunt. Nothing changes that.'

'No…' That small word held a world of pain, of loss. First her sister and now this. Then, as his words filtered through, she said, 'No. That's not right. You don't understand. I didn't… It wasn't…'

'What?' He was looking down at her, but now his forehead was furrowed in a frown, his grip tighter and, when she didn't answer, he gave her a little shake. 'It wasn't what, Grace?'

She looked up at him. She'd promised Phoebe she'd never tell, but her sister would want her, expect her to do whatever it took to keep her baby.

'It wasn't Phoebe's egg, Josh. It was mine.'

CHAPTER FOUR

'But…' Now it was Josh who looked as if he needed something to hold on to. 'They'd been going through IVF,' he protested. 'There were eggs available. Michael told me…'

'Michael…' She swallowed. 'Michael didn't know.'

Grace was propelled back by the shock that came off him in waves. She grabbed for the back of a kitchen chair, then sank down on it as her shaking legs finally refused to support her.

She gestured weakly at the chair beside her. 'Sit down, Josh.' He didn't move and she said, 'Please.'

For a moment she thought he was going to ignore her plea, turn around, walk away, just as he had when she'd told him she was pregnant with her sister's baby. That there was nothing he could do or say to stop her going ahead with the surrogacy.

And so he'd said nothing.

But, after endless seconds, he pulled out the chair beside her and sank down onto it.

'Tell me,' he said. 'Tell me everything.'

Grace looked across at the crib, then back at Josh.

'I couldn't bear to see what they were both going through after the failure of that last cycle, when the consultant called a halt, saying that Phoebe wasn't strong enough to go through any more.'

She reached out, wanting him to understand, but there was something about the way he was holding himself, something so taut, so close to cracking, that she didn't quite dare cross that line.

'You have to understand how hard it was for them,' she pressed, wanting him to feel their pain. 'It was as if someone had died.'

'I understood,' he said tersely.

'Did you?'

Josh understood only too well.

Maintaining that cheerful, positive front for Phoebe had been tough on his brother. Michael had taken to calling him late at night when Phoebe had been asleep, pouring out his desperation, his sense of failure. There had been one call, when his brother had sounded so desperate that Josh had dropped everything and flown home, seriously concerned that he was on the point of a breakdown. Something Phoebe had been too wrapped up in her own loss to recognise.

Grace pressed him for an answer. 'Did you really, Josh?'

'I understood that it had become an obsession, that it was destroying them both,' he said. 'I wanted Michael to put a stop to it. Let it go. Adopt.'

'That seems such an obvious choice to the outsider,' she said. 'For a woman yearning for a baby of her own...' She let out a long shuddering sigh. 'I loved them both so much, to see them hurting like that was unbearable.'

'So it was you who suggested the surrogacy?'

'Not until I was sure it was a possibility. Like you, I did my research on the Internet, found a Web site run by and for people who'd already been through this. Then I saw my doctor, talked it through with her. Had all the health checks. I didn't want to raise Phoebe's hopes, not until I had the medical all-clear.'

'You should have had counselling. What if you'd found you couldn't give up the baby? It happens.'

'I know.'

'But then you weren't really giving her up, were you?'

She didn't argue. She could see how it must look to him, but he hadn't been the one lying in the upstairs flat listening to her baby crying in the night, screwing the sheet into knots as she clung to the bed, waiting for Phoebe to call her, ask her to help. A call that she knew would never come.

'When I told them I was ready and willing to have one of Phoebe's fertilised eggs implanted, they both wept.'

'They didn't try to talk you out of it? Either of them?'

Her eyes flashed impatiently. 'Of course they did. Michael said that it was time for them to take the adoption route.'

'But Phoebe was hooked.'

'They weren't that young any more. We all knew that adoption would not have been easy. And I was absolutely certain that it was something I wanted to do.'

'So?'

'Michael had to go to Copenhagen to put in a bid for a new project. He said we'd talk about it again when he got back.' She shrugged. 'While he was gone, Phoebe and I went to see her consultant so that we'd have all the options when he got back. He gave it to us straight. While he was prepared to attempt implanting a fertilised egg, he didn't need to labour the point about how much harder it is to get a result that way.' She was staring at her hands. 'Phoebe had tried and tried, Josh. I'd seen what it did to her. Simple artificial insemination is much easier, much more reliable. By the time Michael came home, it was done.'

Josh rose slowly to his feet.

It was true, then.

Some sound must have escaped him, because Grace said, 'She's still Michael's baby—'

He shook his head and for a moment she faltered, but she quickly rallied and, on her feet, came back at him with a fierce, 'Yes! Posie is still just as much your niece as if Phoebe had given birth to her.'

'No…'

This time the word felt as if it had been torn from the depths of his soul, as feelings that he'd battling with for a year threatened to overwhelm him.

'Please, Josh,' she said, her hand reaching for his, her voice urgent now, desperate. 'Posie needs you.'

'No!' His bellow, reverberating around the high ceiling, was echoed by a startled cry from the baby.

He was beside her in a stride, lifting her from the crib, holding her out in front of him at arm's length.

'Posie Kingsley is not my niece,' he said. Then, tucking the child protectively against his shoulder, he turned to Grace. 'She's my daughter.'

'What?'

'She's my daughter, our daughter.'

'No,' she said, shaking her head, taking a step back, looking for all the world as if she'd just stepped on the tail of a sleeping tiger. 'Don't…'

If ever her eyes betrayed her feelings, they betrayed them now. Then she turned away, as if she couldn't bear to look at him, walked to where she'd dropped the feeders and bent to pick them up.

'Give her to me,' she said.

'It's the truth,' he said, refusing to surrender Posie when, still not looking at him, she held out her arms to take her. He had to make her look at him. Had to convince her. 'Michael would have done anything and, God forgive me, I conspired in his deception.'

She let her arms drop, turned and walked out of the room.

'You can't hide from this,' he said, following her. 'Or bury your head in the sand. You're going to have to fight to keep your baby.'

She stopped at the foot of the stairs, swung around to face him. 'From you?' she demanded angrily. 'Is that what this is all about?' She gestured at the baby still nestled against his shoulder. 'Control of Michael's baby?'

'My baby. Why else would I have tried to stop the surrogacy? What I did, I did for Michael. To ease his torment. If Phoebe had become pregnant, if she'd had a baby, I could have lived with it. Been glad for them. But to know that you were carrying my child…'

'It was the same, Josh.'

'No, Grace. It was completely different. You were carrying my child. Have you any idea how that made me feel?'

That, at least, gave her pause. The anger died from her eyes, to be replaced by some other emotion. One that was far harder to read.

'How?'

'I can't explain…' It was true. There was no vocabulary for the anguish he'd felt, knowing that a woman he'd loved was carrying his child only to give it away. That she would never—could never—know the truth. He'd felt as if he were stealing something from her. Losing part of himself.

'Why didn't you just tell me, Josh? Instead of going on and on about what a fool I was. How I'd regret it.'

'Michael had made me swear…'

'On what? Your mother's life?' Sarcasm dripped from her tongue and he didn't blame her.

'Not even Phoebe knew,' he said.

'I don't believe you. He wouldn't have deceived her.'

'Just like Phoebe wouldn't have deceived Michael?' he retaliated, and colour streaked across her cheekbones. 'I warned you not to put him on a pedestal.'

'So you did.'

'If it helps, with Phoebe's history I didn't believe there was the slightest chance of her carrying any baby to term.'

'No, Josh, adding cynicism to deception doesn't help one bit.'

'No, I don't suppose it does.' Then, 'If it would have changed anything, despite my promise, I would have told you.'

'But I told you what I hadn't told them. That you were too late. I was already pregnant.'

He nodded.

'Maybe, if we hadn't jumped the gun, if we'd waited until he came home,' Grace said, 'he would have told me.'

'Maybe.' But, as their eyes locked, they both knew that it was never going to happen.

'But…' She shook her head. 'I don't understand. Why? Why would he do it? Why would you?'

'Michael was desperate and I had no choice.'

'They were both desperate, but there was no problem with Michael. It was Phoebe. They both knew that…'

'I know,' he said. 'I know. But while he was holding it together on the surface for Phoebe, he was perilously close to a breakdown. She was going through so much to give them both what they wanted. Michael felt so useless and that somehow morphed into the certainty that it was his fault they couldn't have children. I tried to get him to see a counsellor but he just begged me…' Grace was staring at him and he broke off, unable to continue. 'You're not the only one who owed Michael and Phoebe,' he said angrily. 'They took me into their home, too. I only did what you did, Grace.'

'You think?' She lifted one eyebrow. 'A few minutes in a cubicle with a magazine?'

'If you knew how helpless men feel,' he said. How helpless, how confused he'd felt, knowing that she was carrying a child he'd so unwillingly helped make. 'If I'd had any idea where it would lead, I'd never have gone through with it….'

Grace was in turmoil, couldn't begin to think straight, but one message was coming over loud and clear. That while he had been prepared to assist Phoebe to get pregnant, he'd flown half way around the world in an attempt to stop *her* from having his baby.

'It's okay, Josh. No need to labour it,' she snapped. 'I get the picture. Phoebe could have your baby, but I wasn't good enough.'

'No! That's not right. How could you not be good enough?'

'Then why?'

'Phoebe was just Phoebe. Michael's wife. You…' She'd never seen Josh struggle for words like this.

'What?' she demanded. 'How bad can it be?'

'Not bad. Far from bad, but we were lovers, Grace.'

'Lovers?' She'd never thought of them as lovers. 'Were we lovers?'

'I was the first man who knew you.'

First, last… She didn't want to think about how pathetic that was. 'I still don't understand what your problem was.'

'Don't you?' He looked at Posie for a moment, then back at her. 'My problem was that when Michael told me you were going to have a baby for Phoebe—not his, but my baby—it made me feel the way I did when I left you sleeping after the night we'd spend together, flying away like a thief in the night. I felt as if I was stealing your virginity all over again.'

'You didn't steal my virginity, Josh, I gave it to you with a whole heart, but we were never lovers.'

It struck her now so clearly. All those years she'd clung to something that had been unreal—nothing.

'To be lovers is more than sex. For lovers the whole person is engaged. Not just the body, but the head and heart. My head was missing that night and so was your heart. I don't believe you know how to love.'

She might as well have slapped him. Yesterday she'd wanted to, now…

Now she had to deal with the fact that it was Josh, not

Michael who was the father of her baby. That it wasn't simple biology, a surrogacy without emotional involvement or ties, but that, ten years too late, her darkest dream had come true.

She didn't want to slap him, she wanted to hold him. Wanted him to hold her, tell her that it would be all right…

It was never going to happen.

He'd made his feelings plain. He hadn't expected or wanted this child. But then he'd once told her, when she'd found him burning photographs of his father, that he would never have children.

Later, when Michael and Josh had gone to the sports centre to beat a squash ball to pulp, Phoebe had told her that there had been an announcement in *The Times* that morning, telling the world that his father's new young wife had just given birth to a baby girl.

'I have to deal with this,' she said, clutching the pack of feeders to her.

'You can't run away from this, Grace. Can't hide. Can't curl up in your armchair and make it go away. Posie is our daughter and we're going to have to sit down and decide what's best for her.' He looked down at the dark curls of the baby who was chewing at his shoulder. 'Make decisions that will alter all our lives.'

'She's Phoebe and Michael's daughter,' she replied, a touch desperately. She wasn't ready to talk about anything else right now. She needed time to come to terms with what he'd told her. That she'd had Josh Kingsley's baby. 'It says so on her birth certificate, as you've just taken great pains to remind me.'

'All the more reason…'

'No. You didn't want her, Josh. You never wanted her. You flew from Australia to try and stop her from being conceived.'

'And failed.' He came close to a smile. 'Not that I'm the first man to face that situation. Although I'm probably the first not to at least have had the fun of getting myself there.'

'Sorry, I can't help you with that one, Josh,' Grace said with a desperate flippancy that she was far from feeling. 'You'll just have to dig deep in your memory for consolation.'

'Not that deep,' he replied without hesitation, his eyes glinting dangerously as he lifted a hand to her face, ran his thumb down the side of her cheek. And for a moment all she could think about was how he'd kissed her—not ten years ago, but yesterday, when he'd woken her. Kissed her, kissed his baby. Because he'd always known that Posie was his. And now he knew that she was hers, too.

This was the first time either of them had ever talked about the night they'd spent together and Grace discovered that at twenty-eight years of age she could still blush like the shy fourteen-year-old who'd first come to this house.

Maybe Josh, too, was experiencing whatever similar response men felt when, without warning, they stumbled into emotional quicksand because, for a moment, neither of them spoke.

Then Grace said, 'You're okay, Josh. I don't have a father who cares enough to get out his shotgun and make you do the decent thing.'

'I know all about uncaring fathers, Grace. You're right. Having seen the dark side, fatherhood is not something I ever wanted, but here I am, like it or not.'

And Grace, who hadn't thought beyond the next hour for more than a week, realised that she had better start putting in some serious thinking time about what future she saw for Posie. For herself.

'This changes everything, doesn't it?' she said, sinking onto the stairs.

Josh sat down beside her, put his spare arm around her, pulled her against his chest. 'Everything,' he agreed.

They sat there for long minutes, both of them contemplating the future. Until last week, each had seen the road clear ahead of them. Two separate paths. One a quiet small-town road, the other a challenging climb up a twisting mountain path with the end lost in the clouds. Now their ways merged in a pothole-strewn lane that was shrouded in swirling mists.

It was Posie, waving a hand and grabbing a handful of Josh's hair, who finally brought them back to now, this minute and, as he yelped, Grace lifted her head, smiling despite everything as she rescued him from Posie's tight little grasp.

'Did she pull it out by the roots?' he asked, rubbing at his scalp.

'Not much. Get used to it.'

'Will you help?'

'I'm in it for the duration, Josh.'

And that, she realised, was all that mattered. She was now the only mother Posie would ever have and she just had to get on with it. If Josh wanted to be a father… Well, that was good, but she wasn't holding her breath.

And, with that, the world steadied and, realising that she was still clutching the feeders, she got to her feet. Milk. Shower. Work. Concentrate on one thing at a time. Do what had to be done and the rest would fall into place….

'I'll be as quick as I can,' she said, glancing down at him.

'You're leaving Posie with me?' She saw panic flash across his face. 'What do I do with her?'

She paused, the words *'Be a father'* burning in her brain. Not fair. She wanted him around for Posie, but she wouldn't stoop to blackmail.

He hadn't asked for—or wanted—this.

'Just keep her amused for a while,' she said, forcing herself to walk up the stairs, away from them. She got very nearly halfway before she looked back.

He hadn't moved, but was looking up at her, dark hair still ruffled from bed, ancient jogging pants sagging below his waist, exposing a band of paler skin, feet bare. Posie propped in his elbow, happily sucking at his naked shoulder.

If she had trawled her imagination for a perfect picture of fatherhood, she couldn't have bettered it.

Don't go there, she warned herself. It might only take one little tadpole waking up from deep freeze and eager to explore to make a baby, but being a father required a lifetime of commitment.

Josh thought one night made them lovers. He couldn't even stay married to the same woman for more than a year. He saved his energies for the really important stuff, like dominating his own field of engineering.

'Better still,' she said, a catch in her throat, 'let her amuse you.'

Josh looked at the baby, then back up at her. 'What does she do?'

'Do? She's not a performing seal.' Then, because he was clearly so far out of his depth he was in danger of drowning, she threw him a lifeline. 'She's just learned to roll over. If you put her down on the carpet, she'll show you.'

She didn't wait to see what he did, but ran up the two flights of stairs to her own flat, her brain pounding out the words *Josh's baby* over and over.

She'd been carrying Josh's baby inside her for nine months and not known. Had given birth to Josh's baby and had given her away.

How could she have done that?

How could she have looked at her and not seen? The little eyelid tuck. The grey eyes flecked with amber. A little curl that fell over her right eye.

He was right not to have told her.

To have known and have to give her up, even to her sister, would have been like tearing her heart from her body and, without it, she would never have survived.

* * *

Once she finished expressing her milk, Grace took a shower, then sorted through her wardrobe for something suitable for their trip into Maybridge, ignoring her usual bright colours as inappropriate, choosing the navy trouser suit she normally kept for visits to the bank.

She'd suggest walking into town. Apart from avoiding the hassle of parking, it would be good to stretch their legs, get some fresh air. They could cut through the park on the way home, maybe take some crusts. It was way past time that Posie was introduced to the joys of feeding the ducks. Phoebe had always loved doing that.

To the outside world they'd look like any ordinary family, she thought. Mother, father, baby. All they lacked was a dog.

She put her hand over her mouth, squeezed her eyes tight shut. Hung on until the urge to howl passed.

Grace's baby...

The words thumped through Josh's head as he took the stairs down to the basement flat. Last night he'd stood for a long time in the shadows of the nursery, watching his child sleeping, as every shade of emotion raced through him.

Anger, confusion, guilt. Grief at not just the loss of his brother and Phoebe, but of this last year when he'd walled himself up, unable to come to terms with what he'd done, what his brother had done. Feeling somehow cheated, used. Worst of all, having deep buried feelings for Grace stirred up to torment him.

The minute he'd stopped concentrating on something else, his mind would sandbag him with memories of how it had felt to be buried to the hilt in her sweet, hot body, her legs wrapped around him as she'd cried out his name. Creating pictures of her carrying his child, as if the one had led from the other.

He'd never wanted to be a father. No man had ever been

more careful to avoid it. Even when he'd gone to that clinic, done what was necessary, he had managed to distance himself from the reality of it. Any baby would be Michael's, not his. And it had worked until he had discovered that it was Grace who'd be carrying his seed, at which point dispassion had deserted him.

Now, lifting his little girl from his shoulder, holding her in front of him, he was faced with more reality than he could handle.

'So, Posie,' he said, 'are you going to amuse me?'

Posie, head wobbling slightly, frowned in concentration as if considering his question, just as her mother had once frowned over her homework.

'Your mother said you can roll. Is that the extent of your repertoire?'

That earned him his first smile.

'What? You think that's a funny word, do you?'

Posie made a grab for his cheek, found the short stubble of his beard and tugged.

'Oh, no, you don't, young lady,' he gasped and, eyes watering, put her down on the carpet, pulled on the sweater he'd discarded the night before, then settled down on the floor beside her.

Posie stuck her fingers in her mouth and flung her legs up in the air.

'Oh, please,' he said. 'Is that any way for a lady to behave?'

Posie blew a bubble.

Grace put the feeding bottles in the fridge, laid the table for breakfast and then, since Josh and Posie had still not appeared, she went looking for them.

They weren't in the living room—the most obvious 'rolling' territory—or anywhere else on the ground floor.

The internal door to the basement flat was still open.

She crossed to it, but hesitated on the threshold. It wasn't that she never went down there. She had always volunteered to prepare it for him when he'd been expected home, whisking through it with vacuum cleaner and duster, checking the bathroom was stocked with everything he might need, the fridge contained the essentials. Smoothing Phoebe's best linen sheets over the mattress, fluffing up the pillows.

She had always avoided going down there when he had actually been in residence.

She'd even weaned herself off going down there once he'd gone, wallowing in the scent of him clinging to sheets, towels.

It had been years since she'd taken a pillowcase he'd slept on to tuck beneath her own pillow. Her own comfort blanket.

As she hovered at the head of the stairs, the rich, deep sound of his laughter drifted upwards and, drawn by this unexpected, wonderfully heart-lifting sound, she took one step, then another and then she was standing in the small lobby, looking through the open door into Josh's bedroom.

Unaware of her presence, he was lying face down on the floor, his back to her, playing peekaboo with Posie. Lifting the hem of the sweater he'd thrown on, hiding his face and then popping out with a, 'Boo.' Posie responded by throwing up her legs and wriggling with pleasure.

Josh laughed. 'Again?'

Posie waved her arms excitedly.

The two of them were locked in their own intimate little bubble, totally focused on each other. It was touching, beautiful, unutterably sad, and Grace was torn in her emotions, wanting to laugh with Josh and Posie and weep for Michael and Phoebe.

She did neither.

Instead, determined not to disturb father and daughter as they discovered each other, she clamped her lips together, took a step back, then turned and, as silently as possible, went back upstairs.

CHAPTER FIVE

Josh couldn't have said whether it was a movement of air, some almost imperceptible sound or something else, but he looked over his shoulder, certain that he'd just missed something.

'I think we'd better go and see if your mummy is ready for us,' he said, scooping up the baby and heading for the stairs, dodging as she grabbed for his beard, catching her hands.

'No, you don't, miss.' She stuck out her bottom lip and he laughed. 'You're going to be a handful.'

His handful…

Then, catching a faint whiff of the faintest scent, he let go of her hands and didn't stop her when she grabbed hold of his ear, distracted by a familiar combination of soap, shampoo, something more that was uniquely Grace, and he knew exactly what had disturbed him.

It was this scent that had always been the first thing to greet him when he'd unlocked the basement door and walked in, usually at some unearthly hour in the morning after a non-stop flight from Sydney.

It was on the sheets when he'd stretched out to sleep, but had instead lain awake, imagining her leaning over to pull them tight, tuck them in, smooth the pillowcases into place.

Leaning over him, her long hair trailing over his skin, the

scent of her shampoo—everything about her so familiar and yet completely new.

It had been so real that he had almost fooled himself that this time it would be all right, almost believed that this time she would look at him and the intervening years would be wiped out.

Instead, when he saw her, he'd get a quick, surprised smile as if his arrival was the last thing on her mind and he'd know that she hadn't given him a single thought since the last time he had been home. An impression confirmed when she'd appear at dinner with some decent, straightforward man in tow. A man who'd get the real smile. And he'd be certain that this time she'd found what she was looking for. Not him. Never him.

And he'd tell himself that he'd always known this was how it would be. Tell himself that it was right, that he was glad for her because he was the last man on earth she needed in her life.

Tell himself that he'd imagined the scent.

But he hadn't imagined the scent on his sheets, his pillows. She'd been there time after time in his basement flat, preparing things for his arrival, just as she'd been there a minute ago, watching him with Posie.

As he walked into the kitchen she turned from the stove where, apron wrapped around her, she was laying strips of bacon in a pan as casually as if it were the only thing on her mind.

'I thought you'd be hungry,' she said brightly enough and, if he hadn't known that a minute earlier she'd been down in the basement, he might have been fooled.

'Why didn't you say something?' he challenged. 'When you came downstairs.'

'Peekaboo?' she offered, not looking at him.

'That would have done.'

'You two were having such a good time I didn't want to butt in and spoil your game.'

'Three wouldn't have been a crowd.'

'Peekaboo is a game for two.' She half turned. 'What gave me away?'

'Your scent.'

She frowned. 'I'm not wearing any scent.'

Posie, tired from her games, was falling asleep against his shoulder and he gently lowered her into her crib, held his breath as her eyes flew open, felt something inside him melt as they slowly drifted shut. Awake, playing, she'd been a bundle of energy, but lying asleep he could see just how fragile, how vulnerable she was. Being a parent wasn't just a full-time job, it was a twenty-four/seven responsibility. There was no time off. No putting the job first.

Phoebe hadn't worked since the day she had married Michael. With two tricky teenagers and a large house to run, she hadn't had time. Grace was different. She had her own business, small by his standards, but it had taken years of hard work to build it up from that first market stall and it was her life. Had been her life. Now there was Posie and she couldn't do it on her own. Maybe she wouldn't get that chance.

He'd tried to lay it out in words of one syllable, warn her what might happen, but he knew he could never let anyone take Posie from her mother. His mother could be bought. His father worked in a politically sensitive environment and he wouldn't want his personal life plastered over the tabloids. But that wasn't the end of it. Grace was going to need help, support. And Posie would need a father. Not just a reluctant sperm donation, but someone like Michael.

He felt his chest tighten painfully.

Not him.

He wasn't like Michael. He didn't take in strays. Wasn't a nest-builder. His apartment had been decorated by a professional, looked like a show house rather than a home. He still had worlds to conquer. She needed someone like Toby Makepeace…

He looked up and realised that while he'd been thinking about her, she'd been watching him standing over the baby. She wasn't exactly smiling, but there was a softness about her eyes, her mouth…

He straightened. 'No scent?' he said, stepping back from the abyss yawning at his feet.

'None,' she said, turning away to lift a basket of eggs from a hook.

'I beg to differ,' he said.

'Oh?' She looked over her shoulder at him. 'And just how are you going to prove it, Josh Kingsley?'

He joined her at the Aga. 'Like this,' he said, bending to her hair, the feathery wisps tickling as he breathed in the scent of her shampoo.

'All you'll smell if you stand there is bacon,' she said, twitching away.

'You're using one of those herbal shampoos,' he said.

'Me and the rest of the world.'

'No…' This wasn't something mass-produced. It came from some little specialist shop; it was a national chain now, but it had started in Maybridge and Phoebe had been a fan. 'Rosemary?'

She said something that sounded like, 'Humph.'

As she made a move to escape him, he put his hands on her shoulders and kept her where she was while he lowered his head to lay his cheek against the smooth, fair skin of her neck.

She twitched at the touch of his beard, trembled beneath his hands just as she had when, eighteen years old, she'd come to him. When they'd made love….

'Lemon and myrtle,' she said abruptly. 'From Amaryllis Jones in the craft centre.'

That was it.

The scent on his sheets. The thought acted like an aphrodisiac and he backed off before he embarrassed them both.

'I had the lemon,' he said. 'I'd never have got the myrtle. What is that?'

'A bush. Small white flowers, long stamens, lovely scent. There's one in the garden,' she said, picking up a fish slice and holding it up like an offensive weapon. 'If you'd rather shower first, I can put this on hold.'

A cold shower might be a good idea. But he couldn't quite bring himself to leave her.

He'd dreamed about Grace. Hot, sexy dreams that left him aching with need, but he'd never responded to her physical presence with such an instant hard-on before. Not since the night when, trembling in his arms, she'd kissed him and he'd lost his mind.

But then, since that first night, she'd held him off with all the force of a quarterback scenting a touchdown.

'I'll eat first,' he said, pulling out a chair, sitting down, watching her as she fussed with the breakfast, avoiding eye contact, flustered in a way he'd never seen her before. But then she'd always had someone on hand to run interference for her when he'd been home. All those good, steady men. Never the same one twice... 'So,' he said, 'what game can the two of us play with Posie?'

The fish slice slipped from her fingers and clattered on the quarry tiles.

'I thought I might walk into town,' she said, picking it up, rinsing it under the tap, drying it. 'Posie and I could do with some fresh air. You could take my van if you like.' Then, when he didn't say anything—since not saying anything was prompting her mouth to run away with her—she pulled a face. 'Maybe not. It doesn't quite fit the tycoon image, does it? Phoebe's car is in the garage.' He saw her eyes dim as she thought about her sister. Tried to imagine what this last week had been like for her. 'Eggs?' she asked. 'One, two?'

'Just one, thanks. I'll walk in with you and Posie, Grace. I seem to have spent the last three days sitting in a plane and I need to stretch my legs.'

Grace, who he'd seen handle the tiniest beads with the precision of a surgeon, missed the edge of the pan and, as the egg shattered against the hotplate, sizzling and burning, she leapt back with a tiny scream.

'Did you burn yourself?'

He was with her before she could answer, taking her hand, turning it over to see what damage she'd done. Leading her to the sink to run it under the cold tap.

She shook her head, not looking at him but back at the stove. 'It's nothing, just a splash. I need to clean up…'

'I'll do it,' he said, leaving her with the utmost reluctance, but knowing that, if he didn't, she'd do it herself. He removed the pan with the bacon from the hotplate and picking up the slice that was having a very hard day, used it to scrape burnt egg off the cooker.

She turned off the tap.

'Grace…'

'It's fine. Nothing. There's so much to do.' She pushed long slender fingers, which could conjure up an original piece of jewellery out of nothing, through her short hair. 'I need to go and make up a bed for your mother. Did you say she's coming this morning? Someone will have to be here to let her in. Maybe I'd better stay. She'll want to see Posie, too. I asked one of my friends to take care of her on the day of the funeral. I thought she'd stay on for a while…'

He saw her stop, think about that and then, as she remembered what he'd said about her being at the back of the queue when it came to Posie's future, turn to him for reassurance.

Thinking that if she hadn't stayed, couldn't spare the time

to wait and see her baby granddaughter, there was no possibility that she'd be interested in custody.

He would not give her that. Could not. Not until he knew whether Michael had made a new will. If he had, then he would surely have named Grace as her guardian. If not, it would be open season…

'I have no idea what my mother will do about Posie, Grace. But you can be certain that, whatever it is, it will be for her own benefit rather than as a result of grandmotherly instincts belatedly kicking in.'

He wanted her to understand that she was going to have to fight to hold on to her baby. His parents, her mother, maybe even him.

She stared at him. 'You really do hate her, don't you? Your mother.'

'No,' he said, grabbing the kitchen roll to wipe the surface of the Aga. 'I don't hate her.'

For a long time he'd thought he did but he'd learned, over the years, that relationships were never that simple. He'd come to understand that people were driven by desires, forces beyond their control.

Maybe that was the dominant trait that both he and Michael had inherited—the selfish gene that allowed them to fix on a goal without thought for the havoc created in the wake of achievement.

His father had left them both for a younger woman and, in her misery, his mother had jettisoned him to chase her own second chance of happiness.

Much in the same way that, justifying himself that it was in her best interests, he'd walked away from Grace. Had pursued and married the girl every other man he knew had wanted to bed, without a thought what marriage to him would be like. Alone for weeks on end. Not anger, no sense of betrayal, only relief when she'd found someone to console her…

Then, realising that Grace was still watching him, trying to read his expression, he said, 'If I could have hated her, it wouldn't have hurt so much when she left.' Facing a truth he'd fought since she'd left him with Michael. Sharing it with Grace because she was the one person he knew would understand.

'I tried to hate my mother, too,' she said. 'Hate is so much easier. But the bad stuff is mixed up with all kinds of good memories.'

'What good memories?' he asked. She had never talked about her life with her crazy hippie mother, her life on the road, and he'd never pushed her, even in teasing, instinctively knowing that it was beyond painful. 'What good memories?' he repeated.

Grace thought about it as Josh returned the bacon to the hotplate, cracked an egg into the pan and dropped a couple of slices of bread in the toaster.

'Stringing beads is my first stand-out memory,' she said. 'My mother was making jewellery to sell at a craft fair and, to keep me from bothering her, she gave me a thin piece of leather and a box of big bright beads so that I could make my own necklace.'

She remembered sitting at a table in the old minibus they were living in, sorting through the box of painted wooden beads, totally absorbed by the smooth feel of them, the different sizes, vivid colours. Laying them out in rows until she found a combination of colours and sizes that pleased her. Her delight as each shiny bead slid down the dark leather and the vision in her head became real.

Best of all, she remembered her mother's smile of approval.

'I bet you still have it somewhere,' Josh said, bringing her back to the present.

'No.' She grabbed the toast as it popped up, put it on a

plate, reached for a clean slice and flipped the egg over. 'Someone saw me wearing it at the craft fair and asked my mother if she had another one like it.'

'Absolutely not,' he said, smiling at her. 'It was a Grace McAllister original. Your first.'

'Absolutely. My fate was sealed with that first sale.'

'Sale?' His smile faded as he realised what she was saying. 'Are you telling me that your mother sold the necklace you'd made for yourself?' Shocked didn't cover it. 'That's a good memory?'

'Of course. I'd made something someone liked enough to pay for,' she said, glancing up at him. 'That made me feel special. I bet you didn't feel a bigger thrill when you signed your first contract, Josh. And I made myself another one when I got home.'

'She still shouldn't have done it.' He made no attempt to disguise his disgust. 'If that is as good as it got, I dread to think what the bad stuff was like.'

There were the times they'd been hungry, cold, but she and her mother had cuddled up together—they weren't the bad times. Bad wasn't her mother. It was other people...

'Bad was angry people. Shouting, forcing us to move on in the middle of the night.' She stared at the bacon sizzling in the heavy-bottomed, expensive pan standing on the Aga. The kind of luxury that she took for granted these days. 'Bad is never knowing where you're going to be when you wake up. Another new school where the kids call you filthy names because you live in a camper van parked on the land of someone who wants you gone. Seeing your mother dragged off by the police, arrested, just because she lashed out at someone who'd smashed the windscreen of her home. Running into the woods to hide so that the police wouldn't take you away, put you into care...'

She stopped. Where had all that come from? All those

long-buried memories. Things she'd hadn't thought about in a long time. A world she'd left behind on the day Phoebe and Michael had picked her up from Social Services, brought her home. On the day that Josh had tossed her his spare crash helmet and taken her into school on the back of his motorbike.

Memories that she'd almost blotted from her mind. Apart from that apparently everlasting residual fear, the one about waking up and not knowing where she was. The one that still had the power to give her nightmares. That still brought her out in a cold sweat when she had to spend a night away at a craft fair….

Then, having apparently rendered him speechless, she said, 'There's juice in the fridge, Josh. Help yourself.'

'Why didn't you tell me?' he asked, pouring juice into a couple of glasses she'd put on the table, bringing one over to her. 'I knew your mother was a "traveller", that she'd got into a bit of bother with the law. That Phoebe rescued you from care and was granted a Parental Responsibility Order so that your mother couldn't take you back on the road. But not the rest.'

When she didn't answer, he looked up.

'I thought we were friends, Grace.'

Were. Past tense. Because once you'd spent the night naked with a man, utterly exposed, all barriers down, it could never be that simple ever again.

'Are you saying that you told me everything?' she said flippantly. 'I don't think so.'

'Everything that mattered. Do you think I talked to anyone else about my parents the way I talked to you?'

She knew exactly how much his father's desertion had hurt him. What it had done to him when, six months later, his mother had flown off to the other side of the world with someone new.

He'd put on a couldn't-care-less face for the rest of the

world but, a few weeks after she'd moved in, when life was suddenly unbelievably wonderful, she'd rushed into the garden with a letter that had arrived for him from Japan. Thrilled by the strangeness of it.

He'd taken it from her, glanced at it and then, without bothering to open it, he'd torn it in two, then torn it again and again before finally discarding it, letting the breeze take the pieces, the savagery of it shocking her into a little scream.

'It was from my mother,' he said, as if that explained everything. Then, 'Sorry. Did you want the stamps?'

The line had been a study in throwaway carelessness, but a shake in his voice had betrayed him, as had a suspicion of brightness in his eyes that she'd recognised only too well. And she'd put her thin arms around him and hugged him while he cried.

This was the first time either of them had ever referred to that moment and their eyes connected as they remembered, relived that moment of anguish when he'd been more completely hers than even at the moment of sexual release.

'So?' he said. 'Why didn't you tell me how it was?'

'Fear.' Faced with the disaster of the last week, the deceit, how could she be anything but honest with him?

'Fear?'

Fear that if he knew, he'd look at her the same way those other kids had.

Not that honest…

'I was afraid that if people found out about me, they'd be angry that I was living here. That I'd be forced to leave. And Phoebe, too.'

'But that's ridiculous.'

His response was natural. How could he possibly know how savage people could be when they felt threatened by those who didn't conform to the rules they lived by, who chose to live a different way?

'I know that now. Michael loved Phoebe too much, was too big a man to have buckled under disapproval, peer pressure.'

But she had often wondered what Michael's parents had thought of his wife. While her own mother had been accepted, welcomed on her rare visits, neither of his parents had ever been to this house while Phoebe was alive. And there had been no attempt to reconcile Josh with his parents, something that would normally have been a priority for Michael. He'd never talked about them. Had dismissed without consideration her tentative suggestion that he invite them to Posie's christening. There had to have been more to that than just a messy break-up and divorce.

'Back then,' she said, 'I didn't know, didn't understand how special your brother was.'

'I don't suppose anyone does until it's too late to tell them.' He looked across at Posie, sleeping peacefully in her crib, and said, 'It's going to be up to us, isn't it?'

'Us?' She took a sip of the juice, put the glass down, reached up for a plate.

'To make sure that Posie only has good memories.'

'Oh, right. And how exactly do you intend to do that, Josh? Are you planning to phone them in from whatever exotic location you're in at the time? Tell her about the great beaches, the palm trees?' Then, 'Or maybe send her postcards? That would certainly give her a head start on a stamp collection...'

She stopped. Swallowed. She'd spoken without thinking but he'd think she'd mentioned the stamps deliberately. 'I'm sorry. I—'

'Maybe I should take her back to Australia with me,' he cut in, stopping her apology in its tracks. 'So that she can experience them for herself. It's a great place for kids to grow up.'

Her grip tightened on the handle of the slice but she refused to be rattled.

'The best place for a child is to be with people who love her enough to put her needs first,' she said, keeping her back to him. 'Who'd look after her in Australia when you're off conquering new worlds?'

'You?'

Now he had her attention and she swung round to face him. 'Excuse me, but are you offering me a job as my own daughter's nanny?'

Maybe it was just as well that the doorbell saved him from answering because this was a conversation going downhill fast.

'Your breakfast is burned,' she said coldly, handing him the slice and, leaving him to take it from the pan or not as he pleased, went to answer the door.

The slender woman standing on the doorstep was swathed in bright silk, jewellery dripping from every possible location. As exotic as any bird of paradise.

'Mum...?'

She didn't reply, just dropped the bag she was carrying, stepped forward and wrapped her arms around her, cloaking her in the faint aroma of some exotic spicy fragrance. For the first time in a very long time Grace did not resist or pull back as soon as she could. Right now she needed her mother in ways she barely understood and they clung together for a long time, not needing to speak.

It was, finally, her mother who drew back first, her gaze fixed on something behind her, and Grace didn't need to turn around to know that Josh had followed her into the hall.

'Hello, Dawn.'

'Josh...' she said, acknowledging him, but her eyes were on the baby he was holding with a possessiveness that made Grace's blood run cold. 'Hello, my sweetheart,' she said, holding out her arms. 'Come to your grandma.'

For a moment Grace thought Josh wasn't going to surrender her, but Posie, attracted by the bright colours, was smiling at this interesting new arrival and, after what felt like the longest hesitation in history, he gave her up.

'I'm going to take that shower, Grace,' he said. 'If you can be ready to leave by half past eight?' Then, 'You do still want to come into town? Dawn can let my mother in if she arrives while we're out.'

She had never wanted to go into town, but she couldn't put it off any longer. And they had unfinished business to discuss that she didn't want anyone else overhearing.

'Will you be all right, Mum? I had a commission for a tiara that has to be delivered by the end of the week.' Then, straightening for a fight she hadn't anticipated but would not duck, 'And you're right about the workshop, Josh. It's my livelihood and I need to make arrangements to keep it ticking over while I think about how I can fit it around Posie's needs.'

That brought something that could almost have been interpreted as a smile to his lips as he recognised the challenge. 'You're not interested in hearing my offer, then?'

'Posie and I are happy here.' And, before he could say any more, 'We'll be ready to leave at half past eight.'

Neither her mother nor Grace spoke until they heard the basement door shut, at which point they let go of the breath they'd been collectively holding.

'That man is so intense,' her mother said. 'Not a bit like his poor brother.'

'No. But they were very close.'

'Were they?' She turned to the infant in her arms and they inspected one another, her mother with a searching look, Posie with her little forehead wrinkled in a frown. 'What offer did Josh Kingsley make you, Grace?'

'He didn't make an offer.' Well, he hadn't. She'd cut him off before he'd said the words. 'It was just a joke.'

'Really? He didn't look as if he was joking. Only I did

wonder, if he's been appointed guardian, whether he'll want to take Posie back to Australia with him.'

'He can't do that.'

'Oh?' she said. 'Are you quite sure about that? She's a beautiful child and he seems…attached.'

'He wouldn't. He's never in one place for more than a week and children need stability. Order. He knows that.' They both knew that.

'They are important,' her mother agreed, 'but knowing that they're loved is what really counts.' Then, looking at her granddaughter, 'Phoebe must have been so happy. I'm glad she had these few weeks when her world was complete.'

'Yes…' Grace tried to say more, but there was just a great big lump in her throat.

'And you, Grace? What will make your world complete?'

She shook her head. Some things were never meant to be.

'Come on through to the kitchen. I'll get you something to eat,' she said, anxious to change the subject.

'I'm not hungry, just tired.' Then, 'I'm sorry I didn't get here in time to share the burden, help with the arrangements.'

Grace shook her head. 'They'd left instructions. They chose a woodland burial site. It's very peaceful. I'll take you there when you've recovered. Josh hasn't seen it, either. He only arrived yesterday.'

Her mother nodded. 'I need to make a phone call, let someone know I've arrived. Then perhaps a bath and a nap?'

'Why don't you use my flat? I'm staying down here with Posie so you'll be quiet up there,' she said, picking up her mother's bag and heading for the stairs. 'Private,' she added, wondering quite how Josh's mother would react when they met.

'Nice idea, but I'm not sure that I could cope with all those stairs.' She pulled a face. 'Years of damp and cold, living in vans, hasn't done my hips any favours.'

Concerned, Grace stopped. 'Are you okay? I could sort you out something on the ground floor for sleeping, but there isn't a shower on this floor.'

'I'm going to need replacement joints sooner rather than later but I can just about cope with one flight. I'd like to make my call before I go up, though. I need to tell a friend that I arrived safely.'

That was such an unexpected thing for her free-as-a-bird mother to say that Grace said, 'A friend?' Then, 'You've met someone?'

'You think I'm too old?'

'No, Mum. I'm just jealous.' Then, 'Help yourself to the phone in Michael's study. I'll put your bag in the front bedroom on the right—it's the one nearest to the stairs. Then I'll get Posie ready for her outing.'

'You're taking her with you?' She sounded disappointed. 'I would have taken care of her.'

'You need a rest and, to be honest, we could both do with some fresh air. I thought we'd come home through the park so that she can feed the ducks. You know how Phoebe loved to do that.'

Her mother laughed. 'Phoebe?'

'Wasn't it Phoebe who once gave all the bread we had to the greedy little beasts?'

'No. She gave the bread to you and you gave it to the ducks.'

'Are you sure?'

'Oh, yes. She was supposed to be looking after you so that I could put together some stuff to sell at a craft market.'

Grace had vivid memories of her mother bent over a table, working long into the night to put together her intricate necklaces and bracelets. Easy in hindsight to understand how hard it must have been for her, a single mother trying to make enough money to keep her girls fed and clothed as she lived the travelling lifestyle that she'd taken to with the man she'd loved. Had never left, even when he'd disappeared one day. How lonely it must have been.

A scenario that she was now faced with. Not that Posie would ever be hungry or afraid. Not while she had breath in her body.

'Leaving us all without supper was her way of letting me know that she had much more interesting things to do than babysit her little sister.'

'No!' Grace found that hard to believe. 'Phoebe was always so protective. So caring.' So…*good*. Or was that the grown-up Phoebe she was thinking of?

'It was me she had a problem with, Grace. Not you. We both know that I would never have made the shortlist for greatest mother in the world. Something she made very clear when I came to fetch you after my twenty-eight days for vandalism and disturbing the peace.'

'You came for me?' Her mother hadn't just abandoned her, taken the easy option, the get-out-of-jail-free card? 'I never knew.'

Phoebe had never told her. It seemed that her big sister was better at keeping secrets than she'd ever imagined.

'We agreed that it was for the best. You didn't have her rebelliousness, her toughness. You needed to feel safe. I loved you more than words could say and it was like cutting off my right arm to leave you, but I knew you'd be happier with her. That it would be easier for you if you weren't torn by any foolish loyalty to me.' She kissed Posie's downy head and handed her over. 'She would have been such a wonderful mother. But you will be, too. Much better than I ever was.'

There was such a world of need in her eyes that Grace put an arm around her, held her and said, 'You gave me up because you loved me. That's the hardest, finest thing for a mother to do.'

'Oh…' There were tears in her eyes as she pushed her away, saying, 'Go and pretty yourselves up. I've got a call to make.'

CHAPTER SIX

DRESSING Posie, putting together everything she'd need for the morning, took nearly all the time Grace had so that 'prettying herself up' consisted of little more than pulling a comb through her short hair.

Then she fastened jade button earrings to her lobes and a matching necklace of overlapping disks of the same stone around her throat. Make-up she could live without, but jewellery was her business and she'd never been anywhere since she'd been a toddler without something fancy around her neck or wrist—her 'sparklies'—and she'd feel naked without them.

She settled the necklace into place, trying not to think about Josh, his hands on her shoulders as he'd leaned into her neck to hunt down some elusive scent. The feel of his beard brushing against her skin, sending gooseflesh shivering through her.

The last time they'd been that close, that intimate, they'd been naked. This morning, when she'd felt the warmth of his breath against her ear, been swamped by the scent of a man still warm from his bed, she'd wanted to be naked again.

She slipped on her suit jacket, buttoned it up and, without bothering to check her reflection, fetched Posie from the nursery and went downstairs.

Josh looked up, said nothing, as she hurried into the kitchen ten minutes later than she'd promised. He just looked at her and she was convinced he could see every hot, wicked thought that had been running through her mind, distracting her, slowing her down.

'Ready?' she asked.

Stupid question. He was showered, wearing faded jeans and a soft suede jacket that emphasized the width of his shoulders and brought out the amber flecks in his grey eyes. He had obviously been there for some time since all trace of the breakfast disaster had been removed and he was sitting at the table, looking through the local paper.

He closed it, got up and said, 'Can I do anything?'

'G-get the buggy? It's in the mud room,' she said, opening the fridge, fitting a bottle into its own special little cold box, slipping it into the carrier that contained all Posie's essentials, exactly as she'd seen Phoebe do dozens of times. Keeping her hands behind her back to hide fingers itching to help.

What she wouldn't have given for that yearning now. To see Michael instead of Josh setting up the buggy, take Posie and fasten her into the little pink nest. Put the carrier in the rack beneath it.

'Not bad,' she said. 'For a first effort.'

He didn't answer but took the handle of the buggy, wheeled it into the hall.

The steps weren't exactly easy to navigate, as she knew from experience, and, having opened the door, she made a move to help. Unnecessary. Josh just lifted the buggy, with Posie and all her belongings in it, and carried them down the steps as if it weighed no more than a feather.

A nice trick if you could manage it, she thought and, since possession was nine-tenths of the law, by the time she'd shut the door and reached the footpath he was already walking away from her, forcing her to trot to catch up.

'Slow down,' she said crossly. 'This isn't a race.'

Without taking his hand off the buggy, he lifted his elbow and, glancing down at her, said, 'Hang on. You can slow me down if I'm speeding.'

He wanted her to put her arm through his? Walk along arm in arm as if they were Michael and Phoebe…?

As if they were a couple. Lovers…

She swallowed, imagining her hand against the soft suede, her fingers resting on the hard sinewy flesh beneath it. She wanted that closeness in a way that was beyond imagining. Wanted it too much to be able to risk it.

'You're all right,' she said.

He didn't argue, simply stopped, took her hand and placed it under his arm. 'Whatever happens, you're not on your own, Grace,' he said, then, without giving her time to resist, to object, he continued, rather more slowly, on his way.

The suede was as soft to the touch as a baby's breath, while beneath it the familiar muscular arm seemed to burn through to her fingers, setting light to the memory of him standing in the kitchen, naked to the waist, in the early light.

As a girl she'd clung to his waist when she'd ridden behind him on his bike, pressed to his back, sheltered from the force of the wind by his body. That had been a secret thrill, one that had given her more of a rush than the speed at which they had been flying along. One that Josh hadn't ever known about.

This was different. This closeness was not some careless thing, just part of being on the back of a motorbike. He'd made a deliberate choice, just as he had on her first day at school when he'd tossed her his spare helmet. As he paused, turned to cross the road, and his sleeve brushed against her cheek it was like the sun coming out. She wanted to lean into it, suck up that protective warmth.

All illusion. This was not his world. In a week, two at the

most, he'd be gone, chasing endless horizons. That was fact.
He'd be somewhere out of reach and she'd be alone.

And, with that thought, the true finality of what had
happened crystallised in her mind. Until now she'd been
skimming along, keeping the wheels ticking over, taking care
of Posie. Coping with the details. Standing numbly in the
church through hymns and eulogies. Even watching her sister
and her husband being lowered into the dark earth, it hadn't
seemed real.

Each morning, her first reaction was that momentary panic
at waking in an unfamiliar room, the remembering that she
was in the guest room next to the nursery because her sister
was away for the weekend.

Only after that came the sickening moment when she remembered that Phoebe was never coming home again. But
then Posie claimed her attention and there was no time for
anything but the essentials. Laundry, feeding, bathing her,
changing her. She was a full-time job all by herself.

Now, walking with Josh in Michael and Phoebe's place, an
icy hand gripped at her stomach, her heart. This wasn't just
for a few days. This was her life. There was only her to be responsible, make decisions, make sure that this precious
baby…little girl…teenager…had the best life that she could
give her.

'Grace?'

Josh stopped as she pulled away, gasping for breath, and,
ignoring her as she took her hand off his arm, as she tried to
keep him away, he let go of the buggy and, catching her by
the shoulders, pulled her against him.

'They're gone, Josh,' she said, looking up, wanting him to
see, to understand. 'They're never coming back.'

His only response was to wrap his arms tightly around her,
press his cheek, his lips against her hair as if he could somehow keep out the world.

'Hush… It's all right.'

All right…

All right!

'How can anything be all right ever again?' She pulled back, flinging up her arms to push him away. 'It needs more than a hug and words to fix this, Josh. It isn't just us, there's a baby involved, one that you and I made, and we're responsible.' She knew she was making a scene, that people on their way into town were turning to look, but she didn't care. She had to make him see. 'It's not just for this week, or next week, but for *ever*. We're not just spectators in Posie's life, we're her—'

Josh grabbed her by the arm and pulled her, pushed Posie off the street and into the quiet of the park.

'—parents.'

Except it wasn't 'we'. It was her.

Or was it? Josh had said he had gone through Michael's papers last night. What had he found? What had made him warn her that she was bottom of the heap?

'Do you know what guardianship arrangements Michael made for Posie?' Because a man who'd taken time to plan his own funeral to make things easy for whoever was left to pick of pieces in the event of his death wouldn't leave something really important like that to chance. 'Stupid question. Of *course* you know. You're his executor. Even when you weren't talking to him, Michael still told you everything.'

'I can't tell you anything until I've spoken to Michael's lawyers.'

He let go of her arm, leaving a cold empty space, but that was what he always did. Went away. University, gap year, for ever. He leaned forward over the buggy, tenderly tucking the blanket around Posie where she'd kicked it loose in her sleep, then began to move on through the park.

'Can't? Or won't?' she demanded, planting her feet, refusing to take another step until he gave her an answer. 'What is it you're keeping from me?'

He stopped. 'It won't help.'

'I think I'm the best judge of what helps me, Josh.'

He glanced at her. 'You're wrong about Michael telling me everything. He didn't share whatever decision he'd made with me, which suggests there were unresolved issues.'

'I think we can both guess what they were.'

He shrugged. 'Maybe. There was some correspondence with his lawyer regarding the surrogacy and it's clear that Michael and Phoebe intended to draw up new wills once Posie was legally theirs, but as far as I can tell nothing had been signed.'

'So that means…?' She lifted her shoulders.

'I won't know for sure until I've talked to the lawyer. Even a draft setting out their wishes would be something.' He stretched out a hand. 'Come on. The sooner I get there, the sooner we'll both know where we stand.'

He didn't move to take her hand as he had before. This time he waited for her to choose, to meet him halfway. And, ignoring his hand, she tucked her own back under his arm. A gesture of trust.

'Maybe I should come with you.'

'You can trust me, Grace. I'll look after your interests. You'll be better occupied at the craft centre.'

'But…'

'As soon as I'm done, I'll join you. Once we know what we're faced with, we can talk it through. Make decisions.'

It made sense, she supposed. Then, as another thought struck her, 'Will you tell him? About Posie? About…' She swallowed. There was something so intimate about the fact that they'd created a baby together—even though they had been at opposite ends of the earth when it had happened—that she couldn't quite bring herself to say the words. Couldn't bring herself to say *us*.

'About our involvement in Posie's conception?' he filled in for her.

Involvement.

Good word. If you wanted to eradicate any suggestion of intimacy. And why not? There had only been one night of us and while for her it had been the only night, he had been the only one, she had no illusions that he'd spent the last ten years dreaming of her. That dream had been shattered the day he'd turned up with a beautiful young woman and announced they'd stopped over in Bali on their way to England and got married.

'That would be the involvement you just announced to a street full of people?'

Her hand flew to her mouth. 'I didn't!'

'I'm paraphrasing, but "…there's a baby that you and I made…" just about covers it.'

She groaned.

'Relax. Most people just wanted to get away from the mad woman as fast as they could.'

'You're just saying that to make me feel better.'

'No. I swear. At least three people crossed the street.'

'Only three?' She shook her head, but she was smiling.

'That's better. And, to answer your question, I don't think there's anything to be gained by telling him about us and robbing Phoebe and Michael of something they'd longed for with such a passion. It's nobody's business but ours, Grace.'

Ours. Us.

Josh savoured the words, drinking them in like a man who'd been wandering in the desert.

He'd locked himself out of Grace's life a long time ago. He hadn't fully understood why she'd been trapped like a fledgling, too scared to fly the nest that Phoebe and Michael had made for her. He'd accepted that it was somehow mixed up with her childhood, but he'd never pushed her to explain.

Maybe he hadn't wanted to, preferring to tell himself that it was for the best, that she'd have slowed him down, instead of being honest with himself. Facing his own demons.

But those two tiny words—*ours, us*—like the infant who'd dropped off to sleep in the buggy, joined them in a unique alliance that set them apart from the rest of the world. They were a family.

He was a father and that was a responsibility he couldn't run away from.

They reached the corner where their ways divided but, instead of parting, they stood, her hand linking them together, and for a moment it seemed that she was as reluctant as him to break the connection.

He was on the point of suggesting that perhaps, after all, she should go with him to talk to Michael's lawyer, when she finally took her arm from his and said, 'I'd better let you go.'

He caught her hand. 'We're in this together, Grace.'

'Are we?'

'I'll do whatever it takes to protect Phoebe and Michael. I owe them that.'

'And Posie?'

'I'll protect her with my life.'

As he would Grace. He couldn't begin to guess how hard this was going to be for her. Desperate with worry about the future of a child who she had never, whether she'd admit it or not, truly given up, when she should be left in peace to grieve for her sister.

'This is all my fault,' she said. 'If I hadn't—'

'Don't!' He'd done everything he could to prevent her from having this baby, prevent himself from becoming a father, but he couldn't bear to hear her put what he'd wished into words. Not now he'd held Posie, seen her smile. 'Please, don't do that to yourself.'

Or to him.

She lifted her stricken face.

'But it's true. I wanted them to go away for the weekend, planned it, gave it to them as my treat because I wanted to have Posie to myself. Just for the weekend. Only for the weekend…'

Oh, dear God. It wasn't colluding with Phoebe that was tormenting her. She was blaming herself for the accident.

'No,' he said. And, when she would have argued, he said it again. 'No. It's always like this when someone dies,' he said. 'The guilt kicks in. You can only think of the things you did wrong. Or didn't do at all,' he added, thinking of his own miserable, selfish response to something that had made his brother so happy. 'They can overwhelm you, take on an importance completely out of proportion to their true meaning.'

She shook her head.

'You have to remember the good things. Remember how happy you made them both.' He squeezed her arm reassuringly, then touched the sleeping baby's head. 'I'll see you both later,' he said, taking a step back, saving the picture of the two of them in his mind before tearing himself away.

Grace unlocked the door to her workshop, kicking aside the mail so that she could get the buggy in, turning on the lights.

She'd expanded from her original tiny workroom, moving into this wonderful airy space when it had become vacant a couple of years ago.

She'd kept the walls and furnishings a stark black and white to accentuate the vivid colours of her jewellery. At one end there was a secure walk-in storage space for the basic tools of her trade and a tiny office. There was her working area, with her drawing board and the workbench where she put together her designs.

The centre of the room offered a display area for photographs of some of the special pieces she'd made, as well as the dramatic spiral stands that Toby had designed and made to display examples of her work.

There was a comfortable seating area for clients who came to discuss special commissions and at the far end was another long workbench where she worked with the students who took her classes.

She didn't waste time going through the mail, but put it to one side to take home with her. Instead, she made the most of the fact that Posie was asleep to download and pack up the Internet orders for beads, findings, the jewellery kits that kept the cash flow ticking over.

After that she called Abby, a stay-at-home mum who'd taken one of her classes and proved to be one of her most talented students. She was happy to come in for a few hours a day for the next couple of weeks and, while Grace was waiting for her to arrive so that she could walk her through the Web site ordering systems, she took the armature for the tiara she'd designed from the workroom, the tray with the teardrop pearls and each size and colour of semi-precious stone she would use, counted and placed in individual compartments. Then, with the deceptively simple design in front of her, she began to build the sparkling fairy tale confection that a young bride would wear on the most special day of her life.

When, finally, it was finished, she sat back and looked at it, glad she'd come here. Glad she'd done something positive. Something life-affirming.

Posie, who'd been an angel and had slept while she'd worked, finally woke and began to make her presence felt.

'Well, haven't you been a good baby,' she said, as she lifted her bag from the carrier and plugged in her bottle-warmer before changing her.

She was just about to settle on the sofa in the customer area, when there was a tap at the door.

Josh would have just walked in despite the 'closed' sign

on the door and, expecting it to be Abby, she called out, 'It's open.' Then, as she realised it was neither, she said, 'Oh, Toby…'

Her disappointment must have been evident because he didn't come beyond the doorway.

'I know you're not open but I saw your light on and I thought I'd come over and see if there was anything you need. If it's a bad time…'

Toby Makepeace restored and made bespoke rocking horses across the cobbled yard of what had once been a huge coaching inn, but had long since been converted into craft workshops and small boutiques. He was easy to get along with and she'd taken him home as her 'date' the last time Josh had come home on a proper visit.

Still trying to prove to him, or maybe just to herself, that he didn't mean anything to her. No, definitely to herself. He hadn't given her a thought a minute after he'd left her sleeping in his bed.

Toby, unlike her other 'dates', had quickly cottoned on to the reason for his presence and had played his part to the hilt. Michael had teased her about him for weeks afterwards, referring to him as her 'lovelorn swain' until Phoebe had finally told him to stop embarrassing her.

Had Phoebe seen, understood more than she had ever let on? She had never said anything, but she'd never pressed her about boyfriends, either. She'd never remarked on the fact, that despite the fact that Grace had always said she was too busy to get involved, she had always managed to have a date when Josh had come home.

It must have been blindingly obvious, now she came to think about it. Bless Phoebe…

Toby had laughed when she had told him and it had somehow cemented a genuine friendship and he had been the first person she'd thought of when she'd needed help at the hospital.

'No,' she said, 'it's never a bad time to see a friend. I don't think I ever thanked you properly for what you did.'

'Don't even think about it,' Toby said, closing the door, coming across and giving her a hug. Leaving his hand on her arm. It was no more than a gesture of comfort from a friend, but it was where Josh's hand had so recently lain. It felt so much like an intrusion that it took all her concentration not to pull away. 'Anything I can do, you know you only have to ask.'

'Actually, I'm just about to feed Posie. If you really want to make yourself useful, you could put on a pot of coffee.'

Posie, growing impatient, began to whimper.

'Poor little angel,' Toby said, touching a finger lightly to her cheek before taking himself off to fill the coffee-maker. 'But at least she's still got her real mummy to take care of her.'

Grace sighed. There really was no point in explaining the finer points of surrogacy. She supposed most people would think that. She'd thought it herself until Josh had put her straight. She glanced at her watch. It had been more than an hour since they'd gone their separate ways.

What on earth could be taking so long?

Nothing good, she was sure. But there was nothing she could do about it now and she crossed to the sofa, settled herself in the corner against the arm and offered Posie the bottle. She sucked for a moment, then pulled away.

'What's up, sweetpea? I thought you were hungry.' She offered her the bottle again and this time she seemed to settle.

'Do these need posting?' Toby said, distracting her.

'Sorry?'

'These packages,' he said, nodding towards the pile of padded envelopes on her desk as he spooned coffee in the filter. 'I'm going that way at lunch time. I'll drop them in at the post office if you like.'

'Oh, right. Yes. That would be a huge help,' she said, seizing on his offer. 'If you're sure.'

'I wouldn't offer if I didn't mean it.'

'You're a brick. Pass me my bag and I'll give you some money.' Then, 'They all need to be sent "signed for",' she apologised as she handed over the notes.

'No problem,' he said, tucking the money into his back pocket before sitting beside her. 'It'll mean all the more time to chat up that dark-haired girl behind the counter.'

'Sarah?' She smiled. 'Good choice. She's absolutely lovely. So how long has that been going on?'

He shrugged. 'I've been taking my post to her about twice a week since she started there.'

'And that would be what—five, six months?'

'I thought I'd take it slowly.'

'Er… No. That's not slow, Toby. That's pathetic. Why don't you just ask her out?'

'Because, if she said no, sheer embarrassment would mean I'd have to go all the way into town to the main post office whenever I wanted a stamp.'

Grace clucked like a chicken and he laughed. 'I know, it's pathetic. But the main post office is a mile away.' Then, as Posie spat out the bottle again and began to grizzle, he said, 'What's the matter with her?'

'It's my fault. I usually wear something of Phoebe's when I feed her,' Grace replied. 'For the scent,' she explained. 'But I didn't think to bring anything with me.' She slipped a couple of buttons on her shirt. 'Maybe this will help. Phoebe used to hold her next to her skin.'

'As if she were breastfeeding?'

'What do you know about it?' she asked, laughing.

'I've got sisters,' he said. 'And sisters-in-law. Half a dozen of them. I've lost count of the number of nieces and nephews I have.'

'Right. Well, if I need any advice I'll know where to come,' she said, pushing aside her shirt a little and holding the baby close so that her cheek was against her skin. Drawn by the warmth, Posie immediately turned towards her and, after a moment or two, took the rubber teat of the feeder.

'That's so beautiful,' he said.

'Oh, Toby…'

And when, without warning, her eyes stung with tears that she could do nothing about, he put his arm around her, pulling her against his shoulder so that her tears soaked into his sleeve.

'I'm sorry,' she said. 'This is stupid.' She didn't even know what she was crying about. Phoebe and Michael. Posie. Josh…

Maybe all of them.

'It's okay,' he said. 'Go ahead. Let it out. It'll do you good.'

He still had his arm around her when the door opened and Josh walked in, coming to an abrupt halt at the sight of the three of them.

For a moment no one said anything, then Toby murmured, just loud enough for him to hear, 'I'm sorry, Grace, I thought I'd locked the door.'

The shock on Josh's face at finding her with Toby's arm around her was very nearly as ridiculous as her own sense of guilt.

She had nothing to feel guilty about.

Toby was a friend—he'd been there when Josh had been communing with his guilt up a mountain.

But Josh was clearly reading something a lot more significant into the situation. And why wouldn't he, when she'd gone to such lengths to convince him that she was involved with the man?

But enough was enough and she pulled free of his arm, rubbing her palm across her wet cheek. 'Haven't you got an urgent date with the post office, Toby?' she reminded him before he completely forgot himself.

'You're going to throw me out before I have a cup of that

fabulous coffee I've made for you?' he said, apparently determined to give Josh a reprise of his 'lovelorn swain' act.

'Abby will be here when you get back with the receipts,' she said, cutting him off before he could get going. 'Buy her a cake and I'm sure she'll take the hint. My treat.' Then, 'Buy two,' she said meaningfully.

'Two?'

'A red velvet cupcake is supposed to be irresistible,' she said.

'Got it,' he murmured, finally getting to his feet. Then, as he made a move, she put her hand on his arm, detaining him. 'Thanks for the shoulder.'

'Any time,' he said, covering her hand with his own, kissing her cheek, going for an Oscar. 'Anything.' Then, touching his finger to Posie's cheek. 'Bye, baby. Be good for Grace.'

Then, gathering the packages from her desk, he headed for the door, where Josh was blocking his way.

'Makepeace,' Josh said, his acknowledgement curt to the point of rudeness.

'Kingsley,' he responded mildly. 'I was sorry to hear about your brother. I liked him a lot.' The mildness was deceptive. If he'd actually said, *'Unlike you…'* he couldn't have made himself plainer. 'We missed you at his funeral.'

Josh said nothing, merely stepped aside to let him out, then closed the door after him and slipped the catch.

CHAPTER SEVEN

'I'M EXPECTING someone,' Grace protested.

'Whoever it is will knock,' Josh replied, crossing to the coffee pot. He turned over a couple of cups, opened the fridge. 'There's no milk. Shall I call back your gallant and ask him to bring you a carton?'

Gallant.

It was marginally better than 'lovelorn swain', she supposed. But only marginally.

'Don't bother for me,' she said, and he poured two cups of black coffee and placed them on the low table set in front of the sofa.

'You were a lot longer than I expected,' she said, glancing up at him as Posie spit out the teat, with a finality that suggested that any further attempt to persuade her to take any more would be a waste of time. 'What took you so long?'

'There was a lot to go through, but clearly I needn't have worried that you'd be lonely.'

Feeling trapped on the sofa, Grace got up, lifted the baby to her shoulder and, gently rubbing her back, began to pace.

'I didn't realise you and Toby Makepeace were still a hot item.'

Hot?

Hardly…

'When Toby saw the light, he came over to see if there was anything he could do, Josh. It's what friends do.'

'Yes, I got the "any time, anything" message. Including the shoulder to cry on,' he said, as she turned and came face to face with him. 'You'll forgive my surprise. I had assumed you were, momentarily, unattached.'

He invested 'momentarily' with more than its usual weight, bringing a flush to her wet cheeks, drawing quite unnecessary attention to them.

Josh produced a clean handkerchief and, taking her chin in his hand, he gently blotted first her eyes, then her cheeks, before unbuttoning one of the pockets on her thin silk shirt and tucking it against her breast.

She opened her mouth but no words came and she closed it again. Then jumped as he carefully refastened the buttons she had slipped open for Posie, her entire body trembling as the warmth of his fingers shot like an electric charge to her heart.

'Don't...' was all she could manage. 'Please.'

It was too painful. Too sweet...

He let his hands drop, stepping away from her, and it took all she had not to scream out a desperate, *No...*, because that felt wrong, too.

'In view of the fact that you were carrying a baby for Phoebe,' he continued calmly, as if nothing had happened. As if he hadn't just touched her, switching her on as easily as if he'd flipped a light switch, undoing, in a moment, ten years of keeping all her feelings battened down.

She stared at him, uncomprehending, having entirely lost the thread of what he was saying.

'I don't imagine there are many men who could handle that. Not even Toby Makepeace.'

Toby. The surrogacy...

Got it.

'Actually, you might be surprised. There are surrogates who, having completed their own families, want to help childless couples achieve their own dreams. They're fully supported by their partners.'

She'd done her homework, knew the answers without having to think.

'And is that what your friend Makepeace did? Support you?'

'Friend' was loaded, too.

Okay. Hands up. She was the one who'd gone out of her way to give Josh the impression, over the years, that she had a continuous string of boyfriends. Not that he'd taken much interest on his flying visits.

It was as if, after their one night together, he'd totally wiped her from his mind. As if the minute their relationship had changed from friendship to intimacy she'd become just like any other girl he'd ever dated.

Just like the girls she'd once almost pitied because she'd always known he was going to leave the minute he had his degree in his pocket.

Dispensable.

Which made it doubly surprising that he'd remembered Toby's name. They'd only met once as far as she was aware.

'Well,' she said, 'on the plus side, he didn't arrive in the middle of the night like some avenging angel, demanding that I stop being such a fool. Does that answer your question?' Then, tired of playing games, 'I have no idea how Toby felt about Posie, Josh. I didn't discuss what I was doing with him. It was none of his business.'

'That's pretty much what you said to me a year ago.'

'I didn't know…'

Her mouth dried and, suddenly afraid, she held Posie a little more tightly because it had everything to do with him. Maybe, then, if she hadn't responded with outraged anger, but had taken the time to sit down, listen, he might, despite his sworn promise to Michael, have told her the truth.

'You should have told me.'

'What would that have achieved? You were already pregnant.' Then, 'You're quite sure that Posie is mine?'

'What?' That was so far from what she'd been thinking that Grace took an involuntary step back, stumbling against one of the chairs at the work table.

As Posie let out a startled cry, Josh reached out for her and steadied her, then laid his palm against Posie's head, calming her, giving Grace a chance to catch her breath.

'Is she?' he repeated, so intently that she knew without doubt that he wanted it to be so. That, despite his opposition, despite everything, he desperately wanted this little girl to be his child. For a moment it felt as if the world had truly been made over. But the joy swiftly faded into something closer to fear.

Her mother had warned her. *"He seems attached."*

For ten years she'd been living in a fantasy world in which Josh Kingsley was her hero, the boy she'd fallen in love with. But what did she know about the man he'd become? At home he was just Josh, but in the real world he was a power to be reckoned with. A man who'd built an empire from nothing. Who'd broken her heart when he'd brought home a laughing bride, then on his next visit announced, without apparent emotion, that the marriage had been a mistake. A man who other men treated with respect and, maybe, fear. A man who saw only the prize…

She'd wanted him to bond with Posie and, against all the odds, it seemed that he had. Now, too late, she realised that it was not his mother, or hers, who she'd have to fight to keep her baby. It was him.

'I've only your word for that, Josh,' she said, crossing to the buggy and tucking Posie in, fastening her safely, freeing herself for the fight before turning to face him. 'It never occurred to me to doubt you, but maybe we'd both be easier in our minds if we had a DNA test.'

'What? No…'

Not the answer he'd expected, she noted with a glimmer of satisfaction as he took a step towards her.

Her feet wanted to take another step back, keep a safe distance between them, but her head demanded she hold her ground. One step could be put down to shock. Two looked like retreat and this was a moment for standing her ground.

'Just in case Michael came to his senses,' she continued, as if he hadn't spoken. 'That would let you off the hook, wouldn't it?'

She knew that wasn't what he'd meant, but the alternative was too shocking to deserve acknowledgement.

'You made it very clear that you were simply going through the motions to keep him happy,' she said. 'That an actual baby was the last thing you'd anticipated or wanted, and I can understand why you wanted to put a stop to it…'

She faltered, stopped, hearing what she was saying and realising that it wasn't true. She didn't understand. Worse, she was still pretending, still hiding, protecting herself from hurt. But this was more important than her feelings. More important than his.

Overwhelmed by a heart-pounding rush of anger at his selfishness, she said, 'Actually, no, I can't imagine why you'd be that cruel, but then I do have a heart.'

The raw slash of colour that darkened Josh's cheekbones was a warning that she'd gone too far, but she discovered that she didn't give a damn. He'd just insulted her beyond reason and she wasn't going to stand there and take it.

'Unless,' she continued with a reckless disregard for the consequences, 'you really think that I'd cheat my sister, foist a child conceived out of careless passion rather than a clinical donation on a couple so desperate that they would have done anything, even lied to the person they loved most in the world—'

If she'd hit him the effect couldn't have been more dramatic.

'No!' he said, and it was too late to step back as he surged forward, seized her, his fingers biting into her arms. 'No!'

'No what?' she demanded, meeting his fury head-on and refusing to be intimidated, refusing to back down. She owed it to Posie, owed it to herself, to stand up to him.

'No what?' she repeated, when he just stood there, staring at her as if he'd never seen her before. Well, he hadn't. Not like this. Empowered by motherhood and ready to take on the world.

He took a shuddering breath that seemed to come from deep within his soul and then, never taking his eyes off her, said, 'No. I don't need a DNA test. No. I don't want to be let off the hook. No. I don't believe you'd lie to me…' He broke away, as if he couldn't bear to look at her. 'I'm sorry, but when I saw you with Makepeace, his arm around you, you looked like a family and it just all seemed to make perfect sense…'

He looked so utterly wretched and where a moment before she'd been angry, now she didn't know what to think. She only knew what she felt. Grief. Confusion. Fear at the enormous responsibility for a precious life.

And maybe part of her anger was because she suspected he'd been right when he'd accused her of being too scared to risk a relationship, move on, make a life away from the safety of Phoebe and Michael's home.

Had pining after him been the safe option?

'Josh?'

The muscles in his jaw were working as he clamped down to hold back the tears and in a heartbeat the tables were turned. She could weep, but he was a man. Faced with loss, all he could do was get angry, lash out.

He was grieving, too, and just as he'd reached out to her that moment when she'd woken in the kitchen, now she reached out to him.

'I know,' she said, lifting her hand to his face, feeling the silkiness of the close-cut beard against her palm, the bone that moulded the face she knew as well as her own. Every mark, every tiny dint that life had put into it. The creases that bracketed his mouth when he smiled. The white fan of lines around his eyes where the sun never quite reached. The thin scar on his forehead where he'd fallen as a child. 'It's okay to cry.'

And, laying her cheek against his heart, she wrapped her arms around his chest and held him close.

'You're frightened and that's okay. I understand. I'm frightened, too.'

Josh, crushing her to him, didn't think there was a snowball's chance in hell that she understood one damn thing about what he was feeling. She had never understood and why would she when he'd never told her?

She would never know how he'd felt when he'd come home after that first year, expecting to find her waiting for him, green eyes sparkling, the way she'd always been there. Knowing that he'd let her down.

He'd spent the first week away expecting a call from Michael, hauling him back to face up to what he'd done. When that hadn't happened he'd known that Grace had protected him and that had made him feel even worse.

He'd tried to write, but had been unable to write the words he knew she'd want. But he couldn't stay away for ever and he'd known that she'd be waiting for him, eyes shining with that look he hadn't been able to get out of his head. The look in her eyes when he'd kissed her, undressed her, taken her. It was a 'forever' look. A look that would hook a man, haul him in, nail him down, because a decent man couldn't walk away from a look like that. Not from a girl like Grace.

But she hadn't been home when he had pitched up after twenty-four hours travelling with a ring weighing down his pocket. And when she had eventually turned up, only just in time for dinner, she was not alone, but had brought a boyfriend home with her and those sparkling green eyes had been only for him.

And that had been worse. He'd wanted to grab the guy, beat him to a pulp, then drag Grace down to the basement and make love to her until that look was back in her eyes, but only for him.

And better. Because that selfish gene had been consumed with relief.

Relief, as she'd listened to what he'd been doing with less than half an ear, had won. He could relax, knowing that what had happened between them had meant nothing more than a rite of passage for a girl eager to become a woman.

That she hadn't been sitting around waiting for him to come back and claim her, but had moved on from the jewellery stall and, with Michael's help, had rented a small space at the craft centre, had started her own small jewellery-making business. Had her own tiny van to take her to craft fairs.

Had found someone new, someone closer to home, to share her days and nights with.

That night he'd tossed the ring into the rubbish bin in the tiny basement bathroom, cut short his visit, flown back to his new life. Had found his own substitute for Grace. Lovely blonde, blue-eyed Jessie, who'd had him standing in front of a registrar in the blink of her silky lashes. Jessie, who'd realised her mistake and left him just as quickly. Jessie, now happily married to someone who appreciated her, whose face he could barely remember, while Grace…

She didn't understand but, wrapped like this in her arms, drowning in the warm scent of her, a wisp of hair tickling his chin, he wasn't about to argue with her.

'You're tired. Grieving. In shock,' she said.

No. She hadn't a clue…

'And,' she said, lifting her head to look up at him, her clear green eyes demanding nothing less than the truth, 'I suspect you've got bad news for me.'

'Not bad.' He hadn't thought so, but maybe she'd see it differently. He continued to hold her, meeting her unwavering gaze.

'But not good.'

'Mixed,' he said. 'It was pretty much as I thought. Michael instructed his lawyer to draw up new wills for them both. There were some bequests, but the bulk was left to Posie.'

'That's what I expected,' she said impatiently. 'Tell me the rest.'

'His lawyer had advised naming a guardian for Posie and Michael named me without consulting Phoebe.'

'Because you were her biological father.'

'He didn't tell me about the guardianship, Grace, I swear it. I imagine he thought I'd never know, but it must have seemed to him to be the right thing to do. And maybe he hoped that Phoebe would accept that, as his executor, it made sense.'

'But she didn't.'

'How could she?' He wanted her to know that he understood. 'She apparently blew up in the office, reminding Michael, with every justification, that I had been anything but supportive. That you had given birth to Posie.'

'And?' Then, when he couldn't bring himself to say the words, 'Tell me, Josh!'

'Joint custody was suggested as a compromise, but she just said that with us living on opposite sides of the world that was ridiculous. She didn't stay to argue, but left, leaving Michael to wrap up the meeting.'

'So nothing's been settled? It's all still in the air? Open season on Posie?'

'No…' Then, again, 'No. Michael—because you know how loose ends drove him crazy, how he liked everything to be just so—signed his own will, just a temporary measure until they'd talked it through, before he followed her.'

It took a moment for exactly what that meant to sink in and then she said, 'Oh, dear God.' He caught her as her legs crumpled beneath her, held her, but, before he could reassure her, she said, 'She told him, didn't she? That's why they left the hotel so early.' She looked up at him, her face stricken. 'Why Michael went off the road.'

'No—'

'Yes! He was always so careful, but the police said that he was driving close to the limit on a winding country road. That he couldn't have seen the mud slick that had run off the fields onto the road until it was too late.'

'You can't know that, Grace!'

'They set out before breakfast and I thought it was just because they were so eager to get home. At least I had the comfort of believing they were happy, excited at coming back to their baby, but if she'd told him…'

'Please, Grace, don't do this to yourself.'

'If he'd told her, Josh.' She shook her head as if to drive the desperate thoughts from her mind. 'What state would they both have been in?'

'Maybe they were relieved. Happy that they didn't have any more secrets. Maybe they just wanted to get home so that they could tell you that.' He thought about the calls he'd ignored on his BlackBerry. Had Michael called him, thinking that if everyone knew the truth, he'd be okay with it? 'Listen to me, Grace,' he said, grasping her by the shoulders, shaking her. 'Look at me.'

She obeyed, raising lashes clumped with the tears she'd shed, eyes stricken with grief that tore at his heart.

'Whatever happened is not your fault. You gave them

what they wanted most in the world. We both did what we thought was best.'

'Damned with good intentions.'

She rubbed her hand across her cheek, glancing at it in surprise when it came away dry, then straightened, took a step back and, breaking free, said, 'Well, at least you'll have your daughter to console you.'

'Posie is our daughter, Grace. Yours and mine.'

'You keep saying that, but you'll be the one to make all the decisions about her future. To say where she lives. Who looks after her.'

'Phoebe wanted you to take care of her. I want that, too.'

He saw a flash of hope brighten her eyes. 'Then give me custody, Josh,' she begged. 'As her guardian you can do that, can't you?'

'Yes,' he said, 'but—'

'You could come and see her whenever you want,' she said. 'She could even come and visit you when she's—'

'I could,' he said, cutting her off before she betrayed exactly how little she thought of his ability to make an emotional commitment. 'But I won't.'

He turned to look at Posie, who was watching the spangle of lights spinning across the ceiling, making excited little sounds as she reached up to catch the colours.

He'd been thinking about her ever since the lawyer had told him that Michael had left her in his care.

He'd been so sure that he was going to be able to hand her over to Grace. Put in flying visits, offer advice, be there for them both when they needed him. But basically keeping his distance.

But Michael had wanted him involved, had wanted his little girl to know her father. And as he'd walked back to Grace's workshop it was Posie's smile as she'd grabbed for his beard, her warm baby smell, the joyful way that she stretched for each new sight, experience that had filled his head and he'd known that.

'I'm the only father that Posie is ever going to have and she deserves more than that from me.' He turned to look at Grace, white-faced at the bluntness of his refusal, her hand to her mouth. 'From us.'

CHAPTER EIGHT

GRACE watched him cross to the buggy and crouch beside Posie, catch her tiny hand, hooking it in one of his long fingers—strong, darkly tanned against her pale pink, almost transparent skin. The baby noises grew more excited as she grasped it tightly, kicking her little feet as she smiled up at him.

'This is something we have to do together,' he said. Then, looking back at her when she didn't respond, 'You know I'm right.'

'Do I?'

'Of course you do. You want what I want.'

Grace stared at him.

'Are you sure about that? You never wanted her, Josh. You never wanted children at all. Remember?'

She did. Remembered, as if it were yesterday, the day he'd heard that his father's new wife had given him a baby daughter and he'd said, "…another kid for him to let down…" That no way, never was he going there….

Easy to dismiss as the angry response of a hurting youth, but he'd never changed.

For a moment their eyes met and she saw he was remembering that moment, too.

'It's easy to say you don't want them, Grace, but Posie isn't some faceless baby. She's real.' Then, with a catch in his throat, 'She's mine….'

Grace swallowed, unable to bear the raw love with which he was looking at Posie.

'I'm so sorry, Josh. You never bargained for this.'

'No? The minute I spilled my seed into a plastic cup it was always a possibility. What I hadn't bargained on was the emotional backlash. I told myself that it was anger that kept me away. I'd signed up for Michael's deal with my eyes open, but he'd changed the rules and I'd been used. That you'd been used, too…' He bent and kissed the tiny fingers. 'I clung to that through nine long months, clung to it when she was born, when I ignored Michael's plea to come and stand as her godfather.'

'You convinced us,' she said, a touch shakily.

'Fooled you. Fooled myself. The truth, Grace, is that I knew that if I saw her, I'd never be able to leave her. Let her go. I'd have fought Michael, Phoebe, even you, to keep her.'

'Are you going to fight me now?'

He took one long look at the baby and then rose to his feet. 'I hope not. I want us to be partners in this, not adversaries.'

'How can we? Phoebe was right. You're in Australia, I'm here. Unless you really do expect me to give up everything I have here, come to Australia and be Posie's nanny.'

'You're her mother, Grace. I wouldn't insult you with anything so crude.'

'I'm sorry.' Then, when he didn't elaborate, 'So? What did you have in mind?'

'I told you. A partnership. As Michael and Phoebe's executor it's my responsibility to interpret their wishes.'

'But…'

'We know what they wanted individually. But if they'd both been in full possession of the facts I know that Michael would have wanted you, that Phoebe would have wanted me to be fully involved in her life.'

Grace frowned, trying to make sense of what he was saying, then, giving up, she said, 'The obvious solution is that I keep Posie. You visit any time you like. Move your headquarters to Maybridge if you want to be a full-time father. The world's a global village these days, so everyone says.' Then, when he didn't answer, 'How much simpler can it get?'

'You think that would be simple?'

She shook her head. 'Of course not, but we've established that we both want the same thing. The rest is just details.'

'Not quite. For a start you're assuming that you'll be able to stay in Michael and Phoebe's house.'

'It's Posie's house,' she reminded him. 'Isn't that what you said?'

'The house is part of Michael's estate. It will have to be valued for probate purposes. I'm not up to date with the property market in this area but I do know that prices have rocketed since Michael bought it fifteen years ago. It's certainly going to be in the seven figure bracket.'

'Over two million. One very like it, a couple of doors down, sold last month.'

'Well, that makes it inevitable. Apart from the fact that it's a very large house for just the two of you, with big running costs that would have to come out of the estate, the likelihood is that it will have to be sold to cover inheritance tax.'

'But it's her home,' Grace repeated, bewildered by this sudden turn of events.

'No, it's your home,' he said, but not unkindly. 'Posie's not four months old, Grace. I don't imagine she's likely to notice where she's living for quite some time, do you? Only who she's living with.'

She swallowed down her protest, knowing that he was right. 'What else?' she asked, knowing that there had to be more.

'I'll set up a Trust with the residue to provide adequate

funds to care for Posie, pay for her education, provide all her needs, just as Michael and Phoebe would have done.'

'That's just money. Things. Tell me about the important stuff. About who'll hold her when she cries, who'll take her to ballet lessons, hold her hand on her first day at school. I'll be there, but where will you be?'

'Grace…'

'No! I've heard you say a dozen times that you practically live out of a suitcase. Even if you move your office to Maybridge, you'll never be here.'

'You think I can't change?'

'I think you might mean to,' she said. 'I'm sure you'd try. But how long do you really think changing nappies will be enough? How long before the horizon calls? Can Posie's first step compete with that? Her first word? And what happens when she's sick and you're off somewhere communing with a mountain? You're talking about a partnership, but what's the split? Not fifty-fifty, that's for sure.'

'Is that what you're offering?'

'That's my point, Josh. I can't offer anything. I don't have any rights, remember? You hold all the cards.'

'I could change that.'

'Oh…' The fact that he'd actually been thinking that far ahead took the wind right out of her sails. 'How?'

'Very simply. We'll get married, officially adopt Posie so that we have equal rights as her parents. Fifty-fifty,' he said with a wry smile. 'That is what you wanted?'

Grace felt her heart stop.

Marriage? He was proposing till-death-us-do-part, in-sickness-and-in-health, for-ever-and-ever *marriage*?

Everything that she wanted in one package. Josh, Posie… Except, of course, it wasn't and slowly her heart began to beat again.

'That's a huge commitment just to give me what I want, Josh. As her guardian you could simply put her in my care.'

'I could, but that way neither of us would have any real security.'

She frowned. 'What do you think I'd do, Josh? Run away with her?'

'No, of course not.'

'Then what?' she demanded.

'You might meet someone.'

'Someone?' Then, 'If this is about Toby—'

'No. You told me it's over and I believe you, but it's hardly beyond the bounds of possibility that you'll meet some decent man who'll become part of your life and when that happens, it's inevitable that he'll become the father figure in my daughter's life.'

Then stay with me....

The cry from her heart went unheard, unanswered, as he continued, 'I accept everything you say, Grace. Even if I wanted to, I can't shed my responsibilities just like that. Any change is going to take time and, besides, Posie has had enough disruption in her short life. She needs you.'

Far from delight at getting exactly what she wanted, all she felt was a dull ache at this confirmation that when he said marriage, he did indeed simply mean a partnership, but what choice did she have?

'It's going to take a few weeks to sort things out here, too, Josh. Wind up my business.' Then, trying to make a joke of it, 'Maybe you'd better marry me before you go, just in case I get swept off my feet before we join you in Sydney.'

'Join me?' He looked stunned. 'Would you do even that for Posie?' he said, taking her chin in his hand, lifting her face so that she could not avoid amber and grey eyes that were unexpectedly tender.

Not for Posie. For him....

'Australia is just another island, Josh. It's just bigger than the Isle of Man and you have to cross more sea to reach it....'

A shiver ran through her at the thought, but if that was the only way that Posie could be with her father, the only way Josh could be near his daughter, then, for the two people she loved most in the world, she would do it without another thought.

'No.' Josh's response was abrupt and his hand dropped to his side. 'I'm not asking you to uproot yourself. Leave everything you know.'

'Only marry you.'

That wiped the tenderness from his eyes.

'Only that,' he said. 'In return for your freedom, I'll buy Michael's house from his estate so that you and Posie can stay there.'

He'd buy the house? Just like that? Without having to even think about it?

'And you? Where will you be, Josh?'

When his baby was crying in the night.

When she was alone...

'At work, like any other father,' he replied. 'As you were quick to remind me, I've got commitments that I can't walk away from, but I'll spend as much time in Maybridge as I can, so keep the bed in the basement flat aired.'

Which answered any questions she had about what kind of marriage he had in mind. Could she live with that? Could he? Living on the other side of the world, did he intend to?

'What happens if I tell you to take your partnership and stick it on the wall?'

'She's my child, too, Grace,' he said, not taking the offence she'd intended. 'I'm prepared to do what's necessary so that you can keep her, but I will be part of her life.'

'In other words, if I don't agree I'll have to fight you for custody.'

'You can try.' He tilted one dark brow. 'Do you think you can afford it?'

'Don't you dare threaten me, Josh Kingsley! Phoebe wanted me to take care of Posie. You know that. Michael's lawyer knows it, too.'

'He knows they were going to talk about it. There's nothing in writing,' he pointed out. 'And the last thing Michael did was sign his will, which suggests that, whatever his wife thought on the subject, he was absolutely clear in his own mind.'

'But he didn't know the truth!'

'Whose fault is that?'

She looked away. Not his. And he was right, she didn't have a case. She'd embarked on a surrogate pregnancy with the sworn intention of giving her baby to her sister. Clear evidence that she had no attachment. And Josh could, if she chose to make a fight of it, make it look as if she was clinging to the baby not just as a free meal ticket, but for the roof over her head.

He wasn't threatening her. He didn't need to. He was simply telling it like it was. And what, after all, was he asking of her? Nothing that she'd hadn't, in her deepest heart, wished for with every fibre of her being. To be his wife.

There was a saying.

Be careful what you wish for.

She managed a careless shrug. 'Well, I suppose a paper marriage is just about one step up from being offered a job as her nanny.'

'You don't have the qualifications to be a nanny, Grace. Marry me and you'll keep your baby, keep your home.'

This was surreal, Grace thought. If they were total strangers, it couldn't be any colder.

Grace had scarcely expected him to go down on one knee, declare undying love, but as a proposal of marriage this lacked just about everything.

'That's it?'

'Would you like me to dress it up with fancy words?'

She shook her head. 'No. It's just a business transaction so we'd better keep it plain and honest.' And, since they were being blunt, she said, 'I imagine you'll want the protection of a pre-nuptial agreement?'

'Imagine again. This isn't a short-term contract. We might be on opposite sides of the world, but we'll be together, partners in Posie's life until she's grown up. Independent. After that… Well, I'd consider half my worldly goods well spent in return for my daughter.'

'I don't want your money. Now or ever,' she managed through a throat apparently stuffed with rocks. 'The only currency worth a damn in this exchange is time and love. Can you spare half of that?'

'Posie will have all I have to give,' he assured her. 'What are you prepared to sacrifice?'

Hope. All her dreams… 'Whatever it takes.'

'Then I have your answer.'

'Yes, I suppose you have,' she said.

And that was it. Two people pledging their life to each other, not with a kiss, not to the soundtrack of champagne corks and cheers but with an awkward silence that neither of them knew how to fill.

'Maybe,' she said with forced brightness when her ears were ringing with the silence, empty and hollow as the years that stretched ahead of them, 'since we're in this for the duration, in a year or two, we could pay another visit to the clinic and make Posie a brother or sister.'

He captured her head, leaning into her and, with his lips inches from her own, his eyes molten lead, his voice crushed gravel, he said, 'Sorry, Grace. If you want me to give you another baby, you're going to have to look me in the eyes while I deliver my fifty per cent.'

Someone tried the door. Then knocked.

She didn't move. Couldn't move as he continued to look down at her, his eyes dark, unreadable, drawing her to him like a magnet until they were standing as close as two people could who weren't actually touching. Until she could feel the heat coming from him, warming her through the thin silk of her shirt, through the navy linen trousers. Until her breasts yearned for his touch and her mouth was so hot that in desperation she touched her lower lip with her tongue.

Closer…

'Grace? It's me…' Abby called, tapping again.

It was Josh who spun away from her, crossed to the door and unlocked it.

'Grace,' Abby said, reaching out for her. 'I'm so sorry….'

They hugged wordlessly for a moment, then Grace turned to introduce Josh.

'Abby, I'd like you to meet Josh Kingsley, Michael's brother,' she said. 'Josh, Abby is a genius with enamel.'

'Hello, Abby. Thanks for stepping in to help Grace.'

'No problem. I'm glad to do it. I'm really sorry to hear about your brother.' Then, glancing at her, Abby said, 'You never said he had a beard.'

'It's a temporary aberration,' she said rapidly, before he could wonder just what she had said about him—she couldn't remember saying *that* much, but when you were working together… 'Josh, this is going to be boring. Why don't you take Posie home?'

Josh didn't want to go anywhere. He wanted to stay right here and stare at the gleam of her lower lip where her tongue had touched it. Wanted to rub his thumb over it, lick it, taste her just as he did in his dreams….

'Your mother will probably have arrived by now.'

Not much of an incentive, even if she had trusted him with Posie.

'I'll wait,' he said. Then, before she could object, 'You wouldn't want to disappoint the ducks, would you?'

She looked up and for a moment their eyes closed the distance between them.

Then, without another word, she turned to Abby.

He wandered around her workshop. It was his first visit and he was impressed by the drama, the simplicity of the design, the uniqueness of the display shelves. There was nothing to detract from the jewellery—each piece was individually lit within its own compartment—which alone provided the colour, the richness. Drew the eye.

He touched a collar of gemstones, closing his eyes as he imagined Grace wearing it. Imagined fastening it around her neck… He glanced across at her, head to head with Abby as they went through something on her computer.

As if feeling his eyes on her, she looked up, a slight frown puckering the smooth space between lovely arched brows. Then, as Abby asked her something, she turned back to the computer.

"You never said he had a beard."

She'd talked about him to her friends?

He rubbed his hand over his chin. A temporary aberration, was it? Maybe…

Posie whimpered. 'What's up, angel?' he said, bending over the buggy. He was rewarded with a smile and an excited wiggle. Did she know him? So soon?

Oh, no. The wiggle had an entirely different cause.

'Grace, Posie needs changing.'

'You'll find everything you need in her bag,' she said, not turning round, but concentrating on the screen. 'Wipes, clean nappy, plastic bag to seal up the used nappy.'

'But—'

'The washroom is behind my office.' Then she did turn round, one exquisitely arched brow challenging him to put all

those big sentiments he'd been throwing around, all his pro-
testations about wanting to be a father, to practical use. 'Put
a couple of towels on my desk.'

He had two choices. Throw himself on her mercy or get
on with it. He kicked the brake off the buggy and wheeled
Posie into Grace's office, closing the door firmly behind him.
He did not need an audience for this.

Then he looked down at Posie.

'It's my first time, kid,' he said. 'Be gentle with me….'

Grace had been holding her breath. As Josh shut the door
of her office, she let it go and Abby said, 'Bless.' Then, 'Has
he ever changed a nappy before?'

'I shouldn't think so.'

She raised her eyebrows. 'You're that mad about the
beard?'

Josh, feeling much as he'd done when he'd secured his first
contract—exhausted but triumphant—put Posie to his shoulder and continued his exploration of Grace's workshop.
Flipped through sketches for a new design.

Then he saw a fairy-tale confection sitting on a stand.

'Ready?' Grace asked, reaching for Posie, apparently finished with her briefing.

'This is pretty,' he said, picking it up, turning it so that it
caught the light. She didn't answer and he turned to look at
her. 'Do you get much call for tiaras?'

'Only from brides.'

It was much too late to wish he'd looked the other way, kept
his mouth shut. Impossible to just put it down and walk away.
'What stones did you use?' he asked, sticking with practicality.

'Pearls, obviously. Pink jade and quartz to match the embroidery on the bride's dress. Swarovski crystals.'

'Lucky bride,' he said, replacing it carefully on the bench.
'You've come a long way since your first bead necklace.'

'There's more than one way to travel, Josh,' she said, tucking Posie into the buggy. 'Give me a call if you need anything, Abby. Help yourself to the drawing board if you want to work on your own designs.'

'How good is she?' Josh asked as they headed for the park, eager to get the *'bride'* word out of his head.

'She's got real flair. I was going to offer her an exhibition later in the year—nearer Christmas when everyone is looking for something special….'

'Was?'

'I'm not in any position to make promises at the moment. I've got to put Posie first. I need to be able to see a way ahead.'

'You seem to work well together. You obviously trust her. Is she serious about making a career in jewellery design, or is it a pin-money hobby?'

'She came along to a class after her marriage broke up. Therapy, she said. She obviously doesn't need to work, probably doesn't need the pin money, but you do reach a point at which making jewellery to give away is no longer enough. I think she's passed that.'

'She sounds as if she'd make you an ideal partner.'

Grace stopped, staring at him. 'Partner?'

'You'd halve the workload and costs, double the stock,' he pointed out. 'It's worth thinking about.'

'I can see why you're a tycoon, skimming the stratosphere, while I'm still bumping along on the cobbles.'

'Hardly that. You've obviously managed to maximise all your skills and you have a wonderful selling space,' he said, taking her arm as they crossed the road and entered the park. Then, as he was assailed by the scent of frying onions, he realised just how long it had been since breakfast, 'Mustard or ketchup?'

'What?' Spotting the hot-dog van, she said, 'Oh, no…'

He tutted. 'It's lunch time and you're the one who can't afford to miss meals.'

'It's half past eleven.' Then, with a grin like a naughty schoolgirl, she said, 'Ketchup. No onions. And chips if they've got them.'

'I'll catch you up,' he said, surrendering the buggy.

It was the half-term holiday and the nearest benches were all occupied by mothers watching small children and she wandered alongside the path, following the lake until she was out of sight of Josh. It didn't matter. He'd find her, she thought, trying to remember the last time they'd eaten hot dogs from the park van.

He must have been at university, home for the holidays... Her musings were brought to an abrupt halt by the sight of a small boy teetering dangerously on the edge of the lake as he strained to reach a football that was getting further away from him with every lunge.

Letting go of the buggy, she grabbed the back of his sweater just as gravity won.

'What on earth do you think you're doing?' she said as she hauled him back from, at best, a very cold bath, at worst...

'I can't go home without the ball or my dad'll kill me.'

'Now, is that really likely?' she asked, trying not to think how very much she wanted to shake him herself.

'If he doesn't kill me, my brother will. It's his ball.' Then, looking up at her with big brown eyes, 'You're bigger than me. You could probably reach it.'

They both studied the ball as, driven by a light breeze, it drifted slowly, but inexorably, towards the centre of the lake.

'No one could reach it.'

'You could break a branch off one of those bushes, miss,' the boy suggested helpfully. She wasn't, for a minute, taken in by the 'miss', but even if she had been prepared to indulge in such vandalism, it wouldn't have helped. The ball was too far out for anything but direct action.

She looked around. There was no sign of Josh, but with the children off school there was probably a queue.

She looked again at the ball. While she didn't, for a moment, believe that either his brother or his father would kill him, she did know that, as soon as she turned her back, he'd try to get it himself and, without pausing to consider the wisdom of such a move, she parked Posie by the bench, kicked off her shoes, rolled up her trousers as far as they'd go. Then, with a stern, 'Watch the baby!' she waded in.

A gang of loutish ducks who'd gathered in anticipation of a free lunch flapped away in a flurry of outrage at the invasion, driving the ball even further into the centre of the lake.

'No crusts for you,' she muttered, sucking in her breath sharply at the coldness of the water and doing her best not to think about the slimy stuff oozing over her feet as she took a step towards the centre of the lake. Or how slippery it was. How easy it would be to lose her footing. Instead, she grabbed a low overhanging branch for safety and she eased herself closer to the ball.

Josh, cardboard tray holding cartons of tea, hot dogs, Grace's chips came to an abrupt halt as he saw Posie, parked on the path with a small boy clutching the handle of the buggy. Saw her shoes. Then, as he saw Grace wading out into the lake, his heart turned over.

'What on earth are you doing, Grace?' he thundered.

Josh. *Now* he turned up, Grace thought, wishing she had kept her shoes on as she felt something hard beneath her toes and belatedly thought of all the things that got thrown into the lake.

'Going for a paddle,' she tossed back, without turning round to see if his face matched his voice, afraid that if she made any sudden moves, she'd slip. 'Why don't you roll up your trousers and come on in? The water's lovely.'

'Say that again without your teeth chattering and I might just believe you.'

'Wimp,' she countered, keeping her eye on the ball, which her own movement was driving further towards the centre of the lake.

She didn't need Josh Kingsley to tell her—from the dry vantage point of the footpath—that this was probably the worst move she'd made in a very long time. Too late now, she thought, gritting her teeth as the water edged above her knees and soaked into her trousers.

Then she ran out of branch.

It was much too late to wish she'd stuck to looking helpless on dry land. Instead, she made a sideways tack, taking the long way round to come at the ball from behind.

It was only as she turned to face the path that she realised just how far out she was.

She had no one to blame but herself, she reminded herself as she scooped up the ball, tucked it under her arm and waded back, grabbing for the safety of the branch.

There was a crack like a pistol shot as it broke off and, before she could save herself, she was sitting up to her armpits in water.

The shock of it drove the breath from her body and, unable to move, unable to speak, unable to think, she just sat there clutching the ball to her chest.

CHAPTER NINE

Josh abandoned the tray and plunged into the water, grabbed Grace by the arms and hauled her upright. He wasn't sure which of them was shaking the most as he said, 'I'm sorry I was so long. I had to wait for the chips.'

'That's good. That means they're fresh,' she said. 'Hot.' Then, 'Did you remember—'

'Salt and vinegar,' he said, and suddenly he was grinning as he said it. Laughing.

He'd remembered. He remembered everything about her.

Her legs buckling beneath her as she'd climbed off his motorbike the first time she'd ridden pillion.

The happy way she'd danced at her first school disco. Phoebe had asked him to keep an eye on her, something he hadn't been exactly happy about—he'd had bigger plans than babysitting a fourteen-year-old—but she'd been having such a good time that it had made him almost envious.

He remembered the way she'd flung her thin arms around him, her tears soaking into his shirt, when he'd bought her a puppy. The way she'd rolled her eyes at his choice of girls, music, clothes. Her quietness. The way she'd listened to him when he'd told her his dreams…

Remembered her face as he'd left her asleep in the tangled sheets.

She was always there. When he thought of home, it was always Grace who filled his mind. Always Grace who was the '…ever fixed mark…'

'I remembered,' he said, and her lovely mouth tilted up at the corners, a snort of laughter escaped her because it was beyond ridiculous that two sensible adults would be standing up to their thighs in a muddy lake, talking about chips. 'So, are you done with paddling for the day? Only they'll be getting cold.'

'C-cold?' That made her laugh again so that she was in danger of dropping the ball. He took it from her, turned and tossed the ball to the boy. 'There you go. And keep away from the water in future,' he called after him as he grabbed it and ran.

'H-he d-didn't even say th-thank you,' she said, and that seemed to make her laugh even more.

'No doubt he thought he was in trouble,' he said, picking some waterweed from her shoulder, before taking her hands and helping her back up onto the path. He took off his jacket and wrapped it around her shoulders.

'It'll be ruined,' she protested.

'Then it will be a match for the trousers and the shoes. Here, drink this,' he said, handing her a carton of tea. And they sat dripping on the bench, drinking scalding tea, eating hot dogs.

'Aren't you going to eat the chips?' he asked, taking one. 'They're very good.'

She groaned. 'I shouldn't have vinegar,' she said, looking at them with hungry longing. 'Because of the milk.'

'Right.'

Then, as he took another one, 'I don't suppose one would hurt…'

'Better?' he asked a couple of minutes later as she wiped her fingers on a paper napkin.

'Brilliant,' she said, unpeeling herself from the bench and

tossing the rubbish in a litter bin, while he fished out the bag from under the buggy and hurled a handful of crusts far into the lake, sending the birds spinning and flapping to reach it. 'Greedy little beggars. They've no manners.'

'That's what I love about them,' Grace said, watching him, hair blown by the breeze, shirt clinging to shoulders broad enough to prop up her entire world. Muddy trousers, wet shoes where he'd come to her rescue. 'They go for what they want. No pretence. No hang-ups.'

Then, because she didn't want to think about what she couldn't have, she told him about the time Phoebe had used up all the bread, not just to keep her amused, but to annoy her mother.

'Are you telling me that perfect Phoebe was once a terrible teenager?' The idea seemed to amuse him.

'Apparently.' And she smiled, too. 'Once she slipped away when we were packing up to move. She took the bus into town and didn't come back until dark, forcing everyone to stay another night.'

'I'll bet that made her popular.'

'Most of the kids loved the freedom, but Phoebe just wanted to have a proper home. After that, Mum called someone she'd known at school, got her a pocket-money job as a home help with bed and board and a part-time business course at the local college. She never looked back.'

'And you? Was that what you wanted?'

'I didn't know what I wanted.' In hindsight, though, she could see why her mother had decided to leave her with Phoebe once she'd been released from custody. She must have known it was only a matter of time. 'Thanks for jogging my memory,' she said, when she realised he was waiting for more. 'Perfection would have been an impossible ideal to live up to.'

'You think?' He took her hands. 'I don't believe you have

a thing to worry about on that score, Grace,' he said, his grip tightening, his gaze suddenly more intense. 'You were born a giver. Ducks. Kids with lost balls. A sister desperate for a baby. You're always there.' Then, rubbing his thumbs over the backs of her fingers, 'And, speaking of giving, you'll need a ring. Do you want to design it yourself? Or will you allow me to choose something for you?'

'There's no need for that,' she said. A ring was a symbol, a token of deep and abiding love. Then, because that sounded ungrateful, 'It seems…inappropriate to make a big thing of this.'

'Because it's so soon?'

Josh had known from the moment the facts had been laid out in the lawyer's office what he had to do. Maybe he'd known it from the beginning. He'd told himself that it was no more than a piece of paper that gave Grace back her baby. It wasn't as if he'd planned to repeat the mistake of marrying a woman who'd want more than he could give.

Then, coming around the corner, seeing her wading out into the lake, imagining glass, rusty cans, imagining her slipping and getting tangled up in weeds or rubbish while he was stranded on the path, hands full, unable to move, it had hit him, like running full tilt into the Rock of Gibraltar.

That he didn't want a paper marriage—he wanted Grace. Had always wanted Grace.

Now, hearing the hesitation in her voice, he wanted to wrap his arms around her, kiss away her doubts, put that laughter back into her eyes. Somehow reassure her that if she'd give him the chance, he would strive to make her happy. Give her all the children she wanted, with love, passion, the two of them becoming one in that precious moment of conception.

Instead, he did the very opposite, because to say those things would be selfish beyond belief. In two weeks, three at the most, he'd be on the other side of the world and she'd be on her own, picking up the pieces, making a life for their little girl, while he came and went as he always had, pleasing himself.

The one selfless thing he could do was give her Posie. A home that would be hers for ever. Security.

She deserved that. They owed it to her—Michael, Phoebe and, above all, him.

'People will understand,' he said.

Grace, her hands clasped in his, understood just one thing. Josh didn't have to do this. He was, incredibly, doing it for her. That he was everything she'd ever wanted and now they had a common purpose that would bind them together more tightly than fleeting passion.

'How soon?' she asked.

'I'd like to settle everything before I leave.'

Grace remembered the way he'd made lists on a lined pad—an organisational skill he'd learned from Michael. He'd numbered each item, ticking it off as each task was accomplished so that he could forget it, move on.

And she had, of course, copied her hero.

It was a good system. It kept you focused on what was important. But the idea of being an item on a list, something to be ticked off, was so mortifying that she said, shivering, 'Leave it to me. I'll contact the registrar when we get home and check what we need to do.'

'Let's worry about that later. You need to get home and out of those wet things.'

They went in the back way through the mud room. Grace hung up Josh's jacket so that the lining could dry while Josh eased off his wet shoes, peeled off his socks, tossed them in the sink while she struggled with the buttons of her own jacket.

'Here, let me do that,' he said, bending to tackle them, so that she was staring at his thick, dark, wind-tousled hair.

He peeled it away from her shirt, draped it over the draining board, then, while she was still struggling to catch her breath, slipped the button at her waist. The zip, always dodgy, peeled back under the added weight of water and the lot fell in a crumpled heap at her feet.

'I can manage,' she said, kicking free of her trousers, slapping his hand away as he set to work on her shirt, clearly believing her incapable of undressing herself.

'Sure?' he said.

'P-positive…' Even if she had to rip it off. 'If you leave your trousers, I'll put them through the wash….'

Her mouth dried as, taking her at her word, he slipped the buckle on his belt, undid the button at his deliciously narrow waist and slid down the zip.

Later. She'd meant later, she thought as she groped for the door handle, backing into the kitchen. She was almost sure she'd meant later, she told herself as she turned and found herself face to face with her mother, who was at the table preparing vegetables. Josh's mother, who was watching her.

While Grace stood there, too embarrassed to speak, Josh eased her aside so that he could push Posie into the kitchen, then, looking round, said, 'This is probably a good moment to tell you all that Grace and I are getting married as soon as we can make arrangements.'

Josh's mother reacted first.

'Married? Well, congratulations, Grace. And at least no one will put the obvious construct on the unseemly haste since you've already had the baby.' Then, while Grace was still cringing with embarrassment, she turned to Josh. 'I suppose you'll be giving her my grandmother's engagement ring, too?'

About to step in and read his mother the riot act, he saw the compassion in Grace's eyes and realised that she had seen what he, on the defensive, protecting himself and Grace from

her barbs, had missed. How, looking beyond the plastic surgery, the perfectly applied make-up, the exquisite black
designer suit, his mother was a fragile, desperately unhappy
woman who'd just buried her oldest son—a son she'd lost
years before.

'Would you look after Posie for me, Mrs Kingsley,' Grace
added, 'while I go and take a shower?'

And he saw how like Phoebe she was.

Her gentleness. Goodness.

She would never look back with regret on an unkindness.
Cling to hostility, as both he and Michael had done. And he
knew at that moment that he wouldn't want to die with that
leaden weight in his heart.

He wheeled the buggy closer to his mother, touched her
shoulder and said, 'I'll take your bag upstairs, while you and
Dawn get to know your granddaughter.'

His reward was a smile from Grace. It was a moment of
revelation. Truth.

'Mum?' Grace prompted, obviously wanting to get any un-
pleasantness out of the way in one fell swoop. 'Have you anything to say?'

'Only… What happened to your clothes?'

'What are you looking for?'

Grace looked up as her mother stood at the study door. 'My
birth certificate. I know it's here somewhere because I had to
get a copy when I needed a passport for a school trip to France.'

'I didn't know you'd been to France. You've never mentioned it.'

'No…' She'd spent the week before the trip in a state of
rising panic. On the surface she'd been just as excited as all
the other kids in her class, but deep down she'd known with
a cast iron certainty that when she got back everything would
have shifted. That it wouldn't be Phoebe, but some stranger

from Social Services waiting for her… 'I was sick the morning we were due to leave and couldn't go,' she said.

'That's a pity.'

'It happens…' Then, looking back at the drawer, she saw her name typed on a neat tab and lifted the surprisingly thick folder from its sling, put it on the desk and opened it. 'Good grief.'

'What is it?'

'My entire life, apparently.'

At least everything that related to her life since she'd come into Michael's house. Correspondence with Social Services, the Parental Responsibility Order they'd applied for when she had come to live with them. All those horrible Grace-tries-so-hard-but…end of term school reports.

She'd known a lot of stuff—far more about some things than the other kids—but not in an organised, exam passing way. But she'd shone in art and that had got her a place at the local tech.

And then, at the back, tucked away in plastic wallets, she found her medical card, passport and, finally, her birth certificate.

She took it out, unfolded it on the desk and looked at this public record of who she was. Wondered what a stranger would make of it. Josh, even.

Date and place of birth: 28 July 1980, Duckett's Farm, Little Hinton.

Actually, in a van illegally parked in a field at Duckett's Farm. She'd been told the tale a hundred times. How Grace Duckett, ignoring her husband's fury at having a dozen New Age 'travellers' pull over and set up camp on one of his fields when her mother had gone into labour, had been so generous, so kind that, instead of being called Aurora, a twist on her mother's name, she'd been called Grace after the farmer's wife. As a little girl she'd longed for the exotic Aurora. These days she was deeply grateful to Grace Duckett.

Name: Grace Louise.

She turned to her mother. 'Who was Louise?'

'One of the women in our group. A herbalist. She helped me with your birth.'

'I don't remember her.'

'You wouldn't. She met someone at a music festival and settled down with him in a semi somewhere near Basingstoke.'

'Oh. Right.' She turned back to the document.

Father: Steven Billington, wood-carver.
Mother: Dawn McAllister.

'Did you ever hear from him?' she asked. 'My father? Ever try to find him? For maintenance?'

Her mother shook her head. 'What would have been the point? He'd found someone else, they had a baby and he never did have any money. It hurt, but that's how life is, Grace.' She smiled. 'I loved him enough to let him go.'

As she'd let Phoebe go. And her.

'I can't let Posie go,' she said. 'I've lost so much….'

'I'll stay as long as you need me,' her mother promised. 'Once you're married…'

'It's just a piece of paper,' she said, not even bothering to pretend to her mother.

'For Josh, maybe.' Her mother touched her shoulder. 'You always did light up around him, Grace.'

What could she say? Denying it wouldn't change anything. Or convince her mother.

'It seems indecent to be even thinking of a wedding so soon after burying Michael and Phoebe. Almost like dancing on their graves.'

'The human spirit needs to affirm life at these dark moments, Grace. To celebrate new beginnings. Rebirth.'

'We weren't planning on a celebration. A ten minute in-and-out job at the register office rather than a fertility ceremony,' she replied. Then wished she'd kept her mouth shut. 'Josh has to get back to Australia as quickly as possible. He's just got some big new contract in China.'

'You're not going with him?'

'He'll be all over the place and I've got commitments here. The house. My business…'

'I'll keep the fertility dance on hold for the time being, then.'

'That's probably wise,' Grace replied. 'At least until you've had your hips fixed.'

Her mother laughed out loud at that, then said, 'So? What are you going to wear?'

'Wear? I hadn't thought about it.'

She didn't want to think about it. About the design for a tiny sparkly tiara that she'd drawn years ago and never made. About walking down the aisle in the dream dress on the dream day when she married her dream man.

'It's not important.' And, firmly changing the subject, she said, 'Were you looking for me for something special?'

'Oh, yes.' Her mother opened the book she was holding and handed it to her. 'I've been looking for some way to commemorate Phoebe and Michael. I know a man who carves words into slate stepping stones and I thought maybe a quotation from this one. Elizabeth Barrett Browning…'

Grace recognised it instantly. Had learned it by heart years ago at the height of her teenage infatuation with Josh. She had no need to read it, but closed her eyes and said the words out loud. '"How do I love thee? Let me count the ways…"' But when she came to the final line, it was Josh who completed the poem.

'"—and, if God choose, I shall but love thee better after death."'

Her eyes flew open and he was there, standing right in front of her, and she swayed towards him.

'Steady,' he said, catching her. 'Standing with your eyes closed can do crazy things to the balance.'

'I'm fine,' she said. She wasn't. But she would be.

'Right.' And after a moment he let go of her. Then, taking the book from her hand, he turned to Dawn. 'That last line. It's perfect.'

'I thought so.'

'You do understand, Dawn? Why we're getting married so quickly.'

'You're giving Posie a family,' she said. 'That's a noble thing, which is entirely different from being solemn about it.' She lifted her hand to his cheek. 'You're allowed to be happy, too.'

'Mum…' Grace warned, afraid she was going to start on her earth mother, circle of life, fertility thing again. 'I called the registrar, Josh. We need some paperwork. Birth certificates…'

'And?'

'Your decree absolute.'

He nodded. 'I've got them both at home. I'll get Anna to courier them overnight.'

Anna, the personal assistant.

She slammed the door on that thought and said, 'Right. Good. So all we have to do is call in at the register office, present the necessary documents and give sixteen clear days notice of our intention to marry.'

'Sixteen days? I thought maybe a week…'

'Is that going to be too long? Once we've given notice, we have a year in which to go through with it. If it's not convenient, we could wait…'

Josh put down the book and took out his new BlackBerry. 'It's going to be tight. Let's see. It's the twenty-seventh tomorrow…' he checked the diary '…which makes the first available day the twelfth of June. I have to be in Beijing on the fifteenth… It's just do-able. I was coming to London next week for meetings. I've managed to bring them forward.'

'Not too much of an inconvenience then,' she said.

'No…' He made a note, then slipped it back into his pocket.

When he looked up he realised that both Grace and her mother were staring at him.

'I think I'll go and see what Laura is doing,' Dawn said, picking up her book and heading for the door.

Josh didn't take his eyes off Grace.

'I've just been incredibly insensitive, haven't I?'

He'd watched a variety of expressions chase across her face since she'd opened her eyes when he'd finished her poem.

She'd hadn't been this easy to read since she was a girl, he realised. All those years ago, he'd watched her putting on a brave face for Phoebe, but it had been obvious to him that she was scared out of her wits at the prospect of facing a new school. He knew she was right to be scared. Knew how bad it could be for anyone arriving in the middle of the school year when friendship groups had been established.

And she had 'outsider' written all over her.

She was a quick study, though. Maybe it was living in the wild, but she'd been swift to adapt, learning the most acceptable labels to have on her clothes, the right way to fix her hair. And that most vital survival technique—how to keep her feelings under wraps.

Right now there was too much going on. Too many feelings to hide. He'd just had a glimpse of one more loss she was being forced to bear, this time by him.

He wished he could blame his complete boorishness on the fact that he'd retreated to the basement to deal with things that could not be put off. He'd had to reorganise meetings, arrange for busy colleagues to stand in for him, reassure his Chinese partner that he was going to be there to hold his hand at the next round of meetings with the bureaucrats, but it wasn't that.

It was the glow that had lit her up as she'd recited that poem listing every way in which a woman could love a man, knowing that he could have had that if he'd cared about anyone but himself.

'You don't have to answer that,' he said. 'I already know the answer.'

Grace sighed. 'It's all right, Josh. You don't have to pretend with me. We both know that you're only doing this so that I can keep Posie. I'm truly grateful.'

Pretend?

Grateful...

'Dammit, Grace, you don't have to be grateful.'

He turned away, raking his hands through his hair, locking his fingers behind his head to keep them from reaching out to touch her lovely face. From telling her what she truly meant to him. Telling wouldn't do it. He was going to have to show her....

'I'm the one who's grateful and I'll say now what I should have said earlier.' Then, because some things had to be said face to face, he dropped his hands, turned to look at her. 'You're the mother of my child and I'll do my best, whatever it takes, to make you happy.' And in a gesture that he'd have sworn was completely alien to him but now seemed as natural as breathing, he laid his hand on his heart. 'You have my word.'

She looked up at him, her heart in her eyes. 'Anything?'

It was what, when he'd challenged her, forced her to face reality, he'd demanded of her. He could offer no less.

'Anything,' he affirmed with all the conviction he could muster. Then, rather more gently, 'Tell me, Grace.'

'Well, it's just that I was wondering if we could hold the

actual wedding ceremony somewhere other than the register office.' This was so far from what he'd been expecting that he was left floundering for something to say. 'It's where I had to go to register Michael and Phoebe's deaths…'

She faltered, clearly unable to find the words to express what that had done to her.

She didn't have to.

She shouldn't have had to ask. He should have thought, at least discussed it with her.

'I'm sorry, Josh. You've got more than enough on your plate without me being a pathetic wimp about something so unimportant—'

'Don't!' He caught her to him, held her close. 'It's important to you and that makes it important to me. I should have talked this through with you instead of just assuming that because it's the simplest solution it's the right one.'

'But it is. Simple is good. Just…'

'Just not that simple.' He leaned back a little so that he could look at her. So that she could see that he meant what he said. 'It's not a problem. We can have the ceremony wherever you like.'

'Thank you.' Her smile was exactly like the one she'd given him when he'd tossed her his spare crash helmet. Thrown her a lifeline… 'I'm sure we could find somewhere with a licence that isn't all white doves and string quartets,' she added and, with her this close, looking up at him as if he were her white knight, he felt a surge of hope that this could, truly, be more than a paper marriage.

More than hope.

An almost unbearable need to kiss her, show her that if only she would take her courage in both hands, trust him…

Trust. It kept coming back to that. He had asked her to trust him and she had, despite the fact that he'd not walked, but had run from her after that night when she'd given him everything.

He'd told himself that it had been the right thing for her, but it been his own fear, the prospect of his vaunting ambitions being hampered by a girl who needed more than he could ever give that had sent him out into the cold dawn.

Rebuilding the trust that he'd shattered so selfishly would have to be earned with bone-deep commitment. Kisses would have to wait.

'What exactly have you got against doves, Grace?'

'Well,' she began, quite seriously, 'for a start they're not ducks…' Then she shook her head and without warning that smile hit him again. 'You know what I mean.'

'Yes, I know,' he managed. 'Simple.'

'I thought that's what you wanted, too. Especially as you'll be flying off to China the minute the ink's dry on the certificate.'

Josh hadn't thought about what might happen after the event. Now he did. Did she expect them to say their vows and go their separate ways? That he'd have his bag packed and the taxi waiting to take him to the airport? The idea so appalled him that he said, 'Perhaps not the *very* minute. I thought I'd wait until the following morning. Just for appearance's sake,' he added when she started nervously. 'We both know that the wedding is no more than a formality but there's no reason to share that fact with the rest of the world. In fact, I think your mother might have a point.'

'She might?' she squeaked. 'And what point would that be?'

'That there's a fine distinction between a quiet wedding and something that is, to all intents and purposes, invisible.'

Invisible meant the marriage would pass unnoticed. He suddenly discovered that he wanted the entire world to take note. Having always steered well clear of the gossip column lifestyle, right now he'd actively welcome the prospect of a ten-page spread in *Celebrity*.

'We will need two witnesses. And convention suggests I

should have a best man. Maybe,' he said, 'Posie would like to be your bridesmaid?'

'My bridesmaid? That would be the person who's supposed to lead me astray on my hen night, help me with my make-up, carry my train and catch the bouquet?'

'You could have one of those, too. Posie is going to need a little help.'

'I don't think so.'

'Don't be a spoilsport. She'd love being dressed up in pink frills.'

'Oh, please,' she said, trying not to laugh, but a giveaway dimple appeared in her cheek. How could he have forgotten that dimple?

'You think pink is too much of a cliché?'

'You don't want to know what I think.'

'You do know that she'll hold it against you. When she's older. Feel deprived. Just ask her…' Then, 'Where is she?'

'Asleep,' Grace said firmly, the dimple back under control. 'I put her upstairs after lunch so that she wouldn't be disturbed.' Right on cue, there was a gurgle from the baby monitor sitting on the desk. 'Was asleep,' she said. 'I have to go.'

He caught her hand. 'Leave the wedding arrangements to me, Grace. I'll organise everything.'

'I thought you had to be in London all next week for meetings?'

'All you'll have to think about is what you're going to wear,' he said. 'I promise.'

'No problem. I'll have that navy-blue trouser suit cleaned. It'll be perfect.'

CHAPTER TEN

FOR a moment Josh actually believed her. Then Grace laughed and said, 'I'm going to give Posie a bath before teatime. You can be in charge of the plastic ducks if you promise not to say another word about her being a bridesmaid.'

'You asking me to help?'

'You've already proved yourself in the nappy department. Bathing is next on the agenda. If you can spare the time?'

'Yes… Thank you.'

'Save your thanks until afterwards.'

'How hard can it be?' he said with a flippancy that earned him another smile. One that suggested he'd just said something very foolish. That was okay. Making a fool of himself would be a small price to pay for raising one of her precious smiles.

Actually, it wasn't that difficult. Between them, Grace and Posie made short work of cutting him down to size.

'You undress her while I run the bath,' Grace said.

Easier said than done. He was still wrestling with a minute vest when Grace came looking for him.

'The water's going cold while you two are playing,' she said, leaning against the door, apparently enjoying the spectacle of him reduced to a wreck by an infant.

'I'm not playing,' he protested. Playing he could do. 'It's

Posie.' Then, 'No. It's me.' His hands were too big and Posie was so small, her skin so delicate. 'She's so tiny.'

'Oh, please. She's a great big hulk,' Grace said, picking her up with the confidence of practice. Kissing her, then gently tugging the little vest over her head, pausing for a quick peekaboo, before pulling it free, then kissing her again. 'You should have seen her when she was first born,' she said, then looked away, clearly afraid that she'd said something hurtful.

'I wish I had been, too, Grace.' Been there at the birth to hold her hand, do whatever it was that useless men did while the women they loved suffered to give them sons, daughters. Except that would never have happened. He'd have been the outsider, excluded, while Phoebe and Michael supported her through the birth.

She put a hand on his arm, rubbed it gently in a gesture of comfort. 'The first time Phoebe let me bath Posie I was certain I was going to drop her.'

And in that one brief phrase—'Phoebe let me'—she told him that she knew. Understood.

'It's just a question of holding gently but firmly,' she went on as if she'd said nothing of importance. 'Come on. You'll soon learn.'

The small baby bath was on a low stand and Grace sat on a stool with Posie on her lap. She gently washed her face and only then did she lower the baby into the water. Posie immediately went rigid with excitement, then drew back her little legs and kicked.

Water erupted over the end of the bath, where he was poised with a bright yellow plastic duck, hitting him full in the chest.

Posie screamed with pleasure and, while he was looking down at the damage, she did it again, this time showering his head.

He was kneeling in water, was soaked to the skin and his

hair was dripping down his back. It was the second time that day he'd been soaked. The second time that they had been laughing together.

Half an hour later he left a smiling, composed Posie, dressed in a tiny white T-shirt and soft blue overalls, in complete command of the nursery while he retreated, dripping, to the basement. Dripping but wrapped in the warmth of the towel Grace had taken from the heated rail and draped around his neck.

'You'll soon get the hang of it,' she said, and he felt like the victor at some ancient games who'd just been garlanded with laurels. 'Next time you'll be ready for her.'

Personally, he didn't care how wet he got if he could be shoulder to shoulder with Grace as, together, they'd bathed their baby.

The undercurrent of tension that had seemed to stretch to breaking point since he'd been home had completely evaporated in the splashing, the laughter, the play of Posie's bath time.

'Ready for her? You mean, you knew that this was going to happen?' He indicated his sodden T-shirt and trousers.

'Why do you think I chose the end that doesn't kick?'

'Oh, I see.' He bent to tickle Posie, who was sitting like a little princess in the crook of her mother's arm, to kiss her downy head. 'I think your mummy set me up.'

'It's a rite of passage,' Grace said, still laughing, as he straightened. Then, as he looked down at her, the laughter died away and in that instant it was as if the last ten years had never happened. They were both still young, untouched, with all their dreams intact.

He was twenty-one, about to embark on the greatest adventure of his life so far, skirting around unsettling feelings for this girl he'd watched out for ever since she'd arrived in his life. A girl who'd come downstairs to bring him a pair of cufflinks she'd made for him, to say goodbye. Except they hadn't been able to say goodbye. Instead, her huge green eyes had provoked an explosive, straight-to-hell physical response that neither of them had had the will or desire to resist.

Her green eyes had that same look now and the effect was, if anything, more devastating. But older, just a touch wiser, he recognised it for what it was. Need, fear of change, of losing someone you care for—only this time it was not him she was afraid of losing, but Posie. And he stepped back, turned away before he embarrassed them both.

Dawn met him as he crossed the hall. 'I was going to ask you how you got on, but I can see,' she said, laughing. 'You're having a very wet day.'

'I'm not complaining,' he said, pulling the towel from around his neck and rubbing at his hair.

'Seize every moment, Josh. They grow up far too quickly.' Then, 'Your mother was talking about ringing an agency to engage a nanny.'

'A wedding planner would be more use right now.' Then, 'No, forget I said that. Grace wants simple.'

'I thought you had simple,' she said.

'Simple,' he said, 'but more complicated.' Then, hearing Grace at the top of the stairs, 'Let's go into the sitting room,' he said. 'Can I get you a drink?'

'I don't,' she reminded him. 'But you go ahead.'

He poured himself a Scotch, sat on the leather footstool that wouldn't suffer from his damp clothes.

'Grace isn't happy with the idea of having the ceremony at the register office,' he said. 'It has too many negative associations. And, since we've decided to invite a few more people, we're going to need somewhere that can provide lunch.' Actually, that was his idea, but she hadn't out-and-out vetoed it. 'Any thoughts?'

'To be honest, Josh, very few of the people I know actually bother with the paperwork. I didn't myself.'

Her sigh was, he thought, unconscious.

'Do you regret that?'

'Maybe. Not that it would have made any difference. Once a man's eyes begin to wander there isn't enough paper and ink in the world to keep him from following them. I wish he'd made an effort to keep in touch with the girls.'

'It must have been hard for you.'

He found it difficult to imagine this slender woman taking on a bunch of thugs who'd been hell-bent on destroying her home. But that must have been easy compared with giving up her precious girls so that they'd have a more settled life than the one she'd chosen for herself.

'I managed. Mostly.' She smiled. 'It's different for the two of you, of course. You're marrying to give Posie a family.'

'I thought it would make adoption simpler, especially in view of the fact that we live in different hemispheres.'

'Maybe that's the problem you need to address,' she said, giving him a very straight look.

'We both have commitments, Dawn,' he said, staring into the glass he was holding as if that somehow held the answer. 'Maybe later…'

'So what's the rush to get married?' She tilted her head to one side, looking for all the world like a small, brightly plumaged bird. 'What are you afraid of, Josh?'

'Of losing her.' The words slipped out. He hadn't intended to say them, but there it was. Plain and honest.

'Posie? Or Grace?'

'Both of them.' He glanced up. 'You do know that she's Posie's natural mother?'

'Not just the shell, but the egg, too? How generous. I'm so proud of her.'

'You raised an amazing daughter, but one who, right now,'

has no legal rights as far as Posie is concerned. Michael named me as Posie's guardian in his will.'

'And why would he do that?'

'Because Posie is my biological daughter, too, Dawn. Michael had problems of his own…'

'I see.'

'Do you? I'm doing what I can to give Grace a legal right to her own child.'

'While protecting your own?'

'You think that's selfish?'

'I think it's a very natural instinct,' she said, which didn't answer his question. Or maybe it did. Maybe instinct, the urge to survive was, at heart, selfishness. 'But thank you for telling me. It explains a great deal.' She tilted her head again. 'Although not, perhaps, everything.'

'Everything is, for the moment, beyond me, Dawn. I'm adrift. I can't cry. I feel guilty when I forget for a moment…' He looked up. 'Guilty for not being here. If it wasn't for Grace and Posie…'

'Love is the most powerful emotion there is, Josh.'

Love?

'It gives us the strength to hold on long after reason suggests that all is lost. The courage to let go when it feels as if you're tearing your heart out.'

'I let go once. I convinced myself that it was the right decision but I've come to realise that it was a mistake.'

Was he making a mistake now? Still being ruled by that selfish gene?

'How do you know?' he asked. 'How can you tell?'

'Ask yourself who will gain most from the choice you make. Who will be hurt. Whose happiness you truly care about.'

'It's that easy?' he said with a wry smile.

'I didn't say it was easy. Being honest with yourself is the hardest thing in the world. But if you truly love someone, you'll have the courage to face the truth.' Then, 'But you wanted me to help you find somewhere for the wedding. Why don't you go and get into some dry clothes while I take a look at the local paper? That might give me some ideas.'

'You won't mention any of this to Grace? I told her that all she'd have to do was turn up and say "I do",' he said, getting up, then moving to help her as she struggled to get off the sofa.

'Wretched hip,' she muttered.

'How bad is it?'

'A bit like Melchester Castle. A crumbling ruin.' Then, waving away his concern, 'Did you know that they hold weddings there?'

'In the ruin?'

She gave him a look that he recognised. Grace didn't look much like her mother, but that cool, please concentrate, I'm being serious, look was familiar from a hundred teasing exchanges.

How he'd missed that.

Missed her.

'I know they hold those big glossy affairs in the manor house that was built much later,' he said hurriedly.

'They also have a folly—a mini Greek temple affair—that overlooks the lake. I believe they hold less formal weddings there. I'll make some enquiries.' Then, 'And, to answer your question, no, I won't mention this to Grace. She's just about holding herself together for Posie. Anything that feels like a celebration is beyond her.'

'I can understand that. At least she was here…'

'That was not your fault, Josh. You'll honour Michael and Phoebe's memory far more by bringing up his daughter than by standing in church, singing hymns.' Then, patting his hand, 'It's hard when you're young. Everything is so sharply defined. Right, wrong. Black, white. Pleasure, pain. As you get older you realise that life is mostly a greyish muddle and the best you can do is embrace each moment, learn each lesson and move on.'

'Easier said than done.'

'You can't change anything that's happened. Regret is futile. Only the future matters.'

'I wish there was more time but I don't know when I'll get back and I don't want to leave Grace in limbo. I want her to feel safe.'

'Don't worry. Between us we'll make it as painless as possible. Give her a wedding that at the moment she can't allow herself to believe she has a right to enjoy.'

'Thank you. I'll arrange a credit card for you, Dawn. Do whatever you think best. Invite whoever you think she'd want to be there. Just—'

'Keep it simple.'

'Actually, I was going to ask you to make sure my mother doesn't get carried away.'

'Don't worry, I won't let her sell the exclusive to *Celebrity*.'

He managed a smile.

He'd never given Dawn much thought in the past but now he thought he was going to like her rather a lot. Then, remembering Grace's very specific reservations, 'And absolutely no string quartets or doves.'

Josh had been dreaming. It was the same dream that had haunted him for years. Grace, sensuous, silky, fragrant and forever—tormentingly—out of reach.

He'd come awake with a start and for a moment he just lay there, almost awake, not sure where he was.

Then his memory kicked in and the past week came rushing back like a news bulletin that he couldn't switch off. The loss of his brother, the discovery that Posie was not only his daughter, but Grace's, too.

The first small steps towards reconciliation with his

mother. He wouldn't let one more night pass without making his peace with his father.

Now he had to face something bigger. His marriage to Grace. The fact that in two weeks she would make a vow that tied her to him. That she would be coming to him, not as a bride should in a once-in-a-lifetime gown, a delicate tiara sparkling like raindrops in her elfin hair as she walked towards him down the flower-decked aisle of the local church, but in a ten-minute ceremony in some mock Greek temple.

Not with her heart in her hands, but to be tied to him by a paper marriage because there was no other way she could keep her baby.

His in name, but still forever out of reach.

He threw back the sheet, sat on the side of the bed, his face in his hands.

As he'd walked back from the lawyer's office, everything had seemed so simple. He and Grace would get married, they would bring Posie up together. She had, after all, said she'd do anything and he'd hoped, believed that their baby would bring them together.

And then he'd walked into her workshop and she'd been wrapped around the guy she'd brought to dinner the last time he'd been home.

Funny, attentive, too good-looking by half, he'd known then that Toby Makepeace was the man who was going to take Grace from him once and for all.

He'd told himself, as he'd flown away, his heart like lead in his chest, that all he wanted was for her to be happy. Had waited, expecting every phone call, every e-mail from Michael to tell him that they were engaged.

Instead, he'd got a phone call from Michael telling him that Grace was going to act as a surrogate mother for Phoebe. The unspoken subtext a silent reminder that he had sworn to keep his role in that pregnancy a secret.

In his desperation, knowing that she was carrying his child, he'd clung to the one small crumb of comfort in the whole business—that if she'd loved Toby Makepeace, it would have been his baby she would have wanted. Taking reassurance from the fact that when she had Mr Perfect at her feet, Grace had still been looking for something more and there was still hope that one day she'd look up and see him, waiting for her, to let go of the side of the pool, cast off, swim out of her depth to join him…

He'd never truly understood her fear. Only now began to have a glimmer of why, after a childhood spent being dragged around by her hippie mother, Grace had clung to this house as her rock, her refuge.

He, on the other hand, had begun life with certainty only to have it ripped out from under him. He didn't cling, didn't believe in roots put down by other people, but instead had spent every day since his parents deserted him plotting his escape, eager to travel the globe, build his own world. One that no one could ever take from him.

He'd thought he had that. Had everything.

He got up, pulled on tracksuit bottoms, a T-shirt, needing air. But, as he came up from the basement and heard Posie's thin wail float down the stairs, he knew that he'd been fooling himself. That the universe was nothing beside the power of a love you would gladly die for and he took the stairs to the nursery two at a time.

The only light spilled in through the doorway, gleaming off the thin silky wrap that floated above her bare feet, giving a glimpse of ankle as Grace turned to look at him. He quickly looked up but her face was in the shadows, all dark hollows around her eyes, in her cheeks that told of nights without sleep.

'Josh… I'm sorry if we disturbed you.'

'No. I was awake. How long have you been up?'

She shook her head. 'I don't know. Half an hour, maybe longer. I thought she was hungry….'

She was trying to coax the baby with a bottle but Posie, fractious, turned away, refusing to take it and all he could think was that he must do something.

Be a father.

'What can I do?'

Grace shook her head. 'I don't know. I was just about to go and wake my mother.'

'You're that worried?' He moved closer.

'She had two of us. She's got to know more than me.'

'Let me take her for a while.'

She surrendered Posie without an argument and he laid the infant against his shoulder where she clung to him, snuffling and nuzzling into his neck like a tiny puppy, for a moment quiet. Then she pulled away and resumed her miserable little grizzle.

Grace hadn't moved. 'Do you think she might be sick? Maybe we should call the doctor?'

We.

Such a small word to mean so much.

He felt Posie's cheeks. 'She's not hot,' he said. 'I think she's just like the rest of us. Feeling the strain. In need of comfort.'

'Who isn't?' she snapped, then, as he put his arm around her, she collapsed against his other shoulder and for a moment, with both arms full—even if both shoulders were getting wet—his world seemed complete. 'I don't know what to do!'

He rubbed his hand against her back, feeling the warmth of her skin through the thin silk. Silk?

'Where's Phoebe's robe?' he asked. Grace was a couple of sizes smaller than her sister, even with the fuller curves that motherhood had given her, and this soft, silky robe tied loosely about her luscious body was out of an entirely different wardrobe.

'In the wash.'

Guilt welled up in Grace. If she'd been more careful....

'You did warn me,' she said, pulling free of the comfort of his arm. Comfort she didn't deserve. Then, palming away tears that were clinging to her lashes, 'I'm sorry. I'm trying so hard to hold it together, but I hadn't realised what it was like. Being a mother, totally responsible for a precious life, has nothing to do with whose egg made the baby, or even giving birth. This is what's real....'

'I know, Grace. I'm here.'

'You're here now,' she said. 'But what about next month? Next year…?'

It wasn't fair, she knew that, but she'd been struggling to settle Posie for what seemed like forever and was at her wits' end.

'I used to lie awake upstairs, listening to Posie cry in the night, and I actually envied my sister,' she confessed. 'I wanted to be the one to go to Posie, pick her up, comfort her.'

'That's perfectly natural, Grace.'

'No. You were right. I should have gone away.' She looked up at him. 'I saw the fear in Phoebe's eyes. Every time I picked her up. That's why I did everything I could to get the paperwork through so quickly.' She sighed. 'Be careful what you wish for, Josh.'

'You did not wish for this.'

'No.' She hadn't wished for this. 'I had no idea how alone new parents must feel. How frightened. She's so little, Josh. So vulnerable…'

'Hush…' For a moment she wasn't sure whether he was talking to the baby or to her. 'Try to relax—'

'Relax!' She shook her head. The baby was picking up her tension, they both knew it. 'I'm sorry. Shouting at you won't help.'

'Maybe we all need a good shout,' he said. 'But not right at this moment.' He lifted the baby from his shoulder, held her for a moment, kissed her head, then laid her in the crook of his arm and, taking the feeder from her, offered it to Posie.

She turned her head away.

'She won't take this, Grace.' Then, 'Maybe you should try feeding her yourself.'

'No…' She swallowed. 'No, Josh, I couldn't.'

Even as she said it, Posie started to grizzle again and, without saying another word, Josh took her hand and led her from the nursery and into her own bedroom.

'She wouldn't…'

'Just try,' he said.

'For Posie?' If it was for Posie, she could do it.

'For Posie. And for you, Grace.'

He pulled at the knot tying her robe and the silk slithered from her shoulders, leaving her standing in a thin nightgown that clung to her breasts, her legs, and she felt naked, exposed, in a way she hadn't on the night they'd made love and she let slip a little cry. Anguish. Heartache. Longing…

'Will you trust me?' he asked.

She looked up at him. With his tousled hair, the dark stubble of his chin, he didn't look like any baby guru, but yes, she would trust him with her life. He had been—was still—her hero. Her white knight. And she sat on the edge of the bed, eased herself back against the pillows.

'Ready?'

As soon as he'd laid the baby in her arms she began to cry and Grace instantly tensed again.

'Forget Posie,' he said, sitting on the edge of the bed, turning to her. 'Just relax. Let your shoulders drop.'

But she was shaking. Afraid. 'What if I can't do it?'

'You can.' And he laid his warm hands on her shoulders and began to gently knead the tension from knotted muscles, soothing, relaxing her so that her breathing became easier and the shivering stopped.

'Trust me,' he said, briefly laying his hand against her cheek, before letting it slide down her neck, slip beneath the thin strap of her nightgown.

She tried to speak, to protest, but the only sound that emerged was a tiny squeak from the back of her throat. The truth was that she couldn't have done or said a word to stop him. Didn't want to stop him....

Josh held his breath, knowing that they were both on the precipice of something special. Keeping his eyes fixed firmly on her face. She was wearing something soft, silky with narrow straps and he slipped one over her shoulder, let his hand slide down over the full, soft mound of her breast where once her nipple had hardened eagerly for him, as if begging for his touch.

But this was not a girl's breast. Not the small, high breast that tormented his dreams. It was full, womanly, filled his hand as he lifted it, bent to kiss it.

'Please…'

'Anything,' he said, his eyes never leaving hers, 'you said you would do anything.' And, seized by some atavistic need to make his own mark, he touched his tongue to her nipple.

It leapt in response and, feeling like some great hunter bringing home food for his tribe, he offered it to his baby.

Grace gasped as Posie's eager mouth found her nipple, fastened on. Groaned as she began to suckle and Josh, not knowing whether it was pain or joy that sent the tears cascading down her cheeks, took her face between his hands, brushing them away with his thumbs.

'This is for Posie, Grace,' he said, kissing each of her cheeks, tasting the salt on his lips. 'For your baby. Our baby.' And he silently swore to cherish them both for the rest of his life.

Grace, feeling closer to being a mother than she had since the cord had been cut, looked down at her baby who, eyes closed in ecstasy, fed with serene contentment.

'Well?' Josh asked.

'Very well…' She palmed away the stupid tears and smiled. 'How did you know?'

'Just call me Mr Spock,' he said.

'I think you mean *Dr* Spock,' she said, catching her lower lip to stop herself from laughing. And then she knew he'd done it deliberately, just as he had when she was still a kid and he was halfway to being a man. He'd always known what to do. When her dog had died, it was Josh who'd dug a grave for him at the bottom of the garden. Who'd carved his name into a piece of wood and hammered it into the ground. 'Thank you, Josh. I don't know what I'd have done without you.'

He touched her cheek. 'You'd have figured it out.' Then, 'Can I go and make you something to drink? Something milky to help you sleep?'

'I'll be fine now. But you must be exhausted,' she said, shuffling up to make more room beside her. 'Put your feet up.'

'I don't need much sleep,' he said, but he settled down beside her. 'I got up for some air. I'm used to being outside.'

'In your penthouse? On top of a skyscraper?' she teased.

'It has a deck.'

'Oh.'

'And a pool.'

'For goldfish?'

'For swimming.'

'Ouch.'

'No. You're right. It's wasted on me. I'm never there,' he said. He was never anywhere….

Posie stopped suckling, looked sleepily up at her. 'Had enough, baby?' she asked.

Her mouth began to work and Grace turned her round, jumped as she latched on to her other breast.

'Does that hurt?'

Her laugh was slightly shaky. 'Not hurt, but it does take your breath away for a moment or two. She's very strong.'

'I'm sure your mother would have something to say on the subject of the life force.'

Grace smiled. 'My mother has a lot to say about almost everything.'

Whereas Josh…

'I suppose you let friends use it when you're not there. The pool?' she said.

He glanced at her. 'Why would you think that?'

'Isn't that what people do?'

'Not if they've got an atom of sense,' he assured her. 'Besides, most of my friends have pools of their own.'

'In that case, maybe you should do something about your security because someone was there when I tried to get you on the phone.'

He frowned.

'Anna Carling?' she prompted. 'Your personal assistant?'

'Anna? Oh, right.'

Wrong, wrong, wrong!

'She wasn't actually in my apartment. My number is diverted to hers when I'm away.' Then, looking at her, 'Has that been bothering you?'

'No,' she said, much too quickly.

'She's a married woman, Grace.'

'Really?' And since when did that make any difference…?

'Married, with three grown-up kids and at least two grandchildren.'

'She didn't sound that old.'

'Grace?' When she wouldn't look at him, he leaned forward. 'You didn't think…'

'Stop it.'

'Of course you did.'

He was grinning while she was blushing like a girl. It

wasn't as if she had any right to feel jealous, but when had that ever stopped her? She might have pitied the girls who Josh had dated way back when, but that hadn't stopped her hating every minute of every night he had been out with each one of them.

'You've never talked much about your life in Australia, Josh. Where you live. Your friends. Only about your work.'

'It's been my all-consuming passion,' he said.

'You've really never found anyone?'

'I found a lot of someones. They all suffered from the same problem.' He leaned across and kissed the frown from her forehead. 'They weren't you,' he said, yawning, settling lower into the bed. He muttered something else, then turned towards her, so that the entire length of his body, relaxed and fluid, seemed to mould itself to hers. His face against her naked breast, Posie's toes against his chin.

'Josh?' She stared down at him. His eyes were closed, but he couldn't be asleep. Not just like that. 'What did you say?'

No response. Jet lag had finally caught up with him and it would be cruel to disturb him. Instead, she turned to Posie. Her little girl was asleep, too, and she eased herself from beside Josh, put her back in her cot. Stood over her for a while before going back to bed.

Josh was dreaming again. It was the same dream that had haunted him for years. Grace, sensuous, silky, fragrant and forever—tormentingly—out of reach.

He turned, trying to escape the image, but it only made things worse. The scent so familiar, but warmer, closer. And the silky body so real beneath his hand that he could feel the slow beat of her pulse.

He opened his eyes and discovered that dreams really did come true. He was lying beside his sleeping love, his arm draped over her waist, her lips temptingly within kissing distance.

He resisted that temptation, knowing that once he kissed her she'd wake up, and this was a moment he never wanted to end. Then Posie woke and Grace opened her eyes.

Grace woke to the sound of Posie shouting joyfully from the nursery to let her know that it was time to get up. She lay for a moment, relishing the pleasure of a warm bed, the fact that she'd slept soundly, that the only weight pinning her down was Josh's hand on her hip.

Josh's hand.

And then she remembered.

What Josh had done. How, last night, when she'd been in despair, Josh had been there. Had made her truly a mother....

Had fallen asleep beside her.

She opened her eyes to look at him, only to find that he was watching her. That he hadn't just fallen asleep, but that he had stayed with her.

'Thank you,' she said.

He didn't answer, just gave her the sweetest kiss. A close-your-eyes-and-feel-the-tingle-in-your-toes kind of kiss. A first-kiss kind of kiss that was making her body do giddy little loop-the-loops.

And she knew that was where they had gone wrong. They hadn't started at the beginning but had gone for no-holds-barred, straight-to-hell passion. From here to eternity in one night. No words, all action.

He eased away to look at her. 'This is nice. Maybe we can do it again very soon?'

Now. Her body was screaming now and he was close enough for her to be aware that he was heading the same way. But she wasn't making the same mistake again and, lifting her hand to his lips, she said, 'We need to talk, Josh. I have a thousand things to tell you.'

Or maybe only one....

'Now?'

Posie was shouting for attention and then her mother called up the stairs to let Josh know that his driver had arrived to take him to London. Even so, she knew that if she'd said yes, now, he would have stayed right where he was. But then there would be no conversation.

'It will keep,' she said. And then she returned his kiss with a sweet, soft touch of her lips to his. A promise that she would be waiting. Always.

CHAPTER ELEVEN

'You're getting married, Grace. I know you want a quiet, simple wedding and we all respect that, but you do have to have a new dress and the wedding is the day after tomorrow.'

'That's plenty of time to buy a dress.'

Grace saw her mother and Laura Kingsley exchange meaningful looks. Whoever would have thought those two would become bosom buddies? Arranging a wedding made strange bedfellows.

The thought made her smile.

'We had a look in that boutique in the craft centre the other day,' Laura said casually.

'The one next to the aromatherapy place. I needed some lavender oil,' her mother added, as if to establish the fact that they hadn't actually been *looking* for a dress.

'Yes?'

'Gorgeous clothes,' Laura said. 'I fell in love with a jacket. I think I might go back and get it today.' Then, 'They had a beautiful dress in your size.'

'Really? I didn't know they did large sizes…'

'Layers of different fabrics cut asymmetrically,' her mother continued, ignoring her attempt to distract them, force them into reassuring her that she wasn't fat.

'Simple but very stylish,' Laura added.

They made a great double act.

'Stylish sounds good,' she said, playing along. 'What colour?'

'It was cream.'

'Cream? Outsize and frumpy, then.'

'Did you have any particular colour in mind?' Laura asked, and she just knew that the pair of them had been through every shop in Maybridge and, whatever she said, they'd have an answer.

'I always thought that if I ever got married, I'd wear one of Geena Wagner's designs,' she said absently. 'She has a small showroom in a department store in Melchester, but her workroom is in the craft centre. She commissions me to make the tiaras to match her gowns. Have you seen her work, Laura?' Josh's mother was a fashion plate and probably knew every hot designer who could stitch a seam. 'She uses appliqué, embroidery and beading to stunning effect. One of her dresses was featured in a spread in *Celebrity* last year,' she added. 'With one of my tiaras.'

'Yes…' Laura cleared her throat. 'I believe I saw it. Quite lovely. But I think you've left it a little late to go for a hand-made designer dress.'

'She's a friend. And I wasn't thinking of anything elaborate. A simple ankle-length column dress with one of those little jackets that just covers the shoulders and arms?'

'Even so. These things take months…' Then, 'If you don't like cream—and I admit it can be very draining—what about peach? We did see something in peach, didn't we, Dawn?'

'Not white, you think?' Grace interjected, all innocence.

'Grace…' Her mother's eyes narrowed as she belatedly twigged to the fact that they were being teased.

'Sorry. I couldn't resist.'

Laura was looking from one to the other. 'Am I missing something?'

'I called Geena last week, Laura. When I went to check that Abby was still managing without me.' Which she was. Brilliantly.

It was the day she'd woken in Josh's arms and she'd known that they weren't just going to have a wedding, but a marriage.

They still had to talk, but she'd known, deep in her heart, that after that night, after what he'd done for her, it would never be just a marriage on paper. And she wanted, when she stood beside him and said the words that would make them man and wife, to show him that it really meant something to her. Wanted it to be a day that neither of them would ever forget.

'I'm going for a fitting today. In fact,' she said, making a point of looking at her watch, 'if you can be ready in twenty minutes, you can come with me.'

There was a moment of stunned silence and then a frantic scramble as the pair of them rushed to change. Well, Laura rushed. Her mother was slower, but just as determined.

She was still grinning to herself when the phone rang and she picked it up, knowing it would be Josh. He'd phoned her morning, noon and night while he'd been in London. He was later today.

'You're late this morning. Did you oversleep?' she asked, without preamble.

'I had an early meeting and didn't want to call you before six.'

'Good decision. How are you?'

'Busy. Lonely without my little girl. How is she?'

'Thriving. Sleeping through without any problems now.'

'Good. And the grannies?'

'I'm not asking and they're not telling, but your credit card—or maybe it's Laura—appears to have totally corrupted my mother.'

'I'm delighted to hear it. Sufficiently to give up her principles about jumping the queue and allowing me to pay for her hip replacement, do you think?'

'Oh, Josh…'

'I have to go, Grace. I'll call you later.'

'Later,' she repeated, but was talking to the dialling tone.

Josh smiled as he shut off his cellphone, pushing open the door to the kind of jewellery store that had been beyond his wildest dreams when he'd bought that first ring for Grace.

Something unusual, antique, he thought. Emeralds to match her eyes….

He'd just handed over his credit card when his phone rang.

Still haunted by the thought that he might have missed a call from Michael, missing Grace's call, he moved away from the desk to check the caller.

It was his Chinese partner calling from Beijing. He let the call go to voicemail while he punched in his pin code. He wasn't due back in Maybridge until tomorrow, but he planned to surprise Grace, take her out, ask her to marry him. Be his wife.

'Congratulations, sir. I hope you'll be very happy,' the jeweller said as he handed him the ring.

His smile lasted until he was in the back of his limousine, when he listened to the frantic voicemail, the you-have-to-be-here-tomorrow bureaucratic foul-up that he couldn't ignore. It was his responsibility and his alone. He'd signed a contract. There were billions of dollars, thousands of jobs at stake.

He could call Grace, explain, put off the wedding until he could get back. She'd understand. But what would it be next time? How long would it be before he could get back to see Posie again? Months. She'd have grown, changed, forgotten him. And that was how it would be through all the years. He wouldn't be a father, or a husband in anything but name.

He'd be the stranger who turned up once in a blue moon, when it fitted in with his plans.

And he thought about what Dawn had told him to ask himself. Who gained, who would be hurt by the choices he made? But it was the latter that was important. Whose happiness you truly cared about.

He didn't, he discovered, have to agonise over that one. He knew.

It was late, long after Josh would normally have phoned, when a courier arrived with a package addressed to Grace and she knew—just knew—that whatever it contained she didn't want to know.

She shut herself in the study and opened the envelope. The letter inside was handwritten, brief and to the point:

Grace,
By the time you receive this I will be on my way to Beijing. It seems that you were right all along. I was fitting in our wedding, not because I was making time for it, but because it fitted in with my own schedule, just as I would fit Posie into my life.

I asked your mother how you knew what was the right to decision to make. She told me that if I was honest with myself it would be clear. It's time to be honest and admit that my life is not one that lends itself to either marriage or fatherhood. Posie is your child in every conceivable way and it is right and proper that you should have full care of her.

Enclosed with this letter you will find a copy of my instructions to Michael's lawyer that he should apply to the courts for a Parental Responsibility Order on your behalf. If you wish, later, to formally adopt Posie, I will make no objection.

I will, of course, stand by my agreement to buy the house once Probate is granted. Arrangements have also been made for the estate to pay a maintenance allowance for Posie and you as her carer, as well as any other necessary expenses.

I have no idea when I will return to Sydney, but if you need any further help in the future please contact Anna Carling. She has been instructed to treat any request from you as if it were my own.

Yours, Josh

'Why?' She waved the letter at her mother. 'Why is he doing this? What did you say to him?'

Her mother said nothing.

Laura looked as if she might say something but, when Grace turned on her, she shook her head. Then, 'He was marrying you to keep Posie? Why would he do that?'

'Because she is his daughter, Laura. Our daughter. My egg, his sperm…'

'Oh.' Then, 'But…' She shook her head. 'I don't understand any of it.'

'I think I do,' her mother said. 'It's a sacrifice move.'

'Sacrifice?'

'He's giving her up, surrendering her to you.'

'What?'

'We talked about it. About love. The choices you make. Holding on. Letting go. Whether you loved enough to let go even when it felt like tearing your heart out of your body.' Then, 'I think he just did that, Grace. Tore out his heart and gave it to you.'

Grace said something completely out of character. 'He's

giving up his daughter just because he had to fly off to Beijing and sort out some emergency and miss a ten minute ceremony in a *folly*? What kind of idiot is he?'

'I'm sorry. It never occurred to me… I thought…'

She shook her head. 'No, Mum, this isn't your fault. It's mine. I kept telling him he wasn't committed, that he'd never be here for Posie, when I should have been telling him that I love him.' She got up, walked to the phone. Picked it up. 'Clinging to my safe little nest instead of telling him that wherever he was I wanted to be, too.'

'Who are you calling?'

She stared at the phone. 'Good point. Who do you call when you want to book an airline ticket?'

'The Internet?'

'Right.'

'Where are you going?' Laura asked.

'Where do you think? Bei-flipping-jing.'

'Why don't you let me do that?' her mother said, taking the phone from her and replacing it. 'While you go and pack.'

'Two seats,' she said, backing out of the room. 'Or whatever they have for babies. On the first available flight.'

Her mother, flipping through the telephone directory, stopped. 'You can't take Posie.'

'I have to. I'm breastfeeding…'

'But you haven't got a passport for her.'

For a moment the world seemed to stand still. Then she said, 'Phoebe had. They were going to France this summer…'

Josh swiped the key to his suite and walked in, desperate for a shower, a drink, sleep.

It was finally sorted. Something or nothing that would have been fixed in ten minutes in Australia had required delicate diplomacy, tact, face-saving manoeuvres, when one phrase in a contract had been incorrectly translated.

He opened the mini-bar, took out a Scotch, put it back and took out a bottle of water instead.

His body was in enough trouble without adding alcohol to the mix.

He tossed his jacket on the sofa, loosened his tie, opened the bedroom door and stopped. When he'd left it, this room had contained nothing except the carry-on grip he used when travelling.

Now there was a bright pink holdall, a box of disposable nappies, a very familiar buggy and a cot had been set up at the foot of the bed. The cot contained a sleeping Posie and in the bed Grace lay, fully dressed, flat on her back with her arms thrown out.

Grace?

It couldn't be. The longing, the need, the unbelievable loneliness were inducing hallucinations.

He closed his eyes. Opened them again. She was still there but, needing to convince himself that she was real, he put out a hand and very gently, so as not to wake her, touched her cheek. Then kissed her just as gently.

No illusion, but warm, real flesh.

Grace, who never went anywhere, who had made herself sick rather than go on a school trip to France, had flown half-way round the world to… What? He'd given her everything she wanted.

He turned to Posie. She was lying exactly like her mother. Flat on her back, arms flung wide.

He didn't think he could bear it.

He wanted to hold them both, tell them how much he'd missed them, how much he loved them. But he'd made his decision and, leaving them to sleep, he shut himself in the bathroom, showered as quietly as he could, half expecting that when he opened the door, they would have disappeared.

He was half right. Posie was still asleep, but the bed was empty and he walked through to the living room where Grace was signing the bill for room service.

'I tried not to wake you,' he said.

'Kissing a girl when you've got a beard is not something you can do without repercussions, Josh,' she said, as she poured two cups of tea. Helped herself to a sandwich.

'You're not giving me much of an incentive to shave it off, Grace. I thought you'd be asleep for hours. Why are you here?'

'You have to ask? You bailed out on our talk, Josh. The one we were going to have about the future, about us. And you bailed out on our wedding, too. Okay. It happens. You walked out on me after the most incredible, most perfect night of my life and I should have been ready for you to cut and run again.'

Perfect?

'If it had just been me,' Grace went on, 'I could have lived with it. I've lived without the man I love for ten years so the rest of my life would be a breeze. But I'm here to tell you that I don't believe you'd run out on your daughter, Joshua Kingsley.'

'Ten years?' He shook his head. That didn't make sense. The fact that she was here didn't make sense. 'I did what I thought was for the best, Grace,' he said.

'I'm here to tell you that you're wrong. And that I'm really tired of you leaving before the credits have rolled. Before I can tell you that I love you. That I've always loved you. You're an impossible act to follow, Josh Kingsley.'

There. She'd said it. It was over. And, right on cue, Posie woke up and began to chatter to herself.

'Your daughter is awake, Josh,' she said, getting up and

walking back into the bedroom. 'I've left a couple of feeders of breast milk in the fridge to keep you going until you can buy some formula and there are enough nappies to keep you going for a day or two. Anna is interviewing nannies.' She picked up the pink holdall and began to walk to the door.

'Grace?'

She didn't stop. Didn't turn round.

'Where are you going?'

'Home,' she said, not missing a stride. 'I've done what I came for. I've brought you your daughter.'

'No!'

She reached the door.

'Please, Grace.'

Opened it.

'I love you.'

She let out the breath she'd been holding but still didn't turn round.

'I've always loved you. I came back that first year with a ring in my pocket.'

'No…' That couldn't be true. He'd scarcely looked at her. 'No,' she said, turning to face him. 'You never called. Never wrote. Not even a postcard.'

'I meant to, but I didn't know what to say. Sorry? Thank you? There was only one thing you'd want to hear and I couldn't write it.'

Plain and honest… She was certainly getting what she'd asked for.

'So why the ring?'

'I couldn't face you without it and then, having screwed myself to the sticking point, admitted that I wanted you, I discovered that you'd found someone else.'

'And you just accepted that? Didn't bother to put up a fight? Josh Kingsley, who always got what he went after?'

'I was…relieved.'

'Off the hook, you mean. That wasn't love, Josh. That was guilt. And you were married to Jessie within a year. Still, when you've got a ring…'

'I didn't give Jessie your ring. I threw it in the bin, then I realised that Phoebe would find it, so I took it out again. I still have it.'

She shook her head, not wanting to believe it.

'It's in my apartment in Sydney. At the back of my sock drawer.'

'No…'

It was a cry from the heart for everything she'd lost and in a second he was there beside her, his arms around her, but she had to tell him. Now. This minute, before her heart shattered.

'There was never anyone else, Josh. There has never been anyone else. They were all just camouflage. You'd left me and I didn't want you to know how much that had hurt me. One word. If you'd just said one word…'

'I was afraid. I thought you'd slow me down.'

She looked up at him. 'You were right.'

'Was I? Truly? If I'd had an ounce of your strength, purpose, if I'd had the courage to tell you that I loved you, you would have braved anything to come with me.'

She shook her head, but he caught her chin, forced her to look at him.

'It's true. How did you do it now, Grace? Where did you find the strength to fly into the unknown?'

'Love,' she said. 'Your love, your sacrifice gave me wings.'

'And now you're prepared to do the same?'

'Actually, Josh, I was banking on the fact that having done it yourself, you'd finally get the message.'

'Tell me anyway.'

'"…whither thou goest, I will go; and where thou lodgest,

I will lodge…" We're a family, Josh. It doesn't matter where we are, so long as we're together.'

Josh felt as if his heart were bursting. He'd given everything and in return he'd gained the world.

'There's just one more question,' he said. 'Will you marry me? Not a paper marriage, but a making babies, till-death-us-do part, forever and a day marriage. In a wedding with flowers and bridesmaids and doves and string quartets. I'll even shave off the beard.'

'No,' she said. Then, while his heart was still recovering from the shock, 'No doves, no string quartets and I'll take a rain check on the beard until I've road-tested it.' Then, when he just grinned, 'That's a hint, Josh. We've got ten years to catch up on.'

From the Maybridge Gazette:

DUCKS ADD DELIGHT
AND DRAMA TO WEDDING

Local businesswoman Grace McAllister and Maybridge-born tycoon Joshua Kingsley were married today in a charmingly simple ceremony in the folly at Melchester Castle.

The bride wore a Geena Wagner gown in ivory silk with a matching high-collared bolero that had been appliquéd and embroidered in shades of green and turquoise. Her matching tiara was designed and made by the bride's business partner, Abby Green.

The couple's niece, Posie Kingsley, and the groom's half-sisters, Lucy, Alice and Maude Kingsley were bridesmaids.

The ceremony was followed by a country picnic for

family and friends beside the lake where the guests were entertained by a traditional fiddler, folk singers and morris dancing. A dozen white ducks, decked out in emerald bows, added rural charm to the scene, but during the afternoon they escaped their handler and made for the lake. So far all attempts to capture them have failed.

The couple, who have now left on an extended honeymoon that reportedly includes India, the United States and Japan, have homes in Maybridge and Sydney, Australia.

ALEJANDRO'S
SEXY SECRET

AMY RUTTAN

I couldn't have written Alejandro's story without Amalie, Tina and Annie. You ladies are the best to build a world with.

Annie – Mad Ron's wouldn't exist without you!

Also I want to thank Amalie and my editor, Laura, for taking on the monumental task of whipping this quartet into shape.

PROLOGUE

Las Vegas, Nevada

KIRI WALKED OUT onto the patio of the private villa her friends had rented at one of Vegas's most luxurious five-star resorts. It was getting too crazy inside. There was a lot of alcohol and antics, including a very dirty cake that would make her *naanii* blush.

Heck, it made her blush just thinking about the racy genital-shaped cake.

There were some shrieks from her friends as the bride-to-be opened up another questionable gift. Kiri chuckled and then shouted through the open window.

"You're surgeons, you've seen those parts before!"

Her friends began to giggle again and Kiri just shook her head and sat down on one of the lounge chairs that overlooked the private pool and walled garden. Sandy, the bridezilla-to-be, was accusing her of being a party pooper on this bachelorette weekend and maybe she was, but she was thinking about her final residency exam that was coming up. Also, she was envious. Sandy had it all. She was getting married, she had a career and she knew Sandy and Tony wanted to start a family right away. It was everything that Kiri had always wanted.

The problem was she couldn't find the right guy.

Once she'd thought she'd found the right guy, the only problem being she hadn't been the right woman for him.

To get over her heartache she focused on her work. Never really cutting loose. If she couldn't have a husband and family right now, she'd have her career.

"You're my maid of honor, Kiri. You're coming to Vegas, whether you like it or not!"

"Professor Vaughan is tough, Sandy. He only picks the cream of the pediatric surgery hopefuls to work with him. I have to study. Go have fun without me."

"No, you're coming to have fun. The last three men you went on dates with you blew off because of studying. You need to have fun every once in a while too."

Kiri had come to Vegas, but had brought her books with her. She'd smuggled them like contraband in her luggage. She reached down and pulled out a notebook from where she'd stashed it. She flipped to where she'd left off, brought up the flashlight app on her smartphone and tried to cram like she'd never crammed before.

Except it was kind of difficult with that music blaring in the background.

Lord.

She rammed her fingers in her ears and held the book open with her elbows pressed against her lap and read until her glasses began to slide down her nose.

Blast.

She couldn't study this way.

Her friends had already completed their exams, knew where they were going to be practicing their surgical skills. The pediatric surgical residency exams weren't until next week. She should be back in New York and studying, not here. Of course as a maid of honor she had a bit of a duty to Sandy. And she was failing miserably. At least Sandy's sister had picked up some slack. Like arranging this weekend.

Blast that Sandy for getting engaged to Tony and having a wedding so close to exams. Who does that?

Tony was already a surgeon and was apparently somewhere in Florida, enjoying a golf weekend. Florida was probably warmer than here. She closed her notebook and shivered in the evening chill.

"I thought Vegas was supposed to be hot," she muttered to herself, and took a sip of her Bellini, which was a poor choice to have when she was already chilled.

"It's the desert. At night it gets cold. So *very* cold."

Kiri spun around to see who was speaking in the thick, Latin drawl that sent a shiver of something down her spine. Her mouth dropped open at the sight of the tall, muscular, Latino god who was leaning casually against the French doors. He had a dimple in his cheek as he grinned at her, perfect white teeth and those dark eyes sparkled in the light that shone out through the doors, promising something sinfully delicious.

"P-pardon?" Kiri said, pushing up her dark-framed glasses, which had slid down her nose again and were beginning to fog up. She cursed herself inwardly for forgetting her contact lenses in New York.

"The desert. It's very hot during the day, but at night it's *muy frio*. It's cold."

"Who are you?" she asked.

A lazy grin spread across his face. "Your friends sent me out here to lighten your mood. They said you've been a bit of a party pooper this weekend and you need to loosen up."

Oh. My. God.

She glanced over his shoulder and could see another group of bronzed muscular gods dancing to music while her friends cheered them on. This was the "entertainment" Sandy had been talking about. Male exotic dancers.

Apparently the best that Vegas had to offer.

Heat flushed in her cheeks as he took a step closer to her. He took her hand and led her into the room, sitting her down on the couch.

"Why don't you sit back, *mi tesoro*?" he whispered in that honeyed drawl against her ear that made her forget that she was always just a bit awkward around men. "Let me take care of you."

"Um…" A million thoughts were racing through her mind, but then all those thoughts melted into a pile of goo as he pushed her back against the cushions.

A familiar song that she'd heard so many times when she'd been young came across the stereo system. The kind her and her high-school friends had giggled at but which the school would never play at a dance.

Sandy and her friends began to shriek as the group of exotic dancers began to move together in a choreographed, erotic dance.

And as that Latino god began to move, his hips rolling, she suddenly understood why they didn't play that song at high-school dances. Why her parents hated that song. As she sat there on the couch, her friends screaming around her and that gorgeous specimen of a man's dark eyes locked on her, only her, he grinned at her, as if knowing she was completely aroused by him. He rolled his hips and peeled his shirt off, revealing a tattoo on a muscle-hardened chest, and she realized what she'd been missing. Why she'd been uptight. When was the last time she'd been with someone?

It had been a long time.

Kiri's leg began to tap in a nervous twitch she'd had since she was a kid, when she'd been the chubby geek that no one had paid attention to.

He moved toward her and laid a strong hand against her leg, settling the incessant tapping. His touch burned and set her blood on fire, her body reacting to the pure magnetism and sex he was exuding.

And for some reason he was focused on her.

He's being paid to do this. This is what Sandy wanted.

And that's what she was telling herself as he moved closer to her, pushing her back against the pillows, dancing just for her. He placed her hands on his narrow hips as he moved above her.

"Um…" slipped past her lips and she was mesmerized. Even though she knew it was all an act, this man held her in complete rapture. His deep, dark eyes were locked on hers and there was something about him that completely sucked her in.

Then he turned his back to her as the song ended and Kiri still sat there stunned. The Bellini she had been holding was no longer slushy but melted as she'd been gripping the glass so tightly before he'd taken it from her, deposited it on a table and placed her cool hands on his warm-skinned hips. Her heart was racing and it felt like she was on fire.

She couldn't remember the last time she'd been so turned on, so enthralled by a man. She couldn't even remember the last time she'd had sex. It had been during her residency and with Chad, the man who had broken her heart, but for the life of her all those moments with Chad were obliterated. All she saw was this gorgeous man in front of her. All she could think about was having him. That much she knew.

The last several years she'd been so focused on becoming a pediatric surgeon she'd thrown every last piece of herself into becoming the best darned surgeon in the program. So much so she'd forgotten how much she missed connecting with another person.

Just wanting a simple touch.

A kiss.

And more.

I have to get out of here.

The exotic dancers were now focused on Sandy, which was good. She left her glass of sludgy, melted Bellini on the side table and slipped out of the villa, putting some distance between her and the bachelorette party as fast as her little legs could carry her before she did something she'd completely regret.

"That was a good show tonight. Don't you think, Alejandro?"

"What?" Alejandro asked. He hadn't been really listening to Fernando, one of the dancers in his troupe, as they sat in the lounge of the hotel after entertaining that group of women at the bachelorette party. His thoughts were strictly on the beautiful woman he'd given the private dance to at the beginning. The one who had slipped out of the party when his back had been turned.

The one who was now sitting alone at the bar, nursing a glass of wine. Alejandro couldn't take his eyes off her. She had curves in all the right places and though she was short, her legs looked long and were crossed in a ladylike way and she was swirling her one foot around.

Maybe it was the tight black dress or the stilettos that accentuated her beauty; either way, he couldn't tear his eyes from her gorgeous legs.

"Yo, Alejandro? Snap out of it." Fernando waved a hand in front of his face.

"What?" Alejandro said again.

"I asked you if you thought it went well tonight. I was a bit surprised when Ricky decided to fly us in from Miami to Las Vegas, but now, with this cut from that bachelorette party and being put up at this swanky hotel until tomorrow night, I'm never going to question a thing he says again."

"Yeah, yeah, for sure." Alejandro got up from the table

where he'd been sitting with his fellow dancers. "I think I'm going to stick around here tonight, rather than go out."

"You sure, bro?" another of them asked.

Alejandro nodded. "Yeah. I'm tired."

And he really didn't want to spend the large cut he'd just received on gambling and drinking tonight. Not when this was the last bit of the money he needed to pay off his student loans. This was finally his freedom from exotic dancing.

His freedom from Ricky.

He'd made it all through medical school without his older brothers finding out about what he did. They'd offered to help him pay for medical school, but they had sacrificed enough for him so he'd told them he worked down at the docks, gutting fish, and had been adamant he'd pay his own way through medical school. They didn't need to know he'd started as a dance host in a seedy samba bar before being discovered by Ricky and moving into this. Next week he was starting a residency in transplant surgery in Miami in the pediatric department of Buena Vista Hospital and he wouldn't have to dance again.

This had been his last dance and he'd never had a client walk out on him before. It was bothering him a bit.

As his friends left the bar to seek other pleasures for the rest of the night, Alejandro drummed up enough courage to go over and talk to her. He hoped he wouldn't offend her. That was the last thing he wanted to do.

He'd been a little unnerved when he'd been sent out to retrieve her from the villa courtyard. When he'd seen her, he'd been stunned by her beauty. She was curvy, but he liked a woman who was curvy. Her long black hair had shimmered in the moonlight and those large, dark eyes made him melt just a bit.

There were a lot of beautiful women he'd been drawn to over his years of dancing, but nothing like this. It was like a bolt of pure, electric attraction. He wanted to run his hands over her body, taste her lips, touch her silky hair. He was asking for trouble just approaching her, because clients were against his rules, but he had to know why she'd been so disgusted with him.

Walk away, Alejandro.

"I'll have a mineral water and a twist of lemon," he said to the bartender as he took the empty seat beside her, his heart hammering against his rib cage. He'd never felt so nervous around a woman before.

What was it about her?

"Sure thing." The bartender moved away and the woman glanced over at him, her dark eyes widening in shock. A blush tinged her caramel cheeks and Alejandro knew that she recognized him but didn't want to admit it.

"You slipped out," he said, not looking at her, keeping his gaze fixed on the rows of bottles behind the bar.

"Pardon?" she said, her voice quivering a bit.

He turned to her. "You slipped out of the show at your friend's villa."

"I don't know what you're talking about." She fidgeted with the stem of her wine glass. He leaned over and caught the scent of coconut in her dark hair and he drank it in.

"Ah, but you do, *mi tesoro*," he whispered in her ear.

The bartender brought him the mineral water and Alejandro paid him. He picked up the highball glass and took a sip, watching her as she fidgeted, obviously uncomfortable in his presence.

"Well, perhaps I was mistaken. Have a good night." He turned to walk away.

"Why would it matter?" she asked.

He turned. "Why would what matter?"

"You noticing me leaving."

"Yes, I did."

"I'm sure women leave you…" She cleared her throat. "I'm sure they leave your shows all the time."

Alejandro sat back down. "Not *my* shows."

She snorted and he was enchanted. "You're awfully arrogant."

"I have every right to be. I'm good at what I do." He winked at her and she smiled. He was getting through the walls she'd built up. Not that he knew why she'd built such impenetrable walls, but he knew when he'd been dancing for her that she'd been keeping a part of herself locked away and that was very intriguing to him.

Why would she hide herself away?

"So you're telling me that in a nightclub you notice if people come and go?"

"No, I'm not saying that."

"You just did!" Then she imitated him. "'Not *my* shows.'"

He chuckled. It was sexy the way she tried to get her high voice to deepen. Her brow furrowed and her lips pursed a bit when she did it. "That's a very good impression."

She blushed again. "So are you denying you said that?"

"No, I'm not, just that I don't dance in nightclubs, which is a polite way of saying strip clubs."

She pushed back an errant strand of her inky-black hair. "Strip clubs, then."

"I don't dance in strip clubs. I used to dance in samba bars, but the clothes stayed on. Now my services are primarily hired for private sessions like tonight. I'm *that* good. Women are willing to pay my agent whatever I desire."

She rolled her eyes. "You're laying it on thick. No one is that good."

"I am. I take pride in my work. Don't you take pride in your work?"

"I do. In fact, I'm one of the best there is."

He cocked an eyebrow, even more intrigued, and he couldn't help but wonder what else she was good at. "Really?"

"Yes. Which is why I left the party early. Work is *that* important to me. I had things to look over."

"Then how do you unwind?"

"Unwind? What is this mythical thing you're talking about?" she teased.

Alejandro couldn't help but laugh. His older brothers often teased him about working too hard, never relaxing. Only he didn't really feel like he had the right to unwind. He had to work hard. He had too much to live up to.

"Perhaps you're right. For those of us dedicated to what we do, there is no down time. Also, there is no perfection until all parties are satisfied, and I don't think you were satisfied with my performance."

And the blush tinged her cheeks again. "I'm sorry for walking out."

"Then allow me to show you what you missed."

What're you doing?

"What?" she said, her voice hitching. "I don't have that… I don't even know your name. I can't go off with a stranger."

Alejandro reached into his jacket pocket and pulled out his business card.

"My name is Alejandro. There is all my business information. I'm fully bonded. I take my work seriously and wouldn't jeopardize that. I dance. That's all. I'm not a gigolo and nothing untoward would happen. It's hands-off."

She took the card. "Why do you want me to go with you?"

"Like I said, I don't like leaving a customer unsatisfied." He held out his hand. "Your friend paid me to put on a good show for her bridal party. Please let me finish it."

Never had he ever approached a customer, but it bothered him that she'd walked out of his performance. Or maybe it was the fact he thought she was the most beautiful woman in the world. He couldn't remember the last time he'd seen someone so beautiful.

Either way, he waited with bated breath for her answer, expecting her to say no.

She drank down the rest of her wine. "I'm probably crazy, but this is Vegas and what happens in Vegas stays in Vegas, right?"

His pulse thundered between his ears as he held her soft, delicate hand in his. "Absolutely."

CHAPTER ONE

Five years later. Miami, spring

"You know you married the ugly brother, right?" Alejandro was teasing his new sister-in-law Saoirse Murphy on her marriage to his brother. His ugly brother.

Saoirse, a fiery Irish beauty, had recently married Santiago, who was rolling his eyes as Alejandro and the twins, Rafe and Dante, joined in the good-natured ribbing. They were all the "ugly brothers," but right now Santi was taking the heat because he'd been the first of the Valentino brothers to take the plunge and marry.

"It's your fault," Santi shouted, pointing at Dante and Rafe. "You two are the elders. You should be married already, then I wouldn't be getting this teasing from the baby."

Alejandro chuckled and moved out of the line of fire. He knew Dante and Rafe didn't like to be referred to as the elders, but Santi and he had always done that behind their backs.

The elders were surrogate fathers to him. As Santi had been, before he'd run off and joined the Marines. All because of a robbery in the family bodega. A robbery that had almost cost Alejandro his life, as well. He'd been caught in the cross fire, taking a bullet in the chest at the age of ten.

He'd be dead if it hadn't been for his father's heart saving his life, and because of his father's death he carried a piece of his father with him. It was a huge responsibility he carried proudly. Which was why he was now one of the best pediatric transplant surgeons at Buena Vista Hospital.

Speaking of which...

"I'm sorry, I have to get to the hospital. The new head of pediatric surgery starts today. Apparently she's a bit of a *culo duro*."

"Culo duro?" Saoirse asked Santi.

"Hard ass," Santi said to his new bride, and then he turned to Alejandro. "Don't judge the new head just yet, baby brother. She might not be as bad as the rumors make her out to be."

Alejandro ground his teeth at Santi calling him "baby brother." He hated that, just as much as Rafe and Dante hated being called the elders, but, then, it was all in good fun and he deserved it a bit for calling Santi the ugly one.

Instead of sniping back, Alejandro took Saoirse's hand in his and kissed her knuckles. "Sorry for not sticking around too long, so let me say *felicitaciones les deseamos a ambos toda la felicidad del mundo.*"

Saoirse's brow furrowed. "Congratulations...wishing both of you..."

"All the happiness in the world." Alejandro kissed her hand again.

"Suficiente idiota!" Santi said, slapping Alejandro upside the head.

"Ow, I'm not an idiot." Alejandro winked at Saoirse, who was laughing, obviously enjoying the show of them tormenting Santi.

Dante snorted and Rafe rolled his eyes while Alejandro grinned at Santi, who was busy shooting daggers at him.

"Well, I guess we should be happy he kept speaking Spanish after Mami and Pappi died," Dante groaned. "But does he have to upstage us?"

Alejandro winked at Dante. "Always, old man. Always."

He left the bodega before his older brothers started a brawl. He waved to Carmelita, who'd run the business since he was eleven. She waved back, but was focused on her work.

Outside the bodega the heat was oppressive, which was strange for a spring day. It was always hot in Miami, but this was like summer. Moist, sweltering heat. Palm trees lining the street of the old neighborhood were swaying, but the wind didn't suppress the cloying heat. A storm was brewing to the south.

Fitting.

He'd heard people refer to Dr. Bhardwaj as the Wicked Witch of the East, so it was only fitting her arrival be marked by a storm.

As he walked to his motorcycle a group of boys playing soccer in the street kicked a ball toward him and he kicked it back, waving at them. He knew most of the kids because their parents were people he'd gone to school with. People who had never left the old neighborhood, which comprised a tight-knit community of people from Heliconia, a small island nation in the Caribbean. He'd never been there as his parents had fled the country because of the horrible conditions long before he'd been born.

Only that didn't matter. Everyone here in this neighborhood was family. Everyone stayed together.

Only he had left.

His apartment was in South Beach. He was disconnected from this place because it reminded him of his parents dying, his brothers sacrificing so much of their youth for him.

It was also the place he'd first met Ricky at a scuzzy samba bar where he'd danced with lonely women. Ricky had started in the more lucrative exotic dancing, just so he could make his own way in the world.

Don't think about it. That's all behind you. Focus on now.

He had to keep his head in the game. He'd worked hard to become an attending in pediatric transplant surgery at Buena Vista Hospital. There was no way he was going to let some new head of pediatric surgery force him out.

He usually wouldn't be so worried, but apparently Dr. Bhardwaj wanted to make changes.

And changes meant cuts. He had no doubt the arrival of Dr. Bhardwaj was down to Mr. Snyder, current president of the board of directors. Ever since Snyder had taken over he'd been looking for a way to cut every single department's pro bono fund.

It was a fairly easy ride from Little Heliconia to Buena Vista. The only change was the darkening clouds rolling in.

Yes. Definitely a storm.

"Where have you been?" Dr. Micha asked the moment Alejandro walked into the attendings' locker room.

"My brother Santi just got married," Alejandro replied casually. He didn't really want to engage in conversation with Dr. Micha today.

"Mazel tov," Dr. Micha said sarcastically. "The witch is on her broom, by the way."

Alejandro cocked his eyebrow. "Oh, yes?"

Usually he ignored Dr. Raul Micha's gossip. The man was a paranoid worrywart and thankfully worked far from Alejandro, in Pediatric Dermatology, but for some reason Raul thought he and Alejandro were best friends forever.

"She's made cuts to my program already." Dr. Micha shook his head. "Cuts, can you believe it? Snyder is behind it, I'm sure. Snyder was friends with Dr. Bhardwaj's mentor up in New York, Dr. Vaughan."

Alejandro was impressed as Dr. Vaughan was a world-renowned pediatric surgeon. So at least Dr. Bhardwaj should know what she was doing, but then he recalled the word that sent a chill down his spine.

"Cuts?" Alejandro's stomach churned. This was exactly what he'd been afraid of.

"Yes. She's slashed all I've worked for."

"Buena Vista is a wealthy hospital. It's not like Seaside. Why is the board making cuts?"

"Buena Vista was wealthy," Raul said in a snarky voice. Then he peered out the door. "Oh, man, here she comes. You're on your own."

Alejandro rolled his eyes as Raul slipped out of the locker room. He pulled off his street clothes and pulled out his scrubs. Before he'd slipped his scrub top on the door to the attendings' locker room opened. Alejandro glanced over his shoulder and then did a double take as he stared into the dark eyes of the one who'd got away.

Kiri.

His one and only one-night stand from his days as an exotic dancer was standing right in front of him. He'd finished the private show five years ago and she'd kissed him. Alejandro knew he should've pushed her away, only he'd been unable to.

"Please, don't think badly of me, I've never done this," she whispered. *"Never slept with a man I just met."*

"I don't do this either." He ran his hands through her hair. *"You're the most beautiful woman I've seen in a long time."*

Her mouth was open, her eyes wide behind those dark-framed glasses she still wore. She recognized him. This was bad.

"What…? I…" She was at a loss for words.

"Sorry," he apologized, slipping on his scrub top. He held out his hand. "Dr. Bhardwaj, I presume?"

He was going to pretend he didn't know her.

Which was a lie.

He knew every inch of her. It was still fresh in his mind

five years later. The taste of her skin, her scent and the way she'd sighed when he'd nibbled her neck just below her ear.

This was bad.

"Uh. Yes." She was still staring at him like he was a ghost, an unwanted ghost at that. She took his hand and shook it quickly before snatching it back. "Yes, I'm Dr. Bhardwaj."

He nodded. "I'm Dr. Valentino. Senior Attending on the pediatric transplant team."

Dr. Valentino? His name is Valentino?

Kiri had never known her Latin god's last name. Of course, she hadn't stuck around after her one indiscretion in Las Vegas.

A stolen night of passion that had led to a pregnancy, even though they'd used protection. And then that had led to a late miscarriage at twenty-three weeks, which still hurt all these years later. Staring up at the father of her lost baby boy reminded her in an instant of all the things that could've been.

Even though the pregnancy had been an inconvenience, she'd wanted her baby. She'd wanted to be a mother so badly. It hadn't been how she'd planned to start a family, but she'd been thrilled at the prospect of motherhood. And she'd tried to track down Alejandro, but when she'd called his number she'd learned he'd quit and the agent, Ricky, had refused to give her any information about Alejandro's whereabouts.

Alejandro reminded her of pain.

Yeah, lots of pain. And the wound of losing their child was fresh and raw again.

And he clearly didn't remember her, which was like a slap across the face.

What did you expect, sleeping with a male stripper?

"Yes, sorry, Dr. Valentino. It's a pleasure to meet you."

Come on, Kiri. Get it together.

She was still in shock.

Alejandro smiled, that charming, sexy smile that had melted down her walls and inhibitions five years ago.

"A pleasure to meet you too. Well, excuse me, Dr. Bhardwaj. I have a consult."

He wants to finish changing in privacy.

"Of course. Perhaps after your consult we can arrange a meeting to discuss the expectations of your department."

"Yes. It would be my pleasure."

"I want you," she whispered. "And I've never wanted a man like this before. Please take me."

"My pleasure." And he ran his lips over her body, kissing her in places no one had ever kissed her before.

Kiri turned on her heel and got out of that locker room as fast as she could.

Ugh. You're the head of the department.

Kiri was angry at herself for turning tail and running. When she'd miscarried she'd promised herself she'd never run from the father if she ever saw him again.

She'd tell him everything she was thinking. Those dark thoughts she'd had as she'd recovered from her loss. Everything that had crossed her mind when she'd learned that her baby was gone.

Turn around.

Alejandro was leaving the locker room. He looked so different in scrubs and a white lab coat. Given that she'd had her one-night stand with him five years ago and he was an attending in pediatric transplants, no less, in a world-class hospital, it meant that he must've been a doctor when he'd been dancing.

Which made her angry.

Why had he been doing that? Disgracing himself?

"Dr. Valentino, a moment, if you please."

He turned.

Ha. You can't get rid of me that easily.
"Yes, Dr. Bhardwaj?"
"I'd like to join you on your consult."
He frowned. "Why?"
Good. She had him on edge. She had the power back.
"Why not? I have no patient load yet and I'd like to see how you run your practice. The chief told me you are quite the star when it comes to pediatric transplants."
Which was true. Though she had a hard time believing it until she saw it for herself. Perhaps because she'd learned long before she'd met Dr. Alejandro Valentino that you really couldn't depend on anyone but yourself.
And she wanted to throw him off his game.
One thing she had learned while going through her department's finances when she'd first arrived in Miami had been that Alejandro's department had a lot of pro bono cases. It was admirable, but the board had made it clear to her in no uncertain terms that the pro bono cases had to stop. The board wanted Buena Vista Hospital to be for the elite of Miami.
All those who couldn't afford to be a patient at Buena Vista had to be moved to Seaside or County. The aim of the board was to cater to the rich and famous. The "beautiful people," as one board member had put it.
It was a shame, but she understood that Buena Vista wanted to be at the cutting edge of health and it was a dream Kiri wanted to share.
Perhaps once they had that distinction she could convince them to open up their pockets to pro bono cases once again. Although Mr. Snyder had made it clear that pro bono cases were finished. And she almost wondered why she'd taken the job, because since her arrival it had been a headache dealing with the board of directors. In particular Snyder.

Then again, she'd have felt a bit guilty if she hadn't taken the job her mentor had put her up for.

"Kiri, this is an opportunity of a lifetime. At your age, you won't get a position like this in Manhattan. Buena Vista is a world-class hospital. Take the job I trained you for. Snyder is a friend of mine and I know he runs a good hospital and you'll be treated right."

She snorted at the memory, because it had been too good to be true.

"Of course. If you want to follow me, you can meet with my patient," Alejandro said.

She nodded and followed him down the hall. It was awkward walking beside him, both of them pretending that they didn't know each other. Of course, they really didn't know each other, other than intimately.

Kiri could remember clearly what he looked like naked. How he tasted and how he felt buried deep inside her. Yet he acted like they were strangers.

He should have some recollection of her.

He's forgotten you.

She had after all probably just been a forgettable experience for him.

Kiri knew that she wasn't particularly memorable to many men. Which was probably why she didn't really believe in love in the traditional sense. Even though her parents loved each other, but that was rare.

All Kiri believe in was science and medicine.

Her work.

Although science and medicine had failed her that night five years ago when she'd lost her baby. That pregnancy was the closest she'd ever gotten to love and it had been snatched from her in a cruel twist of fate.

Don't think about that.

Alejandro grabbed the patient's chart from the nurses' station, smiling at the women behind the counter. She could see the effect he had on them—there were a few dreamy expressions—but as he walked past a male nurse he received a fist bump from the man.

He was charming and had everyone fooled. Just like she'd been.

"The patient we're seeing is one of the pro bono cases sent over from Little Heliconia. The patient is an eight-year-old boy with cystic fibrosis. The family only speaks Spanish. Do you speak Spanish?"

"No, well, only a bit, not enough to keep up."

Alejandro frowned. "Well, before we go in I'll fill you in on his condition and what I'll be explaining to the parents. That way I don't have to keep stopping to interpret for you." The way he said it made it sound like her presence was an inconvenience but she didn't care. He wasn't scaring her away and she knew that was his current tactic.

Kiri nodded. "Okay."

"José Agadore has end-stage liver failure. Intrahepatic bile obstruction led to the deterioration of the liver tissue. By the time County sent him to Buena Vista there was nothing to be done to help the liver and I placed him on UNOS. Today I'm going to be updating the family on his condition."

"There's no liver match yet, then?" Kiri asked, making notes. Snyder wanted notes on all current pro bono cases in her department. Each head of each department of the hospital was doing the same.

Alejandro shook his head. "And the boy is not doing well. His last panel of blood showed ascites and a bilirubin count of three point one."

Kiri flipped open the chart to see the labs and sighed. It didn't look very promising. The more a body took a pounding while waiting for a liver, the less chance the patient had to pull through the surgery. "Has he passed cardiovascular and respiratory tests?"

Alejandro nodded. "He's just waiting. Like so many are."

Kiri nodded and followed Alejandro into the patient's room. The little boy was jaundiced and was sleeping, a nasal cannula helping the poor mite to breathe. Kiri's heart went out to the family. A mother and father huddled on the room's couch, dark circles under their eyes. They immediately stood when Alejandro stepped up to the bedside, hope in their eyes, but they didn't even glance in her direction.

"Buenos días, Señor y Señora Agadore, cómo está haciendo José esta mañana?" Alejandro asked.

"Tan bueno como se puede esperar," Mr. Agadore said, then his glance fell on Kiri. She gave them a friendly smile, but it was clear they didn't trust her. Not that she blamed them. They were scared, tired and there was a language barrier separating them.

"As good as could be expected," the father had said. Kiri had understood that. She'd heard that same phrase in several languages from countless parents whose children had been fighting for their lives, the same haunted expression in their eyes.

Alejandro turned and nodded at her. *"Permitame presente Dr. Bhardwaj. Ella es el jefe de cirugía pediátrica."*

The Agadores smiled politely and nodded. *"Hola."*

Kiri half listened, catching a few words here and there as Alejandro spoke to the frightened parents about what was happening with their son and how they had to continue to wait until a match for their son was found.

When Alejandro reached across and shook the Agadores' hands, they turned to her and she shook their hands as well. Alejandro opened the door and they walked out into the hall. She followed him as he returned José's chart to the nurses' station.

The charming, easygoing smile was gone, replaced by a man who was subdued because, like her, he knew that José didn't have much longer to live.

"How much time does he have left?" Kiri asked.

"Days," Alejandro said. "I keep my phone on, just waiting for the call from UNOS."

"Well, I hope the call comes soon. Thank you for letting me in on your consult. We'll speak again soon." She tried to leave but Alejandro stopped her.

"You can't cut my program."

"Pardon?" She asked stunned.

"I know that you've made cuts. I've heard the rumors," Alejandro whispered. "You can't cut the transplant program, any part of the transplant program."

She crossed her arms. "This is not the time or place to speak about this, Dr. Valentino."

He grabbed her by the arm and led her outside, into an alleyway. Thunder rolled in the distance and she glanced up at the sky to see dark clouds, but the heat was still oppressive. It was a bit eerie.

"What is the meaning of this?" she demanded.

"You can't make cuts," he repeated.

"I'm the head of the department. If cuts need to be made, I'll decide," she snapped.

"If you make cuts there will be hell to pay," he said through clenched teeth. His eyes were as dark and wild as the storm rolling in.

"Are you threatening me?" she asked.

"No, I'm just telling you that you can't make cuts to this program."

"I have no intention of making cuts to the program, Dr. Valentino." Then she sighed. "I'm making cuts to the pro bono program. That young boy, he's the last pro bono case that you can take."

"What?" Alejandro was stunned. "You can't."

"The board is cutting pro bono funding. They still want a world-class hospital, they'll fund research programs and equipment. They'll even fund staff, but pro bono cases must be referred to County."

"Cases like José's can't be referred to County. County doesn't have the equipment to handle children like him. Sending them to County is a death sentence. County sends cases like José's to us for a reason. We're the best."

"My hands are tied. Only those who can afford to pay for the services at Buena Vista will be treated." Then added, before she could stop herself, "You know all about what it's like to cater to the wealthy, don't you?"

His eyes were like thunder as they narrowed danger-ously. "You do remember me, then."

"And you remember me. Given your age and your standing here, you must've been, what, a resident when we met?"

Alejandro cursed under his breath. "Yes."

"And does the board know what their precious Dr. Val-entino did before becoming an attending at a prestigious hospital?"

"Are you threatening me?" Alejandro asked, angry.

"No." Even though five years ago when she'd miscar-ried and had had no one to help her, no one to hold her hand, she would've gladly threatened Alejandro then. She'd wanted him to hurt, to know the pain she'd been feeling.

"I danced to pay off student loans. That's all. Once I'd earned enough money, I quit."

"I don't care," Kiri said. "What I care about is protect-ing the reputation of the hospital. What if word gets out that a surgeon was an exotic dancer?"

"I haven't danced in five years. My last show was in Vegas."

Kiri's cheeks heated and he took her right back to that night so long ago. "Why did you pretend not to know me?"

"Why did you?" he countered.

"I was surprised to see a stripper as a surgeon." And she regretted the hateful words the moment they'd slipped past her lips.

"I'm not a stripper. I'm a surgeon. That's all I am. Of course, it's hard to practice as a surgeon when your program is being slashed."

"Your program is not being slashed. Only the pro bono fund. You can practice on patients who can pay."

Alejandro opened his mouth, but then a thin, long wail sounded from behind a Dumpster. It was weak, frightened.

"Was that a baby?" Kiri asked.

"Yes." Alejandro turned and they listened, trying to drown out the sounds of traffic and thunder. Then they heard the small wail again.

Weaker this time.

Alejandro dashed over to the Dumpster and behind it saw a grease-stained box filled with newspapers. Kiri knelt down beside him and gasped as Alejandro peeled back the papers to uncover a small, blue-gray baby. Very small and obviously newly born, because the cord was still fresh and hastily cut off.

"Oh, my God," Kiri whispered. "It's a baby."

A tiny infant that had been abandoned in an alleyway of a hospital. Alone and afraid.

"Fools," Alejandro cursed. "Who would do such a thing?"

And Kiri couldn't help but agree. Someone hadn't wanted this poor mite, but to abandon the baby in the heat next to a Dumpster? That was dreadful.

It was times like this that the loss hurt even more. It reminded Kiri again that life was cruel and dirty.

Life was unfair.

Alejandro whipped off his jacket and gently lifted the

infant, wrapping the boy up. "Let's get him inside. It's sweltering out here and, with the storm coming, that's the last thing he needs."

Kiri nodded as Alejandro gingerly picked up the baby. She opened the door and they ran inside. All she could do was keep up with Alejandro's long strides as he called out for nurses, residents and equipment. They laid the baby down on a bed; he looked so small on the large gurney.

Alejandro moved quickly, giving him oxygen, holding the mask over his nose while they waited for an incubator.

"Who would do such a thing?" Kiri wondered out loud as she stared down at the small baby, new in this world and all alone.

Alejandro shook his head. "I don't know, but it's a good thing we found him. He wouldn't have lasted long out there. Look, his stats are very low—I'm surprised he's lasted this long."

The incubator was brought in and a resident took over respirating the baby while they ran an umbilical line to get fluids into him. Kiri reached down and stroked his tiny hand between her finger and thumb. The hand was so small it made her heart skip a beat. It made her yearn for what she'd lost.

And what she'd probably never have since her obstetrician had said she'd probably never again conceive or carry a pregnancy to term. Motherhood was not meant to be for her.

"How old do you think he is?" Alejandro asked, invading her thoughts.

"I think probably about thirty weeks. Maybe. More like twenty-eight," she whispered as they intubated the baby and transferred him over to the incubator to take him up to the nursery. She'd lost her son at twenty-three weeks. He had only been slightly smaller than this boy.

Alejandro nodded. "We probably just missed the mother. I'll let the ER doctors know to be on the lookout for her."

Kiri nodded as the resident team wheeled the incubator and the baby up to the nursery. "Good call. I'll take the little one up to the nursery and arrange for his transfer to County."

"County?" Alejandro asked, stunned.

"Yes," Kiri said. "I told you, the hospital has cut the pro bono cases."

Alejandro frowned and crossed his arms. "He won't survive the trip to County and County doesn't have the facilities of a level-one NICU."

"Then Seaside," she offered. "He can't stay here."

He shook his head. "We have the foremost neonatal intensive care unit here at Buena Vista. He needs to stay here."

Kiri didn't want to send the baby to County either, but her hands were tied.

"And who will pay for his medical expenses? He doesn't have a family. He's an abandoned baby."

A strange expression crossed Alejandro's face. "I will pay for his medical expenses. I'll take responsibility for him. I'll act as his family."

CHAPTER TWO

"PARDON?" KIRI SAID, because she wasn't quite sure she'd heard Alejandro correctly. "What did you say?"

"I said I would pay for the child's medical expenses," Alejandro snapped. "You're not sending him to County."

Before she could say anything else to him he stormed out of the room. Kiri stood there stunned for a moment, taking in the ramifications of what he'd said.

He was going to pay for him?

She wasn't sure what she was feeling at the moment because she thought about the moment she'd planned to tell Alejandro about their baby five years ago. She'd expected him to be horrified and angry, what she'd thought would be a typical reaction in a man who was finding out he was going to be a father after a one-night stand.

Maybe her assumption of him had been wrong, because he was offering to take this sick infant as his own.

She ran after him. "You're planning to adopt this boy?"

Alejandro froze in his tracks and spun around. "What're you talking about?"

"You just said you're going to be the boy's guardian."

"No, I said I was going to pay his medical bills. I didn't say anything about adopting him."

"Well, usually when someone offers to become financially responsible for a child like this they intend to invest in their health care and adopt."

Alejandro frowned. "I have no interest in adopting him, but I'll give him his best shot at a family. People who actually want children."

It was like a splash of cold water.

People who actually want children.

So it was clear he didn't want children. Just like she'd first thought when she'd found out she was pregnant. It still hurt, though. She'd been hoping for better from him.

His rejection of having a family, of children, was a rejection of their baby as far as she was concerned.

"You'd better get a lawyer involved," Kiri snarled.

"Why?" he asked.

"Because you'd better make sure you can be financially responsible for this child. If you try to take action and the board gets wind of it and doesn't approve, I won't back you."

She tried to leave, but he grabbed her arm, spinning her round to face him. His dark eyes were flashing with that dangerous light she'd seen before.

"Are you threatening me again?"

"No, I'm not. I'm telling you the reality of the situation." She shook her arm free. "You're one of my surgeons, Dr. Valentino. I am only looking out for your best interest."

"Best interest? It would be better if you didn't let the board cut the pro bono fund. That would be in everyone's best interests."

Kiri glanced around and could see staff were watching them now. What she did next was crucial as the new head of the department. She couldn't let Alejandro upstage her here. If she did then she'd lose any kind of footing she had.

"Dr. Valentino, if you value your career here at Buena Vista I suggest you speak to me privately about any issues you have with the board's decisions in this matter. If you continue to bring up confidential information like this in a public manner I will have no choice but to reprimand you. Do I make myself clear?"

Inside she was shaking. She'd never stood up to someone like this before and she wasn't 100 percent sure he wouldn't just quit. Which would put her ass on the line as Dr. Valentino was a valued pediatric surgeon and brought in a lot of money.

"Crystal," he said. Then he turned on his heel and stormed away.

Kiri crossed her arms and stared down everyone who was still staring at her. They quickly looked away. Once she was sure she had sufficiently stood her ground she walked away as quickly as she could before the tears brought on by adrenaline began to fall.

"Are you out of your mind?"

Alejandro groaned as his best friend and legal counsel, Emilio Guardia, lambasted him on the other end of the phone.

"Probably," Alejandro groused. "But can it be done?"

There was a sigh on the other end. "Usually the state of Florida doesn't allow health professionals to become guardians of wards of the state. Unless we can prove that there is no conflict of interest."

"There is no conflict of interest. I'm not gaining anything financial from helping this baby."

Which was the truth. He wasn't. In fact, according to Kiri, he was risking it all by helping him. She'd made that perfectly clear to him, but he really had no choice. If the baby was sent to County he'd die.

"Can you send me over the medical records you do have on the boy and I'll apply for an emergency injunction? I don't see why a court wouldn't approve of you having guardianship over the boy, especially if they can't locate the family in the next forty-eight hours. For now, I can at least keep him at Buena Vista."

"Thank you, Emilio." Alejandro was relieved. "I'll get those medical records over to your office as soon as possible."

"I'll watch for them."

Alejandro hung up the phone and ran his hands through his hair. He hadn't believed it when he'd heard that little cry from behind the Dumpster.

He'd been so angry that the board was cutting the pro bono cases that when he'd heard the cry it had shocked him. And then to find that little guy, premature, barely clinging to life in the hot Miami sun...

It had infuriated him.

There was no one to fight for this baby. Just him. Dr. Bhardwaj had made it clear that the onus was on him. Last night he'd tossed and turned, thinking about how Kiri had appeared to be angry about the fact he was willing to pay for the baby but not adopt him. Having a family was something he'd never planned on. Not with his uncertain future. His heart, his father's heart, which beat inside him, could fail. In fact, the median survival rate for a pediatric transplant patient, such as he had been, was twenty-two years. He was nearing that. Once he started to have problems, he'd be put back on to UNOS to wait for a new heart that might never come. And Alejandro wouldn't leave any child without a parent.

He knew the pain all too well. His future was far too unpredictable.

Yeah, he loved kids, but he knew the pain of losing your parents. He wouldn't wish it on anyone. The best thing would've been to let the baby go to County instead of getting involved, but he couldn't just let this baby get lost in the system.

The baby would die if they moved him now. Of that

Alejandro was certain so there was really no choice, he had to fight for the boy.

Just like Dante, Rafe and Santi had done for him.

He, at least, had had someone to fight for him when he'd been lying in a coma, his parents dead. His brothers had made the decision to take their brain-dead father off life support and direct their father's heart to him because it was a good match and without it Alejandro would also have died that night because of the robbery.

Alejandro had been a priority on the list back then. And at least he hadn't been an infant. Children as young as six could receive a heart from an adult. It was harder to find an infant or a child's heart.

Alejandro and his father had been a perfect match.

His brothers had given him a second chance to live. They'd sacrificed so much to give him a life. This little boy had no one and Alejandro seriously doubted that they would find the baby's family.

The baby was alone, fighting for life, and Alejandro was going to make sure he had a chance.

What about after you save his life?

The thought caught him off guard.

You're lonely.

He was lonely, but he was used to this life. This was what he'd resigned himself to when he'd finally been old enough to understand the ramifications of his lifesaving surgery. Any chance at happiness like Santiago had found had died that day. And when his transplanted heart stopped beating, no child would mourn him like he mourned his parents.

There was a knock at his office door and he looked up. "Come in."

Mr. Snyder walked in. "Dr. Valentino, a word."

Great. Apparently word got around fast.

Alejandro gritted his teeth. "Of course. Please have a seat."

Mr. Snyder took a seat. He smoothed down the lapels of his expensive designer suit and cleared his throat. "I wanted to speak to you last night, but you'd left."

"My shift was over," Alejandro said, "so I left for the evening."

"You're certain it wasn't because of your dressing-down?" There was a glint of pleasure in Snyder's eyes.

Alejandro fought the urge to toss him out of his office. "I'm quite busy today. How can I help you, Mr. Snyder?"

"It's come to our attention that you're trying to keep that abandoned baby here."

"Yes. What of it?"

"I'm surprised you're trying to do this. Hasn't Dr. Bhardwaj told you that all new pro bono cases have been suspended pending a restructuring of the board?"

"Yes," Alejandro snapped.

Mr. Snyder sneered. "Dr. Valentino, are you purposely disobeying the board of directors' decision?"

"No, I'm not. That baby is not a pro bono case."

Mr. Snyder blinked. "I don't see parents and the last I heard the infant is now a ward of the state of Florida."

"Not for much longer, Mr. Snyder." It took every ounce of strength not to belt Mr. Snyder across the head. He knew these kinds of men. They got a bit of power and they thought they ruled the world, and he knew Mr. Snyder was taking great pleasure in it.

Mr. Snyder was a pretentious snob.

"What do you mean?"

"I mean I have contacted my lawyer and very soon I will be guardian of that baby, meaning that I will be financially responsible. I will be paying all the medical bills."

"Why would you do that?" Mr. Snyder asked.

"It's my money. I'll do what I like with it."

Mr. Snyder shook his head and stood. "No good can come from this. That child should be sent to County, like all the other wards of the state."

"Well, he's not. And if we're done talking, I do have to get back to my work. Paying patients, as per your request." Alejandro smiled at him a little too brightly. It was enough to tick off Snyder, who left his office in a huff.

Alejandro raked his hands through his hair.

Oh, Dios mío.

This was not how he wanted to start his week at Buena Vista, with the president of the board of directors breathing down his neck and the new head of pediatric surgery being his one and only one-night stand who knew about his sordid past.

There was another knock at the door and Alejandro cursed under his breath, wondering if Snyder had come back to spew more vitriol and threats at him.

"Come in."

Kiri opened the door and his pulse quickened at the sight of her, but he also didn't really want to see her either, since she was the one who had delivered the devastating news about the pro bono program.

It's not her fault.

"Are you okay?" she asked.

"Of course. Why wouldn't I be?" he asked, trying not to look at her.

"You know I had to dress you down yesterday."

"I know," he sighed. "My apologies, Dr. Bhardwaj. I was angry yesterday."

"I get that," she said. "Dr. Valentino, you can't take responsibility for that infant."

"I have to," Alejandro said. "He doesn't stand a chance if he's shipped off to another hospital. Especially not County."

"You know that I don't want to do that either, but the board—"

Alejandro held up his hand. "You don't have to explain board politics to me. I'm very familiar with that. Snyder was just here."

"Oh, great," she said sadly, then she looked concerned. "I told him I'd handle it."

"Your job is safe, I'm sure. It's me he doesn't like and he never has. Probably because I don't kiss his ass," he snapped.

"I don't either," Kiri said defensively.

"And what about Dr. Vaughan?"

"What about Dr. Vaughan?" she asked, confused.

"Oh, come on, I'm sure there was some smooching involved."

"I ought to slug you," she hissed. "I worked hard and Dr. Vaughan recommended me for the job."

Alejandro felt bad about his gibe. He was just on edge. "I'm sorry. Snyder has got me all riled up."

"I can see that. Can I sit down?" she asked. "I hate hovering by the door."

He may be angry at board politics, but that was no reason for him to behave like an animal. Especially in the presence of a lady. Carmelita had smacked him upside the head numerous times in his youth when he'd stepped out of line when it came to the fairer sex.

"Eres todo un caballero. Comportarse como tal."
You're a gentleman. Behave like one.

"Of course." Alejandro stood and pulled out a chair for her. "Sit, please."

She sat down and then he took his seat again. "So what do I tell the board about the baby?"

"My lawyer is getting an emergency injunction to stop the transfer. I'm hoping as the head of pediatric surgery you can delay things on your end for a couple of hours."

She nodded. "I can, but if that injunction doesn't come by the day's end then I have to send him to County."

"Not Seaside?" At least at Seaside he had family who could watch out for the boy.

"No," she said sadly. "Wards of the state are to be sent to County."

Damn.

"Well, I appreciate you doing all you can do to delay it. I'm dead serious about taking financial responsibility for the boy."

A strange expression passed across her face, like pain, but whatever it was it was quickly gone. "Why are you doing this?"

Alejandro shrugged. "Wouldn't you if you could?"

"Your job is worth this?" she asked.

"Are you going to fire me?"

"No."

"Then, yes, it's worth it. The boy needs medical attention, the best medical attention that this city can give him, and that's here at Buena Vista. He needs a chance at life. I can give him a shot, even if it's only financially."

That strange expression passed across her face again. "How very gallant of you."

"What's with the sarcastic tone?"

"There's no sarcastic tone."

He frowned. "Why does this make you so mad?"

"Look, I want what's best for that baby too, but doing this is just throwing it in my face. In the board's face. You're basically saying that you don't care about the new policies being handed down to you by your boss or the board, you're just going to do what you want."

"That's not it at all," Alejandro snapped. "This is about saving that child's life."

Her eyes narrowed. "I understand that."

She couldn't believe that she was trying to talk him out of it. It was so unlike her. When had she changed so much?

When she'd decided to become a pediatric surgeon she'd wanted to save them all too. She was just as idealistic as Alejandro. And then reality had hit her hard. She'd lost patients and had learned how cruel life was. She'd become jaded, but never had she shared those dark thoughts with another surgeon until now.

Strange emotions were raging inside her. Watching him fight so hard to save this little baby melted her heart, but also reminded her that he hadn't been there to save theirs.

Not that there had been anything that could be done about that. She knew that, but he hadn't been there and he'd made it clear he never would be.

It just hit so close to home.

When she'd seen that little baby in the dirty box, covered with newspaper and thrown away, it had cut her to the very core.

And it had ticked her off.

Alejandro had stepped up to take responsibility for the boy.

Would she have done the same as him? Kiri would like to think so, but she wasn't sure if she could as head of the department.

So she envied him a bit, envied his bravery in doing such a thing.

"Look—" Her words were cut off as Alejandro's cell phone rang.

"Hello? Yes, this is Dr. Valentino." He listened to the voice on the other end. "Where is it? I see. I'll be there as soon as I can."

"Is everything okay?" she asked as he hung up the phone.

"Yes, but I have to go." Alejandro stood up.

"Who was that?" Kiri asked.

"A liver for José. It's in New Orleans and I'm going to retrieve it."

She was shocked. "Do you always do your own retrievals? Why don't you send a resident?"

Alejandro shook his head. "I want to make sure that our piece of this liver is done right. I want to make sure everything goes smoothly for José's new liver. This is his last shot."

Kiri nodded. "I'll make a call to the airport and charter a plane."

"Thank you."

Kiri stood. "Can I go with you?"

He was surprised. "You want to go with me? Why?"

"I want to see you in action," she said. "I was planning on observing this surgery once a match was found. And right now I'm still getting my footing."

"I'd rather you stayed here," Alejandro said. "To make sure they don't ship that baby off to County."

Kiri smiled at him. "I've already put a stop to that. The baby is having tests. I have to be the one to release the baby to County. No one else. The baby is safe."

She waited while he mulled that over. He dragged a hand through his dark curls, making them wild and unruly. Sexy as hell too.

"I can't go," he shouted in frustration.

"Why not?"

"No other doctor speaks fluent Spanish and I have to prep José. I'm going to have to leave the recovery to a transplant team in New Orleans and a resident." He cursed again. "I don't want to do it, but I don't really have a choice."

"I'll go and retrieve José's liver. You stay and prep José," she offered.

"Are you sure?" Alejandro asked. "Have you done a retrieval before?"

She shot him a look and he chuckled. "What am I talking about? Of course you can. You sure you don't mind?"

"I wouldn't have offered if I minded. Prep José and I'll call you when the liver is retrieved. Also, call the charter. I want to leave as soon as possible," she said.

Alejandro nodded. "I'll see you at the ambulance bay in fifteen minutes."

"Okay." Kiri stood and then let herself out of his office. She'd be missing a board meeting, but she didn't care. She was a surgeon and this was her job. To help little José out. It would be better for the parents and for the boy if Alejandro prepped them for what was going to happen.

Kiri changed out of her business attire and into scrubs. She grabbed her new identification and a Buena Vista jacket, which would let the Parish Hospital in New Orleans know where she was from, since they were expecting Alejandro.

Fifteen minutes later she was in the ambulance bay. An ambulance was waiting to whisk her to the airport. Alejandro was standing there, waiting for her, holding a cooler that would transport José's liver.

"Thank you for doing this."

"It's no problem. Look, I know I've been a bit of a hard ass and dropped quite a bomb on you yesterday and then we had our public disagreement, but part of my vision for the pediatric team of Buena Vista is working together as a team."

He nodded. "I like that vision. You'd better go. Call me when you have the liver."

"I will."

Kiri glanced back once more to see Alejandro still standing there, watching her climb into the ambulance, an unreadable expression on his face. She knew that look.

He wanted to do the retrieval himself and he'd be pacing until she called him with the news that it was okay.

She understood that. She respected it.

"You ready to go, Dr. Bhardwaj?" the paramedic, Mike, asked.

"You betcha. Let's go."

As much as she hated flying, at least the flight to New Orleans would be short and a life depended on her.

She may not have been able to save her baby or everyone, but she could save this family's son.

And that gave her an inkling of hope that she hadn't felt in a long, long time.

CHAPTER THREE

THIS WAS THE PART she didn't like and Kiri hoped that no one knew that she was shaking in her boots as she was called to the operating table to retrieve the liver. It was the ending of a life.

And she hated that.

The worst part of a job. Which was why she specialized in general pediatric surgery over transplant surgery. She gave props to Alejandro for dealing with this every day. Life and death involving children.

Parish Hospital had a surgical resident helping her as she watched another surgical team remove a kidney. It was decided she would remove the entire liver out of the donor and then an attending from Parish, who was a bit of a specialist in dividing livers, would do just that. One piece for José and the rest of the liver would go to another person, because the liver was an amazing organ that had the ability to regenerate itself.

It was just that in José's case neither of his parents were a good match for him and were unable to do a living donation. Which was why the boy had gone on the UNOS list and why she was here.

She'd done several retrievals, but in New York she had just overseen them as she'd become an attending. The retrieval had been done by the student she'd been teach-

ing, but only when the transplant attending hadn't done it
themselves, that was.

There was a lot of pressure riding on this retrieval. She
was very aware of that. Alejandro had made it clear that
this was José's last shot.

*You should've stayed in Miami. You should've hired
an interpreter.*

No, it was better that Alejandro was there. If she had
been that boy's mother and couldn't speak the language,
she'd want the surgeon she was familiar with to stay and
look after her child. If she were a mother, she'd feel the
same.

*Only you're not a mother and you probably never will
be.*

Kiri stared down at the liver and decided where to start
the resection. The other part of the liver would go to the
next doctor waiting in the wings. A resident stood across
from her, while a scrub nurse waited for instructions.

"Scalpel." Kiri held out her hand and the nurse set the
number ten blade into her palm, handle first. She was the
more experienced surgeon, so she removed the liver from
the donor patient and placed it in the ice-cold preservation
liquid where the Parish Hospital surgeon waited to split it.

José was a child and only needed half of the liver. The
left lateral segment was destined for him.

Thankfully, the liver was healthy. There was no damage, no bleeding, spots or cysts and no signs that the liver
was deteriorating, things they looked for during a transplant surgery. They would go over it once again before
they placed it in José.

Kiri placed it into a stainless-steel bowl of preservation
solution. Another resident whisked it to the general surgeon
who would divide it. Kiri removed her gloves and got the
cooler that would transport the liver part back to Miami.

Once the splitting was complete and she was in the ambulance she would call Alejandro and let him know they were on their way, which would give him time to get José anesthetized and into the operating room, so it would just be a matter of transplanting the organ into José.

It was a delicate dance and Kiri was impressed that a man like Alejandro would take up such a specialized and difficult field, especially given his background. Wasn't he worried about people finding out?

And she could only imagine the public relations nightmare that it would cause if the general public did find out what the respected surgeon had done in his past.

As she mulled over trying to explain that to the board of directors if they ever found out, a memory of Alejandro crept into her mind.

The tattoo of the large eagle covering his chest.

She remembered running her fingers over the tattoo, tracing the delicate pattern and swirls of ink.

"It's an interesting choice for a tattoo," she whispered as he ran his hands down her back and she tracked the gentle ink designs with her fingertip.

"It covers a scar," he said as he kissed her neck.

"A scar? It must be a large scar."

He nodded. "Yeah, ever since I was a kid. When I became an adult I covered it with something meaningful to me."

"An eagle?"

"Sí."

"Why?"

"No more questions."

He grinned and kissed her, causing her to forget all the questions she still had about him and just feel the way his kisses fired her blood.

"Dr. Bhardwaj?"

Kiri shook thoughts about Alejandro out of her head and stepped forward, opening the cooler filled with preservation solution. The surgeon from Parish Hospital gently placed the liver segment inside.

Once they were sure the liver was safe and that the left branches of the artery and bile duct hadn't been damaged, Kiri closed the lid and moved out of the operating room. Once she had got out of her gown and scrub cap she followed a nurse out to the ambulance bay, where an ambulance was waiting to rush her back to the airport.

She pulled out her cell phone and hit the number she'd programmed in to direct her straight to Alejandro.

"Dr. Valentino," he said quickly.

"It's Kiri. The liver is viable and I'm on my way. Should be there in a couple of hours."

"I'll prep him." Alejandro hung up on her and she slipped the phone back into her pocket as she climbed into the back of the ambulance with her precious cargo.

The paramedic who rode in the back with her secured her in her seat. She wasn't going to take her eyes off the liver and it was protocol at Buena Vista. She was responsible for the organ. With her nod, the siren started up and the ambulance raced out of the bay at Parish Hospital.

Even though the sirens were blaring, they were trying to make their way through the crowded French Quarter at dusk. Already there were partygoers out, horse-drawn carriages and tourists everywhere.

The paramedic driving was cursing under his breath. *Come on.*

She glanced out the back window and behind her the crowd of people filled in any space that they had just cleared. Finally the ambulance got a break in the crowds and headed out on Canal Street and onto the expressway that would whisk them on an elevated highway west to Louis Armstrong Airport.

She closed her eyes as the ambulance rocked slightly, whipping down the highway to the private charter plane that was waiting to take her back to Miami.

"Parish Hospital isn't placed in the best location in New Orleans," the paramedic across from her said. "The French Quarter this time of night is bad."

"I can only imagine, but it's not as bad as rush hour in New York," Kiri said, sharing a smile with the paramedic. They didn't say anything else. Kiri didn't have much to say because, like the paramedics, they all knew that a life had ended.

Even though the donor had been an adult they had still been someone's child. Someone who had been loved. Lives would be saved tonight because of the generous donation, but also tonight there would be people mourning.

Loved ones grieving.

Once she was on the plane she'd feel better, but she wouldn't be at ease until the liver was in José and the boy was pulling through.

Only then would she relax.

Alejandro stared down at José lying on the table, intubated and waiting for the liver. The boy was on veno-venous by-pass and Alejandro had almost finished removing José's damaged liver from his body. He wanted to make sure that he left good lengths of vessel so that when he reanastomosed the donor liver it would take.

This was José's one shot.

Just like it had been yours.

Any transplant surgery was hard for him, even after all this time, because at one time he'd been on the table, hooked up to bypass as a young boy, his father being taken off life support in the operating room next to him so that Alejandro could be given a fighting chance at life.

His brothers having to make the monumental decision to end their father's life and become orphans themselves so that Alejandro could go on living. Every surgery stirred those memories in him, but he still wouldn't change it for the world. When he'd visited his father's grave months later, because he'd been in the ICU when his parents had been buried, he'd promised his father he would save others.

He'd dedicate his second chance at life to transplant surgery.

He would help other children. Other families.

The operating-room door opened and Kiri entered, masked, carrying the cooler.

"It's about time," he said under his breath, barely glancing up as he worked over José.

"Like I can control the speed of a plane," Kiri said. She handed the cooler off to Alejandro's resident, Dr. Page, who had fresh preservation solution ready and waiting.

"Are you going to scrub in and assist?" Alejandro asked. He wasn't sure why he asked, but he figured he might as well make the offer, because she was probably going to stay anyway.

"You read my mind."

He grinned to himself and watched her as she headed back into the scrub room to get properly attired.

Once she was scrubbed and gowned she joined him on the opposite side of the table, and the nurse handed her the retractor.

"You've done a nice job of dividing the bile duct," she said. "Have you removed his gallbladder too?"

"Yes, to avoid future complications, and thank you for the compliment, Dr. Bhardwaj."

"My pleasure," she said.

"And I didn't thank you properly for flying to New Orleans and back to retrieve the liver. It was a lot easier on my patient and his family for me to be here."

She nodded. "I thought as much. I'm sure they were thrilled."

"Yes, and scared beyond belief."

"I don't blame them. If it were my child…" She trailed off and cleared her throat. "It's good you were there and I'd never been to New Orleans before. Not that I saw much of the city."

"That's too bad. It's a great city," Alejandro remarked. "The Café du Monde is one of my favorite places for café au lait and beignets."

"Beignets?"

"Fried pastries covered in icing sugar. Beautiful, but evil." And he winked at her.

She shook her head. "I'm not much into baked goods."

"Oh?"

"I'm more of a savory person. French fries."

"I don't think that's a specific New Orleans food."

"I didn't say it was," Kiri said. "Before my parents moved to New York they lived with relatives in London, England. So when we visited my family there before visiting the rest of the family in Mumbai, we had traditional fish and chips on the banks of the Thames. It was the best."

"Were you born in Mumbai?" he asked.

"Nope, New York City. Manhattan, to be precise. Where were you born? You speak fluent Spanish."

"How is the liver looking, Dr. Page?" Alejandro asked, ignoring her question. He had been born in Miami, but he didn't feel like talking about Heliconia at the moment, the country his parents had come from, because it would remind him of that day he'd lost his parents. It was bad enough the ghosts of that memory haunted him every time he went into the operating room, but he wouldn't talk about that day.

The day he'd been shot.

And if on cue his scar twinged in memory of it, his heart skipping a beat to remind him.

"It's looking great, Dr. Valentino. Ready when you are," Dr. Page said.

"I'm ready."

"Walking with the liver," Dr. Page announced, and she stopped beside him. Alejandro set down his instruments and gently reached into the stainless-steel bowl to lift out the liver. The sounds of the operating room were drowned out. All he could hear was his own pulse thundering in his ears as he steadied himself and focused on gently placing the liver where he needed it to be in order to transplant it into José's body.

Giving José that second chance at life, like he'd been granted.

A life of antirejection drugs and taking care of yourself, but for the price of life it was something that Alejandro was willing to pay, just like José and his family were.

"You're awake!"

Alejandro's eyes focused and he saw Dante and Rafe hovering over him. Santi was slumping in the corner, sulking. His eyes were red.

He tried to talk, but couldn't. His throat hurt and it wasn't the only thing.

"Don't try to talk," Dante said. "You've just had surgery to replace your heart and they just removed the tube from your throat."

He glanced over at Rafe, who nodded. His eyes were red too, bloodshot.

"Do you remember what happened?" Dante asked.

Alejandro nodded and winced as tears stung his eyes. The sound of shots still seemed to be ringing in his ears.

"The police are going to come and they want you to look at pictures. Do you remember the men who came in?"

Alejandro nodded, because he would never forget those scary men with the guns. Then he grimaced, his chest hurting.

"You were shot. Remember?" Dante said again. "Don't try to move. You're still recovering. Please take it easy."

And then he shot a look at Santi, asking silently where Mom and Dad were. Santi would know why Mami and Pappi weren't here. He needed them. He wanted his parents.

Santi's eyes were dark, hollow. "Mami and Pappi are dead. You have Pappi's heart."

He heard screaming in his head, realizing that he was crying out in his mind when he was unable to do it physically. Only the screams were the monitors and his brothers were calling for help as he had a seizure.

"It's a nice job," Alejandro said, shaking those memories from his head. He didn't want to think about his parents right now. Those nightmares of the shooting, there was no place for them. He had to stop thinking about them. He needed to focus on the surgery as he began a caval replacement. Usually he would take the approach of navel preservation cavocavostomy, but in José's case his IVC was completely fried so Alejandro used the donor IVC to replace José's.

"I didn't split it, just removed it," Kiri said.

"Still, you kept all the arteries intact. It's a beautiful liver."

Kiri nodded. "It'll give him the best shot."

"It's the best part of the job," Alejandro said, then he grinned at her.

"What is?" she asked.

"Giving them their best shot. Every child deserves a chance at life."

"Y-yes...of c-course." She stammered over her words, like she was trying to swallow down sadness.

Had Kiri lost someone? A child, perhaps, who still haunted her? When she'd come into his office he'd noticed that she didn't wear a ring on her finger, but that didn't mean anything. Not really. She could still be involved with someone.

She could have a family. The thought of her with another man made him angry. Not that he had any claim over her other than a one-night stand five years ago when he'd still been dancing. One heated one-night stand that still stuck with him.

Since Kiri he hadn't seriously dated anyone. He'd just thrown himself into his work, but there were times he recalled her hands on him, the scent of her, the taste of her, and the thought of her with another man was just too much for him to take at the moment.

"How did your family take to moving down here from New York City?"

She cocked an eyebrow above her surgical mask. "I'm an adult. My parents took it fine, I suppose. They really don't have a say over where I go."

"Not your parents. I mean your husband or significant other."

"I'm not married and there's no significant other, not that it's any of your business."

"I was just curious. You don't have to snap at me."

Her dark eyes narrowed. "How about we focus on the surgery?"

"I like to chat when I'm doing surgeries. Besides, you had no qualms when we were talking about café au lait and beignets."

"I suppose I didn't. Still, we should focus."

"I am."

"How so?"

"Chatting helps me focus."

"Really?" she asked in disbelief.

"What helps you keep your focus during surgery, then?" he asked.

"Silence." There was a twinkle in her eyes.

There were a few snickers of laughter and Alejandro couldn't help but smile. This was why he'd been attracted to her all those years ago. She was feisty, fiery. She might act like a bit of a wallflower, but she wasn't.

She was far from it, deep down.

They didn't say anything further as Alejandro finished the surgery. Before he closed they took José off bypass. And he held his breath, waiting for the donor liver to pink up and let him know that it was being accepted by the body for now. There was always the chance that it could be rejected later on, but Alejandro wouldn't close until he saw the blood flow back into the liver.

That would let him know that he'd done his job well for now.

"Take him off bypass."

The machines whirred to a stop and Alejandro watched the liver.

Come on.

The liver pinked up and he said a silent prayer that it had taken so well. "Excellent job, everyone. Let's get this little man closed up and into the ICU."

"Fine work, Dr. Valentino," Kiri said.

He nodded in acknowledgment, but didn't look at her as he finished his job. He probably should let a resident close, but he wanted to see José's case through. He'd brought the boy this far.

And he'd promised José's mother that he would see it through. That he wouldn't leave José's side.

Once it was done and José was stabilized Alejandro finally stepped away and let residents and nurses take care of his charge. He would check on José in the ICU before he left for the night. Kiri was already in the scrub room, cleaning up, as he peeled off his mask, tossing it in the receptacle.

"There's a lawyer pacing the halls, looking for you," Kiri said. There was a hint of censure in her voice.

"It's not a malpractice suit," Alejandro snapped. "If that's what you're thinking."

"I wasn't thinking that. I assume it's your injunction about the baby, but it doesn't look good for a lawyer to be pacing the halls of the hospital, waiting for a surgeon."

"Are you afraid of the image he'll cast?" Alejandro teased as he ran his hands under the water.

"Yes." She toweled off her hands. "Especially as he's looking for one of my surgeons."

He grinned. "I am one of your surgeons?"

"Of course. I am the pediatric head. You're a pediatric surgeon, are you not?"

"Absolutely." He grinned and waggled his eyebrows at her.

She rolled her eyes, but a smile played at the corner of her mouth. "You're pathetic."

"I thought you were just praising my prowess in there?"

"You're very infuriating. Where did you learn to be so annoying?"

"I have three older brothers, all of them in the medical field."

"Oh, good Lord."

He couldn't help but laugh. "Don't you have siblings?"

"We're going to start with the personal interrogation again, are we?"

"Hey, I like to get to know my colleagues."

She cocked an eyebrow and crossed her arms. "Really? Can you tell me a bit about the scrub nurse in there, then?"

Alejandro grinned. "Of course. Her name is Elizabeth.

She's a married mother of four. She's been my scrub nurse for a number of years. I like her because she anticipates exactly what I need during transplant surgeries. Her favorite color is yellow and she loves Cuban food."

Kiri's mouth dropped open. "Are you kidding me?"

"I make conversations in there when things are going well. It's how I can focus. Why do surgeons have to be so serious all the time?"

"We're serious because we're dealing with lives."

Alejandro shook his head. "And we're human too. It makes for a more relaxed atmosphere. Since you're unlikely to be in any of my other surgeries, what does it matter how I run my operating room?"

He grabbed a paper towel and dried his hands, then threw the towel in the garbage. "Now, if you'll excuse me, I have a lawyer to speak to."

He walked past Kiri, leaving her standing there stunned.

And he didn't care.

It was unlikely she'd be in the OR with him again. She was taking over a department and soon she'd have her own patient load to deal with. He would only have to deal with her if there were consults or meetings.

He was an attending, not a resident who needed to be taught a thing or two.

It was better this way. It was better to keep his distance from her, because he'd promised himself a long time ago he would never get married.

Never get involved with someone, not after what had happened with his parents and the pain their deaths had caused. Not when his father's heart could give out. He was very aware of heart transplant stats. His time was limited.

And he would never put someone he cared about through the pain of loss.

It was better this way. He could bear the pain himself. *Can you?*

CHAPTER FOUR

KIRI WAS WALKING *the halls of a darkened Buena Vista. She'd been working late again and as she walked she realized that no one else was around.*

What was going on?

She turned and the lights dimmed. Alejandro was at the end of the hall dressed in a suit, his head lowered, his hands behind his back. She was completely confused.

"Dr. Valentino?"

Music started and he began to dance. Just like that night in his hotel room in Vegas. Right down to the same suit.

Kiri sat down in a chair that suddenly appeared. She wanted to tell him to stop dancing, that it wasn't appropriate to do his routine in the hospital, but she lost her voice and suddenly it didn't matter that he was doing this in the hospital.

She was transfixed as he undid the knot in his tie, slowly pulling it off. Those dark eyes were glittering in the dim light and were focused on her. Holding her captive.

Kiri realized then she was at his mercy. Her body thrummed with need as he pulled off his jacket and shirt. She ran her hands over his body, over his hard, rippling muscles. Then he leaned over her, his lips brushing her ear.

"Mi tesoro," he whispered. "I want you forever. Always. Only you."

She closed her eyes and waited for a kiss.

Instead a blaring noise echoed in the hall and he moved away...

Kiri woke with a start. Her alarm clock was going off. It startled her and as she groggily reached for her glasses, she fumbled to find the alarm and shut it off.

With a sigh she sank back into the pillows. Sunshine was peeking in through the venetian blinds that covered the bank of floor-to-ceiling windows in her apartment bedroom.

"Good Lord," she groaned. Alejandro was invading her dreams again and even though it had just been a dream her body was craving the kiss she'd been waiting for. The kiss that was in her imagination. She hadn't had an erotic dream about Alejandro in a long time.

Any dreams she'd usually had about him since the miscarriage had brought tears to her eyes and reminded her of what she'd lost. What she'd been denied.

So dreams about him were more like nightmares.

Except for the one she'd just had, which still made her blood burn with need.

The sun coming through her windows was a bit blinding, but it was worth it. She'd chosen South Beach because she liked to be near the ocean, she liked the art deco buildings and there was no city obscuring her view of the ocean.

Her apartment was also a decent size and there was a pool for people in the building to use. It was perfect.

Unlike her small rabbit hole of an apartment in Manhattan.

The only downside was that South Beach was loud at night, but no louder than New York City, so it really didn't bother her all that much that there were boisterous nightclubs and loud music at night. It reminded her of home.

She glanced at all the boxes still littering her apartment. She had the day off so she could do some unpacking, but instead she decided that she was going to go down to the pool and soak up the sun. Kiri had been in Miami for just over a week and she'd been in so many meetings that she hadn't had a chance to really make the most of the Florida sun. Checking her weather on her phone made her smile.

In New York City it was raining, dreary and cold.

For the first time she was glad she wasn't there.

She got out of bed and opened her blinds, squinting as the brilliant sun filled her apartment. It was warm and made her feel alive again.

How long had she been living in a fog?

After she'd lost the baby she'd retreated into herself. Work had been the only thing that could numb the pain. Her life had been on autopilot. She couldn't even remember the last time she'd had a day off. Keeping busy had occupied her mind and kept it off her loss.

A vision of Alejandro holding that little baby from the Dumpster had hit her hard. Would he have been so caring if he'd been holding their baby?

How could he? He didn't even know about his son and he'd made it clear that he didn't even want a baby.

And if their baby boy had lived, she wasn't sure she'd have the position she had now at such a young age, and she doubted very much whether, if she had a child, she would've moved so far from her parents and sister.

She would've wanted to give her child a family.

Cousins, grandparents and aunties. The kind of family she'd had when she'd been growing up. They say everything worked out for a reason, but she would gladly give up all she had to have had a chance to keep her child. A chance to be a mother.

Stop it.

Kiri shook her head. There was a no point in thinking about the past. She was going to change into her swimsuit and head down to the pool. It was her day off and she was going to enjoy it.

She put in her contacts, showered and brushed her teeth so she was ready for the day.

She found her bathing suit and grabbed a couple of magazines from the stack she had and headed down to the aqua pool in the courtyard. Maybe later she'd stroll through her neighborhood and walk along the white sandy beaches.

The whole day was hers.

It was warm outside, but not warm enough to tempt her to go swimming just yet, even if the pool was heated. So instead she found a lounge chair and made herself comfortable. As she relaxed in the chair she realized that she wasn't the only one here.

One of her neighbors was swimming laps in the pool.

She watched him, his muscular arms cutting through the turquoise water with ease. She couldn't help but admire him and then he stood and pulled off his swimming goggles, the water running down over his bronzed body, and she found herself staring at that eagle tattoo she knew all too well.

"Alejandro?"

He blinked a couple of times. "Kiri?"

"What're you doing here?" she asked.

"I live here," he said. "What're you doing here?"

"I live here."

Great. Just great.

He laughed. "Well, isn't that so like the universe, trying to make sure we're together?"

"You mean karma? Are you saying I'm being punished?" she teased.

Alejandro laughed and climbed out of the water and she tried not to let her gaze linger too long on his lean, muscular body. Her blood heated as all those naughty thoughts from her dream started creeping back into her head.

He grabbed his towel and dried his face with it before

wrapping it around his waist and pattering over to where she was lounging.

"I hope you put on sunscreen. It may not be that hot out, but the sun packs a nasty punch."

"I'm a doctor. I know and, yes, I did." She began to flip through one of her magazines, trying to ignore him, but it was no good. He sat down beside her and her heart began to race as the memories of her lingering dream filled her head.

"So when did you move in?" he asked.

"About a week ago. I'm on the eighth floor."

"I am, as well. I'm Eight B."

"You're kidding me?"

"No, why? What apartment are you in?"

"A. You're my neighbor?" Just what she needed.

"Well, not technically. You're across the hall from me. I face the ocean and you have a lovely view of the pool here."

"I think I would rather face the ocean." She sighed. "I have a partial ocean view from my bedroom, by the way."

Why did you just say that?

He grinned lazily. "Well, maybe you'll have to show me your view sometime."

"Uh…" She faltered. "Perhaps."

He ignored her. "The ocean is a nice view. Definitely better from where I grew up. You couldn't see the ocean from where I lived as a child."

"So you're a native Miamian. Is that the right term?"

He chuckled. *"Sí."*

"Well, is it a nice place to grow up?"

He shrugged. "Here it is. I've always liked South Beach, but where I grew up it was a bit different."

"Where was that?"

"Little Heliconia. It's a poorer part of the city on the mainland. My parents were from Heliconia and settled near other Heliconians."

"Ah, that explains why you're fluent in Spanish. Were you born there?"

"No, here in Miami," he said. "I've never been to the motherland, as it were."

"I didn't realize both of us were children of immigrants."

He lazed back in the chair. "I believe that all Americans are immigrants. It's just some have been here longer. So you have the day off?"

"I do. And apparently you do, as well." She tried to feign disinterest in him, but he wasn't taking the hint.

"I'm on call," he said absently. "I have one of my best residents taking care of José. I checked on him early this morning and I will probably go in tonight. However, I'm ready to race up there if I get a call."

Kiri nodded. "And the John Doe infant?"

"I was granted guardianship of the baby and he's stable. He's going through a few more tests with the pediatric cardiologist," Alejandro said. "I haven't seen him since we found him."

Kiri found that remark stung. Why didn't he want to adopt the baby eventually? Why else would he offer to be financially responsible and go through all the trouble of being the baby's guardian if he wasn't going to adopt him?

Because he didn't want kids. He probably liked his life the way it was. She was trying to do that, as well. Enjoy what she had been dealt without thinking about what she didn't have.

Which could be rectified if she ever found the right man to settle down with and adopt. That was still a possibility.

Then she realized he'd mentioned cardiology.

"Cardiologist?" she asked, concerned.

"His heart is giving the cardiology team some concern. They think he was born at about twenty-eight weeks, but if he has a congenital heart defect he could be younger."

"Poor mite," she whispered. "You sure you still want to be financially responsible for him? I mean, the costs already racking up…"

"I'm sure," he snapped. "End of discussion. I'm responsible for him. Once he's better, then he'll have a shot of being adopted into a family who will love him."

"You still don't want to adopt him?"

He frowned. "What gave you that idea? I haven't changed my mind. I'm not interested in a family."

"Because you're currently his guardian, I thought you might change your mind."

"No, I'm not cut out to be a father. Kids were never on the plan. I don't want kids. End of discussion."

It was like a punch to the throat. *Kids were never on the plan* and *I'm not cut out to be a father.* The words made her stomach turn and gave her the answer she'd always wanted. Alejandro wouldn't have been happy if she'd come to him pregnant.

He wouldn't have been there for their child.

It just would've been her. Only she'd never got that chance.

She shut her magazine. "Well, I think I've had enough sun for the day. I think I'll go unpack some boxes."

"You just got here," he said. "Stay."

"I really have a lot of unpacking to do."

"You say that like you're about to dive into a pool of scorpions. Why don't I show you around?" he suggested.

No.

Only she did want to get to know the neighborhood and Alejandro had grown up in Miami. Like it or not, he was her only friend here. It couldn't hurt, as long as she kept reminding herself they were just colleagues. Nothing more, because it was clear Alejandro did not want the same things as her.

"Are you sure?"

"I wouldn't have offered if I wasn't sure." He stood. "Say we meet in the lobby in thirty minutes? That gives us enough time to change and I'll take you out on the town."

"I don't know whether I should be thrilled or terrified."

He grinned, flashing those brilliant white teeth at her. "Always thrilled with me. Or have you forgotten? Make sure you wear pants."

"What? Why?"

"I drive a motorcycle. Skirts and motorcycles don't mix. Well, at least I'm sure those who wear skirts think that. I don't mind looking." Then he winked.

Kiri rolled her eyes and tried not to laugh as she collected up her things and headed back to her apartment. She had never been on the back of a motorcycle before and it frankly terrified her a bit.

Live a little. That's why you came to Miami.

She'd come here not only for the job but for the change. To escape the fog she'd found herself in in New York City. Staying in the same place, she couldn't escape the pain of her loss. This was a fresh start.

Not really since you're going out with the father of your baby.

Kiri groaned as she set her things down on her dining-room table, glancing in the mirror hanging on the wall. "What have I done? What am I doing?"

Alejandro was pacing as he stared at the elevator.

What am I doing?

He was still asking himself that question as he waited for Kiri to come down to the lobby. He didn't know what had made him invite her out. That hadn't been his plan. He'd been going to catch up on some paperwork and perhaps drift over to the hospital. That's usually what he did on his days off. Not that he was really off, he was on call. There just hadn't been any calls yet.

The doors of the elevator opened and Kiri stepped out.

He sucked in a quick breath, bracing himself for the fact she soon would be behind him on his bike, so close to him. And she was just as gorgeous as she'd ever been.

Capri pants, espadrilles and a cotton blouse that made her skin glow. Her long silky black hair was tied back and braided.

"You're staring at me. Am I dressed okay? You said pants, but all my pants are woolen and more for winter wear in New York. I haven't had a chance to unpack my spring and summer long pants."

"You're fine. You look nice."

More than nice.

A blush tinged her cheeks. "Thanks. So where are you taking me?"

"Would you like some lunch first? I know a great place."

She nodded. "Sure. What's it called?"

"Mad Ron's."

She blinked. "Mad Ron's? Should I be worried?"

Alejandro shrugged. "Depends if Ron is there or not."

"There's a Ron?"

"Of course, it's called Mad Ron's."

Kiri shook her head and they headed down to the parking garage together. He handed her the extra helmet he'd been carrying and stowed her purse in the pannier. He waited until she climbed on behind him, her arms wrapped around him, before he started the engine and pulled out of the parking garage onto Collins Avenue.

Her grip tightened as they headed out over the McArthur Causeway.

"Relax," he shouted. "Enjoy the view."

Kiri's nails dug into his flesh so he doubted she was enjoying the view, but Alejandro liked taking the causeway. The islands were dotted with beautiful, expensive homes and large yachts were docked in the channel outside the homes.

He could so be a boat person. Then he could sail around the world, not a care in the world. And if his heart gave out then he could die at sea. It would be peaceful.

Only that was just a fantasy. He'd made a vow to be reliable, work hard and not waste a second of life.

He wouldn't let his *pappi* down.

His father had worked hard to get to America and open that bodega to support his family. To give them a better life than they could possibly live in Heliconia. Too many sacrifices had been made on his behalf. Alejandro took his duty very seriously.

It wasn't long until they arrived at Mad Ron's. He just hoped that his brothers weren't inside. He didn't want to have to explain Kiri, even though there was nothing to explain. His brothers would know something more had passed between them.

Even if that something more had been five years ago.

And he couldn't risk his brothers finding out what he'd done.

The dancing had been the only time he'd been free. It hadn't been his favorite job in the world, but it had let him have just a taste of freedom.

It was a secret that only he and Kiri knew about. And he was tempting fate by taking Kiri to Mad Ron's, which wasn't far from his family's bodega and Little Heliconia, but it was a weekday and he was hoping Dante and Rafe were working and that Santi was in a bit of a honeymoon phase with Saoirse and wouldn't be making an appearance.

He parked the bike out front. Loud music was blaring from the open door. The palm trees surrounding the building swayed in a gentle breeze, rustling the fronds and the bamboo wind chimes hanging outside.

Kiri handed him the helmet. "I thought we were going

to explore South Beach. I wasn't expecting a ride over the water."

"You've been stuck in Miami Beach too long. You've driven the causeway in a car before."

"Yes, but there was something about not having the safety of metal surrounding me…"

Alejandro chuckled. "Well, I'll buy you a mojito. That will calm your nerves."

He breathed a sigh of relief when he scanned all the plush red leather booths and didn't see any sign of his brothers or Mad Ron, which was probably a good thing.

Gracias a Dios.

"Would you like to sit outside and enjoy the breeze?" he asked.

Kiri nodded. "That would be nice."

Alejandro waved to Ángel, who was working behind the bar. They took a seat in the farthest corner of the patio. The palms and hibiscus bushes were covered in fairy lights, but they weren't on right now.

Actually, they had the whole patio to themselves, which was nice in one way and a bit awkward in another.

Kiri sighed and leaned back in the chair. "It's wonderful out here."

"Worth the motorcycle ride?"

"Not sure about that. Ask me when we have to drive back over that causeway to get back home."

He grinned. "Well, if you pried your eyes open you could enjoy the sights of the islands with all the beautiful homes and all the big yachts."

"Do you have a yacht?"

Alejandro cocked an eyebrow. "As you're technically my boss, you know how much I get paid. No, I don't have a yacht."

"I figured you had some money stashed away from your

days of dancing." Then she blushed. "I'm sorry. I didn't mean to assume or bring that up."

"No, it's okay. Nothing much is left. I paid off my school loans, if you recall. The rest went to a down payment on my condo five years ago."

"What did your parents think of your chosen career path before becoming a surgeon?" she asked.

"Not much. My parents died when I was ten."

"I'm sorry," she said, and she reached out to touch his hand. "Did you have other family to take care of you?"

"No, my parents were the only ones who came to America from Heliconia, long before I was born. The rest of my family is back on the island, but I have never really met them. It was just me and my brothers. They're all older. The twins Dante and Rafe were legally adults at the time our parents died. Santi was only thirteen and I was ten. My brothers took care of me."

"That was nice of them. You said they were all in the medical world. What do they do?"

"They're all doctors." He smiled as he thought about his brothers. He was proud of them and he was sure that his *mami* and *pappi* would have been proud of them all too. They had all worked hard to get where they were. "Dante is a neurosurgeon, Rafe is a epidemiologist and Santi was in the army as a doctor, but currently he's a paramedic. He recently got married."

"Are the older two married, as well?"

"No, I think they're confirmed bachelors."

Like me.

Only he didn't say that out loud. Usually he did when he was talking about his brothers, but for some reason he didn't want to tell Kiri that.

"Besides, they're too ugly to get married." He winked at her.

"I'm sure they love it when you call them ugly."

"Oh, yes, I'm the baby. I'm *perfecto*."

"Ha-ha, yeah, sure," she teased.

"And what about your family? I know your parents come from Mumbai. Do you have any siblings?"

"Yes, I have an older sister. She's married with a couple of kids. They're great kids. I miss them." There was a hint of sadness in her voice.

"Then why did you move so far away from them?" he asked.

"The job was too good to pass up and the kids are older now. It's not too cool to hang out with boring aunt Kiri anymore."

Alejandro chuckled. The waitress came out and handed them menus. "We'll have one of Ángel's mojitos and a virgin mojito for me, please, as I'm driving."

The waitress nodded and left.

"How strong are these mojitos?" Kiri asked with trepidation.

"Strong enough, or so I hear. I don't drink."

"I remember," she said, blushing again. She picked up her menu. "What should I try? I'm not really used to Latin cuisine. Other than Mexican."

Alejandro grimaced. "That's not the same."

"Then you pick. I'm pretty adventurous."

"Are you?"

"Okay, now you're scaring me with that evil grin."

"If I had a long mustache I would be twirling the ends and laughing maniacally."

She rolled her eyes, but chuckled under her breath. "Well, I guess I'm mostly adventurous. I don't eat beef."

"Really? Why?"

"I'm Hindu."

"Chicken is probably your safest bet, then," he said.

The waitress came back with the drinks then. She set a huge mojito down in front of Kiri, whose eyes widened at the sight of it. His alcohol-free mojito was smaller, but was still a big glass of slushy goodness.

"Would you like to order anything else?" the waitress asked.

"Yes, two orders of *pollo asado* please."

The waitress nodded. "Coming right up."

"What did you order?" Kiri asked.

"It's chicken. You'll like it." He leaned back in his chair. "It's been a while since I've been to Mad Ron's. I've been busy working on my pro bono program at Buena Vista."

She sighed. "I'm sorry about that, but the board was very clear. Or rather Snyder was."

"I know. You're just doing your job but, still, it's not the right decision."

"My hands are tied. José got his liver and this baby will be taken care of. You can't save them all."

"We should be able to save them all," he said.

"You're right," she said soberly. "We should, but it's not like Buena Vista is closing its doors to children. We can still save children."

Alejandro sighed. "It just doesn't feel like it's enough."

"It never is," she said, and that hint of sadness was in her voice again.

"Who did you lose?" he asked, catching her off guard.

"Pardon?"

"I'm a good reader of people and there are moments where you seem so sad I can't help but wonder who you lost. I lost my parents and I'm familiar with that expression."

She shrugged but wouldn't look him in the eye. Instead she poked at her mojito. "I didn't lose anyone. I hate to see children suffer. It's the worst part of the job."

"Of course." Kiri was right, Alejandro knew that. Not being able to save all the children was the hardest part of the job. It tore his heart out when he lost one of his little patients, but there was something more to it than that for her. Something deeper.

He knew that pain. A pain he would never bring on anyone else.

Before he could ask any more questions his phone rang. "It's the hospital."

Kiri leaned forward. "Well, answer it."

"Hello? Yes, this is Dr. Valentino. Yes. Are you sure?" His heart sank as he heard the other doctor on the other end tell him what he didn't want to hear. "Okay, I see. Thank you for letting me know. I'll be in to check on him later."

He hung up the phone and let the words sink in.

Dammit. He'd been hoping for better news. This was not the kind of news he wanted to hear, especially in light of their conversation.

"Is it José? Do you have to go?"

Alejandro shook his head. "It's not José. That was the cardiology team about the baby."

"Oh, I see." And Alejandro knew that she understood exactly what had been said on the other end of the line.

The baby needed a new heart.

The baby had been officially put on the UNOS list, because without a new heart that little miracle baby he'd found in a cardboard box behind the hospital would die.

And the odds of finding an infant heart in time were very slim indeed.

CHAPTER FIVE

THE REST OF the lunch at Mad Ron's was pretty somber after Alejandro had fielded that call about the baby. She wasn't sure if it was because of the cost involved or the fact that they probably wouldn't be able to find a heart in time.

Either way, it hurt her, as well.

She'd never wanted that infant to be sent to County. She'd wanted to keep him at Buena Vista where the top surgeons in Miami could take care of him, but her hands were tied. There was no more money in the pro bono fund for anyone.

Still, she felt responsible. Like it was her fault this child might not make it.

Like you blamed yourself when you miscarried.

She shook that thought away. It had taken her a long time to stop blaming herself for the loss of her child. And who was she kidding? There were moments she still blamed herself.

"I can't believe he survived as long as he did," Alejandro murmured.

"So he has hypo plastic left ventricle, double outlet left ventricle, tricuspid atresia, atrial septal defect, ventral septal defect and pulmonary stenosis?" Kiri asked. "You're right. It's a miracle he made it out in that heat."

Alejandro nodded. "They put him on UNOS because the only way to stabilize his heart, which is totally out of rhythm, is to give him a Fontan procedure. The problem is that the pulmonary resistance is high because he's a newborn. It takes months to drop, so they can't do the Fontan. The baby doesn't have months to wait for the procedure and because his heart disease is so complex, his little heart is swelling, so it's better to wait for a new heart."

Which would be costly. But she didn't say that. He knew. They both did. Usually transplants weren't done on babies so young. It was rare, but they could do it.

"You never know what could happen. It's true that more adults die than children, making infant and children's hearts harder to come by, but since older children can take adult hearts, he has a better shot of landing an infant or a small child's heart. If his current heart is enlarged there should be space to take a toddler's heart."

Alejandro nodded. "Yes, that's not what I'm worried about, though. As his guardian I can't do the transplant surgery. Heart transplants are one of my specialties. I'm the one the cardiology team calls when a heart transplant needs to be done on a child. A baby's vessels are so much more delicate. Especially a preemie's."

"Yes, that is a conundrum. You may not be able to perform the surgery, but you can stand over the surgery and guide a resident."

He shook his head vehemently. "A resident is not touching that baby."

"Oh, no? Who is, then?"

He then stared at her. "You are."

"Me?" She had done pediatric heart transplants, but she wasn't sure if she could operate on that child. Not when Alejandro was the guardian. It hit a little too close to home for her.

"You are the head of pediatric surgery. I want you to be the one to do it."

"I'm not a transplant specialist. You need to have one

of your residents do it," she argued. She didn't want to risk hurting the baby.

She just couldn't.

He shook his head. "No, you're a good surgeon."

"How do you know? I've only ever assisted you once."

"I saw for myself how you retrieved that liver. You may not have split it, but the veins were easy to graft back into José. I also have my sources." He grinned deviously.

"Your sources?" she asked.

"I like to check out my competition. You were Dr. Vaughan's top student and Dr. Vaughan only chooses the best. I'm sure you've done these procedures before under his tutelage. I know he's done infant heart transplants and I know you have, as well."

"I'm not really your competition, I'm the head of the department and I'm not a specialist in transplant surgery."

"Everyone is competition," he said seriously. "Something I've learned the hard way."

"Really?"

He took a drink. "When you have to work and fight your way through a competitive program and specialty and you're a minority, you have a longer way to arrive at the destination. I fought the whole way. I worked hard to get where I am and I'm very protective of what I have."

Kiri smiled. She understood that all too well. Being a woman of an immigrant family, short and a bit of a wallflower when she'd been younger, she'd had to learn to speak up in a very competitive surgical program.

She'd learned to fight for everything she wanted, as well.

Even if she lost that fight. She never gave up.

You've given up on one thing.

And she tried to not think about the fact that she was never going to have another baby. She'd decided after she lost hers that she was never going to put herself through that kind of pain again, and her obstetrician had told her she had a hostile uterus so it would be unlikely she would conceive again, let alone carry a child to term.

"You're sad again," Alejandro remarked.

"What're you talking about?"

"As I said, I can read people." He leaned forward. "You went somewhere else. Your thoughts drifted. Where were you?"

Nowhere.

"I'm not sad," she said, plastering a fake smile on her face.

Liar.

Where she was was a dark place. A place where all her dreams had been laid to rest.

Alejandro stared at her with those piercing dark eyes seeming to read her soul. "Something is bothering you."

"Well, I am far from home. I've spent my whole life in New York City, rarely traveling except once to Vegas…" Then heat flooded her cheeks as she thought of the one time she had traveled there. "And then to see family. That's all the traveling I've done."

"How was the wedding?" he asked, a twinkle in his eyes.

"What wedding?" she asked, confused.

"The bachelorette party from five years ago. You were the maid of honor, I believe? The trip to Vegas."

"Oh, right. It was good. They're still together."

"Well, that's good." He smiled. "So this is your first time in Florida, then?"

She nodded. "It is and I have to say I'm not missing the cold at all. I like this heat and the sun."

"It's not always this beautiful. In the summer it gets humid and then there's hurricane season."

"We've had hurricanes in New York."

"You're right, you have. I guess, then, that Florida—

other than the fact we don't usually get snow and we have alligators—is really no different from New York."

"Alligators." She shuddered. "I'm not a fan of reptiles or bugs."

"Perhaps we'll have to take a drive down to the Everglades and I'll take you out on a fan boat into the swamp. See if we can spot some gators."

"No, thank you!" And Kiri shuddered again. "I'm fine right here, in the city, where it's somewhat safe."

This time it was his turn to have a strange look pass across his face. "The city is not as safe as you think."

"Well, no city is safe," she agreed, but she could sense there was tension between them. "But I seriously doubt that an alligator is going to take an elevator and knock on my door." She was trying to ease the tension between them.

He laughed, his eyes twinkling, his demeanor relaxing. "Not an alligator, but maybe other beasts."

"Now that I've been to Mad Ron's and surprisingly haven't been knocked on my butt by the mojito, probably because of the chicken, is my tour of Miami done for the day?"

Alejandro grinned. "Hardly. There's still so much to show you."

"Should I be afraid?"

He shrugged. "Don't you trust me?"

"I don't know you well enough to trust you," she teased. "Don't you?"

"One night together and one surgery does not equate to knowing each other. I have secrets and I'm sure you do, as well."

And she meant what she said. She was sure that he had secrets, just like her.

Alejandro reached into his wallet and pulled out some money, weighting it with an empty plate so that it wouldn't blow away in the wind.

"What're you doing?" she asked.

He cocked an eyebrow. "Paying?"

"No way. Let me. You drove me here."

He chuckled. "No. I'm paying. You're my guest. I insist." He stood and held out his hand. "Come on, trust me. Nothing will happen to you. You trusted me once before."

And look how that turned out.

Only this time she wouldn't end up in his bed. She was just enjoying her first real day out in Miami. Ever since she'd arrived here it had been nothing but work. Kiri also found that she liked Alejandro's company.

She wasn't so lonely when she was with him. Yeah, she had friends and a loving family, but there was a void in her heart that wasn't as noticeable around him. And he was here, her family was not.

She took his hand and he helped her to her feet. Kiri didn't know where he was leading her, but at that moment she didn't care. There were so many times she didn't live. It was exciting to see where he was going to take her.

He waved to the waitress as they left and headed back to his motorcycle. This time when she climbed on the back she wasn't as nervous as she'd been before, but her pulse still raced because she was going to be so close to him again.

Even after all this time, he still affected her.

She was still attracted to him.

The memory of his lips on her skin, bringing her to ecstasy, was forever burned into her brain. And as she sat behind him on his motorcycle, her arms around him, she could feel those rock-hard abs again.

And instinctively she ran her hands over where the tattoo was, feeling the hard ridge of his scar that the tattoo covered.

She heard him suck in a breath but he didn't say anything. All he did was rev the engine of his motorcycle, causing her to grip tight as he pulled out of the parking space at Mad Ron's and headed out onto the Miami streets.

This time as they drove through the city she was able to appreciate the architecture. The Spanish influence.

He headed toward the Bay of Biscayne and she couldn't help but wonder where he was taking her. They were traveling in the Coconut Grove area of the city on a tree-lined street, which offered nice shade. There was a Spanish gatehouse and Alejandro slowed down, turning into the drive. They drove through a parkland of what looked like an estate before he pulled into the main parking lot for visitors.

"Where are we?" Kiri asked, handing him her helmet again and then running her hands through her hair.

"Vizcaya. It's a European-inspired villa in the heart of Miami. It's one of the most beautiful places in the city and I thought you'd like to see it. I've been here many times, so I can tell you what we're looking at. You don't need to get the audio tour."

"It's a museum?"

"Do you have a problem with museums?"

"No, I like them," she said.

He grinned. "I thought you might."

"Why, because I'm such a nerd?" she teased.

Alejandro cocked his head to one side. "Hardly."

They walked side by side through the gardens. This time Kiri paid for admission into the museum since Alejandro had paid for drinks and the lunch. Vizcaya looked like something that would be found in Spain, in a place like Barcelona. It was very European and totally out of place in Miami, but she was enchanted by the grandeur as they wandered through the main house.

"So who built this place?" she asked.

"James Deering. It was a vacation home in the Jazz Age."

Kiri grinned as they moved through rooms full of art

deco and luxuries of the early 1920s. She could almost picture ladies in flapper attire and liquor flowing freely despite Prohibition.

"It's an interesting name for his home. Vizcaya. I like it," she said.

"There's a lot of speculation about why he named it Vizcaya but, yeah, I have to agree with you, it does roll off the tongue. It's sexy and mysterious, which is probably what he was going for."

They walked out of the main house and she gasped at the sight of the Atlantic Ocean. The water was calm and the sun was sparkling over the gentle lapping of waves. In the distance they could see Key Biscayne. And the water was dotted with large white yachts.

"I wonder where they're heading."

Alejandro shrugged. "The Bahamas or Caribbean. Or nowhere. There are a lot of yachts that just stick around Miami."

Alejandro watched her as she leaned over the garden wall and stared happily out at the yachts in the water. He couldn't help but smile and he couldn't remember the last time he'd had this much fun.

He'd worried that the day he'd originally planned was going to be so boring.

He'd come to Vizcaya before on his own. He liked walking through the gardens and the home, but he'd been here so many times he forgot what it was like to walk through it with someone who had never been.

Alejandro had been worried that she wouldn't like it as much as he did. It was a special place to him. His parents had liked this place. They'd often come here, bringing him. His brothers didn't seem to care much for it, but Alejandro loved it here.

His mother had loved the European gardens and they

would wander for hours out amongst the hardwood trees. She'd said it reminded her of home and his father would always hold his mother's hand. Alejandro loved running along between the hedges, they were so uniform, like green walls. Everything was lush and verdant.

So different from their home in Little Heliconia.

They were happy here.

Carefree here.

And on days like today, with the warm breeze and the calm waters, he could almost feel their presence again. The day of the shooting they had been going to finish up at the bodega and head to Vizcaya to walk around the gardens. His brothers hadn't been going, just Alejandro and his parents.

"Why do you want to go to Vizcaya again?" his father teased his mother.

"You know I like it and on days like this, calm, it reminds me of when Heliconia was just like this. I want to walk amongst the trees. It relaxes me."

"And how about you, Alejandro? Do you want to go to Vizcaya again?"

"Sí," Alejandro answered. "I like it there. I like to run through the grass."

His mother shot his father a look. "You see? He needs to feel the grass on his bare feet."

"Okay, we'll go to Vizcaya again." Then his father took his mother in his arms and kissed her. "You know that I would do anything for you, mi tesoro."

"Put your hands up!"

His mother screamed.

Alejandro shook the horrible thought out of his mind. He'd never forgotten the sound of his mother's screams. The sound of bullets and of him lying on the floor, staring at his father who was unconscious, lying in a pool of blood, his hand outstretched towards his mother.

He didn't want to think about his parents or that horrible moment. He should've died that day too.

"Come on, let's go wander around the gardens." And without thinking he took Kiri's small hand in his and led her away from the water into the gardens. She didn't try to pull her hand away.

He'd almost lost his cool when she had been running her hands lightly over his chest, tracing his tattoo through his shirt.

He knew what it was like to really have those soft fingertips trace his skin. And just thinking about it caused his blood to heat with desire.

Even after five years he wanted her. And he'd never wanted a woman like this before.

It scared him.

What am I doing?

He couldn't lead her on. There was nothing he could offer her and she was his boss. All they could be was friends.

He let go of her hand as they wandered along the outer perimeter of Vizcaya's gardens. He had to get out of here. He had to put distance between them. It was bad enough that they were working together and that they lived across the hall from each other, but he couldn't take her out like this.

To the places which reminded him of his life when it had been happy and easy.

To the time when he'd been an innocent boy, before he'd been forced to grow up.

"Mami and Pappi are dead."

Santi's words haunted him again.

"You know what, I really think I should get to the hospital and check on the baby. I know that I can't be his doctor, but maybe you're right, maybe I should school a resident on doing the transplant. I also want to make sure the cardiology team has got him on the UNOS list."

Kiri tried to hide her disappointment. "Okay, sure."

"I'll take you back to your apartment before I head to the hospital."

"You could just take me to the hospital. I should check on a few things, I planned to anyway. There's no sense driving all the way back to South Beach and then back into Miami just to drop me off," she said.

"I don't know how long I'll be. How will you get home?"

"I can take a cab," she said.

Guilt ate at him, but it was for the best. "Okay. Let's go."

They walked in silence back to his motorcycle. This time when she held him, he could sense the distance in her.

It's for the best, he reminded himself again. He dropped her off at the hospital's main entrance before he headed to the parking lot.

Kiri climbed off and retrieved her purse, handing him back his spare helmet. "Thanks for lunch and Vizcaya. I had a good time."

"You're welcome. I'll see you later." It was a lie. He was going to try and avoid her as much as he could. He wouldn't hurt her. He liked her too much.

She nodded and headed into the hospital.

You're an idiot, Alejandro.

CHAPTER SIX

KIRI HADN'T SEEN ALEJANDRO for a couple of days. Not since he'd dropped her off at the hospital. Something had changed at Vizcaya and she wasn't sure what, but it was probably for the best. It wasn't like anything could happen between them.

He'd made it clear he didn't want kids or a family. He wasn't going to adopt that baby and Kiri didn't want to give up on her dream of becoming a mother.

A dream of a family.

Besides, she was his superior. There was no way anything could happen between them while they worked at the hospital together.

She couldn't jeopardize her career for a man who didn't want the same things she did.

She cleaned her hands with hand sanitizer before she walked into the neonatal intensive care unit to check on some patients.

"Good morning," Kiri said to the head NICU nurse, Samantha, who always seemed to be there.

"Good morning to you too, Dr. Bhardwaj," Samantha said cheerfully.

"How are my two surgical patients today?" Kiri picked up the chart of the first baby, Maya, who had been born with her organs on the outside. Kiri had done the first surgery yesterday to start correcting the problem. It would take some time to slowly return the organs back to their rightful positions, but she had no doubt Maya would make it. She'd done so well in the surgery and was thriving post-op. Hitting all her milestones for recovery.

"Maya's stats are good. Blood pressure and oxygen levels are stable. She's tolerating treatment well," Samantha said. "She's a fighter."

Kiri nodded and pulled out her stethoscope, listening and examining the incision and the bag that covered the organs.

Her next patient was a simple cleft-palate fix. She'd done the first surgery the day before Maya's.

"How's he feeding?" Kiri asked, as she disposed of the gloves she'd used to look at Maya and put on new ones.

"When I feed him, he does well. Mom hasn't been down to feed him. She's not handling the cleft palate well," Samantha said.

Kiri frowned. "Why? It's a simple fix. I mean, parents are never happy their children have to go through this. It's not pleasant, we all want healthy babies, but he's healthy other than this."

She glanced at where the John Doe baby was. The boy who was clinging to life, who had been thrown away.

It could be worse.

"I know, but she refuses to come down and I can't always feed him. I have other patients to care for so he still has an NG tube and receives feeding from there."

"Perhaps it's postpartum depression?" Kiri suggested. "Perhaps that's why she hasn't been down?"

"She's from a very wealthy family on Fisher Island. The family's money comes from a cosmetic line. The baby, the heir, was supposed to be on their reality show next month, but now he can't be. Mom doesn't want him to be seen like this, so she's disengaged."

Kiri shook her head. "Get her a psych evaluation. Money or not, it sounds like postpartum depression."

"Her OB/GYN tried to get that. Snyder put a stop to it because he's friends with the child's father who thinks it's ridiculous."

Kiri rolled her eyes and muttered, "Ridiculous."

The boy would be fine. Cleft palate was a serious issue, but could be fixed. It just took time. Some people wouldn't care about appearances. Some people just wanted a baby.

Like me.

Her gaze fell on the incubator at the far end.

John Doe. The child she and Alejandro had found.

She disposed of her gloves and wandered over. He wasn't her patient, he was on Dr. Robinson's service until a heart could be found. After she did the transplant he'd be on her service, but she couldn't help but check on him.

"How is our little John Doe doing?" Kiri asked, peering into the incubator. Her heart melted at the sight of the small soul hooked up to so many machines.

"He's a fighter too," Samantha said proudly. "It's too bad Dr. Valentino hasn't come to see him. I feel bad because this baby is all alone."

Kiri's stomach clenched. She was alone here too. Miles away from family and friends. She understood.

Life was unfair.

"I'll hold him. I mean, I found him too and I will be his doctor when a new heart is found."

Samantha smiled and nodded in approval. Kiri put new gloves on as Samantha opened the incubator. Together they maneuvered all the wires and cords and wrapped him in a blue hospital blanket.

Kiri picked him up. He was so light, so delicate.

"See that! His stats stabilized," Samantha remarked. "He's benefiting from the touch."

"I can see," Kiri whispered, smiling down at that little

face. John Doe wasn't the only one benefiting from the touch. It did something to her, deep inside. She handled babies all the time in her job, but this was different.

She rarely cradled them. Rarely held them against her own heart to savor the feeling of something so tiny and fragile against her chest.

It felt so right.

So good.

It was wonderful.

Tears filled her eyes as she thought of that brief moment she'd held her tiny son. Holding the little John Doe made her yearn for what she'd lost and what she'd never have. Her child had been in her arms so briefly before he'd been taken away. He'd never taken a breath. Never cried. Never had a chance.

"Okay, I'll put him back. I have to get to a consult." Her voice quivered and she tried not to cry.

"Sure thing, Dr. Bhardwaj." Samantha took the baby from Kiri and together they got him settled back into his incubator.

"Thank you for letting me hold him," Kiri said. "I can see all our patients are taken care of here."

"Thank you, Dr. Bhardwaj," Samantha said. "And your holding him really did help. I'm a huge believer in skin-to-skin contact. Maybe if Dr. Valentino came by he could hold him, as well. It would help him out."

Kiri nodded. "I'll let him know."

She quickly left the NICU and tried not to cry.

She was angry at letting herself feel that way again and when she rounded the corner and caught sight of Alejandro at a charging station, charting, she saw red. He was part of her pain, because he was the one who'd got her pregnant.

The condom broke. It's not his fault.

Only she was too emotional to listen to rationality. Their baby was gone.

"Valentino," she snapped. He looked up, surprised.

"Yes, Dr. Bhardwaj, how can I help you?"

"You're John Doe's guardian. Visit him. Hold him. You're a doctor, you should know that human contact is essential to healing. You should know better."

She didn't wait for his response. She kept walking, not giving him a chance to respond because if she lingered she knew she'd cry.

When she was far away from the NICU and Alejandro, Kiri leaned against a wall and took a deep steadying breath, trying to get her emotions under control.

"Dr. Bhardwaj?"

Kiri opened her eyes to see Dr. Prescott from the emergency room standing in front of her. He looked concerned.

"Are you okay?" he asked.

"I'm fine. How can I help you, Dr. Prescott?" she asked.

"You know your John Doe in the NICU?"

"Yes," she said, but she knew. Deep down she knew what Dr. Prescott was going to say.

"We think we found the mother. We did a blood test when she came in for a postpartum infection, which we treated. The lab work came in and it's a match."

Kiri smiled. "Great work. Is she still here?"

Dr. Prescott nodded. "She is, but she doesn't speak English. Just Spanish."

Dammit.

"I'll get Dr. Valentino. We'll be down to the emergency room soon."

"Okay." Dr. Prescott left and Kiri girded her loins to deal with Alejandro again. Hopefully the mother really did want her child. Perhaps she'd had a change of heart and she wanted to see her baby. Kiri could only hope.

Perhaps John Doe would get a happy-ever-after.

Alejandro was still standing there at the charging station, charting. He saw her coming and did a double take, glaring at her.

"Kiri, what—?"

Kiri cut him off. "They found John Doe's mother."

He cocked an eyebrow. "Are you sure?"

"Dr. Prescott is positive. They ran blood tests. She came in because of a postpartum infection."

"Does she want to see the baby?" he asked.

"I don't know. She doesn't speak English. Perhaps you could speak with her?"

Alejandro nodded. "Let's go."

They walked in uneasy silence side by side down to the emergency room. Which was fine.

She had nothing really to say to him. If the mother wanted the baby back then maybe this whole situation with the John Doe and Alejandro could end. He'd no longer be the guardian and could do the surgery himself.

Dr. Prescott was waiting for them when they got to the emergency room floor.

"Dr. Valentino, thank you for coming down," Dr. Prescott said.

"No problem, Dr. Prescott. You said she doesn't speak English?" Alejandro asked.

"Not well. She could tell us sort of what was wrong. If you could translate for me that would be great."

Alejandro nodded. "Sure thing."

They all stepped into the isolation room. John Doe's mother was very young. That was the first thought Kiri had when she saw her. She saw a frightened young girl whose eyes darted back and forth between the three of them. She was ready to run.

"Hola, soy Dr. Valentino. Cuál es su nombre?"

"Luciana," she said, with a hint of relief in her voice.

Alejandro went on to explain what Dr. Prescott was saying to her about the postpartum infection and the medication. Once that was done Dr. Prescott slipped from the room. It was then time to ask her about the baby.

"Cuándo dar a luz, Luciana?"

He was asking her when she gave birth. That was when the girl became guarded. Even though Kiri couldn't understand what she was saying or what Alejandro was saying, she could see the change in personality. She was lying to him. She didn't want anyone to know about the baby.

Alejandro's words became quick, blunt, and Luciana's eyes narrowed. Then she turned her head and wouldn't say anything more. She was done talking. Kiri's heart sank. This was not the happy ending she was hoping for.

Alejandro shook his head. He stood up and they left the room, shutting the door.

"Well?" Kiri asked, though she knew.

"She doesn't want the baby. I'm going to send legal counsel and a translator down so she can officially relinquish her rights."

"Why doesn't she want the baby?"

Alejandro sighed. "She was assaulted. The father of the baby is unknown. She said looking at the baby reminded her of the assault. I'm going to have Prescott recommend a trauma counselor, as well. I told her what her baby was dealing with, but she doesn't care. She's only eighteen."

"She's just a child herself," Kiri murmured.

Alejandro nodded. "So our little John Doe is officially a ward of the state of Florida. I asked her if her parents or any other family members would want him, but, no, her mother is the one who delivered him and dropped him off at a hospital. She didn't know it was this one or she wouldn't have come here."

Alejandro didn't say anything further to her. He went to speak with Prescott. Kiri glanced back into the isolation room. Luciana was crying, but she was angry. And confused, of that Kiri was certain.

She didn't want or probably couldn't afford John Doe anyway. With the complication of his congestive heart disease, it was probably better that the boy had been dropped off. Someone would want him when he was all better.

Someone would love him.

Why not you?

He'd managed to avoid Kiri for four days after she'd called him out and after being told the baby's mother had been found. Luciana had officially signed him over to be a ward of the state and had given up all her rights.

Alejandro had a lot of mixed emotions about it all. And it appeared Kiri did too. He was angry that the young woman had been assaulted, but it was sad the little boy had to suffer and be born as the result of something so violent.

He just threw himself into his work and rarely went home. Alejandro picked up the chart in the neonatal intensive care unit to check on the child, who was intubated and hooked up to different monitors. He'd been avoiding the neonatal intensive care unit because he didn't want to get attached. Only he couldn't stay away.

Not since that day Kiri had called him out, because before that he'd gone to the NICU and seen Kiri holding the baby close to her heart. Seeing her hold John Doe, her eyes closed and an expression of bliss and agony on her face, had been unnerving.

And an image of Kiri holding his baby flooded his mind. Only he couldn't have that. A bullet had denied him. An uncertain future had also decided his fate. He lived life to the fullest, but he was destined to be alone. He shook that thought away and focused on the child he was legal guardian to. There was so much wrong with his heart.

Hang in there, amigo.

He shook his head as he read over his chart. So young,

born too early, no parents and to have so many problems. It wasn't fair.

Of course, life wasn't fair.

Alejandro knew first-hand what that was like, both personally and as a doctor. He set the chart down and then put on some gloves. Even though he knew he shouldn't, he opened the incubator and touched the little boy, placing his hand over the boy's little head.

So tiny. So fragile.

And then he ran his hands over the boy's body, before that tiny fist curled in a reflex action around his finger. A strange rush of emotions flowed through him as he stared at the little baby.

Other than working with children, he didn't have much experience with babies as he was the youngest of the brothers. He still remembered the first time he'd handled a sick preemie. He'd been so afraid that he was going to break the little girl, but his teacher had given him confidence.

Now he had no problem holding even the most fragile of babies. Which was good considering that he was going to be an uncle soon and he'd have to show Santi a thing or two about holding a baby.

He chuckled to himself, thinking about Santiago becoming a family man.

Santiago was the last person in the world he'd thought would settle down. Saoirse had certainly tamed his brother.

Perhaps you can be tamed?

"Do you want to hold him?" the NICU nurse Samantha asked as she finished charting on the incubator next to infant John Doe. "You should."

He should say no, but instead he said, "Sure, I think that would be good for him."

Samantha nodded. "Yes, it would be, Dr. Valentino. Skin-to-skin contact is sometimes the best therapy for these sick little mites."

Alejandro took back his hand and then sat in the nearby rocking chair. He peeled off his white lab coat.

Samantha looked up from where she was readying baby John Doe. "Dr. Valentino, skin to skin means you need to take your scrub shirt off."

"Do you think that's wise? I understand the importance of skin-to-skin contact, but I'm not related to the baby."

Samantha fixed him with a stern stare. "You're his guardian. He has no one else."

Alejandro understood how that felt. So he peeled off his scrub shirt.

Samantha raised her eyebrows at the sight of his large tattoo, which hid his heart-transplant scar, but she didn't say anything. As a nurse, she'd probably seen worse.

She brought the baby over to him and with a lot of finesse because of the different cords and lines attached to him she placed baby John Doe against his chest and then covered the infant with a blanket.

Alejandro gently place his hands against the baby's back, holding him there. And even though the boy had a bad heart, just holding him like that did something. The monitoring tracking the baby's heart started to stabilize a bit into a steady rhythm, which was saying a lot for an infant with a bad heart.

Samantha smiled at him. "You know, miracles do happen. It's a good thing the parents dropped this little guy off at Buena Vista and that you found him, Dr. Valentino. We all know what you're doing and we want to help any way we can. We heard that the hospital is cutting the pro bono fund."

"It's not the hospital cutting the fund, Samantha. It's the board. Snyder in particular, who is currently president of the board of directors."

"Not surprising, but still you can't bear the financial

burden on your own. We all want to help. We want to do a collection. We want to do something to help this poor baby."

Alejandro smiled. "That is very kind of you."

"My son was born with congestive heart failure. They told me to let him go so many times when he was a baby, but I didn't listen to them. He had a heart transplant when he was ten years old and he's just started college."

"I'm glad to hear that, Samantha. You never know what can happen. Miracles do happen." He said it all the time, but he wasn't sure if he believed it. The statistics didn't lie.

Samantha nodded and moved away to the next incubator.

Alejandro stared down at the little boy against him, so tiny against his chest. It was like holding a delicate bird.

"You'll be fine, amigo. You'll see. We'll get you a heart and you'll be fine."

"You should name him, instead of calling him amigo."

Alejandro looked over to see Kiri standing in the door of the NICU, her hands deep in the pockets of her white lab coat. She wasn't wearing the dark-framed glasses that she usually seemed to sport when she was wearing scrubs and working on patients. Instead she was dressed in business attire, a tight pencil skirt and heels, which elevated her from five feet five to maybe five feet seven.

"How can you walk in those things around here?" Alejandro teased.

She glanced down at her feet. "With difficulty, but I find when I'm addressing the board of directors I want to appear a bit taller, or taller than Snyder, at least." She stuck out her leg and he admired her shapely calf. "That's why I bought these shoes. They were expensive."

"Designer, then?"

She nodded. "I much prefer my sneakers or sandals. And I definitely prefer wearing scrubs and not having to wear panty hose."

Alejandro chuckled. "So why are you lurking around the NICU today if you're supposed to be in meetings?"

"I was checking on a couple of my patients." She nodded in the direction of the other end of the NICU. "They're not as badly off as your little John Doe."

"I don't think any baby currently at Buena Vista is." He glanced down at John Doe. "You're right, though, I should name him. John Doe and amigo don't suit him in the least."

"No, he needs a name and an identity if he's going to win his fight. He's got a long road ahead of him." Kiri took a step closer and reached out as if to touch the child, but then thought better of it. She put her hand back in her pocket and stepped back again, which made no sense as he'd seen her holding him a few days ago. "So do you know any good names?"

"My mother always said that names give us strength and pay homage to our culture. I would like to name him something like that."

"I can't help you with naming. Unless you'd like a completely boring name like John Doe."

"How about an Indian name? Why don't we both name him? We both found him, let's both have a hand in naming him."

A strange expression passed over her face. "No, you name him. I—I wouldn't know... You name him."

He couldn't help but wonder why she didn't want to help name him, but he didn't press the matter. "Gervaso, it means warrior. He needs a strong name."

Kiri smiled. "That's a nice name and very different. I don't think I've heard it before. How do you spell it?"

"*G-e-r-v-a-s-o.* Gervaso."

"It's nice," she whispered.

"My mother liked it. It's my middle name, actually."

"Well, it's better than baby John Doe and definitely better than amigo."

"Are you sure you don't want to give him another name?" Alejandro asked.

"Positive. I'd better go check on my patients." She turned and headed to the far side of the NICU, picking up a pair of gloves before she opened an incubator.

He didn't know what had got into her and he didn't care.

Right now his focus was Gervaso and getting him healthy again so that he could get adopted and live a long, happy life.

You can live a long time. You can be happy.

Only the moment he thought about Gervaso going off with someone other than him it caused him a pang of pain. Would it be so bad if he became the boy's father?

Yes. You can't. What if you die? What if your heart fails? What if...?

It wouldn't be fair to the baby. He needed parents. He needed a stable home.

And Alejandro couldn't give him those things. Everything was so uncertain.

"Samantha?" Alejandro called out.

"Yes, Dr. Valentino?"

"I have to finish my rounds. Can you help me put him back?"

"Of course, Dr. Valentino." Samantha put on fresh gloves and gently took little Gervaso from him and they got him settled back into the incubator.

"Also, make sure you change his chart and the application for his birth certificate. His name is Gervaso, not John Doe. *G-e-r-v-a-s-o.*"

Samantha smiled. "Will do, Dr. Valentino."

Alejandro pulled on his scrub shirt and picked up his white lab coat from the back of the rocking chair. He briefly glanced at Kiri's back and then got out of the NICU as fast as he could, because he was scared of the emotions little Gervaso and Kiri were stirring in him.

They were unwelcome.

Were they?

Kiri had been completely unnerved when she'd walked into the NICU and seen Alejandro holding that wee baby boy skin to skin. It had stirred so many emotions in her. When she'd first found out she was pregnant and had been trying to get hold of Alejandro she'd pictured him holding her child like that.

It was one of the silly fantasies she'd clung to.

She hadn't cared if he didn't want her, but she'd wanted her baby to have a father.

Of course, he didn't want kids and she'd lost her baby and she hadn't thought about that little fantasy in a long time. When she'd walked into the NICU and seen it playing out live it had made her feel weak in the knees. He was so sweet, holding that small baby against his chest. So gentle, so kind.

It had completely unnerved her.

She'd wanted to reach out and touch the baby again, but she'd stopped herself. She didn't want to get emotionally attached to a child who was going to be adopted by a loving family after he pulled through his heart transplant.

And then Alejandro had asked her to help name him. It was almost too much.

She didn't want to grow attached to a baby she was going to lose again. A baby who wasn't hers.

There were a lot of names that she'd thought of when she'd been considering names for her child, but those names were too precious and had been buried along with their son.

She knew that Alejandro had been avoiding her and, truth be told, she'd been avoiding him too. Kiri didn't know what had happened at Vizcaya, but those walls that had been coming down had been built up fast again.

And it had reminded her too that he was able to get past her defenses easily.

She'd known it was better for both of them if she kept her distance so she'd thrown herself into her work. She'd planned meetings, begun to see patients and had got very good at navigating the halls without seeing him.

Until today.

Kiri finished checking up on the babies in the NICU and then discarded her rubber gloves. She made quick notes and instructed the NICU nurses on care. As she was leaving the NICU she glanced at Gervaso's incubator.

He was so small.

She took a step closer and her heart skipped a beat as the image of Alejandro, holding the wee baby skin to skin, invaded her mind and overtook her senses.

And, though she shouldn't, she pulled on a pair of gloves and reached inside to touch the baby. Her eyes filled with tears as she ran her fingers over his little back, over his legs to the tiny feet curled under his bum. The hospital identification bracelet looked so large on his skinny little ankle. There was a hint of dark hair on his head...

This was what she'd imagined her baby to look like and it was almost all she could do not to start sobbing in the NICU.

She pulled her hand out of the incubator quickly and discarded the gloves in the receptacle. She'd thought that by leaving New York she'd been escaping the ghosts that haunted her. Walking the halls of the hospital where she'd lost her son had been too hard for her, and she'd thought that by coming to Miami she'd escape.

Kiri had never counted on the father of her baby to be in Miami.

She left the NICU and headed to her office, until she got paged to the emergency room. There was an incoming trauma. Children were hurt.

Kiri's stomach flip-flopped and she ran as fast as she could in her heels toward the emergency room. There was no time to change. It didn't matter. This was her job. Children needed her. When she got down to the emergency room, it was in chaos.

It was like a war zone almost.

"What happened?" Kiri asked, as she threw on gown and gloves.

"A school bus was in an accident. Multiple trauma," the emergency doctor in charge said. "Most of the kids have minor injuries, but one of them is unresponsive. She's in Pod Three."

Kiri nodded and headed straight for Pod Three.

The little girl was unconscious and the code team was shocking her.

"We have a sinus rhythm," the resident in charge of the team said.

Kiri rushed forward and jumped into the fray. "What do we have here?"

"She was thrown from the back of the bus when the accident happened and was hit by a car."

Kiri cursed under her breath. "I need a CT scan stat. I want her checked for head injuries and internal bleeding." She lifted the girl's shirt and could see extensive bruising on her abdomen. She palpated and she could almost guarantee that there was internal bleeding and the girl would require a splenectomy.

She listened to her chest and could hear fluid.

"I need a chest tube tray," Kiri shouted over her shoulder. It was handed to her and she inserted the chest tube, blood filling the tube as it drained from the lungs. "Let's get this girl up to the CT now."

"Right away, Dr. Bhardwaj." The resident moved fast as they got the little girl stabilized and started to push her gurney through the havoc of the emergency room to get her a stat CT scan.

Once she had the scan she would know how to approach the surgery. Who she would need in there. They got her straight into the CT scan and Kiri waited as the scans came through. As they appeared on the computer screen she was glad to see that there was no intracranial bleeding, but there was a lot of free fluid in the abdomen as well as a few broken ribs, probably puncturing her lungs. She needed a cardiothoracic surgeon to work on her lungs while Kiri removed the spleen, which was the source of the internal bleeding.

"Page Cardiothoracic and let's prep an OR," Kiri said to her resident. "Get her ready."

The resident nodded and Kiri headed straight for the locker room to change into scrubs. This little girl was going to be in surgery for some time.

And Kiri was going to make sure that the long hours that this girl was in surgery were going to be worth it. She was going to make sure this little girl lived to see another day.

CHAPTER SEVEN

"Suction, please," said Kiri as she worked on the little girl's spleen. There was no saving it and Kiri was in the process of removing it. The lungs had not been badly punctured and the ribs had been set. The lungs were patched. The cardiothoracic surgeon on duty, Dr. Robinson, was monitoring her, just to make sure that another leak didn't happen.

"Kids are quite resilient," Dr. Robinson said offhandedly. "I'm sure she'll pull through. She's a lucky little girl. Someone three times her age would have a harder recovery. If this accident had happened on the bridge she could've been thrown into the water or the ambulances might not have gotten to her in time."

Kiri nodded, but didn't respond to Dr. Robinson. She knew very well that this girl was lucky to be alive. She didn't wish to engage in any banter, she just wanted to make sure this little girl was stabilized so she could update the parents, who she knew were in the waiting room.

And as she was working on the spleen she noticed there was damage to the kidneys, as well.

Blast.

"How is her urine output?" she asked over her shoulder.

"She hasn't had any urine output," a nurse responded as she checked the bag.

Dammit.

The kidneys were probably shutting down, which meant this girl might need a transplant if both kidneys were shot. That's the last thing this poor girl needed after all she'd been through. Hopefully they could be repaired.

Though she didn't want to see Alejandro again today, she needed him in the OR. She needed him to check on the girl and assess the kidneys while she continued to work on the spleen.

"Can someone page Dr. Valentino to come to the operating room? I want him to check out this patient's kidneys."

An OR nurse went to the phone and paged Dr. Valentino. She could hear the murmur across the room, but she ignored it. She ignored that her own pulse began to race at the thought of seeing him again.

Focus.

Kiri continued to work on the spleen, but then the left kidney began to bleed. "Hang another unit of packed cells. And suction, please. Where the heck is Dr. Valentino?"

Definitely kidney trauma and Alejandro needed to be here. She needed him.

The doors to the OR from the scrub room slid open and Alejandro, capped and scrubbed, came into the room.

"It's about time," she snapped.

"Dr. Bhardwaj, what seems to be the problem?" he asked as a nurse gloved and gowned him.

"We have a female, age ten, who has blunt-force trauma to the abdomen after she was thrown from a school bus during an accident. Her urine output has been nil and the left kidney has blood pooling behind it. I need your assistance as I'm working on the spleen."

Alejandro nodded and took his spot across from her. "And the spleen is damaged beyond repair?"

Kiri nodded. "I'm performing a splenectomy. Her ribs were broken, but Cardiothoracic has cleared her of any trauma to her diaphragm, heart or lungs. There was a small puncture to her left lung but that was patched by Dr. Robinson. It's all in her abdomen."

Alejandro whistled under his breath. "It must have thrown her far to damage the kidneys."

"She was hit by a car," Dr. Robinson said.

"Poor girl." Alejandro began his examination. "The left kidney is torn, but it can be repaired. I'll place a shunt." Then he looked at the other kidney. "Minor tear in the ureter. Let's get this girl on bypass so toxins don't build up and I'll get to work."

"I'm almost done the splenectomy then I can get out of your way," Kiri said.

And she wanted to get out of his way.

"You're not in my way, Dr. Bhardwaj. I can work around you," Alejandro said without looking at her as he got to work on the patient.

She couldn't help but admire his dedication to the task. How he was able to repair such a small organ. Those strong hands so delicate as they worked on the young girl. They moved in unison, not needing to speak as they focused on their work. It was like they had been operating together for a long time. She hadn't had this rapport with another surgeon since she'd worked with Dr. Vaughan.

"Do we know her name?" Alejandro asked, breaking the silence.

"Casey," Kiri said. "Why?"

"I like to know." He glanced up at her. "It helps me to connect to my patients and I like to talk to them, to let them know that they're going to be okay. And, Casey, you'll be okay."

Tears stung her eyes as he talked to the little girl so gently.

"You have a way with kids," she said.

"I like kids," Alejandro answered as he worked.

"Yet you don't want kids?"

His brow furrowed over his mask. "Liking kids and wanting kids are two different issues. Something I don't want to discuss."

"Hey, I'm just trying to get to know my colleague better."

"It's a very personal question," he said.

"It's no different from you grilling me about my lack of significant other the first time we operated together."

Alejandro's eyebrows popped up and he chuckled. "Touché."

"Wrong use of that word, my friend."

"How so?" he asked.

"It means to touch. We're not touching." And then her cheeks heated when she realized what she'd said. Those dark eyes of his twinkled behind the surgical mask but he didn't say anything else to her.

"Casey, you're doing great," he said. Kiri smiled.

What was with him and names?

And it reminded her that she'd never named her baby boy. Their baby. She'd planned to name a boy after her father. She shook her head. She couldn't think about that right now.

As she finished the splenectomy Alejandro was still working on the damaged kidney and shaking his head, which made her heart sink.

"There is nothing I can do," he said. "I'm going to have to do a nephrectomy."

"And the other kidney?" Kiri asked.

"The ureter isn't that damaged and the kidney is intact and not bleeding. It will be fine. We'll keep her in the hospital and I'll monitor her and give her the right medicines to help with elimination until the ureter on the right kidney heals. A shunt will help." Then he stared at her. "And if her parents can't pay to keep her here, will you ship her off to County?"

It was a pointed barb. And as she'd be the one to sign off on it, she was powerless to stop the board's will.

"You know that's beyond my control. And she has parents. She's not a ward of the state."

"Good, because I would do everything in my power to keep her here if she was going to be shipped off. She's my patient."

"You can't pay for every child."

He grunted in response. What she wanted to tell him was that she'd try her best to keep Casey here so that Alejandro could monitor her, but that was beyond her control. It was bad enough that the Buena Vista board of directors was seriously considering shutting the ER doors, because they were tired of vagrants and those who couldn't pay coming to their hospital, but that was for the head of trauma to deal with. Not her.

In this case of the school bus accident they had been the closest hospital and they were a level-one trauma center. Whether the board liked it or not, they couldn't close their doors to those who were hurt.

Especially not children.

Perhaps that was how she could persuade the board of directors to allow Casey to stay if her parents weren't able to pay the hospital bill. It would be good press for the hospital if they allowed the young girl who was hurt in a school bus accident to be treated by their world-class physicians.

Like Dr. Alejandro Valentino, who was saving this girl's life by operating on her kidneys and probably saving her from going on the already taxed and full UNOS list.

And then she thought about little Gervaso. He was priority, but she was worried that he wouldn't make it to get his heart transplant and what would that do to Alejandro? She knew the pain of losing a child.

"I'm finished with the splenectomy," she said. "I'll go give the parents an update about her condition."

Alejandro nodded. "Thank you, and let them know that once I'm done with the nephrectomy I'll come out to speak with them."

"All right." Kiri headed to the scrub room and peeled off her gown and gloves. This was her least favorite part of the job, telling parents who were scared beyond belief the status of their child. Telling them their child was ill and undergoing a serious surgery to save their life.

At least Casey would probably pull through.

Casey would probably live.

The nephrectomy and the ureter repair took longer than Alejandro had anticipated, but the bleeding in the cavity where the damaged kidney was had stopped and the ureter had been repaired. Casey was producing urine again, thanks to a shunt and some elimination medicines that would help her as she healed. At least Casey still had a viable kidney. She didn't have to go on UNOS. She was broken, but she could be repaired and go on to live a full life.

You can too. You can have a full life. You're just scared.

He shook that thought away. There was no time to feel sorry for himself. He was here to give an update to his patient's parents.

As he walked into the waiting room he was surprised to see that Kiri was still sitting there with the parents, talking with them.

Kiri saw him first and gave him an encouraging smile then stood up, which caused Casey's parents to jump up and stare at him with terrified hope.

There was no other word for it. He knew that look too well.

"You must be Casey's parents." He held out his hand. "Dr. Valentino."

"How is our daughter?" Casey's mother asked, clearly terrified, not taking Alejandro's hand after her husband had shaken it.

"She's fine. She's in the pediatric intensive care unit. She sustained multiple injuries to her abdomen as well as several broken ribs. As Dr. Bhardwaj told you, we had to remove her spleen and one of her kidneys."

Casey's mother covered her mouth with her hands and was trying not cry. "Is she going to be okay?"

"Yes, she will be. People can live with one kidney. I'll refer her to a nephrologist, who will monitor her over time. We're going to keep her in the hospital for at least a week so I can monitor her progress and watch to make sure that the shunt I placed doesn't slip. She will be on some medications for some time to help her eliminate urine and aid in the healing process."

"Can we go see her?" Casey's dad asked.

"Of course," Alejandro said.

"I'll take them up there," Kiri said. She walked by and squeezed Alejandro's arm in thanks as she led the parents out of the waiting room. He was exhausted and he had to find a good strong coffee and take his own medication.

Just like he did every day at this time. The antirejection medication so he wouldn't lose his father's heart.

It's your heart now.

Only it wasn't. Alejandro knew it was his dad's and that was why he was living. The ultimate gift from his father. Which was why Alejandro had dedicated his life to surgery.

He wanted to give back.

For as long as he could, because who knew how much longer he had? How much time his father's heart would beat for him?

He grabbed his wallet out of his locker and then headed outside where there was a coffee cart that sold particularly strong Cuban coffee day and night. The sun was just setting. The city was full of gold and red and he wished that he was back at his apartment, watching the sun set over the ocean.

This was his favorite time of day.

When the world slowed down just a bit. When he could thank the powers that be for another day on earth. Another day of saving lives.

Of course, in South Beach the world didn't slow down all that much and the nightlife would be gearing up. The clubs would be pumping out loud music and hordes of people would be wandering the streets.

Tourists mostly, but still the streets hummed with a different pulse and it had been so long since he'd gone there to feel life, the energy flowing through the music. It had been so long since he'd danced.

"What will it be tonight, Dr. Valentino?" the barista asked.

"Tall and dark with two shots of espresso, please." Alejandro opened his wallet and pulled out the money.

"Coming right up."

Alejandro rolled his shoulders. They were stiff and sore from the surgery, but the pain was worth it. That little girl would go on to live another day. Even if she was minus a couple of organs.

She had another shot at life.

The pain on the parents' faces, though, had been too much to bear for him. Which just affirmed his choice not to have a family.

"Here you go, Dr. Valentino."

Alejandro took the coffee and paid the barista. He wandered over to the row of benches just outside the main hospital doors and sat down. He closed his eyes and listened to the city.

His city. When he'd danced, he'd been working all over

the country, but Miami was his home. It always would be, even though he'd lost his parents here and had even lost a brother who'd gone off and joined the army for a time, he still loved it. He would always come back here.

His parents were gone, but at least Santiago had come back.

There was just something about this place that spoke to him. Miami had a hold on him. It was his first love.

His only love.

Is it?

And then he couldn't help but think of Kiri. After their time in Las Vegas he'd tried to find out more about her. He'd wanted to get to know her, but Ricky hadn't had that information or at least hadn't been willing to share it.

Ricky had been a bit difficult that way and he had not been happy when Alejandro had decided to leave.

"You'll come back. You'll need money and you'll come back. They always come back."

Alejandro had promised himself he would never go back to dancing like that. Which was why it was imperative that no one found out about his past.

Of course, that had never concerned him until Kiri had shown up. It was good Ricky had never shared that information. He had no right to get attached to her. To lead her on when his time was limited.

"Can I join you?"

Speak of the devil.

He opened his eyes to see Kiri standing there. She looked as tired as him. He should tell her to leave, but he couldn't. He was lonely.

"Of course." He slid over and she sat down, slumping over.

"I was not prepared for a splenectomy today," she said.

"Who is prepared for splenectomies?"

"I am, when I plan the surgery because of a preexisting condition, but an accident like that? It's something I'll never get used to." Kiri shook her head. "So much trauma."

"You're a surgeon, you have to live for the moment." He took a sip of his coffee; it was bittersweet, just the way he liked it, and it woke him up.

"I know, it's just… It's so hard watching a kid go through that. I sometimes wonder why I chose to work with kids."

"Why did you?" he asked. "If it weighs so heavily on you, why did you choose to work with kids?"

She shrugged. "I don't know, probably because they're worth saving."

He raised his eyebrows in question.

"And adults aren't?"

Kiri laughed softly. "No, it's not that. I just… I love kids and I want to help them. Why did you decide to become a pediatric transplant surgeon?"

Alejandro sighed and set down his coffee cup. He lifted his scrub shirt. "You see the eagle?"

"I remember the eagle," she said tenderly, and a delightful blush tinged her cheeks.

"And you know there's a scar there. Touch it and tell me what you think it is."

She reached out and traced her hand over it. Not just the touch of a lover, but this time as a doctor.

"I would say heart surgery. Have you had heart surgery?"

Alejandro nodded. "A heart transplant, to be precise. When I was ten."

She gasped. "I'm sorry to hear that."

"Well, I'm okay now." He winked at her. "I decided when I was ten that I wanted to be like the surgeon who saved my life. I wanted to save other kids. I wanted to help. So I worked hard to become the surgeon I am today."

"Why did you cover it with an eagle?" she asked.

"To remind myself to always soar and because women don't particularly find it sexy if their exotic dancer has a big old ugly scar across half their body."

She chuckled. "I guess not."

"Tattoos are hot," he teased, waggling his eyebrows. "Although it did hurt like you wouldn't believe and took a few sessions to complete."

"I don't doubt it."

"Are you off tonight?" he asked.

What're you doing?

He didn't know. She was his boss, it was probably a bad idea, but he needed to be with someone. Someone he didn't have to pretend around.

Someone who knew him.

Not many did.

"Yes, I'm done now. How about you?"

"I was on my way out the door when you paged me."

"Sorry about that," she said. "I thought if she needed a transplant you would know right away. I should've paged someone else."

"Never be sorry. It's my job and I take it very seriously. I want you to know that. You know who I was before I was a surgeon. No one else does."

"I wouldn't tell anyone your secret. Our secret, remember? I was there that night and indulged too."

His blood heated as he thought of that night. Not so much in the private villa where he'd been dancing for her and her friends, but when he'd seen her at the bar. Alone and sad.

And even though he shouldn't, he couldn't help himself.

"What're you doing tonight?" he asked.

"Nothing. Why?" she asked, frowning. She looked confused.

"We're going dancing."

"Dancing?" She sounded panicky. "Do you think that's wise?"

"I know. It's probably not right, but I think I'm your only friend here in Miami and we're just going dancing. That's all. It's harmless."

"I don't dance," she said.

He slugged down the rest of his coffee. "Tonight you will. I'm taking you to a samba bar and we're going to dance. We're going to celebrate saving Casey together."

"Well, then, shouldn't we invite Dr. Robinson, as well? He helped," she teased.

Alejandro wrinkled his nose. "No, it's just going to be us two. Have you seen Dr. Robinson dance?"

"No, I haven't." Kiri chuckled. "Have you?"

"Yes. It's bad."

"No worse than me, then."

"You've seen me dance, though." He grinned as she began to blush. "I can teach you. Come on, there's a samba bar near our apartment. We don't even have to take the motorcycle. We can walk."

She bit her lip and he waited with bated breath to see if she would take him up on his offer. One part of him hoped that she wouldn't, but another part of him really hoped that she would. He felt like celebrating tonight. Tonight he wanted to dance and he wanted to dance with her.

He didn't want to be alone.

"I shouldn't," she said. "But I will. Why not?"

"*Excellente.* I will pick you up at ten o'clock. Be ready. Wear a dress." He crushed his coffee cup and tossed it in the garbage bin as he stood. "I'm looking forward to this. I promise you'll have fun, Kiri."

"Promises, promises. I'll hold you to that, you know. I'd better have fun." She was teasing.

"I guarantee you'll have a good time."

"You guarantee it?"

And before he could stop himself he took her hand and kissed her knuckles, before whispering, "Absolutely."

CHAPTER EIGHT

KIRI WAS SECOND-GUESSING the choice of dress as she stared at herself in the full-length mirror in her bedroom. It was short, tight and a one-shouldered emerald-green number that always looked good on her. She always wore this dress when she went dancing.

It was probably dated, but this dress made her feel comfortable.

It had been a long time since she'd worn it, though.

What am I doing?

Not only had it been ages since she'd been dancing, but she shouldn't be going out with Alejandro. Not when he was one of her surgeons. It could be detrimental to their careers, but Alejandro was the only person she'd connected with here.

The only person she knew.

She almost canceled. She was going to, except he knocked on her door.

"*Hola*, I..." He trailed off as his gaze raked her from head to toe.

A blush crept up her neck and bloomed in her cheeks. Her pulse raced as those dark eyes settled on her.

"You look...stunning."

"Thank you. You said to wear a dress."

"Yes, well, that dress suits you." He cleared his throat. "Are you ready to go explore South Beach and samba bars?"

"I think so," she hedged.

"You only think so? You don't sound very certain."

"Should we really? I mean, given my position at the hospital…"

He held up his hand, cutting her off. "We're going as colleagues. Nothing more. We're celebrating, that's all. We're friends, yes?" He held out his hand. "So are you coming?"

No. Don't do it.

It had been so long since she'd had fun. Kiri took his hand and went with him. Once they were outside the cool chill of air-conditioning gave way to a sultry night. It wasn't too bad as a breeze was rolling in off the ocean.

"How far are we going?" she asked.

"Not far. Stick with me."

Kiri did exactly what Alejandro suggested as they moved through the crowds. She stuck close to his side as they moved through the crowded streets toward a samba bar on the busiest street of South Beach. She could hear the Latin music pouring out onto the street. It was loud, but not obnoxious. It seemed to fit with the mood of the crowd, the vibe in the air.

"Slow down, you have longer legs than me," she teased as she tried to keep up.

Alejandro stopped and looked at her legs, grinning. "They look fine to me. Damn fine. I happen to like your legs. If I haven't said so already, I'm so glad you wore a short, tight dress."

"Be serious," she said, but she was pleased he thought she looked good. The last time she'd felt even remotely good about herself had been in Vegas.

Don't think about that night.

"That's not the point. Slow the pace down. I can't keep up with your march."

"I'm just eager to dance with you. To dance in celebration of our success with that little girl today." And as if to hammer his point home, he spun her around in the crowds.

Kiri laughed at his enthusiasm.

Alejandro gripped her hand tight as he moved through the crowds. Or actually it was almost as if the crowds parted for him. And as they moved through the people she could see more than a few women who stopped to check him out.

And to check out her as well, the competition, as it were.

It made her feel slightly uncomfortable to be sized up by other women. It reminded her of the times when she'd been a little girl, chubby, in hand-me-downs from her older sister, a bad haircut and big, thick glasses.

You're not that girl anymore.

She was a confident, talented surgeon with a great job at a respectable hospital. Although she couldn't blame the women for checking out Alejandro. He looked so good in his tight white shirt and dark denim. He had perfect hair, he was tall and ripped and had a devastatingly charming smile, with a dimple to boot.

So sexy.

It wasn't just his looks, though. It was his personality. His charisma. He had this hold on people. Kiri was pretty sure that he was aware of this and he used it to his advantage, and given that it was Friday night and the street outside the club was packed, she was glad he knew his way around.

Alejandro spoke with the doorman. They shook hands and laughed and the velvet rope was lifted for them to enter the club, much to the protests of the crowd waiting.

"Come on," Alejandro said.

"How did you get in? There's a huge line waiting to get in here."

"I grew up with the bouncer and the club owner. Plus, I started dancing in a club like this."

She stopped in her tracks. "You mean…"

"No," Alejandro said quickly as he led her into the darkened club. "I just danced. My friend would hire dancers to dance with lonely women who were on their own. That's how I was discovered by Ricky, who got me into the exotic dancing side. Of course the club Ricky found me in was in Little Heliconia. The club owner I know has become very successful."

The club was filled with people dancing and there were dancers on a stage by the bar in brightly colored costumes covered in feathers dancing to the Latin beat. It was like being at Carnival in Rio, only more contained.

It was overwhelming. She gripped Alejandro's hand tighter as she took it all in. It was like an attack on the senses, but then she felt excited to be here. The music made her sway a bit. She'd been dreading this, but now that she was here she thought this might actually be fun. As long as she kept her cool around Alejandro and didn't let her attraction to him sway any of her decisions.

"Why did you choose dancing for Ricky over this?" she asked, shouting a bit over the noise.

"Dancing for Ricky paid way more. I would still be dancing here, trying to pay off medical school, if I hadn't taken that job." And then he spun her as they headed out onto the dance floor. "I was one of the best dancers here."

He brought her out of the spin and tight against his body as he led her into a dance. Her pulse was racing, being so close to him. His arms wrapped around her as their bodies moved together.

"I don't doubt it," she said, and then she cursed herself inwardly for sounding a bit like a schmuck. She tripped and he caught her.

"Legs wobbling still from the forced march?" he teased.

"No, I don't dance very well. I'm not very coordinated

in heels. I can barely walk in them. And, besides, I told you I don't dance."

He smiled down at her. "You're doing fine."

"Ha-ha. You're too kind."

Alejandro frowned. "No, you're doing fine. Just grab the rhythm."

"Says the man to the woman who is rhythmically inept."

He chuckled and then his hands moved from hers and he put them on her hips, guiding them to the rhythm of the music. "Just feel the music. Close your eyes and forget everything else."

It was hard to forget everything else while his hands were on her hips, guiding her in a very sensual dance. Her body was very aware that Alejandro was touching her and she was glad a layer of clothes was separating them.

"There you go," he said. "You've got it." He took her hands again and led her into the middle of the dance floor, his hands holding hers as he led her through a very simple dance. His dark eyes twinkled and that irresistible grin made her feel a bit weak in the knees. She couldn't help but admire the way his body moved.

She'd enjoyed watching him in surgery; his fingers working on the most delicate structures was like a dance in itself and this was just an extension of that. It was an assault on her senses.

He had been the only man to ever make her feel something. He'd made her feel desirable, sexy, and it was a rush to feel that way again in his arms.

Five years had not dulled the desire she still felt for him.

He spun her round again and she laughed as the colorful dancers all around her and the flashing lights blurred in a dazzling light.

He was laughing too as he pushed and pulled her through the dance and she just listened to his advice and found the rhythm of the music and moved her hips. His eyes were dark and she recognized that look, the lust in his eyes, and her heart fluttered.

She had to be careful tonight or she might be swept away.

The song began to wind down and he spun her round and then brought her close, holding her tight against him. His breath was hot on her neck as their hips moved together.

The song ended and people began to clap. She pushed herself away from his embrace and joined in applauding the live band.

Another song started up and before she had a chance to say no, because she was still trying to regain composure from the last dance, he brought her close, holding her tight. His hand held hers as he led her through a slower dance.

She glanced up to see him staring at her.

"What?" she asked.

"Nothing." He looked away. "I was just going to compliment you on your supposed lack of dancing skills."

She stepped on his foot and they laughed together. It was nice to be real with him. Kiri didn't have to pretend.

"See, I told you I'm no good at this."

"You're very good at this." He smiled at her.

Kiri's heart skipped a beat. She thought he was going to kiss her and she wasn't sure if she'd be able to stop him.

"It's hot out here on the dance floor. Do you mind if we stop?" she asked over the din of music.

"Do you want something to drink?" Alejandro shouted.

"Yes. Some water would be great. The crush of people in here, it's so hot."

He nodded. "Let's go that way, where there's a quieter bar."

Kiri took his hand and he led her off the dance floor. They found a small table tucked into the corner of a bar.

She sat down and he went to get the drinks. He brought back two bottles of what looked like expensive water.

"How much did that cost you?" she asked.

"Probably more than an alcoholic drink. This water might be made of gold."

She laughed and took a drink. It was ice cold and heavenly. "Thank you for the water. This place is popular."

Alejandro nodded. "It's one of the best in South Beach and a definite tourist trap."

"I can see why. Not only are people dancing but this place is crawling with professional dancers."

"They often do a dinner show early in the evening, but you need reservations for that."

"I'm sure those are hard to come by."

He nodded. "That's really for all the tourists." He took another swig of his water. "You did so good out there. You can dance, you're just being modest."

"I'm not being modest. I really can't dance, but you're a good teacher."

"*Gracias.* I did do a bit of that too."

"What?" she asked.

"Teaching dance, but again Ricky paid me so much more to do exotic dancing." He frowned. "I loathed it so much, but it afforded me my freedom."

"Aren't you afraid that one of our patients would've seen you? I mean, look at me."

He shrugged. "I have thought of that, but I didn't do my exotic dancing in Miami. I was quite insistent that I be sent outside the greater Miami area. I didn't want my brothers finding out. They didn't know that I was doing any sort of dancing as a way to pay for my schooling. They thought I was working at the docks in a fish-processing facility."

Kiri wrinkled her nose. "And that was better?"

"To my older brothers, yes. I didn't have the guts to join the army like my brother Santiago."

"Who taught you to dance?" she asked.

"My mother. She taught me and I just kept dancing, even after she died." He smiled wistfully. "She wanted me to be a dancer, I think, like her brother Jorge. Jorge died when she was young, before she came here. She always talked about Jorge's dancing."

"And your bothers didn't know you danced even then?"

"No, they would've teased me so it was a secret. Just me and my mother knew about it." He cleared his throat. "If someone were to recognize me I'd pretend I didn't know them. Honestly, most people don't remember a male exotic dancer's face. The only reason you remember me is because of what happened afterward."

His gaze was intense and she looked away.

"Yes," she whispered, and the reason his face was burned into her brain was because no other man had made her feel that way, because she'd stepped out of her comfort zone and allowed him in, and look where that had got her.

"Come on, let's have another dance." He stood and held out her hand and as much as she wanted to, she just couldn't.

"I'd rather not press my luck. I think I'll sit this one out."

"Are you okay?" he asked, squatting down in front of her. "Too many people?"

She nodded. "Yeah, I just need some air. It's really crowded in here."

He nodded. "Okay, let's get out of here and take a walk on the beach. It's been an exciting day."

She was relieved that he understood her need to get out of the crowded club. She took his hand and let Alejandro lead her out of the overcrowded club. Her head was pounding because of the loud music, but it wasn't that. Being with him like this, getting to know him was going to make it harder to walk away. She liked being with him, but they didn't want the same things. There was no future for them.

It ate away at her soul.

They crossed the street, dodging the cars that were pretty much at a standstill because of people looking for parking and partygoers going from bar to bar.

Once they were on the opposite side of the street it was a short walk over some small dunes and through some long grass to the beach. It was dark and overcast. There was a strong breeze blowing in from the ocean, but it was nice. They kicked off their shoes because sand was starting to fill them.

Even though it was dark, the sand was soft and warm against her feet.

It was exactly what she needed at that moment.

"Looks like a storm is rolling in," Alejandro remarked. "Or rather it feels like a storm is rolling in. I can't tell since it's dark."

Kiri glanced out over the water, but all she could see was darkness, though she understood what he meant. The air felt different. The wind was stronger, with a haunting whistle to it. And then there was a distant roll of thunder.

"Maybe we should head for shelter?" she asked.

"It's still far off. We can walk on the beach back to home. Would you like that?"

"Yes. It will be better than the crowded street."

They walked in silence, right down by the shoreline, letting the cold water wash over their toes. It felt so good. There was another flash of lightning, this time closer, and they stopped to watch it light up the sky in the distance. And then a bolt of thunder cracked across the sky over the ocean.

"Beautiful," Kiri murmured.

"It is. I never tire of watching it."

"Have you ever watched a hurricane come in?" she asked.

"Only when the whitecaps come rolling in. I'm smart

enough to know that when a hurricane is coming you seek shelter. As one man said once, it's not that the wind is blowing, it's what the wind is throwing around that causes the most damage."

"Sound advice."

"Though I do understand the appeal of chasing a storm. The danger in it. I find them fascinating."

She stopped to look up at him. In the streetlights shining down onto the beach, and as the lightning flashed, she could see the wind rippling his white cotton shirt.

"You like to live dangerously, then?"

"No, but I like the idea of living dangerously. The only time I lived dangerously was when I came up to you in that bar five years ago." He took a step closer and tilted her chin so she was looking at him. Her heart hammered against her chest and her body ignited in a thousand flames. He still had a physical effect on her.

So much so that she lost all sense of control around him.

And she didn't like to lose control. She couldn't lose control when it came to Alejandro. She'd learned the hard way what it was like to lose control around him. He cupped her face, strands of hair tickling her cheek, and no matter how much she wanted to fight it, how much her inside voice screamed that she should push him away, she just couldn't.

She closed her eyes and let him kiss her.

His lips were gentle against hers, familiar, and so many emotions came bubbling to the surface. Anger, sadness and lust. It had been so long since she'd been kissed by a man she couldn't remember when it had been.

She'd only been on a couple of dates after she'd lost the baby, but now, with Alejandro's arms wrapped around her, she couldn't recall them.

All she could remember was him.

Everything else was forgotten as she melted in his arms.

Kiri wanted to stay there. He made her feel safe, he made her feel alive again.

What're you doing?

She pushed him away. "I can't."

"I'm sorry, *mi tesoro*," he whispered. "I didn't mean for that to happen."

My treasure. Only she wasn't his treasure and she resented the term of endearment.

Kiri nodded as his words hit her with a cold dose of reality. "It's okay, but please don't call me that. I'm not your treasure. I never will be."

A strange look passed on his face. "Of course. I'm sorry."

"I'd like to go home now. I have some more meetings tomorrow that I have to prepare for. It was a long, emotional day. This was probably not wise. I should've just gone to bed."

"Of course. I'll take you home." There was no lingering by the beach this time. They walked the rest of the way in awkward silence along the beach until they got to their condo.

They rode the elevator up to their floor in silence. She tried not to look at him. If she did, she might cry or do something she'd regret.

And Alejandro walked her to her door only because his own door was across the hall from hers.

"Kiri," he said gently, those dark eyes of his making her melt, "I am sorry if I made you feel uncomfortable."

"It's okay." She was trying not to let her emotions overwhelm her.

He rubbed the back of his neck. "I got carried away, but I want you to know that I don't regret what happened between us. Not then, not now."

What he said made her pulse race.

"I don't regret what happened between us. Not then, not now."

Kiri didn't regret it either, but she knew that if Alejandro knew what had happened he might regret ever having laid eyes on her. He might regret ever sleeping with her.

The thing was, even after her loss she'd never regretted the choice she'd made. It had hurt, but she'd never regretted going with Alejandro that night. That night had been the most wonderful night in her whole adult life.

No man had ever treated her like that before. Or since.

So, no, she didn't regret it either. She wished that she could have more, but there couldn't be any more between them. She was technically his boss. She'd come here to prove herself, not to fall in love. She couldn't fall in love with a man who didn't want kids. Still, she wanted him to know. Wanted him to share it with her.

He had the right to know.

For so long that pain had been very hard to bear and she'd sworn to herself five years ago that she would never ever go through it again. Telling him would probably push him away for good.

So it was better this way. He deserved to know.

It was better to keep Alejandro at a distance. That kiss had been too dangerous.

It was too dangerous for her heart.

"Alejandro, five years ago, after our night together, I fell pregnant."

"I... What?" he asked, his eyes widening. "Pregnant?"

"I lost the baby. I tried to find you but..." Tears streamed down her face. "I can't ever go through that pain again. You deserve to know. I'm sorry. So sorry."

She didn't give him a chance to respond because she began to cry harder. She had to get away from him. Kiri pulled out her keys, her hands shaking as she unlocked her door.

"Kiri…"

She shook her head. "I'm sorry." She slipped inside her apartment and shut her door quickly so she didn't have to see the stunned expression on his face or the hurt. She didn't want to talk about it because she couldn't handle it right now.

At least he knew now.

At least now she could move on without him, without the guilt of keeping the loss of their child a secret, because she was sure he wouldn't want anything to do with her again.

CHAPTER NINE

SHE'D BEEN PREGNANT?

The words sank in and he was still numb. Still in shock. *Kiri had been pregnant?*

After standing in the hallway, feeling stunned, for a few moments he unlocked his own door and went into his apartment. It was so hard to walk away from her door when all he wanted to do was ask her how she'd lost the baby. He wanted to hold her, console her, because she'd faced that loss on her own.

He hadn't known.

He'd almost been a father and that thought scared him. She'd also been the only one to ever get to him.

He'd had a couple of other casual flings, but nothing compared to Kiri.

And now the more he got to know her, the more he wanted her.

Which was a dangerous thing. He needed to know her pain. He wanted to console her, process it, but at the core of all the rush of emotions swirling around inside him he wanted to make love to her again.

To let her know in the only way he knew how that it was okay.

He was okay.

They could separately be okay.

When they had been out on the dance floor together,

his hands on her hips, all he'd been able to think about had been taking her, making her his. And he'd been very aware of the way other men had been looking at her and that had infuriated him.

She was his.

She's not, though.

And he had to keep reminding himself of that fact. When they'd been standing out on the beach, watching the storm roll in, it had reflected exactly what he'd been feeling in his very soul at that moment, watching her standing there, wisps of her silky black hair escaping and blowing across her face.

The absolute peaceful smile on her face, but then the pain. He hadn't wanted her to feel pain. He'd wanted to take it all away. It was all he'd been able to do not to carry her off.

Alejandro had wanted her. Just like he'd wanted her back in Vegas. Nothing had changed, she was still the woman he desired above all.

So he'd kissed her.

And he'd sworn he could feel her melt into him. For one crazy moment he'd been lost and then she'd brought him screeching back to reality. She'd lost his baby. He couldn't be with her because he didn't want to hurt her. She deserved a man who could give her everything. Everything she wanted. Marriage, children. He couldn't give her those things. He may have got her pregnant once before, but he couldn't do that again.

Though he'd been shot and injured, they'd told him his father had died because of a brain hemorrhage, but Alejandro was certain that the hemorrhage had been caused by the shock of seeing his wife and son fall first. His father had truly died of a broken heart and subconsciously given up the will to live. In the foggy recesses of his brain from that moment, he recalled his mother being shot first, of crumpling into his father's arms while his father had screamed her name, and then he'd felt the sting of a bullet.

Alejandro shook his head, trying to drown out the sounds of his father screaming. He rubbed his scar, which burned.

He couldn't imagine loving someone so deeply and then losing them. And he couldn't do that to another person. It was too much to bear. Which was why he never opened his heart. Had never let another person in. Yet Kiri always seemed to find a way in. His walls weren't safe when he was around her, which was why he had kissed her on the beach.

Why he couldn't resist her. He would never be able to resist her.

She lost our baby. He had already caused her pain and hadn't been there.

And she had tasted so sweet.

Outside the storm raged, just like a storm raged in his heart. Thunder rumbled and he leaned against his window in the darkness, staring out. He could see the once calm ocean was becoming choppy as the storm rolled onto shore.

Go to her.

And though he knew that he shouldn't because of their positions at the hospital, he couldn't help himself. He needed her. He turned and left his apartment and knocked on her door, his heart jackhammering, his blood on fire.

She answered. Her hair was down and brushed out and she'd changed out of the dress into a nightgown. Her dark eyes were swollen and red from tears.

"Alejandro?" she said, surprised to see him.

He didn't answer her; instead, he reached down and kissed her again. Possessively. He wanted to let her know that he wanted her. He would always want her, and even though she was not his to have, he would never not desire her. And he wanted her to forgive him for not being there when she'd needed him most.

She was under his skin, burned into his memories.

No one could live up to her.

Though he could never have her, she was his.

Kiri melted and kissed him back, her arms around his neck and her fingers tangling in the hair at the nape of his neck. He pushed his way into her apartment, almost expecting her to stop him again, but she didn't. He closed the door with a swift backward kick.

"I'm so sorry, Kiri, for your loss. For what you went through alone. I don't know how to help you. How to make things better. I just know that I want you. More than that night in Vegas…"

"Alejandro," she whispered, laying her head against his chest. "What're we doing?"

"I don't know." He cupped her face and ran his thumbs down her cheeks. "I don't know. I want you, but if you need more from me, if you need a promise of something more, I can't give you that and I'll leave. I just swore a long time ago that I wouldn't ever…" He sighed and dragged his hand through his hair. "My heart transplant."

"You're afraid it will fail?"

He shook his head. "Yes, when I was ten I had the heart transplant because I was shot when my parents' bodega in Little Heliconia was robbed. My mother died at the scene, but my father died during surgery to save his life. My life was hanging in the balance and since my father was brain-dead my brothers directed my father's heart to me as we were a perfect match. I carry a piece of a man I admire greatly inside me. It's a huge responsibility and it reminds me every day that I have to work hard to be the best doctor I can be. I can't be selfish. I promised him that I would dedicate my life to medicine." He was going to say more about how he didn't know how much time he had left, how he'd never hurt her again, but he couldn't.

Her eyes filled with tears for the horror that he had endured at such a young age and her heart went out to him for the brave decisions he'd made since that dark time. "I'm so sorry for your loss, Alejandro. You went through a shocking and terrible ordeal—and at such a young age. I'm wowed that you've dedicated your life to saving others as you yourself were saved. Your parents would be filled with pride to see what you've achieved. It's so admirable. I understand."

"It's not a burden, it's just how I've lived. I had to tell you, I just had to know if you still wanted me even though I can't promise you anything beyond this."

She bit her lip. "I do want you and I don't need a promise. You've made it clear about how you feel, but what about our jobs?"

"No one has to know. We can just have tonight."

"I just need tonight," she whispered. "To chase away the ghosts."

"Are you sure? You deserve more than I can give."

Kiri shook her head. "All I want is you. Right here. Right now."

A flash of lightning illuminated her apartment and he heard the rain splash against the glass of her windows. The storm had come and there was no turning back now. No stopping it now. He scooped her up in his arms and carried her to the bedroom. He set her down and then cursed under his breath.

"What?" she asked.

"I don't have protection. Seducing women is not something I do very often."

"I can't get pregnant again," she said sadly. "I'm unlikely to conceive. Added to that I have a hostile uterus, which makes the odds of carrying a baby low as well... I won't get pregnant again. I refuse to, so I take birth control."

"Are you sure you want me to continue?"

She nodded and then undid the buttons to his white shirt. "I want you, Alejandro. I've always wanted you."

The moment her hands pressed against his bare chest he lost it and he knew he had to have her. There was no going back and perhaps he was putting his heart at risk, but it was just for this moment. Another stolen moment.

He kissed her again, running his hand down her back, cupping her bottom to pull her closer against him.

"I've thought only about you for the last five years," he whispered against her neck. "Only you."

"Me too." A little moan of pleasure started in her throat as he kissed that spot on her neck that he remembered so well. Alejandro nearly lost his mind with desire. This was what he'd been dreaming about for so long.

"If I'm not careful I'm liable to take you right here."

"Is that bad?" she teased, running her hands down his back.

"Yes, I plan to take my time with you."

Alejandro pressed her against the mattress, running his hands over her body but pressing his body against her so he could feel her curves pressed against him. He reveled in the softness of her skin, her hair, as he kissed her again.

"Touch me," she whispered. "Please."

"With pleasure." And he cupped her breasts, squeezing them, but that wasn't good enough for him. He wanted to kiss every inch of her skin.

Apparently it wasn't enough for Kiri either because she pushed him away and took off her nightgown, baring her beautiful naked body to him. Her skin glowed in the darkness, the flashes of lightning illuminating her.

With hurried fingers she helped him out of his clothes

so that nothing was between them. She ran her hands over his skin, causing gooseflesh to break out over his body.

"I love your hands on my body," he whispered.

"I can tell," she teased. Then she teased him with the tips of her fingers. Running a finger lightly down his neck, over his chest and then tracing the tattoo. Her hand splayed against his abdomen and slipped lower, gripping him in the palm of her hand.

"Dios," he groaned.

"I love it when you speak Spanish." Still holding him, she leaned forward and nibbled his neck. "You're completely at my mercy."

"Sí."

Her dark eyes glittered and she grinned devilishly as she stroked him. He sucked in another breath. His whole body was alive, every nerve on fire as she touched him. He tried to hold back a moan but he couldn't.

Kiri touching him was driving him wild and he was afraid that if she kept it up he would come. Only he didn't want her to stop.

"Oh, mi Dios, no se detienen," he grunted, bucking his hips at her.

"What did you say?" she asked, dragging her lips over his chest.

"Oh, my God, don't stop."

"Then I won't." Her mouth was on him then and his hands slipped into hair and he started speaking in Spanish, not even knowing what he was saying because he was being driven wild with pleasure.

Growling, he pushed her against the mattress, pinning her there below him.

"Now who is at whose mercy?"

She bit her lip and tried to wrap her legs around him, but he let go of her wrists to push open her legs.

"I want you, Alejandro."

"I know, but now it's my turn. I've wanted to taste you for so long."

"Taste wh...? Oh, *mi Dios*," she gasped as he did exactly just that. Torturing her the way she had tortured him.

"You've picked up Spanish quite well," he teased her.

"How do you say 'I want you inside me now'?"

"Te quiero dentro de mí ahora."

"Te quiero dentro de mí ahora."

"Sí."

"That wasn't a question. That was an order."

"Was it, now?" he teased her again, running his tongue around the most sensitive part of her, making her cry out. "Say it again. I want to make sure you're saying it right."

"Te quiero dentro de mí ahora. Please."

"Por favor."

"Sí," she said, arching her hips at him.

"Okay." He moved over her, staring down into her eyes. Kiri pulled him down for another kiss as he entered her with one quick thrust.

"Dios," he groaned. She was so tight, so hot. It took all his control not to take her too fast, but her body arched and she began to match his rhythm so that he sank deeper into her, and he couldn't hold back. He slipped a hand under her bottom, bringing her closer and angling his thrusts as he quickened his pace.

It was hard to hold back, but he managed it until Kiri came, crying out his name as she tightened around him. Only then did he allow his own sweet release.

When it was over he rolled away, trying to catch his breath, and he realized that he wanted more of her.

"That was amazing," she whispered in the darkness. He could hear her panting and he grinned.

He rolled back over and grabbed her, dragging her across him, her soft body against his. She kissed him gently on the lips.

"That was amazing," he said. "You're amazing."

She smiled at him. The wind howled outside as she settled against him and he stirred to life again. He wanted her again. And she seemed to want more as she sat astride him, sinking down on him, riding him, but this time making love to him slowly. Tenderly.

Yes. He wanted so much more of her. So much that it scared him and he realized that he was a lost man.

Kiri woke with a start. She reached out, expecting to find Alejandro there, but he wasn't. This time he'd left, instead of her. Her stomach knotted as she thought of him sneaking out, but really he was just doing exactly what she'd done.

And they hadn't made any promises.

He'd told her he couldn't offer her anything and she'd accepted that because she couldn't give him anything either. And since they worked together, what they'd done wasn't right.

All they had were these couple of stolen moments and a lost child.

That's all they had together.

Outside the sky was gray, the ocean was gray and turbulent, and the beach was littered with driftwood and seaweed. It was a miserable day outside as the remnants of the tropical storm lingered into the morning.

She got up, because she couldn't lounge around in bed all day, though that's what she wanted to do. The moment she sat up she caught sight of his white shirt lying crumpled on the floor where she'd tossed it.

Kiri picked it up and held it to her face, drinking in his scent. Tears stung her eyes and she thought of what she'd almost had with him. While he'd expressed remorse for her he hadn't seemed to feel much at all about it himself, which confirmed her belief that he didn't really want children. That saddened her because being with him had been so much more this time because she knew him. She understood him. She loved being with him. She enjoyed his company. He was a friend.

No, he was more than that.

I'm in love with him.

And the thought scared her because it was something she'd been trying to deny for a long time. She could talk herself out of it before because all Alejandro had been then was a one-night stand. She hadn't known anything about him, not even his last name.

Now it was different. Kiri knew a lot about him. She knew his last name. Knew he'd grown up in Miami and his parents had been immigrants from Heliconia. He was dedicated to his work, he rode a motorcycle, he loved to dance and he was charming.

He treated his patients and his coworkers with a level of respect she'd never seen from a brilliant surgeon before.

He was charming, sexy and passionate about medicine.

And he'd suffered a devastating tragedy as a child. With far-reaching consequences. Only he'd turned his life around, had turned the darkness of his past into something bright and wonderful.

Alejandro was the perfect man. Only she couldn't have him because he didn't want the same things she did.

She was in love with a man she could never have. She tossed the shirt away.

Get a grip on yourself.

Alejandro had made it clear to her last night that he couldn't be in a committed relationship and she had done the same. She'd promised him that it would be okay, that he didn't have to commit to her.

She was a big girl.

She was independent. Things could carry on like they had before. She would make sure of it. Only as she stared at the crumpled shirt on the floor she knew that nothing would be the same between them again.

Kiri only hoped that she hadn't totally jeopardized her career in Miami.

Even though she missed New York City like crazy, Miami had grown on her. She loved the weather and the culture. Loved working at Buena Vista.

This was her home now.

And she wasn't going to let anything stand in her way. Even her feelings.

CHAPTER TEN

"YOU'RE LATE, DR. BHARDWAJ."

Kiri tried not to roll her eyes as she walked into the small boardroom where she was meeting with the head of the board of directors today. She really detested these meetings with Mr. Snyder, who only saw the bottom line instead of the lives.

"Thankfully, Dr. Prescott was able to meet with me in your time slot," Snyder snapped.

"The head of trauma?"

Mr. Snyder glanced up at her briefly from his paper-work. "The former head of trauma."

Her stomach sank into the soles of her feet. So they were planning to close the trauma department, and Prescott had been so helpful in finding Gervaso's birth mother.

Dr. Prescott didn't deserve this. This was not how a hospital should be run. A hospital needed a trauma department.

"Do you think closing the trauma department is wise?" she asked.

"We're not planning on closing the trauma department. Dr. Prescott quit. He took another job. He was just handing in his resignation. I'm on the lookout for a new head of the trauma department, so if you know anyone or can recommend someone out of the pool of attendings we have here

I would appreciate any recommendations. Besides, your only concern is pediatrics. You're not Chief of Surgery."

It was a barb, meant to keep her in her place.

Kiri took a deep breath and counted to ten. "I'll keep my eye out. I haven't quite met all the attendings outside the pediatric department."

Mr. Snyder nodded. "You're running your department like a tight ship. I have to say, the board of directors is quite pleased with your summary."

"Thank you," Kiri said, but if Snyder was pleased with her she didn't take that as a compliment. The cuts she'd made when she'd first arrived didn't sit too well with her.

"We just have one concern, about Dr. Valentino," Snyder said.

Her stomach did a flip again. "What about him?"

"We want to keep him, he's the best specialist in pediatric organ transplant that we've ever seen. His survival rate is high, but these pro bono cases have to stop. We're trying to save money and attract a very specific clientele here."

"I couldn't very well send José Agadore elsewhere. He was too ill to move and Alejandro spoke his language. The family were at home with him. It wasn't long before UNOS called and we were able to give him the liver transplant."

Mr. Snyder cocked an eyebrow. "Yes, but the antirejection meds aren't being paid for by the family. They should be, but Dr. Valentino is paying for them."

Kiri was taken aback. "What?"

Mr. Snyder ignored her and pulled out another file. "And this John Doe in the NICU, why wasn't he shipped to County? That's where wards of the state of Florida in Miami go. They don't stay here."

"I'm aware of that, but you'll notice that Dr. Valentino was approved to be guardian of the baby. He's footing the bills. The child needs a heart transplant."

Mr. Snyder pulled off his glasses and rubbed his eyes.

"We don't want to lose Dr. Valentino, he's too gifted, but this has to stop. This charity. The only way to keep away the people who require pro bono services is to stop all charitable donations."

Kiri clenched her fists under the table. She knew exactly what Mr. Snyder was implying. He meant riffraff. Whatever riffraff was. "Dr. Valentino is not doing the baby any harm and it's his money."

"You need to talk to him." Snyder sent her a pointed stare that made her blood boil.

"I'll talk to him. That's my job," she snapped.

Snyder glared at her. "Remind him that while it may be his job to save his patients medically, it's not his job to save them financially."

"Is that all? I do have *paying* patients to see."

"Yes." Snyder waved his hand, effectively dismissing her like he was a lord and she was a lowly serf.

Kiri stood and left the meeting. She was fuming and she had an inkling this wasn't the board of directors speaking but Mr. Snyder personally. How could Dr. Vaughan, a man she admired so much and who was all for pro bono cases, be friends with someone like Mr. Snyder? She had to find a way to appeal to the rest of the board about their pro bono fund.

Babies like Gervaso and others didn't deserve to be shipped off to County because they were unwanted. They deserved to be cared for by the best team of pediatric doctors in Miami. She was worried about Alejandro forking over so much money. It was attracting the wrong attention and he had to lie low for now.

Until she could get the heads of the hospital together to convince the entire board that the pro bono fund needed to be reinstated.

She found Alejandro in José's room. He was talking to José's parents, and before she could even knock on the door she saw him reach into his pocket and bring out bottles of prescription medicine.

Dammit. What're you doing?

Kiri was angry at Alejandro for endangering his job like this. With Gervaso's case he'd gone through a lawyer and a judge had approved it. The hospital's hands were tied, but this? This was going too far.

José would be on antirejection medications for the rest of his life. Alejandro couldn't be doing this. José's family had to be on some sort of drug plan. The boy had cystic fibrosis as well. Was Alejandro supporting the medication for that too?

Now he was stepping out of line with the doctor-patient relationship.

She knocked on the door. "Dr. Valentino, can I speak with you privately?"

He glanced over his shoulder and nodded, holding up a hand to let her know that he would be one moment.

Kiri moved away from the door and headed into a private exam room, waiting for Alejandro to come in.

It wasn't long before he was there.

"Close the door, please," she said, not looking up at him. She was fuming. He was putting his career at risk. If he was fired for conflict of interest he wouldn't be hired by another hospital if Snyder had any say over it. Then who would take care of Gervaso?

It was highly irresponsible.

"You're very serious." Alejandro closed the door behind him. "What's wrong?"

"I just got out of a meeting with Mr. Snyder."

"I can tell from your expression that your meeting with him didn't go too well."

"No, it didn't." Kiri sighed. "I don't know how to say this, but they're concerned about your behavior recently, first with baby Gervaso and second with José."

He frowned. "What do they have to be concerned about?"

"They're worried about you paying for too many things." Kiri scrubbed a hand over her face. "You're too charitable."

"I don't understand. Why is that a bad thing?"

"It's not, it's just bad here."

"Why?" he asked.

"Mr. Snyder cut the pro bono fund."

"I know, but it's not coming out of hospital funds. It's coming out of my pocket. The bills are getting paid so why do they care?"

"Alejandro, they're worried that it might get around that there's a surgeon on staff who is willing to shell out money. It's a conflict of interest. They don't want to attract the wrong kind of attention."

He snorted. "I know exactly what he means by that."

"Look, I know too. I hate that, but you can't save everyone." And then she paused. She was starting to sound like Mr. Snyder and that bothered her.

"I'm not saving everyone, financially that is. I'm Gervaso's guardian."

"What about José? I heard that you're paying for his medication. You can't do that. It's a conflict of interest. You can't go out of pocket for them. It's attracting attention. You could lose your job and then what will happen to Gervaso?"

"You make it sound like I'm stealing the medication," Alejandro snapped. "For your information, I'm not paying for José's medication."

"You were pulling pill bottles out of your pocket."

Alejandro reached into his pocket and held up the bottles. "You mean these? These that say 'Alejandro Valentino' on them? I was showing José's family the medication that José will be on for the rest of his life. Just like the cystic fibrosis medication. They need to understand the importance of the antirejection drugs."

"Mr. Snyder had a bill showing that you paid for some of José's meds."

He shook his head. "I took José's parents' money and went down to the pharmacy to deal with the pharmacists. The pharmacists here don't speak Spanish. I do. José's parents paid me back. They're on a drug plan through their insurance and their pharmacy is in Little Heliconia, but the hospital won't allow me to discharge José until his parents pick up meds and show the attending physician that the child is taking the antirejection meds. It's hospital policy. Since José's parents don't drive and were planning to take a cab, I didn't think it was right for them to pay extra money that they don't have to get to their pharmacy in Little Heliconia and back again to get their son."

Kiri's heart melted. Alejandro was so good and she felt like a heel for thinking the worst of him, for letting Snyder sway her into believing the worst in him.

Alejandro was good and suddenly she felt like the harbinger of doom and gloom. "I'm sorry. I didn't know. I am very relieved, by the way."

He gave her a half smile. "It's okay. I get it. You were under pressure from the board and Mr. Snyder. I can go speak to the board if you want."

She shook her head. "No, you don't have to do that. I'll explain to them, it makes sense now."

"I hate board politics," he grumbled.

"Me too."

An awkward silence fell between them.

Alejandro took a step closer to her. "Since we're alone…"

He bent down and kissed her on the lips.

"I have been thinking about you all morning."

"What're you doing?" she asked, stunned.

"Kissing you," he said.

"I know, but last night you said it was just going to be one time."

Alejandro took a step back like she'd hit him. "And kissing you to thank you is taking it too far?"

"Yes," she whispered. "Because kissing me like that makes me want you more."

"You want me?"

This time Kiri gripped his lapels and pulled him down into a kiss that she knew she would regret, because kissing him like this tore down her walls completely, shattered them, and it scared her that she wanted him this badly.

You're at work. You can't have him. He's bad for your heart.

It was that sobering thought that made her push him away. Why was she so weak when it came to him? Why couldn't she control herself when she was around him?

"We can't do this," she said.

"We can."

And she glanced up to see those dark eyes full of lust, the same dark, burning desire that she was feeling for him.

"I want you too, Kiri. You make me crazy with wanting you."

This was wrong. She should stop him, but she couldn't. She wanted him so badly she didn't care anymore.

She'd been numb and living in a fog so long. She wanted to live again.

To feel.

And not feel the blinding, raw pain she'd buried deep inside.

She just wanted passion. Release.

In this room it was just the two of them.

Just them, and that's what she wanted, even though she knew he didn't want that. It wasn't a permanent thing so right now she'd savor every moment that she had with him.

She crossed to the door of the exam room. Turned the key in the lock, sealing them in, shutting out the real world.

Hot and wild with need, she shimmied out of her underwear and hiked up her skirt as she helped him undo his scrub pants. He was hard and ready for her. Just like she was ready for him. She'd been ready for him the moment she'd laid eyes on him.

Alejandro hefted her up and pressed her against the wall, inching up her skirt. She wrapped her legs around his waist, her hands gripping his shoulders, holding on for dear life as he thrust into her.

"Kiri," he moaned. "Why do I want you so much?"

Kiri didn't answer; all she did was bite her bottom lip so hard she tasted blood. She was trying not to cry out in pleasure.

If all she could have was this moment with him, she was going to revel in it.

"You feel so good… *Dios*…" he moaned against her neck as he thrust into her.

She wanted to tell him she loved him. There was so much she wanted to say to him but couldn't because she didn't want to get her heart broken. He'd been so clear that he couldn't give her anything.

You should've resisted him. You should've kept far away.

And she'd tried to resist him, so many times, but each time she'd failed. He was always there and she was drawn to him. She was a weak fool and she tried to stop the tears of emotion that were welling up inside. The last thing she wanted to do was cry. She didn't want Alejandro to see her tears.

Right now she just wanted to savor this moment of being with him. Of him buried inside her, their bodies pressed together as they moved as one.

She came quickly and he followed soon after.

This was all so wrong. Wanting him when he didn't want more, but when it came to Alejandro she was so weak. So very weak.

Hot tears streaked down her cheeks and he saw them.

"Are you okay?"

"No."

He wiped the tears away with his thumb. "Tell me about it."

"What is there to tell?"

"A lot more. How did it happen? How did you lose our baby?"

She sighed. "Because of my hostile uterus, my cervix dilated. They couldn't stop it. I was only twenty-three weeks along. There was nothing to be done."

His head dropped. "A boy or a girl?"

"A boy." Her words caught in her throat. "His lungs weren't ready. He never took a breath."

He nodded. "I'm sorry that happened to you. Was he buried?"

"In Manhattan."

Alejandro nodded again and she began to cry more as he held her tight. "I'm so sorry."

"I know. Me too." She gave him a wobbly smile, but still couldn't help the tears.

He smoothed the tears from her face as her sobs subsided. He kissed first one damp cheek and then the other. Carefully, tenderly. Then he caught her lips with his own in a slow, lingering kiss that ignited the fires of passion in her once again.

What're you doing? Stop this.

Only she couldn't because she was so helplessly in love with him. He was the only one for her. He was the only one she wanted. She was completely ruined for all other men. It was him or nothing.

You're a fool.

"I can't get enough of you, Kiri," he murmured as he broke the contact momentarily. "Why is that?" he asked.

"I don't know."

"Do you want me to stop?" he asked, kissing her neck now. "I'll stop if you want me to."

Yes, the rational part of her screamed, the part of her that wanted to protect her already fragile heart from being hurt again. Only she couldn't say no. She didn't want to say no.

"No, I don't want you to stop."

I never want you to stop.

"Good, because I don't think that I can," he moaned as he thrust into her.

"Then don't," she whispered, pulling him down to kiss him again.

So very weak.

He held her tight against him as their breathing returned to normal. This was not how he was going to get over her. Last night, being with her, he'd realized it wasn't just that he desired her or that he was attracted to her.

He was in love with her and it terrified him to his very core.

His plan had been to avoid her for the next few days, but he was slowly coming to realize that he needed her. Like air or water. He wanted to be with her. He wanted to forget about the pain he'd caused her. The guilt ate away at him. He hadn't been there. She'd been alone. Yet one moment with her and what had happened? They'd locked themselves in an unused exam room and he'd taken her twice. He just couldn't get enough of her when he was around her. He just had to have her again and again.

There's a solution to your problem.

He shook that thought away. He couldn't give her all she deserved.

"I'm sorry," he whispered. "I didn't mean for that to happen." He helped her back up from the exam table, which wobbled slightly as they got up.

"It's okay, neither did I." She straightened her skirt and hair, while he pulled up his scrub pants.

"This is going to be tricky."

"What is going to be tricky?" she asked.

"Us around each other."

"Agreed," Kiri said. "Very tricky."

"So what're we going to do about it?" he asked.

"Try harder not to succumb?" she suggested.

"Unless we just say screw it and date." The words shocked him as well as her. He didn't want to date her, or that was the plan, but being around her he couldn't get enough of her. He'd been very clear when they'd first got together and now he was reneging on the deal. Alejandro could see the disappointment on her face. She didn't want to be serious with him.

Which was what he'd wanted in the first place. And all the percentages of heart-transplant survival rates swirled around in his mind. Twenty-two years was the median and he was at twenty-one. He could be on the UNOS list next year. He was being selfish in wanting her.

It terrified him.

"Alejandro…" She was going to say something more, but then her pager went off. "It's the baby!"

"What?"

"Gervaso, it's a 911 page."

"Oh, God, no." He ripped open the door.

His heart raced at a thousand beats a minute as he thought about all the things that could go wrong with Gervaso's heart. And all the variables terrified him. They ran out of the exam room toward the neonatal intensive care unit. When they got there Dr. Robinson and his team were working on Gervaso. The NICU had been cleared of all nonessential personnel and Alejandro winced as he saw them use the defibrillators on the tiny infant.

Gervaso couldn't die.

He was supposed to live. That's why the mother had dropped him at the hospital, wasn't it? That's why he and Kiri had been destined to find him. Gervaso was supposed to live. He wasn't supposed to die in a world-class facility while waiting for a heart. He wasn't supposed to die like his son had died.

The child he hadn't even known he'd had until recently.

The child he'd never wanted.

The child he'd lost.

His blood. His flesh.

Now Gervaso was dying. He could see that.

You can't let this happen. This is not how it's supposed to be.

Alejandro took a step in but Samantha stopped him. "You can't, Dr. Valentino."

"I'm his doctor. His transplant doctor," he said fiercely.

"You're not, though, Alejandro," Kiri said gently. "You're his guardian. You're not allowed in there."

"You're all the family he has," Samantha said. "And family is not allowed in there when the doctors are working. You know that."

It hit him hard. Like a punch to the gut.

Gervaso's family. That was him. He didn't want to be that baby's family. He just wanted to help the baby get a new heart. To have a second chance and then find his real family.

You can be his family. You are his family.

And as the boy's family he couldn't go in there. His hands were tied and he felt completely useless standing there.

"What am I going to do?" He cursed under his breath

a few choice words and raked his hands through his hair. "He needs me. I'm the best transplant surgeon there is."

"I know you are," Kiri said. "But he doesn't have a heart yet. There's nothing you can do and legally there's really nothing that you can do because you're his guardian."

"Someone has to be there, someone who can help," he pleaded with her.

"I'll go," Kiri said. "I'll take care of him."

Alejandro nodded as Kiri slipped inside the NICU to help. And all he could do was stand by and watch helplessly as his only chance for any kind of family was on the other side of a glass partition.

And it was slipping away from him.

"We're losing him!" Dr. Robinson shouted. "I need zero point zero one of epinephrine stat! Damn, this kid's vessels are so small. I can barely get a Norwood done on him."

Kiri couldn't do much to assist Dr. Robinson, but she was there, watching little Gervaso struggling to live. His little heart was giving out and everything was moving in slow motion. So all she did was hold the retractor and try to help Robinson navigate the small, delicate vessels of a preemie's heart.

Gervaso's heart.

And she was taken back to that moment when she'd been bleeding out and learning the sad truth that her baby was gone.

Even though Gervaso wasn't her child, she didn't want him to slip away. Alejandro may deny that he was that child's family, but she saw the way he was with him. He'd named him. Alejandro was this boy's family.

Alejandro was about to lose another child and it tore her up completely and she felt like it was her fault because at this moment she was useless.

Come on.

She closed her eyes and said a little prayer.

Then she heard a heartbeat and she opened her eyes.

"We got him," Dr. Robinson shouted.

"He's going to be okay?" Kiri asked.

"For now, but this will happen again and the next time he won't survive. He needs a new heart."

Kiri nodded. "I'll check with UNOS again."

"Let them know what happened here today. It will probably bump him up on the list," Dr. Robinson said.

"I will." Kiri looked down at little Gervaso, intubated and so small. In that small face she saw her lost baby and she couldn't help but reach out and touch his little fist. Longing shot through her.

Hold on.

She had to get out of the operating room. She couldn't stand to see Gervaso like this. To know that Alejandro would be heartbroken if the baby died. It was all too much for her because she understood that pain and if she lingered then she was in danger of having that happen to her again. She couldn't let that happen again.

Kiri peeled off her gown and gloves and scrubbed out.

She headed out of the OR and saw Alejandro pacing in the hall. His expression was broken and he looked defeated. Even though he didn't want to admit it, he cared.

"Well?" he asked the moment his gaze landed on her.

"He's stabilized. I'm about to call UNOS and let them know about his progression. We're hoping this will bump him up the transplant list."

"Okay."

Kiri touched his arm. "He's a fighter."

"Can you honestly say that he'll pull through this?" Alejandro asked. "The odds are against him."

"Miracles do happen." Though she was one to talk. She wasn't even sure that she believed in miracles.

"I want you to do the surgery."

"I can't," she whispered. "Don't make me."

"Make you?" Alejandro snapped. "What're you talking about?"

"I can't operate on that baby."

"Why? You're not related to him." Alejandro froze. "You care for him?"

"I… I don't think… You can get a neonatologist to work on him."

"Kiri, he's not a neonate, he's premature, yes, but he falls under your jurisdiction. You've done heart transplants and I need you to do this. I need you to save him. For me. Please."

"Don't make me operate on him. I can't do it. I can't lose another baby." Tears slipped from her eyes, because there was no controlling them now. When Gervaso had coded and she'd watched them trying to bring him back from cardiac death, it had all become too real for her. When she'd miscarried their baby, she'd been far enough along to hold their son in her arms. To weep over him and to bury him in a tiny white coffin.

She couldn't do it again. If Alejandro wasn't going to adopt Gervaso, she was. So she didn't want to operate on him.

"What're you talking about?"

"Our baby," she said. "I lost our baby."

Alejandro frowned "I know. I know you did."

"If Gervaso dies, it will be my fault this time."

"This time?" he asked confused. "Whose fault was it last time?"

"Yours, your fault… I blamed you for so long. You weren't there to help me."

"It was my fault that our baby died?" He shook his head in confusion. "How? I didn't know. I would've helped had I known."

"Yeah, sure, you've made it clear you don't want kids.

You have no idea the depth of my pain. You're not the one who lost the baby," Kiri yelled, all the anger that she'd been keeping pent up inside her coming out. "You don't know what I went through. The pain I felt. I did it all alone. You weren't there!"

"How could I be there? I didn't know!"

"Exactly. It was my pain to bear. Not yours."

"It could be my pain to bear, but you're scared. So scared you won't even help out a child who needs you. Losing our baby wasn't your fault any more than it was my fault, but if you don't do this surgery on Gervaso you will be responsible for his death. It will be your fault!"

Kiri slapped him hard because he was right but also because she wanted to hurt him. She wanted him to feel the sting of what she'd gone through when she'd lost their baby. He would never know the pain, because he hadn't been there.

Alejandro held his cheek, his eyes like thunder.

"I'm not the only one afraid," she said. "You're so afraid of having a family because you lost your parents. You say that you carry a piece of your father inside you, you want to be like the man he was, but from what you're telling me you're nothing like him. Your father brought your family to a new country to give them a new start. It sounds like your father was a brave man and you're too afraid of loving and losing that you're losing what you could have. You're a coward, Alejandro Valentino."

She turned on her heel and ran from him because she didn't want him to see her cry. He didn't deserve to have her tears. To share in this pain. It was a little too late for that, but then again he was right to call her a coward too.

She was afraid of losing a child again.

The pain was too much. It hurt too badly and she was terrified of feeling this strongly for someone. She was terrified of acting on her feelings for Alejandro, of admitting out loud that she was in love with him. And she was terrified of loving Gervaso. Of wanting to be a mother so desperately but too afraid of losing it all.

That she wanted all Alejandro had to offer, even though he wasn't even sure about what he was offering yet.

He didn't even know if he wanted Gervaso for the rest of his life.

Could she really put her heart at risk like that? Especially with someone who didn't want kids?

Her smartphone rang. She cleared her throat. "Dr. Bhardwaj speaking."

"Yes, this is the United Network of Organ Sharing. Are you the surgeon responsible for Gervaso Valentino?"

"Yes," she said, her voice shaking.

"We have a heart at County. It will be ready in the next couple of hours. Are you able to come?"

Her hands shook because it was so close that she would go and retrieve the heart and because it was so close she knew that somewhere in this city someone was mourning a loss. Tears stung her eyes. They could bear the pain and so could she. She had to.

She was a surgeon.

She cleared her throat. "Yes. I will be there within the hour."

She hung up the phone, gripping it tightly in her fist.

She could do this.

She *had* to do this.

CHAPTER ELEVEN

ALEJANDRO STOOD THERE, STUNNED. The imprint of her palm was still stinging his cheek. He'd deserved it, though. He'd said heartless things to her. She had lost their child alone. He hadn't been there; she hadn't deserved that. He should've been there. His child had died.

Things she didn't deserve, but he was still trying to process the rush of emotions flowing through him. Emotions that he'd kept at bay for so long.

He wasn't sure what he was feeling.

And then it hit him that he'd lost a baby and he was on the verge of losing another. He stared at Gervaso in the neonatal intensive care unit, isolated and hooked up to so many machines. The nurses who were handling him were now gowned and masked.

If a heart wasn't found it would be only a matter of days before his little body gave out. And if Gervaso died, what would become of his heart?

Dios mio.

He was completely helpless and lost.

How had his brothers coped?

How had Kiri coped? And then tears rolled down his cheeks. He couldn't remember the last time he'd cried. And then it hit him. He remembered in complete Technicolor the last time he'd cried. It was a memory he'd blocked because it was too painful.

The last time he'd cried had been the night Santiago had left for the Army. They'd just gotten the note and Alejandro had realized that he was on his own. Dante and Rafe were working hard to support them all.

He'd decided that, being fifteen, he was too old to cry, even though being alone in the night had scared him. At night he'd remembered the shooting, losing his parents. Even before then the night had always scared him. He'd cried because he'd missed his mother, who had soothed his bad dreams. He'd cried for his father who'd always had a joke.

He'd cried for Dante's and Rafe's smiles and gentle good-natured ribbing and Santiago, who had always been in the next bed, snoring his head off.

He'd been alone and had missed his family.

So he'd cried one last time when at fifteen and had never shed another tear again, because he'd been on his own. He'd had to take care of himself. He hadn't had a family anymore.

Except now he did.

Kiri and Gervaso were his family. As much as he wanted to deny it, he couldn't. Now he was on the verge of losing another family and it was too much to bear.

You have to bear it.

He couldn't ever have a family. His future was so uncertain. How could he give Gervaso and Kiri any sort of life? He was living on borrowed time. And as he thought of that, his head spun. Beads of sweat broke out across his brow.

Alejandro glanced up to see Kiri coming towards him. He wiped the tears away because he didn't want Kiri to see them. As she got close he saw she was wearing a Buena Vista jacket and was carrying an organ transplant cooler.

She gave a solemn nod, keeping a professional calm

about her, though from her red eyes he could see she'd been crying. Tears he'd caused. "There's a heart at County Hospital."

"Kiri," he said, "you don't have to do this. If you can't—"

"I do have to do this." She glanced through the NICU's glass windows sadly. "There's no one else to do this. Gervaso deserves a chance at life."

"I'm sorry," he whispered.

"I'm sorry too. It will be okay. He'll pull through." Kiri cleared her throat. "It will give him a chance to live. A chance for a *real* family to love him, since it's clear you don't want to adopt him."

It was a dig and he deserved it. He knew in that moment that Kiri's heart was lost to him.

"But you're going to retrieve—"

She held up her hand to silence him, her dark eyes flashing. "I know very well what I'm going to retrieve. I know what I'm walking into. Don't remind me. I'm not doing this for you."

Her voice trembled a bit and he wanted to pull her close and tell her he was sorry that he hadn't been there for her five years ago when she'd delivered their child. He wanted to tell her that it would be okay. She could do this. Only he knew she didn't want to hear it from him now. Not when he was making her do this for him.

This impossible thing that would hurt her and possibly close her heart to him forever.

"Thank you," was all he managed to say.

"You asked me once to give him a middle name," Kiri said.

"I did. Names give strength."

"I know," she whispered. "Aatmaj is my father's name. It means 'son' and I think it's fitting, don't you?"

"Was that what you were going to call our baby?" he asked, trying not to let her see that it was eating him up inside, but it was. He'd lost a child, one he'd never known he'd had.

A child he hadn't even known he'd wanted.

Until now, because it had been with her.

The woman he loved.

The woman he'd lost.

The only woman who had been able to reach him, but he couldn't say those words out loud. If he said them out loud then there was a possibility that it wouldn't come true. That Gervaso would die and he'd be alone.

He'd lose his heart.

It's already lost.

She nodded once and then turned, walking away from him to retrieve Gervaso's heart.

He nodded solemnly and all he could do was drop his head and pray for all the things he'd never known he'd wanted.

All the things he was so close to losing.

And he couldn't leave it like this.

He started to run after her and caught her as she was heading out of the ambulance bay. He caught her by the arm, spinning her round and kissing her.

It caught her off guard and he was almost expecting her to slap him again, but instead she kissed him back, touching his face in reassurance. He needed that.

"Thank you," he said again.

Kiri's dark eyes twinkled with unshed tears, tears she was fighting to hold back. "You're welcome, but don't ever do that again. I don't need your kisses or want them."

Thanking her had not been what he'd wanted to say, but he'd found himself choking on the words. How could he say it when he wasn't sure he could give her his entire self? And she'd made it clear she didn't want him, but what did he expect?

He let her go, watching her as she climbed into the back of the ambulance. Alejandro watched until it left.

He wandered away from the ambulance bay and, feeling lost, he found himself standing in front of the church chapel. There was no priest in there, but that was okay. Alejandro didn't need absolution right now.

Don't you?

He hadn't been inside a church in so long. His brothers had never really enforced it. The only time in his youth he'd gone after his parents had died had been when the nuns at school would force him to go.

He took an uneasy step and then stepped back.

There had been so many things he'd done wrong with his life, would he even be welcome? And his whole life he hadn't even been sure he believed in God. Not after what had happened to his parents. Taking a deep breath, he walked into the chapel.

There were prayer candles burning so Alejandro picked up a fresh one and lit it. He set it down and closed his eyes, sending up a prayer for Gervaso. For Kiri and her strength and for himself. For the child they had lost.

All he wanted was another chance at a family, a chance at happiness, and he was worried that he'd blown it. The chapel began to spin and he felt light-headed.

He was standing there helplessly like a fool, staring at a wall of flickering candles, when he got a page about Casey.

Dios mio. Not another one.

Right now he had to bury all the feelings raging inside him. Right now he had to be a surgeon. He left the chapel and headed up to the pediatric critical care unit where they had been monitoring Casey since her surgery.

When he got to Casey's room his resident rushed the chart over to him and he could see from the catheter bag that Casey was bleeding again.

"She spiked a fever and complained of pain, separate from her incision pain, and then her urine output stopped."

"The shunt has probably become dislodged, which has torn open her ureter most likely." Alejandro cursed under his breath. "Get permission from Casey's parents and prep her for surgery."

"Yes, Dr. Valentino."

Alejandro headed off to the scrub room. He had to focus on Casey right now and he had to bury all the anxiety he was feeling about Gervaso right now. Another child needed him.

Kiri had been dreading this moment. It was like she was reliving her loss over again. She closed her eyes as she waited for the surgeon to call her forward. She'd be the last to go up. The heart was always the last organ to be removed. And then a life would end.

Don't think about it.

She learned that the donor in question had been born with a chromosome disorder and was brain-dead, but it didn't make it any easier and she sent up a silent prayer for that little one, an old Hindu prayer that her grandmother had taught her. Just a simple prayer that would send blessings, for the parents who were grieving, for the little life that had never had a chance.

"Dr. Bhardwaj?"

Kiri stepped forward.

"Walking with the heart," the doctor said, carrying the bowl with the preservation fluid. They placed the heart in a bag with fluid into her container. She snapped it shut. When she was out of the operating room she called Buena Vista.

"Robinson speaking."

"Prep Gervaso Valentino for a heart transplant. I will be there in thirty."

"Will do."

Kiri disconnected the call and moved as fast as she could to the ambulance bay. She was trying to process all her feelings now, to get them out of the way so that she could operate on Gervaso. If Gervaso died Alejandro would never forgive her and she would never forgive herself.

Dr. Robinson would be there, but he'd never done a transplant on an infant this small before. Usually it was Alejandro who handled transplants this small. It was his specialty, only his hands were tied. He couldn't be in there. If he was it could jeopardize any future adoption for Alejandro if he wished to pursue it, though she seriously doubted he would. She hadn't even seen him shed a tear for their child.

At least she had done transplants on babies this small and the two of them could do this together.

They had to do it.

She had to save Gervaso, for Alejandro's sake.

And for you.

That thought scared her, but it was true. She didn't want to lose Gervaso and she didn't want to lose Alejandro. Even though Alejandro had made it clear he didn't want her.

She wanted them to be her family.

For so long she'd been mourning her loss and been too afraid to reach out and take what she actually wanted. She wanted a family. Wanted to be a mother, more than anything.

She wanted love and she didn't want to spend her life alone.

The ride to Buena Vista was smooth. Kiri drowned out the sounds of the siren blaring and held tight to the cooler that held the heart. When she got to the hospital she was whisked up to the operating room where Dr. Robinson and the team were prepping Gervaso.

She handed the heart to a scrub nurse and scrubbed in. The nurse would take care of the heart and place it in preservation fluid. Dr. Robinson would be placing Gervaso on bypass and removing his wee damaged heart while she inspected the donor heart and went over the plan of attack.

You can do this.

She walked into the operating room and saw the little body on the table...

"It was a boy."

Kiri held out her arms and took the tiny boy wrapped in a towel. His eyes hadn't even opened and he was so small.

"My baby." She wept. The pain was too intense, so hard to bear that she didn't know how she was going to go on living. "My baby." Her little boy who she'd been going to name after his father.

She shook the memory away because this baby was stronger. This was her baby and he would live.

Oh, God, please, help me.

The nurse gowned and gloved her. She went over to the heart in the stainless-steel bowl. Such a small heart, but it was good.

"The baby is on bypass, Dr. Bhardwaj, and the old heart has been removed. We're ready for the donor heart," Dr. Robinson said.

Kiri nodded and headed over to the table, taking over the lead position. A nurse placed a head lamp on her head and magnifiers over her glasses so she could see all the small vessels.

"Walking with the heart," a nurse shouted.

"I'm glad you're here to help," Dr. Robinson said. "I'm used to working on teenagers and adults. Alejandro has the lighter touch for the young ones."

"I'm glad you're here too, Dr. Robinson. You're the heart specialist. We can do this together."

Dr. Robinson's eyes crinkled as he smiled behind his mask. "You bet we can."

Kiri took a calming breath as the nurse stood next to her, holding the heart. Gently Kiri reached into the bowl and lifted it out, knowing that right now she was holding everything that mattered to her in the palms of her hands.

You can do this.

Once Casey's shunt had been stabilized and she was back to producing clear urine, Alejandro got her back up to the ICU and on a new regimen of medications that would help with the flow. He talked briefly to Casey's parents and reassured them that their daughter would be okay.

I wonder how Gervaso is?

He glanced at the clock on the wall of the waiting room because he couldn't even go down to the surgical floor and be near the operating room. It wasn't allowed.

Instead, he paced, watching the clock.

How do people wait?

It was driving him mad, waiting. While he waited he tried to take his mind off Gervaso's surgery and he thought about what Kiri had told him about Mr. Snyder and how they'd wanted the baby to go to County. He thought about all the other children who were now being sent to County because Buena Vista wasn't taking pro bono cases.

Alejandro knew that he couldn't work in a place like this anymore. He had to help every child, no matter what their situation in life.

That's what his father would do.

That's what his father had done.

He'd helped those who'd come to his bodega, those who'd been unable to afford to buy anything. His father had helped the needy.

"I came here to make a better life, Alejandro. I couldn't make a good life in Heliconia. There was no life left there to

live, but here I can help. I can take care of you, your broth-
ers and Mami. And I can take care of everyone who needs
me. That is a life worth living. That is a rewarding life."

He scrubbed his hand over his face before he pulled out his phone and punched in a familiar number.

"Hello?" Santi sounded tired on the other end.

"It's Alejandro."

"Is something wrong? You never call me."

"I know I don't," Alejandro said, and then he sighed. "Why did you marry Saoirse? I thought you never wanted to get married."

"I didn't, but I fell in love. I couldn't help it. I fell so deeply in love with her that the thought of living without her outweighed my fear of possibly losing her."

Alejandro nodded. He understood what Santiago was saying.

"You still there?" Santi asked.

"I am. I'm just thinking."

Santi snorted on the other end. "Well, that's a first."

"I'm adopting a baby," Alejandro blurted out.

The other end went silent.

"Now who is at a loss for words?" Alejandro teased.

"That's a huge responsibility," Santi warned. "What brought this on? You're not one for responsibility beyond your work."

"I know, but he has no one. He's undergoing a heart transplant right now."

"You're calling me during a heart transplant?" Santiago yelled into the phone.

"I'm not doing it. I can't, I'm already his guardian."

"Well, that was fast," Santi said.

"Not really. I applied a couple of weeks ago. I found him, you see. He was abandoned and sick and the hospital cut the pro bono fund."

Santi cursed under his breath. "Really? That's not good."

"I know. I'm thinking of leaving. Going somewhere I can help those in need. I thought I was living like Pappi this way, but if I can't help those who need it, then I'm not really."

"Alejandro, you have to do what's right for you. You have a piece of Pappi in you, yes, but that shouldn't define your life. Our parents wanted us to have freedom to choose our paths. Your life is your life. Live it."

"My time is limited."

"Who says?" Santi snapped.

"Medicine? Come on, Santi. You're a doctor too. You've read the reports."

"Yes, I know, but you didn't get a transplant because of heart disease and Pappi was in excellent health when he died. You know the statistics better than anyone else. You've lived this long. Live your life, *idiota*!"

"Oh, yes? Is that what you're doing now?" Alejandro teased.

"Yes." Santiago laughed. "It took me a long time to realize this and you're even a bigger dunderhead than me. You're stubborn."

Alejandro laughed. "Thanks."

"No problem. Do what's right for you, Alejandro. Step out of Pappi's shadow, stop being afraid of what you can lose and just take what life gives you. Live it."

Alejandro disconnected the call. Santiago was right. He had been too afraid to open up his heart because of the what-ifs. There would always be what-ifs and did he really want to live his life not knowing what could come of it? It might be messy. It might hurt, but it would hurt more if he didn't try.

He wanted it all.

And for the first time he wanted what his parents had had.

It was hours that he stood in that waiting room. Alejandro got a taste of what it was like on the other side and he didn't like it much.

Was this what it had been like for his brothers?

Was this what he'd put them through?

It was absolute torture. He was used to being in the operating room, not outside, wondering if Gervaso was alive or not.

He raked his hands through his hair and made up his mind to go to the surgical floor, whether he was allowed to or not.

You could jeopardize your adoption of him.

The doors of the OR opened and Kiri stepped out. She was looking for him and then her gaze landed on him and she smiled, nodding.

"Oh, *gracias a Dios.*"

She nodded. "He survived, but the next twenty-four hours will tell the whole tale. He could still reject the heart."

Alejandro nodded. "I don't care. I will be there for him."

"Good."

"I'm going to adopt him."

"I'm glad to hear that." She grinned. "He's supposed to be your baby."

"This is hard for me to say…"

"What? Have you changed your mind?" And she looked ready to hit him if he gave her the wrong answer.

"No, I want to adopt him, but I wonder… I can't help but wonder…" Only he didn't finish the rest of what he'd been going to say because the world began to spin and his knees crumpled beneath him.

"Alejandro!"

Kiri's screams were muffled but they sounded like his mother's. And as he laid his head against the cold tile of the floor he knew his time was up. His heart was racing, and then it froze, and as he lay there, the world disappearing from sight, he could hear his parents' voices again.

This was the end.

"Alejandro!" she screamed, and reached out to try and catch him, but he fell to the floor, just slipping out of her hands.

"No," she cried out. She checked for his pulse, but there was none.

"I need a crash cart *now*!" Kiri yelled over her shoulder.

A Code Blue was called. She straddled him and checked his airways before starting CPR.

"You're not going to die on me!" she shouted at his lifeless body as she pumped his chest. "You're not going to die. Damn you!"

The crash team came running. She could see the looks on their faces as they realized that their Code Blue was Dr. Valentino.

Then Dr. Robinson was there, fresh from the operating room.

"Kiri," he said gently. "Let me. It's plain to see you're family."

Kiri stopped her compressions and let the crash team take over. Dr. Robinson guided them as she watched the man she loved lying there, no pulse, no heartbeat, on the cold hard floor.

She couldn't lose him; she couldn't raise Gervaso without him.

She needed Alejandro. Always had.

Oh, God.

Tears streamed down her face.

"Clear!" Dr. Robinson shouted, and a shock went through Alejandro's body.

Please. Not him too.

"Charge to one hundred," Dr. Robinson said. "Come on, Valentino, work with me for once in your life!"

Kiri closed her eyes, holding her breath as they shocked him again. Then she heard it. After the thump of the shock a heartbeat, faint on the monitor but it was there. It was a rhythm.

"Good. Let's get him to the CT scanner. Let's see what caused his heart to fail."

"He had a heart transplant as a child!" Kiri shouted.

Dr. Robinson nodded. "I know. Who do you think writes his prescriptions?"

He left Kiri standing there as they carted Alejandro away. She'd never even had the chance to tell him how she felt about him. Just like she'd never got to say that to her baby.

Their baby.

On the floor was Alejandro's phone.

He had brothers and they deserved to know. She picked it up and saw Alejandro had recently been speaking to Santiago.

Alejandro needed his brothers.

She pushed redial and took a deep breath.

"You again?" a deep voice said on the other line. "Now what do you want? You seriously never call me this much."

"It's not Alejandro," Kiri said, trying to keep her voice from shaking.

"Who is this?"

"Dr. Bhardwaj at Buena Vista. Alejandro collapsed and needed to be resuscitated."

There was silence. Then a sharp cry of pain. "Is he…?"

"He's alive, but going in for testing. You need to…" She trailed off as she began to cry. "You need to come down here."

"I'll be there as soon as possible."

Kiri ended the call and then went to wait for Alejandro's family. If she didn't, she might lose her mind.

It was only a matter of minutes and a paramedic faintly resembling Alejandro came running into the trauma department. He made a beeline for her.

"Are you Dr. Bhardwaj?"

"Yes, and you're Santiago?"

"Yes. I couldn't get hold of Dante or Rafe. I figured just me is good enough for now."

"He's in the catheterization lab. There was a block that stopped his heart."

Santiago nodded grimly and they walked to the cath lab, where they watched Alejandro on the table. Dr. Robinson was threading the catheter to remove the block.

"Mio Dios," Santi murmured, crossing himself. "I can't take this. We almost lost him once. I knew a day would come when he'd need to go back on UNOS, but I thought he had more time. I prayed he had more time. I can't lose him, we can't... I just thought he had more time."

"I know," she whispered. "It's been about twenty or so years?"

Santi nodded. "Yes, about that since our parents died. Do you know how they died?"

"He told me," Kiri said gently.

Santi cocked an eyebrow. "I assume you're more than his boss, then?"

She nodded. "Yes."

"He'll pull through," Santi said, turning his gaze back to his brother. "If he doesn't, I'll kill him."

Kiri smiled at Santi, watching him watch Alejandro, worry on his face.

It was more than she could take at the moment. She slipped away and went to the NICU. She saw Gervaso in his incubator, clinging to life, a new heart giving him a chance.

She gowned up and went into the isolation room. She couldn't touch Gervaso. He needed time to heal and touch right now would put too much stress on his body. Knowing that she couldn't touch him made her begin to weep.

She needed to heal too. Needed Alejandro. Needed Gervaso.

She needed her family.

If only God would give her a chance, but even if Alejandro didn't make it Gervaso was hers. It was a done deal with her heart.

Her heart belonged to him and it belonged to Alejandro.

Fully and completely, whether he liked it or not.

CHAPTER TWELVE

Damn.

Alejandro winced in pain as he slowly opened his eyes to see Santiago at the foot of his bed, glaring at him.

"What the…?"

"Shut up," Santiago said. "Do you know how much you scared the ever-loving heck out of me?"

"What happened?"

"You had a heart block, *idiota*."

The monitors began to beep as his pulse raced.

"Don't overexcite yourself. You're fine. No rejection of Pappi's heart. You'll be fine. Scar tissue is not your friend. That was the culprit."

Alejandro relaxed. "Did they do surgery? I'm numb so I can't tell."

Santi shook his head. "No, just a catheterization. You're lucky, amigo. You were put back on UNOS, though, but you're low on the list. There are more options for you and that heart before you need a transplant."

"Good, that's good. Do the elders know what happened to me?" Alejandro asked.

"Yes, they're relieved you pulled through." Santi grinned. "They threatened you with death if you didn't make it."

Alejandro chuckled. "Kind of a moot point by then."

"I did the same. I planned on torturing you when we met up again one day. You scared me."

"I scared you?" Alejandro teased. "Nothing scares you."

"Some things do," Santi said, and he nodded over at the chair beside the bed, where Kiri was curled up, sleeping. "You were lucky. Don't blow it."

"I won't," Alejandro said. "Though I'm on the transplant list again, what kind of life—"

"Let her make that decision. She knows," Santi said. "Live life, you moron!"

Kiri stirred. "Is he awake?"

Santi nodded. "Yes, and I'm going home to my wife." With one last squeeze of Alejandro's foot and a knowing glare Santi left.

"Kiri," Alejandro said.

She sat on the edge of the bed. "You scared me."

"I'm sorry."

"Don't ever do that to me again."

"I can't guarantee that. My heart—"

"Is fine for now. You're on UNOS, but not a priority. I'm a surgeon. I understand the implications," she said, interrupting him. "Your heart is fragile, but so is mine. You can't use that as an excuse to push me away. Not anymore."

He grinned. "So I guess that answers my question from earlier."

She looked confused. "What question?"

"I was going to ask… I was hoping that we can adopt Gervaso together. I'm the father and you're the mother."

Tears filled her eyes. "Can we? I mean, you want me to adopt him with you?"

"Yes."

"I don't know what to say. How can we?"

He nodded. "We can, but we should get married first."

"Married?"

"Sí." And he held his breath.

She sighed. "Alejandro, if you're just asking me to marry you to expedite the adoption application, then I can't marry you. I know you just had an attack, but I won't marry you for that."

"I'm not asking you because of Gervaso. I'm asking for me." He gripped her hand. "I want you, Kiri. I've always wanted you. I want to have a family again. I can't live without you. The thought of losing you terrifies me, but I can't not take the chance. I'll risk everything to have you. To make a family with you."

Tear began to roll down her cheeks. "How can I make a family with you? I lost our baby."

"We'll make a family with Gervaso. You and him, that's all I need."

"And if Gervaso doesn't make it?"

"I'll have you. I love you, Kiri, *mi tesoro*."

She broke down in sobs when he said those words. His hand was still clutching hers and she couldn't believe that Alejandro was saying these things.

"I love you too," she finally managed to say. "I was too afraid to love, too afraid to lose. Losing our baby almost killed me and then I almost lost you. I didn't think I could ever love again, but I love you, Alejandro. I love you."

She leaned over and he wrapped her in his strong arms and then cupped her face, kissing her in his recovery bed.

She still was terrified about what the future held, whether Gervaso would make it or not and whether Alejandro would too, but at that moment she didn't care. It was a risk she was willing to take because it was a chance to live. Fully.

"How is Gervaso?" Alejandro asked.

Kiri nodded and took his hand. "Strong."

"Really?" There was a smile on his face.

"Yes."

"I think he'll live," Alejandro said, as he leaned back.

"Babies are resilient and he's definitely a fighter." She smiled up at him. "I'm scared, though. Scared of losing you both."

"Me too, but you don't have to do it alone this time. I'm here. I'm sorry that you had to bear the pain of loss without me. If I…" He trailed off, his dark eyes moist. "I'm sorry, Kiri."

And she held him. "It's okay. We have each other now."

So they held each other close, holding on as they talked about Gervaso. How they knew he would survive, the boy they hoped would be their son. Planning for a future together.

Praying for a miracle and never letting each other go.

Kiri wanted to wait a week after Alejandro was discharged and given the all clear before they decided to go down to City Hall and make their marriage official. She wanted to stay close to Gervaso's side and make sure that he didn't reject the heart.

Gervaso was strong.

A definite fighter, and each day that went by he grew stronger. Just like his father.

"So is today the day?" Alejandro asked as he came into the neonatal intensive care unit where she had been sitting with Gervaso. She couldn't hold him but she was watching him and checking his stats often. "We got our license four days ago."

"I think so. He's doing well and Dr. Robinson is on duty." Kiri smiled at Samantha, who was hovering. "As is Samantha. I think we can leave for a couple of hours to get married."

"Married?" Samantha shrieked. "That's wonderful! I had no idea you two were an item."

Alejandro chuckled. "We met a long time ago and have been in love since then. We just didn't know it."

"He's stubborn," Kiri teased.

Samantha snorted. "Don't I know it?"

"We're getting married so that we can put in the adoption papers tonight to formally adopt young Gervaso here." Alejandro laid a hand against the incubator. "My lawyer said that we have a better chance adopting him if we get married."

"I'm so happy," Samantha gushed. "For the both of you. It's the right thing to do clearly, and I'm so happy for Gervaso. Such a sad story ending so right."

Kiri shot Alejandro a knowing look. She stood and took Alejandro's hand as they walked out of the neonatal intensive care unit.

"Did you manage to find some witnesses?" Kiri asked. "The only people I know in Miami are you and the people I work with."

"I wrangled up a couple of unwilling participants, but they don't know why."

Kiri cocked an eyebrow, intrigued. "Who did you get?"

"My brothers Dante and Rafe."

"I'm finally meeting the infamous elders?" She grinned. "I can't wait to see what they look like. So if you didn't tell them we're getting married, what did you tell them to get them to go down to City Hall?"

"I told them I was being tried for public indecency. I broke the news of my exotic dancing days to them and they were not happy. So they think I'm being charged with that. They're mad. First the heart block and now this. Getting arrested is on the elders' no-no list for me."

She laughed. "You're terrible."

He grinned. "I know, but I like to have fun with the elders."

They took Kiri's car to City Hall and parked it. When they walked into the building they saw the tall, dark-haired, olive-skinned twins scowling and searching the crowds of people, probably looking to string Alejandro up by his short hairs.

They were devilishly handsome, as well.

Kiri had met Santiago when Alejandro had had his heart issue and had then met Saoirse just after Gervaso's surgery. She'd been taken aback by the brother that Alejandro had called ugly. When she'd first met Santiago she hadn't understood why the brothers all insisted on calling each other ugly when it was far from the truth.

One of the brothers' gazes landed on Alejandro and his fist clenched as he moved through the crowd toward them.

"I think you're in trouble," Kiri whispered.

"I think you're right."

"Alejandro Gervaso Valentino, you have some explaining to do!"

"Dante, that's Dr. Alejandro Gervaso Valentino, if you don't mind."

Kiri squeezed his hand in warning not to provoke his brothers, who looked ready to murder him.

"You're lucky I don't kill you right here, baby brother. I would if it weren't for Pappi's heart," Rafe snarled. "Exotic dancing? Public indecency? You're a doctor, for God's sake, and you're recovering! What are you thinking about?"

"That was all a ruse, old man."

Dante frowned. "For what?"

"The heart block?" Rafe asked.

"No, that was real. The arrest."

"What the…?" Dante looked like he was going to murder someone and that someone was Alejandro.

"I needed two witnesses. I'm getting married today."

Dante and Rafe exchanged looks.

"You're what?" Dante asked.

"This is my fiancée, Dr. Kiri Bhardwaj."

Kiri felt uneasy as the brothers' gazes fell on her, but

they instantly softened and they smiled at her warmly. Just like Alejandro.

"A pleasure," Rafe said, taking her hand and kissing it. "I've heard so much about you from Santiago, but given the fact you're engaged to Alejandro I thought Santiago was just pulling a fast one on me."

Kiri chuckled. "I assure you I'm quite real."

"Why are you marrying this ugly one?" Dante teased. "You're picking the wrong brother."

Kiri laughed while Alejandro scowled.

"I love him," Kiri said, shrugging.

"She's delirious," Dante said in an aside to his twin.

Rafe nodded and then turned to Alejandro. "No, seriously, what is going on?"

"I'm in love with her and we're adopting a baby."

"A baby?" Dante and Rafe said in unison.

"*Sí*, a baby." Then Alejandro proceeded to tell the whole story, right from the first time he'd met Kiri to Gervaso's heart transplant a couple of weeks ago.

"So, you see, I needed two witnesses and I knew you two elders wouldn't come down to City Hall because you would think that I was pulling your legs, so I told a little white lie."

"We're happy for you," Dante said.

"It's about time you grew a pair," Rafe said. "Seriously, Alejandro, Mami and Pappi would be proud."

Kiri smiled as Alejandro hugged both his brothers tight.

"We're going to be late," she piped up. "Our appointment is in ten minutes."

"Right, let's go." Alejandro took her hand and the elders followed them into the judge's chambers.

Alejandro handed the paperwork to the judge and stood in front of Kiri, holding her hand. He grinned down at her.

"I love you, *mi tesoro*."

"And I you."

The ceremony was simple, then Kiri signed the certificate and so did Alejandro.

They were married.

"You may kiss the bride," the judge said.

Alejandro tipped her chin and pressed a kiss against her lips. "Thank you for bringing me back my family."

"Thank you for being my family," she said. "Thank you for helping me find my way to the world of the living again. I was so lost."

"Me too," Alejandro whispered, pulling her close. "Now let's get these papers off to the adoption lawyer so we can make Gervaso a part of our family."

"Sí," Kiri teased.

Dante and Rafe welcomed her to the family and the four of them went to the next building to file their marriage certificate with their adoption papers. After that was done Kiri and Alejandro took Dante and Rafe to the neonatal intensive care unit at Buena Vista to meet the soon-to-be newest member of the Valentino family.

"So should I call you Dr. Bhardwaj or Dr. Valentino?"

"I think there're enough Dr. Valentinos to last a life time," Kiri teased.

"Fair enough, but you know there are never enough Valentinos. Miracles do happen," Alejandro said encouragingly.

"I hope you're right."

And she hoped that miracle would come true, but for now she had all she could ever want.

EPILOGUE

One year later

KIRI WALKED ALONG the beach, watching as Alejandro jogged ahead, chasing after Gervaso, who was toddling at full speed through the sand and the surf. Against all the odds and his preemie start, their little fighter had mastered first walking then running around the time of his first birthday.

He was thriving a year after his heart transplant, though Kiri knew he might have to go back on UNOS again one day. Just like Alejandro.

Alejandro was good about going to his appointments and taking care of himself. He was on the list, but so far with close monitoring there had been no further heart failure.

So Kiri just lived every day to the fullest, enjoying the time she had with her family.

She couldn't believe that she'd been married to Alejandro for a year already. Shortly after they'd married Kiri's parents had descended from New York City to meet their new son-in-law. Her parents were thrilled that she'd gotten married but not that she'd gotten married at City Hall.

So while they'd been in Miami Kiri had married Alejandro again for a second time in a traditional Hindu ceremony, which her parents had always wanted for her.

And Alejandro had teased that there was no escaping him now.

The newlyweds and Gervaso had taken the painful trip to New York City to visit the grave of the child they'd lost, which had allowed Alejandro to mourn and to mourn with her.

And on the anniversary of his parents' deaths she'd gone with him to the graveside to pay her respects to the people who'd raised four strong, proud men.

She still missed her family and friends back in New York City, but after becoming a Valentino and adopting Gervaso she became part of an even larger family.

It was what she'd always wanted.

"Come back here," Alejandro shouted, interrupting her thoughts as he playfully ran past her after Gervaso, who loved splashing through the little waves that broke on the shore. Kiri grinned as little footprints appeared on the sand before the waves washed them away.

The little boy was laughing and screeched when Alejandro closed in on him then hefted him up and swung him around. Gervaso sported a crop of dark curls and had the bluest eyes that Kiri had ever seen. The scar from the heart transplant was barely visible over the top of his T-shirt, but that didn't stop the precocious boy from running amok. It didn't slow him down one bit.

One of Gervaso's first words had been spoken when he'd pointed to his scar and Alejandro's scar and said, "Same."

"Mami!" Gervaso cried out through fits of giggles.

"I'm coming," Kiri called out, but they'd gotten so far ahead of her she had a hard time catching up.

Unfortunately she was moving a bit slower than those two were.

She looked down at her belly. She was seven months along and she was apparently carrying an elephant. Once she'd found out she was pregnant she'd had her cervix sewn up and had been put on a light workload up until last month, when she'd been told she should no longer work.

Which was fine. It was harder to stand for long periods of time now. Not with what seemed like a gigantic child growing inside her.

Her sister-in-law, Saoirse, had warned her that Valentino babies were large.

"Big heads!" she'd teased.

Kiri had laughed then, but now she believed it.

"I have to sit down," she shouted over the laughter. She grabbed one of the many beach chairs along South Beach and sank down into it. It was heavenly, though she didn't know if she'd ever be able to get out of it again. Still, it was nice not to be walking around so much.

They'd spent the day house hunting in South Beach, because Alejandro wanted to live near the ocean and they were outgrowing the one-bedroom condo that Kiri owned. They'd sold Alejandro's condo to pay for Gervaso's heart-transplant surgery, but not long after they'd paid the hospital bill Mr. Snyder had been booted off the board for giving a bad reputation to Buena Vista and the pro bono fund had been reinstated.

It seemed the press had got wind that a surgeon had applied to adopt an abandoned baby to save the baby's life when the hospital had threatened to turn him away.

And since Alejandro was a renowned pediatric transplant surgeon the press had eaten it up. It had been a small victory, but worth it.

Buena Vista was now the kind of hospital they could both be proud to work in.

Kiri leaned back in the chair and put her feet up. The sun was setting over the ocean and the nightlife on South Beach was starting to kick up a notch.

Alejandro came back with Gervaso on his shoulders.

"You know, on second thought I think we should expand our search area."

Kiri cocked an eyebrow. "I thought you loved the ocean. And Gervaso clearly loves the ocean, he's absolutely soaked."

"I know. Sorry about that, but he loves the waves. For what it's worth, there's a huge wet spot on my back."

Kiri chuckled. "I have no sympathy for you. So why do you want to widen the house hunting? I though you loved South Beach."

"I do, but we can go outside Miami. We could go to an island even."

"No way, not an island. I'm not driving over a large bridge every day."

He shrugged. "You do it now."

"Yes, but at least South Beach and Miami Beach are hard pieces of land and not islands that could flood." She shook her head. "No islands."

"How about a yacht?"

"No yachts. Besides, all your stripper money is gone, yes?" she teased.

He glared at her. "I could always go back to it."

"I don't think so. You're mine."

Alejandro bent over and kissed her. "So where were *you* thinking?"

"There're a lot of nice houses down by Vizcaya," she suggested. "On the mainland."

Alejandro grinned. "A good school district too."

"Exactly." She rubbed her belly again. "I'm really dreading having to trade in for a minivan soon."

He laughed. "You'll look good driving a minivan."

"You're driving it, buster."

"I don't think so," he teased. Then he set Gervaso down beside her. He curled up against her belly, rubbing his baby.

"Baby," Gervaso said. "Mine."

Alejandro placed a hand against her belly and the response was a strong kick. "Not long now. We'd better speed up our search. I want to be in the house before the baby comes."

"I agree." Kiri laid her hand over Alejandro's and the baby kicked up at them, as if knowing that they were talking about him or her. Kiri hadn't found out the gender as she wanted to be surprised.

It was a miracle she was pregnant, but she'd heard tell of women who spontaneously conceived after adopting and that's exactly what had happened. Seven months ago when all the final paperwork had come through, announcing they were finally Gervaso's parents, they'd celebrated in style that night.

And now they were on the fast track to a family. If they could only find a house that would suit them both.

"Did you ever think that you'd be here?" Kiri asked. "You were so adamant about not having kids."

He shook his head. "No, I never did, because I didn't think I'd live to see this."

"You're a transplant surgeon—people beat the odds all the time."

He grinned at her. "I knew I shouldn't have walked up to you in that bar in Vegas."

"Well, you told me that what happens in Vegas stays in Vegas. And look where we are," she teased. "It certainly didn't stay in Vegas."

"I'm glad of it, *mi tesoro*."

"Are you?"

He gave that charming smile as he leaned over and kissed her gently on the lips. "Absolutely."

* * * * *

LET'S TALK
Romance

For exclusive extracts, competitions
and special offers, find us online:

- facebook.com/millsandboon
- @MillsandBoon
- @MillsandBoonUK

Get in touch on 01413 063232

For all the latest titles coming soon, visit
millsandboon.co.uk/nextmonth

MILLS & BOON
A ROMANCE FOR EVERY READER

- **FREE** delivery direct to your door

- **EXCLUSIVE** offers every month

- **SAVE** up to 25% on pre-paid subscriptions

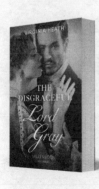

SUBSCRIBE AND SAVE

millsandboon.co.uk/Subscribe

MILLS & BOON

THE HEART OF ROMANCE

A ROMANCE FOR EVERY KIND OF READER

MODERN

Prepare to be swept off your feet by sophisticated, sexy and seductive heroes, in some of the world's most glamourous and romantic locations, where power and passion collide.
8 stories per month.

HISTORICAL

Escape with historical heroes from time gone by. Whether your passion is for wicked Regency Rakes, muscled Vikings or rugge Highlanders, awaken the romance of the past.
6 stories per month.

MEDICAL

Set your pulse racing with dedicated, delectable doctors in the high-pressure world of medicine, where emotions run high an passion, comfort and love are the best medicine.
6 stories per month.

True Love

Celebrate true love with tender stories of heartfelt romance, fr the rush of falling in love to the joy a new baby can bring, and focus on the emotional heart of a relationship.
8 stories per month.

Desire

Indulge in secrets and scandal, intense drama and plenty of siz hot action with powerful and passionate heroes who have it all: wealth, status, good looks…everything but the right woman.
6 stories per month.

HEROES

Experience all the excitement of a gripping thriller, with an int romance at its heart. Resourceful, true-to-life women and stron fearless men face danger and desire - a killer combination!
8 stories per month.

DARE

Sensual love stories featuring smart, sassy heroines you'd want a best friend, and compelling intense heroes who are worthy of t
4 stories per month.

To see which titles are coming soon, please visit

millsandboon.co.uk/nextmonth